The Creative Experience

EDITED BY Stanley Rosner
AND Lawrence E. Abt

GROSSMAN PUBLISHERS
New York
1970

Copyright © 1970 by Stanley Rosner and Lawrence E. Abt
All rights reserved.
Library of Congress Catalogue Card Number: 76–86116
Published by Grossman Publishers, Inc.
44 West 56th Street, New York, N.Y. 10019.
Published simultaneously in Canada
by Fitzhenry and Whiteside Ltd.
Manufactured in the United States of America.
First Printing.

To Blanche and Virginia

Preface

There is an ever-widening interest and curiosity about the creative process among persons in all walks of life, and, accordingly, there is an ever-increasing amount of research and publication on aspects of the subject. Virtually everyone is fascinated about the possibilities of developing talent in himself and others. Among the questions being asked are whether there is a disposition toward originality and whether there are relationships between kinds of education and the development and cultivation of creativity.

Traditionally, there have been two general approaches to the study of creativity, the sociological and the psychological. Ogburn and Thomas,[1] for example, have presented information on the simultaneity of invention; Kroeber[2] on the significance of cultural growth patterns; and others, like Barnett,[3] have placed emphasis on cultural value systems as these relate to creative results. Usually, psychologists have looked at personality factors, such as intelligence, motivation, attitudes, and the like, as being perhaps crucially related to the creative instinct and the development of its expression.

Both approaches to the study of the creative process have yielded a substantial body of information that has contributed to greater understanding of what creativity is and what conditions, social and psychological, are both necessary and sufficient for its occurrence and fullest expression.

As psychologists, the editors of this volume are naturally most inclined toward inquiry regarding the psychological factors involved in creative development, and this book is an expression of that interest. However, our orientation is substantially sociological as well, because we believe the

[1] Ogburn, W. F., and D. Thomas. "Are Inventions Inevitable?" *Political Science Quarterly*, 1922; 37, 38–98.
[2] Kroeber, A. L. *Configurations of Culture Growth*. Berkeley: University of California Press, 1944.
[3] Barnett, H. G. *Innovation: The Basis of Cultural Change*. New York: McGraw-Hill, 1953.

individual can be studied and understood best within the context of his environment, considered in the widest sense.

Works exploring creativity, even those most highly regarded at present, tend to lay stress either upon the creative product or outcome, such as Tuska,[4] or on the creative process itself, such as Ghiselin.[5] We believe that the present work is virtually the only one that places emphasis on the creative experience itself as a basis for approaching an understanding of creativity.

In exploring this new dimension of creativity, the editors have sought out the creative experiences of twenty-three persons in the arts and sciences who are recognized by their peers, and often by the informed public at large, for their creative contributions in their respective areas. Several factors have entered into the choice of those whose creative experiences are examined. Mr. Albert Rosenfeld, former Science Editor of *Life* magazine in cooperation with the editors, identified individuals noted for their achievements in science. Mr. Clement Greenberg, the noted art critic, nominated a group of persons representing many of the arts covered in this book, whom he judged to be especially creative in their respective media. The editors themselves, however, must bear the full responsibility for the final choice of those interviewed and included in this work.

In many cases, because of prior commitments or an expressed lack of desire to participate in our inquiry, specific persons nominated by Messrs. Rosenfeld and Greenberg declined to participate, and others were chosen. But the roster of those who responded to our invitation is impressive and speaks for itself. We wish to express our genuine appreciation to all of them for their generosity and willingness to let us explore the aspects of their lives that seem related to their creative expressions.

In no sense can we regard our inquiry as scientific, if, by scientific, one means an impeccable methodology that meets all or most of the requirements of experimental procedure. Our inquiry has no such pretensions; its principal aim has been a serious interest in a preliminary understanding of creativity *as experience,* which we regard as largely subjective, though nonetheless capable of communication and understanding.

We have been concerned, then, with exploring the phenomenology of the creative experience. For such an exploration, we have relied upon an interview structured to urge the interviewees into examining and evaluating the subjective, highly personal factors that they believe underlie their

---

4 Tuska, C. D. *Inventors and Inventions.* New York: McGraw-Hill, 1957.
5 Ghiselin, B. (ed). *The Creative Process.* New York: Mentor, 1955.

creative expressions. Although our interviews were focused somewhat toward exploring certain aspects of personality which we had reason to believe, on the basis of current research, might be related to the creative process, the actual interview technique itself, as will be apparent, was fully open ended. Thus, the interviewees were encouraged to explore the memories, feelings, and emotions they might associate with the conditions involved in their creative areas.

Wherever possible, we conducted our interview in the person's present working environment, and the interview proceeded at a speed dictated largely by the interviewee himself. Each interview was taped and upon transcription given to the participating individual for corrections, deletions, and additions. Our concern was always that each interview reflect as fully as possible, both in substance and style, what each person wanted to communicate about his creative experiences and the aspects of life which seemed to have a bearing upon his creative process.

As we review our material, we are strongly persuaded that this is only a beginning to the exploration and appreciation of the various factors, both subjective and objective, that compose the creative experiences of persons in the arts and sciences.

Contents

Preface   *vii*

THE SCIENTISTS

Introduction   /   *Albert Rosenfeld*   *3*

Archaeology and Anthropology   /   Froelich G. Rainey   *7*

Astronomy and Physics   /   Harlow Shapley   *27*

Biology and Genetics   /   H. Bentley Glass   *41*

Behavioral Sciences   /   David Krech   *59*

Linguistics   /   Noam Chomsky   *71*

Mathematics   /   Morris Kline   *89*

Medical Sciences   /   Wilder Penfield   *103*

Molecular Chemistry   /   Paul Saltman   *115*

Social Sciences   /   Arthur Koestler   *131*

THE ARTISTS

Introduction   /   *Joseph James Akston*   *157*

Architecture   /   Ulrich Franzen   *161*

Choreography and the Dance   /   Merce Cunningham   *173*

Cinema   /   Sidney Lumet   *187*

Crafts   /   Oppi A. J. Untracht   *207*

Fiction   /   Isaac Bashevis Singer   *223*

Fashion Design   /   Bonnie Cashin   *239*

Industrial Design   /   George Nelson   *251*

Music   /   Aaron Copland   *269*

Painting   /   Raphael Soyer   *279*

Philosophy   /   Sidney Hook   *289*

Photography   /   Edward Steichen   *311*

Poetry / Selden Rodman   *319*

Sculpture / Robert Engman   *343*

Theatre / Neil Simon   *355*

Conclusion and a Review of

the Literature on Creativity   *377*

Bibliography   *393*

Credits for photographs are: Harvard University News Office (Harlow Shapley), W.U.S. van Lessen Kloeke (Noam Chomsky), Stanley Bergson (Morris Kline), Andre Laroze (Wilder Penfield), Glasheen Photographs (Paul Saltman), Jonathan Green (Arthur Koestler), Jack Mitchell (Merce Cunningham), Warner Brothers—Seven Arts (Sidney Lumet), Alfred Sundel (Isaac Bashevis Singer), New York University (Sidney Hook).

THE SCIENTISTS

ALBERT ROSENFELD

"Did you ever know a young scientist?" asks Nina Leeds in Eugene O'Neill's *Strange Interlude*. "He believes if you pick a lie to pieces, the pieces are the truth." This is often the layman's (even the educated layman's) jaundiced view of how science works: by analysis; by cold logic, by taking things apart to inspect them—perhaps changing or destroying them in the act of observation—by studying the parts and ignoring the totality; by reporting the data and mistakenly assuming that the "facts" add up to Truth. All in all, a process that is the opposite of creativity, which is putting things together, seeing them whole.

If anyone had asked me, back in my late teens or early twenties, I would have said that I did not have a mathematical or scientific turn of mind. I had no modesty where the arts or humanities were concerned, but science was hopelessly beyond my grasp. As a matter of fact, among those of my young friends who nursed creative aspirations, it was the prevalent conceit that anyone with *that* kind of mind (scientific) must be a dull, plodding individual without the imagination to soar to any creative heights. "Science moves," as Tennyson put it, "but slowly slowly, creeping on from point to point."

By the time I reached college (as a veteran, after World War II), I knew otherwise. One of the things I certainly wanted to do at that point was learn some science. Several factors had converged to kindle my interest; and, once the interest was high, I discovered that the

3

subject matter was not beyond me after all. I was also convinced by then, and have since become more so, that there do not exist two distinct and separate types of mind, one for the arts and humanities, the other for the sciences. If you have a mind it should be as capable of responding to one as the other. Moreover, you must possess both intuition and imagination to be creative in the sciences as well as the arts—a contention I think this book bears out.

In fact, we know there is science in all good poetry and vice versa. One instance, according to Poe, was his writing of *The Raven*. "The work," he tells us, "proceeded step by step to its completion, with the precision and rigid consequence of a mathematical problem." This statement makes the point that there is method, technique, and usually some overall design, though not always so conscious as Poe's, in the arts as well as in the sciences. I have never heard anyone suggest that the employment of method and technique in poetry, music, drama, or sculpture, disqualifies them as creative activities. Yet this same criterion does, in the minds of many, disqualify science, and there are no grounds for such a double standard of evaluation.

Much scientific endeavor does indeed consist of the painstaking accumulation of detail. Often the accumulator is not creative in any artistic sense (though he *may* be), and his data remain merely data, until a more creative intellect sees a way to apply them or seizes upon them as raw material for a sweeping generalization or a deep new insight into the way things are. But then, how many dull, plodding versifiers are there? Or historians? Or dramatists? Exercises in composition do not necessarily produce art, and much that goes by the name of art scarcely merits being called creative. In any field, the creators are always vastly outnumbered by the workers. The same holds for science.

"At the risk of wearying the reader by endless repetition," says the eminent British scientist Norman Campbell, in *What Is Science?*, "I have insisted on the fallacy of neglecting the imaginative element which inspires science just as much as art." The interested layman can, says Campbell, "if he will take the trouble, appreciate the discoveries of others and experience at second-hand the thrill of artistic creation. For those who have the necessary knowledge, it is as exciting to trace the development of a great scientific theory, which we could never have developed ourselves, as it is to read great poetry or to hear great music which we ourselves could never have written."

But do science's very concerns and attitudes not render it an altogether different kind of activity? According to Poet Archibald MacLeish, science deals only in abstractions while poetry deals with real things. Science can abstract ideas and facts about an apple, but it takes a poet to present the apple itself. One of MacLeish's favorite modern definitions of poetry (Matthew Arnold's, in a letter to Maurice de Guérin) gives poetry the unique "power of so dealing with *things* as to awaken in us a wonderfully full, new and intimate sense of them and of our relation to them." As an example, he quotes George Meredith:

> Mark where the pressing wind shoots javelin-like
> Its skeleton shadow on the broad-back'd wave!

Now, of course, science cannot do that. Nor does it pretend to, any more than it pretends to any ultimate Truth (its truths are always conditional and tentative). But science can give us different kinds of knowledge of the "real thing" in ways that poetry cannot. A poet might describe, say, a certain type of stone in sharp and immediate terms, evoking its lines and textures. But listen to Dr. Harlow Shapley: "We break open a stony ball—this Scottish stonemason and I—a nodular mass of blue limestone, and expose beautiful traces of an extinct world of animals and plants; we find fossilized tree ferns, giant growths from the Carboniferous Period of two hundred and fifty million years ago—and forthwith we lose ourselves in conjecture." In such an instance, breaking open the stone and examining it scientifically surely provided as profound a knowledge, and certainly no less aesthetic delight as any poetic description would have.

Here, perhaps, is one of the key differences between creativity in science and creativity in other areas: The scientific creator has to know more facts. To evaluate the data, to maintain a mind prepared to take advantage of serendipity, to relate miscellaneous assortments of seemingly unrelated observations, to apply the insight, to derive the formula, to formulate the law, to recognize the cure—any of these requires some education in the subject matter, some firsthand experimental experience, or at least a keen awareness of scientific context. This education and experience are often gained by the very kind of taking-apart and analyzing that Nina Leeds decried. In the process, the creative genius surmises how to put things together no one has ever put together before: an entire dinosaur or prehistoric man from a single bone or tooth, an entire cosmos from a few spectroscope readings.

"Microscopes and telescopes," said Goethe, "actually disturb a man's sense of sight." Maybe so. A poet is "seeing" other things. For the scientist, microscopes and telescopes are passkeys to unimagined and inexpressibly lovely realms. His sight is extended to take in the hearts of atoms and the boundaries of galaxies. Thus do microscopes and telescopes, fossils and tables of logarithms and computers and ultracentrifuges give science a kind of power similar to that reserved by Arnold for poetry, though achieved in a different way "of so dealing with *things* as to awaken in us a wonderfully full, new and intimate sense of them and our relation to them."

It is clear that discovery and invention in both science and art require the exercise of creative imagination. And the creative process seems to be basically the same in both fields: a mind trained and attuned to possibilities, an immense amount of work and methodical planning, then leaps of intuitive insight followed by swift consolidation.

I do not mean to claim that the experiences of art and science are equatable and interchangeable. They are rather unique and yet similar. Both are important and complementary instruments for perceiving the world. Each gives us kinds of realities the other cannot. Science deals essentially in repeatable and reconfirmable patterns, and this leaves a lot of loose ends that only art (or religion, or philosophy) can help us with. "It is essential to our happiness," as Mary McCarthy's heroine thinks in *The Company She Keeps,* "to have both the patterns and the loose ends."

FROELICH G. RAINEY

Dr. Froelich G. Rainey, who is Director of the University of Pennsylvania Museum and has been Professor of Anthropology at the same institution since 1947, was interviewed in New York City in November, 1968.

Rainey was born in Wisconsin in 1907. He received his bachelor's degree at the University of Chicago, and his doctorate in anthropology from Yale in 1935. At Yale, he served at the Peabody Museum for almost five years as an assistant in anthropology, and at the same time he carried on field work in the West Indies with the Arawak Indians.

While at the University of Alaska from 1935 to 1942, Rainey did some of the early field research in anthropology in that area. Serving as a member of the Board of Economic Warfare in 1942, he was dispatched during the final days of World War II to Europe, where he served in Berlin as a foreign service officer.

As we talked to Professor Rainey, he spoke of his chairmanship of the Planning Board for the 21st Century Exposition at Seattle and his two-year membership on the U.S. Mission to UNESCO.

Among his more strictly professional pursuits, Professor Rainey had a large share in the search for the lost city of Sybaris in Italy, and he has maintained a long and continuing interest in the development and application of the many scientific and technical tools on which modern archaeology increasingly relies. This interest has been elemental in his producing a large bibliography of publications concerned with physics, electronics, and engineering as they make available techniques and tools for investigations in archaeology.

Chief among his publications are "Puerto Rican Archaeology" (1935) and "Whale Hunters of Tiagra" (1947).

ARCHAEOLOGY
AND ANTHROPOLOGY

Froelich G. Rainey

Do you have any thoughts that you could help us with that have to do with the birth of an idea? Specifically, such issues as dreams, daydreams, fantasies, that you think may contribute to the birth of an idea.

That's a very difficult question for me to answer, because I can't say that I've thought much about dreams in the kind of work we do. Certainly, in the back of everybody's mind that is working in this field are some basic attempts to reconstruct things that have gone before; I mean, history of people and their behavior, and human history in general. And, whether or not in their mind is some sort of a reflection of the past, I wouldn't know. As for me, I'm not much of a dreamer.

Have you had thoughts about somewhat reconstructing your own experience?

Gosh, I couldn't say. How do you mean? This is an odd question.

Would it be possible, for example, to want to see the work of yourself, or of an archaeologist in general, as being an extension of a desire or motivation going way back to find out more about yourself? You know, the history of your family tree, or what have you.

Well, I think that basically everybody's interested in this subject. It's a reflection of his own curiosity about his life, where he fits into the scheme of things. I think that's certainly true. But I really don't think that in my experience in this field I've ever coordinated what I do with a curiosity

9

about my own personal history. From my own point of view, how you get into this business and how you get interested is largely a matter of chance. And, lying behind that chance, you obviously go in directions in which your personality and your character lead you. That's true. But, I never consciously thought about it in terms of my own personal history or through reconstructing my own life. Although I'm sure, like others, I'm certainly concerned about how I fit in the scheme of things.

Well, what made you interest yourself in the Yucatan, for example? How did you get involved in that?

You mean a specific excavation in the Mayan area? This has always been a kind of mystery, the Mayan civilization. Still is, as a matter of fact. In the whole course of human history, we still don't really know whether this is an entirely independent development from the Old World. These are the basic philosophic ideas we're trying to get at. We picked what we thought was, from the evidence, the oldest and biggest city of Tikal, in Guatemala, of the Mayan cities. Settling on this site was an interest in, or a hope that, in a great big settlement like this, which was very ancient, we could really unravel the mystery of who the Maya are, and where they came from, whether they're absolutely independent, whether civilization in America is independent, or part of the Old World development. It's a kind of underlying mystery, of who these strange people are. There's a romantic touch to it.

We've been there, working there now more than 12 years. The interest of everybody working there has been that of trying to figure out whether these great building centers and so on are ceremonial centers, or whether they're real cities, in our sense. We've come to the conclusion that they're probably real cities. Now that's quite a revolutionary idea. We've also come to the conclusion, at least many of us have, that the end of a civilization like that is probably just a sheer breakdown of a political or social structure, because it became so bureaucratic and so top-heavy it couldn't function any longer. These are the kind of challenges that you're trying to solve in your own mind, and as a part of your whole discipline. But, in turning back to the original question about my own motivation here, I find it very difficult to put my finger on it.

Well, why, for example, the highland Maya, and not the lowland Maya? What is your interest in the Guatemalan highland Maya as opposed, let's say, to those in the Yucatan?

We're all pretty well agreed that the Yucatan Maya are a later develop-ment, or at least they flowered in a later period than the Maya of the highlands around Guatemala City. We think the thing began in the high-land areas, and we're really trying to get at origins there. We're trying to figure out what's caused all this, this rather unusual and strange civiliza-tion. This is all rationalizing about why we go into an area. It's all part of the accumulation of knowledge that has been going on for over a century.

In a sense, we're really concerned here about the creation of an entirely distinct civilization. We'd like to know how it came about. Is it an inde-pendent thing or is it stimulated by some contact with the Old World via the Pacific? Is it connected with the advanced civilizations in the highlands of South America? How unique is this business? In a sense, we're trying to get at the whole business of the creative forces in human society, I suppose.

Can we take two word meanings and put them together and see whether they lead to anything? You speak of challenge and you speak of origins.

That's a very curious question, because you know archaeologists are con-stantly concerned with origins of cultures, civilizations, connections, and so on. Are you getting at some idea that there's a personal element in this, that most of us are concerned with origins anyway, and we make a sort of transfer to the origins of cultures and civilizations?

Well, we're just wondering. It's an open question, really.

Could be. I mean, could be a reflection of a natural, human curiosity about one's own origins. That could very well be. I don't know. It's an odd thing to think about it. Archeologists are a peculiar group in the sense that, once you get started in this business, you get really trapped in it. Nobody becomes very famous, or very rich, or anything like that, as an archaeolo-gist. It's an all-engrossing study, which, if you really are bitten, you're in it for good. And, the real motivation in this I find very difficult to put my finger on.

How did you get bitten, Dr. Rainey?

When I think back, it was rather odd. I had taken some courses at the University of Chicago with Ralph Linton. Ralph was a very enthusiastic sort of person. He appealed to young students. I was rather excited about the course. It was anthropology and archaeology combined, both beginning courses. As I think back on it, I suppose what really got me excited about it is that it opened up a whole new world outside my own civilization, my own particular culture, and I began to see a much wider world. I mean, I began to look at human affairs from a worldwide point of view. And this was exciting. It's very exciting to people of that young age, I'm sure. This is one of the fundamental things about it. But, then, a lot of accidents took place. Because Ralph didn't drive, and I had a car, he suggested that I take him down to an excavation at some Indian mounds that the University of Chicago was doing out on the Mississippi River.

We spent a long weekend digging in this Indian Mound. I was perhaps eighteen or nineteen—something like that. This was a very exciting business. We began to find things. I began to see what archaeology was all about, and I think I was bitten right then, as a matter of fact, although I didn't really get back to archaeology for quite a while. I then went to the American School of Research in France. We worked in the paleolithic caves of Spain and France, and so on. And, of course, this gets very exciting, because you're looking back at 25,000 to 40,000 years ago, and you begin to realize that there were people living then that had all the intellectual capacity that we have today. They certainly had the brain capacity of a modern man. And, a lot of things they made and did in those times were not very different from some of the more advanced primitives today. This is a great excitement to the curious mind of a nineteen or twenty year old.

I find among my own students that it's almost unpredictable who really gets steamed up about this. And, then it's a matter of chance whether they stay in it or not. Things have to work out to keep their interest going, and they have to get a job in the field. Or they get distracted by other things. They may keep their interest all their lives, but they don't spend their life in doing it. So there's an original impetus, certainly, inspired by somebody, or something. And, then I think it's a series of accidents that keep men in this particular profession.

The aspect of new ideas in your work—we wonder how they manifest themselves because, as laymen, we would assume that if you're working on diggings in a certain area, once you have the flair for picking the right area to work in, you would feel that there's an ongoing creative process, or that the initial insight comes from the original choice, and then one could spend the rest of his life working on it.

This gets much closer to home than what we do all the time. We have a curious experience in a museum like ours. We have so many researchers working all the time. There are researchers who always seem to find significant things. There are others who don't. And I suspect that those who don't are those who get caught on a particular problem very early on, and they get so wrapped up in that problem, that their mind becomes sort of stereotyped or fixed. They never break out of that. There are others who are always going on to more and more original discoveries. I'm sure this is a matter of personality and character of the individuals.

I am reminded of a very good case of this that interested me a great deal. It's a fellow by the name of Louis Giddings who died as a result of an automobile accident three years ago. Of the many archaeologists I've known, I've never seen one who made so many fundamental, basic discoveries in his field. He was working in the Arctic. This is the best example I know of a really creative thinker in archaeology. He always seemed to spot the unusual, the unlikely, the fundamentally significant. I'll give you just one example of what I mean. Ever since about 1900 or 1910, there have been a lot of Danish, American, British, Canadian archaeologists working up in the Arctic doing archaeology. It's a rather limited, prescribed field, and there are not very many, but there are very good people. I started there in '35 myself, and in those days we were all absolutely convinced that all the archaeological sites in the Arctic were nice green mounds. Along the shore of the Arctic Ocean you'll see these green mounds. These were ancient archaeological sites. That's where everybody dug. Nobody thought about anything else. Giddings arrived up there. He was not an archeologist at all. He was a biologist, studying mosquitoes. He went up there to work with us studying mosquitoes, and he was also studying tree rings at that point for climatic studies for Douglas in Arizona. He was with me and a Dane, Helge Larsen, one day coming back across the tundra, near Point Hope. He saw a lot of what he thought were shallow, rectangular depressions in the ground. He said that he thought they might be house sites or old sites, and so on. Larsen and I, who were trained archaeologists in the Arctic—both of us had been working there for some time—pooh-poohed this whole business and said they were frost cracks and stuff like that. But he convinced us that we ought to go and try there.

Sure enough, these turned out to be old, very, very old house ruins of Eskimos, or Arctic peoples. Once we discovered these, we had discovered a new culture, and it made quite a noise in the Arctic field, because it was an entirely different kind of thing from what anybody had found before, with different horizons and everything else. Since that time, nobody in the

Arctic bothers digging those green mounds any longer. They're all looking for those depressions in the ground. This is just the first one of half a dozen discoveries that Giddings made like that before he died. One of the last ones that's also ingenious and creative in a very real sense, he got the idea that on the Arctic shore there was a series of beach lines, that the sea had moved out and left ridges along the shore, or beach lines. They're sort of rises, with hollow or shallow impressions between.

He conceived of the idea that people in the Arctic would always live right out on or near the sea, because that's where they lived on the sea mammals. So he thought, as you went back on those beach lines, you get older and older remains. He pursued this idea for a couple of years until he found the perfect example, and there he demonstrated that there were about a dozen different cultures on some 114 beach lines. Well, we'd all seen these beach lines. We all knew this perfectly obvious thing, this perfectly sensible, rational conclusion that he came to. But he persisted, and proved it, you see. It's another example of this sort of creative process. This is an unusual mind. It's a mind which is not trammeled by preconviction or what you already know. I think one of the worst things in science, for all of us, is that certain things are true, and certain things can't be true, and then all your life you're stuck right there, because you know that this can't be true or that this must be this way.

And they never go beyond the original facts.

Never go beyond. It's always unique individuals who somehow look at the bumps instead of the depressions, and the depressions instead of the bumps. Put it that way. There are such people, fortunately. Those make the breakthrough, I think. And it's just as true, I'm sure, in archaeology, as it is in physics, or chemistry, or any other science. In a way probably it's less true among archaeologists because, by and large, they're a pretty conservative lot, I think; whereas the physical sciences have been forced into a more original point of view, because of the tremendous strides forward in technology and scientific application and so on. These have forced most physical scientists to think in a different way. Until quite recently, at least, I think archaeologists have been a conservative group, and they find it very hard to look at the other side of anything. Like everybody else, in archaeology these days, we're being forced by technology. You know, application of radioactive carbon dating to archaeology, and many other techniques have been worked out since the last war. They're forcing a more open mind in archaeology, too. A more creative kind of thinking.

It's perfectly obvious to all of us that one of the greatest developments in science and technology in recent years is the development of new tools for research—where suddenly your whole horizon extends because of an applied technique or a new kind of technology, which makes it possible to see deeper into the nature of life or further out into space. These are the things which are forcing us all to think differently. But actually they don't. They make no difference. I mean, I feel that you have to have that kind of mind before you can take advantage of these new tools. No question about it.

Well, we'd like to know more about that kind of mind. What goes into it? For example, when you come up with an original idea, do you have any thoughts about what prompts it? We tried earlier to get at some of the possible unconscious forces. But what about the more superficial forces— exposure to colleagues, some reading, some new idea, or a chance comment of someone's.

This is a constant process with us. You see, we have quite a large staff at the Philadelphia Museum. All are archaeologists or anthropologists. We try to create an atmosphere where people from completely different fields are kicking ideas around among themselves. We even take people from the Near East and send them to Middle America or vice versa. Or we get somebody from the Middle East and send them to South Asia, and so on. For the simple reason that we think that, in this day when there is such a tremendous upsurge of ideas and developments of all kinds, the most stimulating process, the most stimulating thing you can do, is to sort of force people into contact with others in other fields, and a chance word will set somebody thinking in an entirely different way.

This last winter we had a boy who'd been working in Afghanistan and Pakistan, and we thought it would be a good idea to send him to see an operation in Central America. It's a completely different point of view in Central America, from what it is in Central Asia. He came back all steamed up. What comes of being all steamed up I don't know, but I'm sure it's a healthy business. You never know what a chance word, or what thing he sees, starts him thinking in an original point of view. This is what I was saying about Giddings. In our field, and I suppose, like most fields, it's getting outside of those blinders that we all have on us these days, because you're in a specific field. You're trained in specific ideas and have specific limitations. How you break out of that strait jacket that we get in our academic training these days, this is the really critical thing.

Are you suggesting that there's a role for the generalist in archaeology, as well as the specialist?

Well, I certainly hope so, because that's my role. If you're like me you're spending some weeks in Iran, and then some weeks in Egypt, and then maybe in Italy, and then Central America, and so on, or the Arctic. You're constantly running into ideas in those areas. I feel that people tend to get terribly restricted in the way they think about their work, if they remain specialists in their field. On the contrary, you don't get very far these days unless you become a specialist and an expert. Somebody has to play the role of needling, stimulating, pushing them to see some different ideas, or to get in contact with people in other fields.

One of the best examples I've had of that in recent years is setting up an applied-science center at the Museum, where we have physicists, chemists, engineers, electronics experts, and so on, constantly exchanging ideas with archaeologists. Since we're developing all these new tools and techniques, you simply have to have the specially trained people to handle them. The interesting part to me is that particularly the physical scientist develops usually a tremendous interest in archaeology. He begins to see history in a way he's not seen it before. He begins to think of history in terms of tens of thousands of years, instead of centuries, for one thing. The scientists kind of break out of their own Western civilization. By the same token, the archaeologists, I think, are suddenly aware that there is a new kind of technology; I mean, there's a different order of technology today from what they're normally concerned with. You know, they tend to think, since we studied . . . that there is a kind of . . . the slow development of technology and science over hundreds or thousands of years, orderly progression in this business. Once they got thrown into work with contemporary physicists and chemists, and electronics people and engineers and so on, they suddenly realized that it's an era of phenomenal technological change and development, unlike anything we've ever seen before, really. It's really a new order of things. It kind of opens their eyes to the contemporary process that's going on. My role in the museum is to try to cut across not only all the different fields in archaeology, but also different sciences, such as physics, chemistry, climatic studies, and geology, and everything else; because these are very stimulating things, if you can get people to go more deeply into something that's entirely outside their field.

What was there, if anything, in your family background that predisposed you to an interest in archaeology?

I really can't imagine anything, 'cause I was brought up on a cattle ranch in Montana, and my idea of the best life in the world was to be a cowboy. I can't get further away from being an archaeologist, as far as I can see.

Your father was a rancher?

My mother was on the ranch with my father. I was brought up there until I was about sixteen or seventeen years old. I went to the University of Montana, and then I went to Illinois, and Chicago, and finally ended up at Yale. I suppose, in this process, somewhere between that cattle ranch and Yale, I somehow got involved in this business. My father was eighty-seven before he died, my mother's still alive; she's eighty-nine.

And, there was never any question in your own mind, for example, about where you came from, or what your identity was?

In front of psychologists, I don't know if I should say this, but you know, I was really brought up by a bunch of cowboys in a bunkhouse. Actually, it was a very funny bringing-up for a young kid, because I can remember the first time I went to church, the man was standing up there, and in a very eloquent manner, he was cussing a blue streak. And, I couldn't imagine why he was up there swearing at us like that. And he was saying, "Jesus Christ" and "God Almighty." It was an odd upbringing, but I don't think in those days a very abnormal one. My family was very intact, and stayed intact, and they've been very close.

What about this issue of curiosity you spoke of before, this intellectual curiosity. Was there something in those years that sort of stimulated this curiosity by the cowboys?

I can't put my finger on it, I must say. Although you'd be surprised at the discussions that go on in a bunkhouse. You wouldn't call it intellectual, but they're certainly curious. They're interested in what the world's all about and why things happen, what this all means, and so on. There are long sessions among these rather uneducated boys who are herding cows. They have a lot of time to think. No question about it. I suppose that's the way it is with rather isolated people who are spending a lot of time with themselves. They may develop more curiosity about the world around them than somebody who's deeply involved in urban civilization, and who is going at a high pace all the time, and who is distracted by other things, whereas these boys are not. Not educated, but intellectually curious. Intel-

ligent, a lot of them. It could be. I couldn't put my finger on it, but it
certainly may have been something like that.

*Can you address yourself now to the question of the role of intuition in
your work. Do you feel that it plays a role?*

It's certainly very debatable. Yes, I think a lot of us play hunches. But,
you know, when you start an excavation, there are infinite numbers of sites
you may dig at. When you settle on a site, for many reasons there are
infinite numbers of places you can start digging, and a lot of diggers say,
"we just played a hunch. We tried it here. We started here." Perhaps
intuition played a part in this. It's hard for me to say. But, everybody has
to make that kind of judgment. You know there are some enormous sites,
and you can't dig them all. You just have to select a section, and there's no
guide really in many cases, as to where you start. You just play a hunch.
Maybe it is intuitive. Maybe that's why some people hit it lucky and some
don't. Some of our boys just seem to be unlucky. Year after year, they're
just unlucky.

They keep digging, and they never find anything.

They keep digging, and they find, you know, things, but never very significant. The next guy, every site he digs he turns something up, something
very significant. What is this? It isn't just rational intelligence, because,
you know, they're all scholars, and they know, they all read all the published material on that area, and they know the background. That's just
elementary in our field. But, beyond that it's just original thinking somehow. I'm sure I don't know what it is.

Does surprise play an important part in this work?

Well, we're always being surprised, certainly. One never knows what he's
going to turn up. Maybe, in some cases, there are certain individuals who
somehow utilize the surprise elements more. They follow the surprises.
Others, I feel, are so damned conservative, that they probably cover up the
surprise. There are people who are just that set in their ways.

*Well, that's very interesting. We wonder whether we could do anything to
sort of distinguish one from the other. The guy who sweeps over what
would turn out to be a major find for somebody else.*

Well, you know if you're obviously going to find something very interesting, a bronze pot, nobody misses that. But, it's a much more difficult thing if you're working in an area where there's a mud-brick settlement, let's say, and you're tracing a mud-brick wall, and there's damned little difference between that mud-brick wall and the dirt around it, and some fellows are the ones who see a very surprising turn in the wall, or a very surprising junction in the wall. And, they're very intellectually curious, and quick. They'll follow that. Whereas the other guy, who already knows what that's going to do—and a lot of our people think they do, they know from their training and experience that these walls always do such and such, and they turn so and so, and they're so high, and so on—if you're absolutely convinced of that, you don't see the surprise. And, I'm sure that's true of certain individuals. It's capacity, or I don't know if it's capacity, it's an alert mind, an inquiring mind, an innate curiosity that sees something that may be very inconspicuous, but they follow it out. Whereas, the more conservative, the more fixed in his ways, he would just overlook it. I'm sure of it. I suppose that's it.

Is there a role of accident in your work?

Oh, there always is. I had a very amusing one years ago when I was at Yale and I was digging in the West Indies. As a good graduate student, I knew that the only sites in the West Indies were shell heaps. That's where you found everything. Great piles of seashells. I had a big crew. It was during the Relief Administration times, some forty or fifty men, and we were digging long trenches in a shell mound. When we got down to the bottom of the shells, we stopped, because that was the bottom of the site. We knew that. One day, I'd had a very big luncheon and I went to sleep after lunch, it was siesta and a very hot day. The foreman thought, "Oh, well, it's a hot day, let the boss sleep." I slept. Some of our workmen finished one of their squares and sections, finished the bottom of the shell and, nobody was there to tell them to stop, so they went right on down to see what it looked like, absolutely sterile stuff. When they got beyond the sterile stuff, they began to turn up the kind of painted pottery that nobody had ever seen before in the West Indies. At that point they woke me up, and I made my first discovery. I got all the credit for it. This is Arawak Indian country. This is in Puerto Rico.

I always think of that; I got a lot of credit as a graduate student for a remarkable discovery in the West Indies; and I'm absolutely certain it was because I ate too many beans for lunch, and then slept, had a long siesta. But, at least being reasonably intelligent, it was a thing I've never forgotten. One doesn't stop where one is supposed to any longer. You learn one fundamental lesson, that you really look for the surprises, and for the unusual now. You don't really stop any more until you're sure you're down to bedrock. At least, you learn from these accidents, I must say. I think we've all learned from accidents like this. But, surely, accident does play a role, the great chance is the way you happen to approach something. With all the learning you've got, where you actually attack something is either chance or intuition, or luck, or something is involved in this business. As I say, some make use of it, and some don't.

Do you find that your graduate students come in with the idea that there is a particular civilization that they want to study? Or, do they come in with a more general view? Is there something about a particular area that sort of stimulates the curiosity of an individual and, if so, what might be some of the reasons?

Well, I think an awful lot of American anthropologists and archaeologists have, in their childhood, gotten fascinated with Indians. This has gone right on through their lives. I've known many of them that must have had a childhood interest—they collected arrowheads, or they happened to dig into an Indian site, or they had run into an Indian burial area. It made such an impression on them, as children, that they got fascinated with Indians. I wouldn't be surprised if that accounts for an awful lot of American anthropologists and archaeologists who work with the American Indians. Their childhood enthusiasm has been with them all their lives. A lot of our students at Pennsylvania, when they were undergraduates got excited about a new perspective on their own society. This is the fundamental thing. They just get excited about anthropology and archaeology, as such. Then they go on, and in graduate school, they graduate to a certain field. That again is largely luck. For example, we have graduate students who are taking basic courses and then suddenly one of our curators says, "Do you want to go to Pakistan?" He goes to Pakistan, and he's committed, probably, for the rest of his life. A sheer accident. He didn't decide on Pakistan. That's where luck comes in. That's the way I went to Alaska. I'd been working in the West Indies, and Dr. Winder at the American Museum of Natural History asked me if I wanted to go to Alaska. I said, "Good God, no! That's the last place I want to go." But, at that point, I was not getting along very well with some people at Yale, and it was the only thing that turned up in the middle of the Depression, so. I went to Alaska. Pure chance. It was really quite contrary to my bent, at that point. Once I got there, I found it so fascinating, I stayed there for many years.

Could we come back to this question of challenge. We wonder whether there is a challenge within yourself, to prove something in your work?

Well, I'll give you a specific case, first. You know, I've been searching for that city of Sybaris for six or seven years now. We used all kinds of new techniques and so on to do it. This got to be a real challenge, because, damn it, we've been looking for that site for nearly a hundred years, since about 1875. And nobody's found it, and I thought the first couple of years we'd got it, but then, my better judgment told me we hadn't. At least I couldn't prove it. As the years went on we spent more money, more time, it became a tremendous challenge, a kind of obsession to find that place. This is a specific case. This is a real challenge. And now we have. I'm just now finishing up, and saying, "Yes, we have it."

It's a tremendous satisfaction to resolve something that's been an enigma for so long. This is the kind of challenge, I think, many people face in the field. In a more general way I find it more difficult to say. There are many challenges when you come to human history, and you and they get confused. I find it very difficult to pinpoint any specific challenge in world-wide archaeology and anthropology. You know, you think that probably ideas have only sprung up one place in the world, and you must explain the distribution of these ideas around the world on a diffusionist basis. This becomes a kind of challenge to prove that. Or, another time, you're convinced that they can't possibly be diffused, and so you're challenged with the idea, "How does it happen that people on completely different continents will develop the same idea."

Is there something in human nature that simply duplicates this idea, because he's a human being? These are the big, basic challenges in the whole field which we all fiddle around with. We change our minds about these things all the time.

Oh, yes. Could you tell us any more about the challenge of finding Sybaris? What spurred you on? What started you on that track?

Well actually, I got into it in a very peculiar way because, you know, I was at one time chairman of the planning board for the Seattle Exposition. We were trying to plan the science exhibition, and we were trying to look forward into the 21st Century. In doing that planning for the 21st century exposition in Seattle, I had the idea, sitting with twenty scientists in Washington, day after day, for about two years. We had a series of meetings. It struck me that what was having the greatest effect on our everyday, on our ordinary lives these days was, not so much science, but the application of science; that really technology was having the greatest, the most fundamental effect on modern times. This was a result of our trying to look forward into the 21st century. So I thought, if that's true, then we should busily get to work in archaeology, and make use of all these new tools that the technological people are providing for us. I purposefully went to work with a group trying to develop and adapt and discover new tools for archaeological research—dating, interpretation, analysis, search, and all sorts of things. Because of that, I was naturally led to Italy, because here you have a variety of sites of all kinds. It was a marvelous proving ground for these things we were developing. Also I happened to run into an Italian, who was interested in the same things. We sort of joined up. Of the many proving grounds we could use, this was one of the most challenging, because it had been searched for, for so long, and had not been found.

There's a poem by Schiller that every schoolboy in Europe must learn, which refers to Sybaris as a kind of moral lesson—luxury, wealth, and decadence, and so on. It was destroyed and disappeared, and it has been used as a kind of moral lesson by poets, and philosophers, and so on, ever since. All of this built up into a special challenge to see if we could utilize instruments to find this city, and in doing so make all these applications of the new techniques. It was a rational thing in one way, and it was a kind of emotional challenge in another way. That's what focused us on that.

Do you think that that poem by Schiller was responsible for your wanting to find Sybaris?

No. Because, as a matter of fact, I never read that poem by Schiller. I can't recall it at all.

It just knocked our theory to hell!

I'm afraid it did. I wish I could support it. Now, it may be that way back in my school days I did read that poem, but I certainly have no conscious memory of it. Sorry about your theory.

You say once you got on to the city, you were obsessed by it.

Yes!

All right. Could you tell us how that obsession manifested itself? Did you eat, drink, and sleep it? Did you dream it? Did you work on it?

Boy, I should say so! Because, in the first place I was not alone. We were working with a lot of people. And night after night, day after day, we were all discussing, arguing, pondering, where this damned place could be, and how to find it. We'd come up with a theory one day, and we'd all get excited about it—then we'd knock it into a cocked hat the next day, you see. I happened to be living in Italy, with a man named Enrico Mueller, a South African. He'd been obsessed with this thing a long time, trying to find this city. So, he welcomed me with open arms as somebody who was coming with all these new techniques, and was a trained archaeologist, and so on. Of course, this was another impetus in the direction, 'cause I stayed with him for years. Every time I was out there, I stayed with his family. And of course Enrico and I were debating this thing night after night. So, it was constantly on my mind. My God, I thought about it all the time. But, I'm sorry to say, I never had any dreams about it. I only wish I had.

We'd get terribly tangled up in the problems, and certainly would dream about it, like anything else, when your mind is very much involved in them.

Do your excavations show up very much in your daydreams or in your night dreams?

I don't think so. It's not the sort of thing I dream about. I dream about high places and difficult physical situations—almost never about my work except in a case like this where I go to sleep with a problem in my mind. But normally, my dreams are not occupied with my work. They're occupied with, you know, things like being on a very high place, and not being able to get down. I wake up in a sweat. That kind of nightmare thing.

Uh huh—

But they are not associated with archaeology, as a rule.

You said something about overcoming physical obstacles, too?

Yes, sort of. The dreams that I remember are of the nightmarish type. I guess maybe most people do. Like those in which you must get something done, and you can't make it, you can't move. You're moving very slowly, or the damned car breaks down, or something like that. That's a very common sort of problem in my dreams. The ones I remember, at least. Most common one is that of being in a very high place and of not being able to get down. Most common nightmare I have. I have a kind of fear of heights, anyway. Not in planes, but in high buildings and so on, and that expresses itself in my nightmarish types of dreams.

How does it manifest itself when you work on the pyramids or anything like that?

Well, on the pyramids in the Maya country, it certainly does. Jesus! Tikal has the most straight-up pyramids you ever saw, and they give me the absolute jitters. Coming down gives me the jitters. I can remember that we had one of our men, an architect, working on the roof of the tremendous, big temples. I never could get myself up on top there. Oh, I was dying to get up and take a look from that high elevation. But you had to go up on a scaffolding. All open. And the scaffolding swung out over the land. It was 250 feet high. I never could make that. It was my sense of feeling about heights and I just couldn't get up there.

Are those pyramids higher than the ones in The Valley of Mexico?

Oh, yes. They're higher and a lot steeper.

I don't know whether I'm helping you fellows out. I hadn't ever thought along these lines.

Well, we think that a lot of these things that you've said are very interesting.

Well, with regard to your main theme—of course, naturally, I'm concerned always in employing men, creative men, what you're talking about. Because, in our field, it's the creative business, the creative thinking, which succeeds. And I suppose that the biggest job I have is to try to select young men that I think are going to have this. I'll be fascinated with what you find out, because I don't know what rules of thumb to use in selecting young men. I tried for three years to find a man to head our Egyptian Department. And I must have gone through six or eight different countries looking for him: Holland, England, France, Belgium, United States, and so on, looking for an Egyptologist. There are a lot of them. But it took me a long time to find one that I thought was the right one to head up our department. It's a very important department for us. I wanted to get a young man that I expected would have a very original look at this, and a completely fresh, creative way about it. I found, almost everywhere I went, that most Egyptologists—it's a kind of a special subject in archaeology anyway—are all highly specialized; that some of them were Middle Kingdom linguists, and some were art historians of the Old Kingdom, and so forth.

You were looking for another Renaissance man?

That's right. We were looking for somebody who looks at the whole business and can apply all of what we know about Egyptology to a new look at the whole Egyptian field. It's darned difficult to find such a person. How do you sight that fellow? How do you know? In conversation, it's the only way I can judge, if he goes right down a sort of stereotyped line, I think, "He's not for us." But, if he's exploring with an open mind, and asking questions, and shows a curiosity, he's a good bet, anyway. I don't think that assures he's going to be a genius, but a least it's the best bet one can make, the best guide one can find in selecting a man. If you fellows come up with any idea of how you can put your finger on creativity, it'll be something.

HARLOW SHAPLEY

There may be a cultural difference between western Missouri and Cambridge, Massachusetts, but Dr. Harlow Shapley manages to represent the best of both areas. He was born in November, 1885, and today he is a distinguished man of science whose intellectual achievements are complemented by his wry midwestern humor and wit. Long director of the Harvard College Observatory and now Emeritus Professor of Astronomy at Harvard, Professor Shapley retired from the formal academic life more than fifteen years ago.

From meager beginnings in Missouri, Shapley's career has been, on his own testimony, far from easy. It began with a bachelor's and master's degree from the University of Missouri, followed by a fellowship at Princeton University, which awarded him his doctrate for work with Henry Norris Russell. His work then led him westward to the Mt. Wilson Observatory and years under the famous George Ellery Hale.

Returning later to the east again, Harlow Shapley accepted the directorship of the Harvard College Observatory and a professorship of astronomy at the same college. His discoveries over the years are legendary: the determination of the distances of the globular clusters, the calculation that there are more than 10^{20} stars in the universe, and the startling conclusion that our sun is not the center of our own galaxy, as astronomers before Shapley believed.

Dr. Shapley's life illustrates that he is not only a specialist in his field, but in addition has a deep concern for the larger issues facing humanity. This finds expression in a long-held interest in the effects of science upon the modern world and in his joining other concerned scientists, after World War II, in having a voice in the peace that they helped to secure.

It may also come as no surprise that Shapley's scientific contributions are not in astronomy and physics alone, but embrace also entomology and especially the sub-specialty in that science known as myrmecology. In the interview that follows, Professor Shapley tells us something about his interests in the behavior of ants, a subject in which he has made some significant contributions.

ASTRONOMY AND PHYSICS

Harlow Shapley

To begin with, can you tell us how some of the problems that you have attacked came to invite your interest? How did they occur to you? To be specific, do you feel that your inner life, in the sense of your fantasies, has been instrumental?

There's one little item I'd like to put in before I answer your wider question. Did you know that I have a twin brother who is not a scientist? He clips coupons for a living! We have been almost strangers over a considerable portion of our lives, but not recently. Our father was a farmer, or I should say, a hay dealer, in Southwestern Missouri, and we twins grew up in a curious way. When does a person become creative?

Sometimes at a very early age, the early teens.

My brother Horace Shapley and I, in our early teens, were associated in a sort of imaginary operation that I think may have been unique. Later on, I found that Hudson Hoagland of Worcester had a twin with whom he engaged in a similar kind of imaginary operation. In these imaginary operations of our early teens, Horace would do the work and I would use my imagination. He was a dream boy who went along with my ideas, and that comes as near to being a psychological situation as can happen. It was quite a dream life that I had.

And right now, do you feel that your dream life followed you when you went on to college?

I would say so. After I graduated from a Carthage, Missouri, high school, if you want to call it a high school as we know a high school today, I enrolled at the University of Missouri in Columbia. At college I hated physics, but in my undergraduate years I got interested in astronomy.

How did this interest in astronomy develop?

A mathematician, Oliver Kellogg, had more influence on my academic career at the University of Missouri than anyone else and helped me get a graduate fellowship at Princeton. But an important factor was the fact that I needed money, which all of us did, and money meant scholarships which guide your life a bit. Indeed, if I hadn't had a rather difficult start, I might have gone into physics more directly.

At about sixteen, I left our hay ranch and went to Chanute, Kansas, where I got a job on a newspaper. This appealed to me because I soon found out that I could write moderately well, and I therefore decided to become a journalist. You've certainly heard about a fellow by the name of William Allan White, who was a country editor in Kansas at the time. His work represented a goal toward which I could strive, and pretty soon I became one of the editors of a country daily.

I realized that you have to be educated to be a newspaper person, so I returned home and decided to go back to school with my younger brother, John. He's five years younger than I. My twin brother Horace had gone west. Unfortunately, I couldn't get into the Carthage high school. But John and I were lucky because there was a so-called collegiate institute in Carthage where we became students. I spent two semesters there, having skipped one semester, and graduated from this high school. John continued to get a more formal education.

It worked out then that after about a year or so I was ready to go to the University of Missouri where they were to start a new School of Journalism in which I enrolled. As it happened, they didn't start the school that Fall.

I was at the University and I enrolled in the regular undergraduate program. I early came in contact with Frederick Seares, the astronomer. He was a precise sort of man and in every way a good man to study with, but he was also very stiff and had little warmth. This is where Oliver Kellogg comes into the picture. But I was fortunate because Seares needed an assistant, and I became his student assistant. Because I took the second year of physics before the first one, I nearly flunked my first course in physics at the University.

This really made me decide to do well in physics because I really wanted to show them. So I continued with physics, and two years later I graduated from the University with honors in physics and mathematics. I became quite a hero because they punctured me in my first course in physics!   ›

Was this idea of showing people something important to you in later life? Can you relate it to some of the work you subsequently have done in astronomy?

I am afraid that it was important. I suppose it's a matter of vanity because I got nothing but top marks at the University after that disaster in my first course in physics. I remember in French that I got A plus, a grade that they'd never before given, and I was just the cat's pajamas, and that of course excited my vanity. In mathematics, in which Kellogg influenced me, I did very well also.

Would you say that you are an inspirational person in your teaching?

Yes. I think that I have excited the young in their studies for years. I have been able to do this without having much to do with the really young students. At Harvard, where I have done most of my teaching, I have not had undergraduate students. Much of my work at Harvard involved managing the Harvard College Observatory complex, which has branches in a number of different places. At the Observatory I always expected a high level of accuracy in the work, but also some novelty. We've always worked hard for novelty in our undertakings at the Observatory. And I've been lucky to have gotten a number of breaks in my scientific work.

Can you tell us about these breaks? Do you have one or two examples?

When I went to Harvard from the Mt. Wilson Observatory, some people who were interested in my work told me that I was giving up a scientific career. They told me that I had many things yet to do in astronomy. At the Harvard College Observatory at that time, there were only two fields in which research was going forward. These were spectral classification and standard methods of photometry. I enlarged the program a great deal when I went to Harvard. When I originally went to Harvard, there were no doctor's degrees offered in astronomy. There were good people at the Observatory, and I set out to make the whole program outstanding. This wasn't hard to do.

I'd say that I had an ambition to see what I could do at the Harvard Observatory at a time when the very big telescopes were on the west coast, which was the dominant area in astronomy.

I think you should mention a person whom I met early in my career in astronomy, and there's nobody who should be mentioned more often as having had a significant influence in my life in astronomy. This is Henry Norris Russell. I guess Russell was the only real genius that I've ever met. After becoming acquainted with each other, we became chums. I had the good fortune of being associated with him for about three years, and he served as a very important source of my inspiration.

Actually, it worked out that each of us learned from the other one. Both Russell and I had found someone whom each could work well with, and we developed idea after idea, with the result that we were able to publish paper after paper together. During this period, there was much interest in eclipsing binary stars, and as a matter of fact interest in this dominated the field for perhaps twenty years. There was one kind of star that didn't act like a double eclipsing star, in which one component moves in front of the other. In this type of single star, the light goes up and down, and we called them Cepheid Variables. I began playing around especially with these stars as soon as I got to the Mt. Wilson Observatory, and out of this came the Shapley Theory of Cepheid Variation. My friend Russell wasn't in on this work, and when I later tried to give him credit for developing some of the more important ideas about cepheid variation, he refused to accept his share of the credit and insisted that it was all mine.

As it has worked out, the theory has turned out to be correct, and for about forty years I think that I can say that the cepheid theory has been a dominant one and has had its application to other kinds of variable stars as well. The simple fact of the matter is that Russell and I had stumbled upon something which, after much work, turned into a bonanza.

You actually stumbled upon it?

Well, practically so. After being a kind of intellectual stumblebum, if I may refer to myself in this way, I went after the cepheid variables and, out of much work and with the help of others at the Harvard College Observatory, came the theory of cepheid variation. We were working with the period luminosity curve which is concerned with a period of time and its relationship to variations in brightness levels. Our work at the Observatory with cepheid variation led quite naturally to another thing—that of the possibility of calculating the distances to the globular star clusters.

When I was a small boy, the greatest distance that astronomers could measure with security was about 100 light years, and this grew out of certain trigonometric work involving estimating the distances of different stars and projecting from them via trigonometry other distances. I had been interested in this whole matter while I was at Princeton working on my doctorate, and had been able to show that new tools for estimating distance were becoming available. Along about 1917, many years after I had gotten started in this area, I was able to come out with a distance measure of globular star clusters.

There are about 100 of these globular star clusters scattered around the sky that have cepheid variables in them. The cepheid variation theory, as I came to realize later, showed a way of measuring the distance of heavenly bodies, that we had a new concept of the universe that greatly extended a way of measuring heavenly bodies. This provided a new way of measuring distances without recourse to trigonometry and provided the possibility of extending distances up to 100 million light years. This is, of course, a rather colossal change.

Thus it came to be said that up to this point there were two outstanding things that I had done in astronomy. One was the pulsation theory of cepheid variation, the other its application in the measurement of distance in the universe. When the universe came to be extended in this manner, it appeared as if it were lopsided and that man seemed to be located in a somewhat different position in the cosmos. I think that I initially didn't make much of the implications of this finding. Later on it became clearer that we had had a geocentric universe conception that had been reformulated by Copernicus into a heliocentric one which involved a view of the universe as one in which our sun is central. My new views led finally to a galactocentric conception of the universe in which the central pivot is the galaxy. Using this conception and the implications that seemed to me to flow from it, I had a lot of fun in pouring out one paper after another that sought to develop the material.

In this work, which proliferated into so many papers that the astronomy journals finally refused to publish all of them, I was greatly helped by Miss Annie Cannon to whom I owed a great deal of my inspiration during this period. I was able to excite her so that she did an excellent job in classifying the stellar spectra. But during this period there were also about twenty other young women who were extremely helpful.

This work seemed to lead quite naturally to my going to the Harvard Observatory where I would have an opportunity of trying to revive what had become over the years quite dormant. I think what resulted was a sort of revival of interest in and importance of the Observatory in Cambridge.

When you spoke some moments ago about your having stumbled upon the important notions you've been discussing, we suppose you're referring to your intuition. Is this correct?

Yes, yes. But I want to emphasize that it was more, much more, than intuition. It took a great deal of awfully hard work. At Harvard I didn't follow the Mt. Wilson plan of having one part-time assistant assigned to each full professor. I was fortunate in being able to obtain as many as ten or so assistants, and this became a big factor in the number of hours that could be devoted to analytical work that could move forward the ideas that I had.

The first doctoral student I had at Harvard, and indeed the first person who took a doctorate in astronomy at Harvard, was a woman. Her name is Cecilia Payne Gaposchkin, and she has made history. She was a very remarkable person and quite difficult for me to manage, and I think that I could write quite an essay on wild women I've met and worked with. After her, there were many more doctoral students because Harvard had become a good place to work and also have fun at. Mrs. Shapley was always very good to my students, offering them an opportunity to visit us in our home and to enjoy parties there.

When you have worked, have you done so in a systematic or erratic fashion?

I find that nothing is easy. I've had a Dictaphone beside my bed for years, and I've had the good luck to get many people to help me move systematically into the solutions of my problems. Sometimes in the mornings I would loaf, staying in bed and talking to my Dictaphone. Some years ago, the National Academy of Sciences asked me to make a list of my publications and I found out that I had published more than 450 scientific papers. In anybody's schedule, that means a lot of work. It turns out that I haven't made too many mistakes in the course of this work, but I do know that there were two or three blunders.

In retrospect, why do you think you made those blunders, if you now know why?

The worst blunder I made was because of loyalty to one of our staff members, just because of friendship and such like. I just felt that he hadn't been getting a good deal, and I thought that I could help him get out of the mess that he'd gotten in. Most of the work was scientifically clean, and the problem involved determining the distance to the center of a galaxy, which can be quite important. My first estimate was 50,000 light years, and later I dropped this estimate down to 25,000 light years. The error was due to my believing that the work of another astronomer had been correct, and it turned out to be quite wrong.

Can you tell us what the effect of your mood on your work is? Do you work, for example, more productively when you're happy or when you're depressed?

I think I work better when I am depressed. I feel like the devil when I'm not getting things done or when I've not been able to get an idea earlier.

This is interesting, and you seem to be talking about your reactions to frustration. Do you drop something that is giving you difficulty and pick it up later?

I don't drop it. I stick with it right to the limit of my ability. I stick with things I can't quite handle, such as equations, and stay with them until I've licked them.

Do you ever run into dry periods? Does your frustration sometimes lead to blocks?

No, I don't remember such. I don't remember being blocked. I think that I just hammer away. I stay with it because I find so many places where there are loose ends that I can work on, and there is enough pleasure in the whole enterprise to keep me going until I finish it. When I do come to something that's beyond me, that's a different matter. I had a kind of double life at Harvard. One was administrative, the other scientific. Being an administrator makes for many difficulties. For example, I made a number of wrong decisions about how to handle staff members, who can be very difficult. On the other hand, I think the Harvard Observatory was more free of jealousy than any other place I've been associated with, and that was quite deliberate on my part. I worry about a person who I see in difficulty.

In working on a scientific problem, do you have a sense of urgency about it?

Yes, I feel a sense of urgency. I don't like to be bypassed by others. I mean that this is just ordinary vanity.

Has your administrative work offered as much pleasure as your scientific endeavors?

I think that they're about equal. I've done work for UNESCO, for example, but if I hadn't, someone else would have done so.

Do you feel that if you hadn't discovered the Cepheid Star Theory you've told us about, someone else would have done so?

I didn't believe so at the time, but now I do think so.

When you discovered it, did you feel that you simply had to discover it, that it couldn't wait?

I believe so, but I now wonder how urgent it was. I guess that it's only in recent years that I've come to the sane philosophy of saying, "Well, keep your shirt on, somebody else is going to do these things, and perhaps will do them better than you could."

In recent years, have you found use for the computer as a replacement for the young women who earlier did so much of the work you've mentioned?

One day long ago, a graduate-school student, maybe in engineering, came over to see me at the Observatory to ask whether I needed help. We knew that we had a tremendous number of calculations to make, and wondered whether a little bit of machinery would help. I think his original idea may have been that of linking up a number of calculating machines in such a way that they could be helpful generally. We had some very exacting calculating jobs to do, since our calculations for the orbits of Jupiter and Saturn needed to be overhauled.

That fellow's name was Harold Aiken, and I think he must have the credit for introducing, or originating, if you please, many of the new ideas of calculation that permitted us to take on problems that had been standing around for decades, even for centuries, waiting for the time for them to be tackled. You may have seen pictures of the round table at the Observatory where many of these calculations were made. Later on, of course, through the cooperation of Aiken and others, we were able to get increasingly sophisticated equipment to use in the tackling of our problems and in the performance of our calculations.

Mrs. Shapley has been a wonderful companion for you in your work at the Observatory, hasn't she?

Yes, I'm afraid that I've worked her pretty hard. I mean that she's done at least half a dozen papers on star calculations and star theories. She started out as a philologist, and then I wrecked that career for her, and she then became an astronomer. Mainly, as I've suggested, she was a guide to the social life associated with the Observatory. I have a number of grandchildren, and one of them, June Matthews, is exceptionally good in nuclear physics. She has her doctorate in nuclear physics from MIT. She just happens to have an extraordinary gift for handling cyclotrons. My third son, Lloyd Shapley, who is a mathematician, has the mathematical talent that my wife, his mother, has and this trait has also been passed on to June Matthews.

Still, Dr. Shapley, can you tell us more about the role of intuition in your scientific work?

Well, I think I've stumbled quite a bit, such as in the process of getting ideas about the center of the Milky Way. I think I had the thing pretty well worked out about 1917, except for details. I didn't know the corrections to make for the absorption of light in space, and I did quite a bit of stumbling with this problem. I really think that my intuition unfortunately lies more in the areas of philosophy and religion.

I think that you'll get some idea of my interest in this field by just glancing at the titles of some of my books. Take, for example, *The View from a Distant Star*. I think that only about 10 per cent of the articles or chapters in it deal with astronomy. The others lie quite outside that field. I didn't quite realize that I was an "outside operator."

Do you read outside of astronomy?

Yes, I have been concerned, for example, with man's place in the universe. A paper I've written is "Two Moments of Discovery." A third contribution is "Bird's Eye View of Our Galaxy." In my book, *The View from a Distant Star*, I get into the idea of applying the concept of evolution to an expanding universe. I concern myself with what I've called cosmochemistry, but I don't really think that's philosophy. It's rather a combination of science and speculation.

A hobby of mine, by the way, is the study of insects. This area is one of the two I refer to in my essay, "Two Moments of Discovery," to which

I've already referred. I think that I have discovered a throwback of perhaps a hundred million years in the development of the social insects.
Once, while walking in the street in Pasadena, California, I stumbled upon
an observation that has proved to be very helpful. I noticed that there were
some little black spots on the backs of some of the ants. I followed this up
through a series of observations over quite a period of time. The thing hit
me originally, I guess, because I was just keeping my eyes open and was
ready for some kind of discovery.

Somewhat later I went up to the museum in San Francisco and looked
at their collection of ants. It was a poor collection, to be sure, but I was
able to find one of the pterergates that I had seen much further south in
Pasadena. Only about six had ever before been discovered, but now many
more are known, mainly because of my work with them. I was excited by
my original find, and sent it back to Wheeler at Harvard, who considered it
a really worthwhile discovery.

*Dr. Shapley, wasn't it you who originally had the idea of applying the
principles of evolution developed by Darwin to the evolution of the
universe?*

Yes, I really think so. I think we've finally come to the place where we see
that the same principles apply to the evolution of every blasted thing,
including the universe. I think we're always involved in the process of
continuous change. It's a very penetrating, very deep process that touches
the entire universe in many different ways. Originally, the ideas applied to
our own solar system, which is a little tick in the universe. The same
principles that apply to solitary wasps apply equally well, I believe, to
spiral galaxies.

I would like to have you remember, then, that this is my view that
evolution touches the whole world, and somewhere, in one of my books,
I've developed this point fully.

Can you tell us, have you published at all on your hobby, entomology?

Yes, three or four papers. A long time ago, I guess I decided that, instead
of being a poor entomologist, I'd try to be a good astronomer. But I've
continued my experiments with and interest in ants. Just yesterday I was
noticing one in particular. There are about twelve varieties of ants in this
vicinity, five kinds that come on to this porch. There are perhaps 3500

varieties that have been identified, and it's possible that before we get through, we may identify as many as 10,000 species.

I work with ants chiefly with my naked eye, rather than with a microscope. I do a great deal of observation while I'm on my stomach, and that's just one of my indulgences.

I think you'll find some interesting episodes about my work with ants in my latest book, *Through Rugged Ways to the Stars*.

H. BENTLEY GLASS

Dr. H. Bentley Glass is Academic Vice President of New York State University in Stony Brook, Long Island. In addition, he also serves as Distinguished Professor of Biology, a post he has held since 1965.

His large and busy office in the new library was the scene of our interview in November, 1968. Professor Glass is the current president of the American Association for the Advancement of Science and his major field of study is genetics.

Born of American missionary parents in China in 1906, he received his doctorate in 1932 at the University of Texas and has, for many years, been a seminal thinker and research worker in the field of human genetics.

After a long career at Goucher College in Baltimore, Glass transferred to Johns Hopkins University in 1952. As he spoke of his years in Baltimore, we were impressed by his deep humanistic orientation and his concern through science with international affairs and intercultural problems. Clearly these concerns are reflected in a growing and very impressive body of writing.

Since 1965 he has served, in addition to his offices at the University, as a trustee of the Cold Spring Harbor, Long Island Laboratory for Quantitative Biology, and during 1967 he was the national president of Phi Beta Kappa.

Included among his many publications are those that reflect both his humanistic philosophy and his belief in the importance of education: Genes and Men *(1943),* Science and the Liberal Education *(1959), and* Science and Ethical Values *(1966).*

BIOLOGY AND GENETICS

H. Bentley Glass

Our interest is to try to get at some of the dimensions that go into the creation of an idea. And, we're interested in such things, for example, as mood, state of mind, physical condition that you feel might lead to a particularly productive period of thinking on your part. Do you have any thoughts along those lines?

It's hard to say. For a long time I worked along on various genetic problems which seemed to grow naturally from my initial interest in mutation, and the relation of high-energy radiations, especially X-rays, to a deeper understanding of such matters. But, I would say that no one would probably be able to understand my drive, in general, unless he knew, in the first place, that I was a child of missionary parents in China. In spite of the fact that I'm not orthodox in a sense that my parents would have understood, I nevertheless have a very deep social concern and an intense conviction that the pursuit of science (scientific knowledge and understanding) must be made to benefit man. I'm therefore deeply concerned that there are many human problems on which science can throw light, and, perhaps, provide solutions. Also, science itself produces problems of growing concern to man, and very often the technological developments that flow out of scientific discovery are not thought through on a long-range basis before they are let loose from the laboratory.

So, beginning in the 1950's particularly, I would say that in what was perhaps the most active and fruitful period of my scientific life, I became very deeply concerned with such matters as the work of the committee established under the National Academy of Sciences to study the genetic effects of atomic radiation, and to make a general report. I was the secretary, or reporter, for that committee, and helped to formulate its considerations. Similarly, during the forties I had an opportunity, unsought on my part, to tie up with a colleague in a medical school, the University of Maryland Medical School, who was a hematologist, and interested in the new Rh blood typing, and the problem that was developing of maternal-fetal incompatibility, and the possibility of doing something to understand and alleviate these conditions. So, my friend Milton Sacks was instrumental in starting the Rh Blood Typing Laboratory in Baltimore, the first of its kind in the country. After it had been going a year or so, he asked me to ally myself with it and to carry on genetic researches using the rather significant data from the blood typings that they were getting from women who came in for diagnosis.

Whereas previously my genetic research had been pretty much restricted to the fruit fly, and thus to studies of mutation in the classical sense using a laboratory organism, it was this new opportunity that really made a human geneticist out of me. I suppose that now my reputation is probably greater in that area than it is in the classical genetics of the fruit fly. I found it very advantageous to have had the rigorous, more or less classical, kind of training with experimental techniques. I was left with a rather strong feeling that anybody who gets into the field of human genetics should probably approach it that way, rather than from the side of medicine. At least, the two types of persons should cooperate, collaborate, very closely. Our studies in the distribution of blood groups led to various kinds of theoretical papers, dealing with the evolution and change of human populations, for which blood group data could be used. Probably if any papers I've ever published are to be regarded as classics in the field, it is the papers in human genetics, which grew out of my initial association with the Baltimore Rh Blood Typing Laboratory. There was, for instance, a group of studies on the Dunker community in Franklin County, Pennsylvania, in which we, Milton Sacks and I, together with others who assisted, undertook to study for the first time a very small socially isolated group (socially, because religiously isolated) to determine whether they were genetically what one would expect on the basis of their known derivation from a Western European German population, and their present location in the center of a North American white population.

We met with the rather interesting, indeed startling, discovery that, genetically, they have deviated without explanation very widely from this expected pattern, so that in regard to their blood group frequencies they're about as distinctive as Eskimos or Hottentots. In a very short period of time, just 150 to 160 years, this change has taken place and is quite surely attributable to the very small size of the inbreeding group there and to its isolation from others in a marital sense; only a very small minority of converts come in generation after generation. Chance itself would lead to fluctuations that would cause, in the course of time, runs of genetic luck, that are extreme deviations from the expected. Then there was a study of the composition of our North American Negro population, in the light of its original provenance in West Africa and Central Equatorial Africa, and of the degree to which the North American Negro population has been modified by an influx of genes from the white population. We studied the dynamics of the situation. At this point, I began to feel that some of the aspects of the questions were getting beyond my own capacity to analyze, on the basis of my weakness in mathematics, and I teamed up with a Chinese geneticist, C. C. Li. He is a population geneticist, with whom I first had an opportunity to discuss the question at Cold Spring Harbor, at the laboratory here on Long Island, at the time of one of their annual symposia. I posed to him the kind of question that I was interested in: "What are the dynamics of a situation when you have one population about ten times the size of the other, and a definite amount of change that has taken place in the course of a specified, calculable number of generations? What would be the mathematical expression of the equation to describe this transition, and how can you extrapolate it into the future?" In the course of a year or so we had worked this out together, and we then published it. That, too, is a kind of landmark paper on which, I guess, hundreds of people have based similar studies in various parts of the world since that time.

Dr. Glass, both of these, of course, are studies in human genetics.

Yes.

Are you suggesting that, apart from the opportunity provided you by your association with Milton Sacks, it is your relationship with your parents and their missionary background that helped move you in the direction of human genetics and brought you into the field of human genetics, as opposed to biological genetics, in the more general sense?

It certainly had something to do with it. I feel in me something of the social reformer, the missionary spirit, the deep concern for the welfare of human beings everywhere, that is a primary motive. Perhaps, at the time when this opportunity came along to get into human genetics, I could have said, "Well, I'm terribly busy. I'm doing my work with my fruit flies, and that's good enough for me. And I have to teach, and that's hard work. I just can't take it on as an extra burden." But, no; when the opportunity came, I grabbed it, because it lay in a direction that I felt was tremendously important. Now I might mention another thing of this kind. It began in the fifties. I had always stayed out of administration in college and university work. I felt that I was born a teacher, tremendously interested in teaching students and working with them, and administration was just not for me. True, I did get involved in a lot of editorial work. When the editor of "Science" abruptly resigned after a dispute with the officers of the association, I was selected to pinch-hit until they could get another permanent editor. I was, at that time, chairman of the editorial board, so it was a somewhat natural choice. The university gave me a kind of blessing, without reducing my duties any, and said I could take on an extra load of commuting to Washington 3 days a week, and so on. For some six to eight months I served as the editor of *Science* and *The Scientific Monthly*.

Before Dr. Abelson?

Long before. Oh yes, long before. There had been several editors in between. I was also already at that time associate editor of the *Quarterly Review of Biology,* which was published in Baltimore. The chairman of my department, Professor Benjamin Willier, was the editor. I'd been doing most of the legwork in getting out that journal for some years and dating back into the forties. So I was getting a lot of editorial experience. Then I was asked to start in on that series of books you see over there on the shelf, the third from the bottom, at the left—*The McCollum-Praff Symposia* on biochemical problems. Although I'm not a biochemist, I had reached a point where I felt my progress in genetics, in the pursuit of genetical problems, was suffering because of my growing inability to handle the biochemical side. To edit the *Symposia* was a good way of forcing myself to develop a real understanding of a necessary field. So I undertook the job, which lasted over ten years, producing those nine volumes there. For each symposium I wrote a summary which tried to put in a comprehensive, succinct, and critical way the gist of each symposium. Perhaps those summaries established a different kind of reputation for me that made me even more widely known than some of the things I've done in genetics. Some people, I find, are surprised to discover that I'm not a biochemist at all. All of these editorial experiences got me into scientific organizational work. I served as president of the American Institute for Biological Sciences. I was its first president. I've been president or vice-president of most of the genetic or biological societies. My writing was branching out into quite a diversity of areas of interest such as history and philosophy of science and the social concerns of science, as well as the strict analysis and interpretation of experimental results. That got me something of a reputation as a humanist as well as a biologist, and my election first as a senator, and then as president of Phi Beta Kappa. Also in '59 I became the first Chairman of the Biological Sciences Curriculum Study, which has done much to revolutionize secondary-school teaching of biology in this country. I don't know, it's always hard looking back over a career—and mine is getting along now toward a close—to know how I got into things. Part of the problem has been that I could never say "No" when something really exciting and challenging came along. And part of the motivation is certainly this great social concern that I feel for the right place of science in the life of man. Still another part of it derives from my very deep concern for education, particularly for science education, which I think has often been very badly handled and has stood in great need of reform.

Had you ever been interested in studying medicine?

No. I never really had such an intention at all. From the time when I was a child, growing up in China and getting a large part of my education by reading my father's encyclopedia from cover to cover, I intended to be a teacher. To teach was what I wanted to do. When I went to college, even when I graduated from college, the idea of becoming a scientist myself didn't seem within the bounds of possibility to me; for one thing, of financial possibility. Missionaries' children don't have much money. I was quite satisfied when I graduated from college to get a teaching position in a high school in Texas, and I thought that probably would be my metier. But, after two years of that, I had an opportunity to go back to my alma mater on a fellowship, a teaching fellowship, and to work for my master's degree. There I fell in with professors who really encouraged me to go on and assisted me in getting the necessary support to go to graduate school. It was just at that time that Hermann Joseph Muller had discovered that X-rays will produce mutations in fruit flies, a great discovery, the one for which he later received the Nobel Prize. He was at that time in Austin, at the University of Texas. I was nearby at Baylor University. It turned out, very fortunately for me, that the Rockefeller Foundation gave him a sizeable grant to develop a genetics program at the University of Texas, and to support a number of students in fellowships. I was one of the lucky ones to profit from that program.

We'd like to ask you a very difficult question. And, that is, this idea of concern about people, together with the idea of change in the sense of mutations, does carry with it a certain degree of a carry-over of the missionary flavor. And, we're wondering if, for example, in your daydreams, in your fantasies, in your night dreams, whether there has ever been anything that you can recall concerning this idea of bringing about missionary kinds of changes, reforms within large groups of people. You seem to have avoided the one-to-one relationship—patient to doctor, for example.

No, in teaching. I almost became a preacher, a minister, at one time. In fact, I actually reached the point of being ordained, although I never served. I did serve as an assistant minister in a church during my days in Texas before I went to graduate school at the University of Texas. And I did a great deal of speaking in behalf of foreign missions to help raise money for such things at that time. I can't say that my dreams, my fantasies, have ever focused on such matters. Perhaps because reality is so much with me in my waking hours and is a constant goal. Perhaps, I'm not much given to fantasies. One always wonders, as a boy, what one might do if one became President of the United States, for example. But I can never remember dreaming that I would actually become President of the United States, nor would I spend any time figuring out what I would do under such circumstances.

How about your dreaming about changing the world? Changing people? After all, this is the idea of radiation, mutations, genetics. This is dealing with the stuff that could affect them.

All I can say is that the reality is so omnipresent that one doesn't need to dream about it. Instead, I can recall dreams about composing music. I'm very fond of music, and I listen to music during most of my free time, and often at home I do a great deal of my desk work while listening to music, reading while music is going on. I have dreamed, now this is something of a fantasy, that I was a great composer. In fact, it was so vivid a dream that I can recall actually hearing the music note by note as the composition was played. It was so vivid that I thought when I first woke up that I could still hum the themes. But it disappeared quickly, and it was really pure fantasy. I recognize that while I enjoy music very much, I really know very little about the technical aspects of composition and I have very little gift for original formulation of melody, harmony, or rhythm.

Well, in the original formulation of genetic problems, and their solution, where you have your reputation, what are the factors that go into your coming up with a problem? Do you find that this is a problem that grows out of your preceding work, or is it a problem that you decide when some idea suddenly hits you that you want to work on?

Well, there's nothing sudden about it. One of the courses that I most enjoyed teaching and developing during my years as a professor at Goucher College, and later at the Johns Hopkins University, was a course in evolution, which emphasized especially the genetic aspects of evolution. The analysis of the genetic factors in a form in which you can present them clearly to students certainly requires, from time to time, some head scratching, some analysis of the weaknesses in the theoretical structure and of the gaps in our existing knowledge. So, for example, I was well aware that in modern evolutionary theory Sewall Wright in the early thirties had proposed that the effects of chance, of random genetic drift, as he called it, might in very small populations have a considerable influence as an evolutionary factor, if these small populations ever later amounted to anything. Their character might be set, in other words, not so much by natural selection of mutations, as by chance establishment of mutations, without reference to natural selection—provided, of course, that they were not so terribly detrimental that they would be obviously influenced by selection. This would have to relate to the relatively neutral kinds of conditions, such as blood groups, for example. So, when I got into this area of human genetics, knowing that there was really no experimental evidence to support this theoretical structure, I had the idea one day that there was a golden opportunity to test this theory if one could find a human population that was sufficiently isolated, not geographically, but rather by its social structure. To make a study of it and to determine—if you knew where it came from, and you knew where it was, you would know what it ought to be—you could test this theory to a certain extent. That led to the study of the Dunker community.

And this study in turn grew out of a theory advanced by Sewall Wright?

Yes. And the test was actually made, you see, nearly 15 or 20 years later, 20 years later than Wright's theory of random genetic drift.

Could you relate to the question of what it was in Sewall Wright's theory that sort of grabbed hold of you? What motivated you to want to proceed to test it?

Why, in any genetics textbook of the forties that discussed the subject of evolution, you could find enumerated, just as I had done as a teacher many times in classes, four principal factors that determine the nature of the evolutionary process: (1) mutation, (2) natural selection, (3) migration (or rather, the transfer of genes from one population to another, because migrations themselves don't bring about any genetic changes if there's no interbreeding, that is, if the populations remain socially and culturally isolated), and (4) random genetic drift. In human genetics one cannot do much with mutation or natural selection. However, there are these other factors, the gene flow and the genetic drift, which one could work with readily with just the kind of genetic information about the distribution of genes in different populations derived from the blood typing data for a larger number of systems than just the A B O and M N groups, which had been known for a long time, and which had already been used by anthropologists as a basis for study of some aspects of human evolution. So it was a natural choice, not remarkable at all. If you get into a new field, you try to work on the major unknowns that exist. It didn't require any great insight on my part to pick out those types of problems.

But, it was really innovative in terms of what resulted.

Yes, I think you could say it was.

Because a whole series of things developed from that decision on your part.

That decision of mine, yes.

There conceivably were many geneticists who were confronted with the same theory, but who chose not to pursue this. They may have gotten lost with some other kind of problem. You chose to follow this line. And, we're just wondering if we have any leads as to why you wanted to pursue this particular line. We agree, it's a major dimension in your field, but you could have gotten lost with the fruit fly or with something else.

Well, I could have been restricted to it. I think this is what happens to many scientists. From the time of their graduate study, they get a set of blinders, like a horse, on the head. They can see only what is right in front, and they go right down that track without seeing the possibiltities that lie out at the sides. This has its advantage, for it prevents fruitless straying, rambling, and wandering. But it also has its disadvantages for the development of science as a whole. Now, my friend George Beadle, who is a much more distinguished geneticist than I am, has been remarkable among all geneticists for his ability, not just once, but several times during his life, to drop work on a particular organism and to drop work with a particular set of techniques, and with an idea of the problems to be solved and the need for genetics to go in a new direction, to hunt for a new organism to work with, and to develop new methods that open up a new approach. He started out as a corn geneticist, a plant geneticist. Then he shifted to the fruit fly. He became very distinguished in both of those areas. After some relatively conventional work with the fruit fly, he went into developmental genetics, for he was so interested in probing the way in which genes control developmental processes. That was what really interested him. He went off to Paris for a year to work with Borus Ephorussi to develop techniques of transplantation from one genetic type of fruit fly to another, in order to study how a particular characteristic, eye color, would develop if you took the eye buds out of one larva, and put them into the body of another one of a different type. He pushed this technique as far as it would go, and the result was really startling. After a time he got the feeling that that technique was not going to enable him to go any further. Where many geneticists would have continued to try to press it further he dropped it, to look for another organism with which he could really pursue the analysis of the biochemical effects of genes during development. Then he and Edward L. Tatum came up with the neurospora work which won them the Nobel Prize. That started an entirely new kind of genetics, the beginning of molecular genetics.

Has this been your own way of proceeding?

Much less than in the case of Beadle. Where he went from one kind of genetics to another, I've never really done that, except to shift from the fruit fly to human genetics. And even while I was actively pursuing human genetics, I never dropped my studies of fruit fly genetics. I kept that going all during the fifties, until I came here to Stony Brook, in fact. I've never been able to let go an old line of work as he has. I think that's a fault in myself, that I have not been able to shift gears so completely and so smoothly as he was able to do. I could learn about a new field intellectually, but it was something of a tour de force that didn't take me away from active involvement with the older problems and the familiar techniques. Right up until my involvement in administrative work here—I closed my laboratory when I came to Stony Brook—I was still working with the effects of X-rays on mutation in a fruit fly, because I could still see many things that hadn't been properly or fully worked out.

You don't see this as keeping the blinders on because you did carry something through?

Well, there was a difference. When I shifted, I picked up some quite different kind of activity such as editorial work, interest in the history of science or in the philosophy of science, science education, which has occupied me heavily since 1959, when I became the chairman of the Biological Sciences Curriculum Study and started various kinds of international work in science education, too. I've been very much involved in the Pugwash Conferences on Science and World Affairs. That is another indication of my involvement with the social concerns of science, of my feeling that scientists, representing different nationalities, especially the U.S. and the U.S.S.R., have got to get together and try to develop a common ground of informing and warning their governmental leaders about the realities of nuclear warfare and genetic damage, and the problems of developing nations, from a scientific and technological viewpoint, and of science education. My experience with the BSCS led me to appreciate far more keenly than ever before the rapidity of the educational obsolescence which professional people in modern times undergo. I regard it as an absolute necessity that we reform our educational systems so that professional people can, on the basis of a continuous cycle throughout life, keep up their knowledge of the advancement of their own disciplines.

What do you feel is the half-life of knowledge in biology and genetics, for example?

Well, roughly, our knowledge is doubling in genetics in about ten years, so the half-life, I guess, is about five years.

And, it's about five to seven years in medical science.

Yes. To strike the imagination I've been saying that the obsolescence of education is about like the obsolescence of a motor car. In eight years it's truly antique.

We'd like to ask you, Dr. Glass, a question similar to the one we asked Froelich Rainey whom we met with last week. This is because there are some similarities between archaeology and anthropology and what you've been talking about, in the sense of origins: in one case, the origin of certain strains within the human being. Do you have any thoughts about this, about your interest in origins? It's sort of going back as far as one can go.

Well, it would be hard to be a geneticist without being, at the same time, an evolutionist, and being profoundly interested in the whole problem of the evolution of life from its very origins on this earth to the present time and, through extrapolation, into the future. As I have said before, I have enjoyed developing and teaching most of all in my educational career a course in evolution, rather than one strictly in genetics. That course not only involved a discussion and analysis of the genetic aspects of evolution, but dealt also with the origin of life on earth and the historical side of the evolutionary panorama. I have been very much interested in all of those aspects. Also, quite as a side issue, I have been interested in the origins of scientific ideas and the transformation of those scientific ideas as evidence increases. My interest in the history of science is primarily one in the problem of scientific change in ideas, in the history of ideas, and what contributions I've made in this area have been largely in the direction of seeing how certain concepts—the conceptual schemes of science that are current at one time—become modified; in other words, how they are based upon evidence that is always, to some extent, incomplete and faulty. Therefore, as further evidence accumulates and corrections are made, we reach a point very often where our paradigm, our conceptual scheme or model, is not only outworn, but collapses and must be replaced by another. Now, how does this happen? I think Tom Kuhn at Princeton, in his study of this process in the physical sciences, has thrown a great deal of light on it. My own view is that when the model is first introduced, it serves a very useful scientific function. It generates a lot of experimentation; work is very active to test it, to prove it, to extend its applicability. Everybody jumps on the bandwagon. For example, everybody's now writing about the genetic code. Then, after a time, not only do things slow down because most of the main possibilities have been tested, but blinders are put on. The model becomes a dogma. After that, it really requires a heretic of some sort to break down this old dogma and substitute a new model. The old theory of the gene, which prevailed during the twenties and thirties, had to be broken and a new idea substituted before the present concept of the genetic material could prevail and the new period of molecular genetics begin to develop. It's very interesting to me, too, to see how frequently in science the idea we accept today is a synthesis of two ideas that were once thought to be incompatible, or contradictory.

The Hegelian thesis, antithesis, synthesis.

Yes, that is really an Hegelian thesis, antithesis, and synthesis. Our present ideas about the nature of individual development, for example, have in them not only the epigenetic view of development, but also a good deal of the preformationist view. Only the preformation we now conceive not as the actual formation of miniature parts, such as head, limbs, heart, liver, and the like, but rather that the genotype is preformed. Some of the early preformationists, such as Charles Bonnet, were pretty shrewd and sharp in this respect and realized that it wasn't the full form that was present from the beginning, but that nevertheless there must be some kind of prearrangement of matter, of particles, that would determine the development of form in a particular way. You can hardly deny this.

Dr. Glass, it seems to us that your work, as you've described it, has proceeded very much along conceptual lines. Is there a role of intuition, in the more usual sense of that word, in your own work in science as you look back on it? Or has it been very largely conceptual and rationalistic, in the way in which we understand you just to have spoken.

I am afraid that in my own case my work has been largely conceptual and rationalistic. This I see in myself as a defect in that I do not have a sufficiently strongly developed gift of intuition. This is where, in comparing myself with Beadle, I say he is the man with intuition, while I'm the man without it or largely without it.

Have you ever had the experience of having an error you've made lead to something productive? Force you into a new field, or the development of a new conception, or even ultimately, the development of a whole new concept?

No, I don't believe I could say so. I have made unfortunate errors, which have caused me much mortification and chagrin. But none of them, I think, occurred at a time or under circumstances where they would really have led to a profitable redirection. I can easily conceive how it might have been so, but it just didn't turn out that way.

Could we get back for a moment to this question earlier about your interest in origins? We're just wondering again whether this may somehow, in some way, be tied up with your religious background, with its concern for beginnings.

Yes.

Has this kind of thing been on your mind consciously?

Oh, I'm sure it has. You see, my parents were very orthodox Baptists who thought the theory of evolution was a view generated, no doubt, by the Devil to mislead the minds of gullible men.

And, you've become the Devil's advocate?

And now I've become the devil's advocate! Like so many missionary children, I've gone off in a different direction entirely. Yet I must still recognize their influence. The more I felt dissatisfied with any literal interpretation of the Book of Genesis as an expression of the origins of life, the more I have sought for a valid explanation elsewhere, and the more I think I've learned to appreciate the real ethical and spiritual significance of the stories in Genesis. In one of my lectures, which is in my book *Science and Liberal Education*, I discussed the relation of Darwinian evolution to ethics. I ended by pointing out what appears to me to be the significance of the story of the Garden of Eden and the Fall of Man. It is a parable of the dawning responsibility of man as his conscience evolved, and not only his conscience, but also the consciousness of the influence of his actions upon others. There was no sin until one ate the fruit of the true—not, as so many persons wrongly suppose, the tree of life, but the tree of the knowledge of good and evil. In other words, it was the ability to discern that one's own actions would have an effect upon other persons, and upon other beings even though not of our own species, that brought sin into the world. Before that there was innocence—ignorance and innocence. From that conclusion I proceed to the view that the scientist similarly must awaken to the consciousness of the influence of scientific discovery, and of the uses made by technology of scientific discovery upon human beings. It's not proper for a scientist to say, "It's none of our business, what's done with our discoveries."

That they don't believe in value judgments, and so on.

Yes, some scientists say: "Let me find things out; it's the business of others to decide what is to be done with them. I only make the bomb; it's up to other persons to decide whether it shall be used or not. I will make the pesticides, but it's up to others to decide how to apply them." I think we're now reaching an era when many scientists, perhaps a majority of all scientists, are feeling a deep social concern about the nature of the scientific enterprise.

If I can identify myself with anything particular in the scientific world, I would say it's as an exponent of that point of view. My last book *Science and Ethical Values* deals specifically, over and over again, with these questions. I advocate, for instance, that every country, in its development of science education for the welfare of its people, ought to establish an agency, governmental or private, the primary function of which would be to study the long-term effects and side-effects, as well as the short-range effects, of introducing specific scientific discoveries and technologies into their particular culture and economy. I don't know of any country that has anything like such an agency now. I think we're in for a very bad century to come if we don't get busy and start looking at the impact of science and technology on society, looking just as far ahead as we can. Like many others in the area of human genetics, I'm deeply concerned about the effects of the discoveries that have been made in genetics, and those that are surely just around the corner in this area of controlled reproduction. They will at least raise the possibility of taking human reproduction out of the bedroom, and making it a matter for the laboratory and the eugenicist. Who is to make these choices? Who is to decide what values we pursue? And how can we possibly regulate the change in society that would result, without destroying our existing systems of freedom and value?

That's a very real problem. It's one thing to do it with cows and another thing to do it with humans.

That's it. We know how to do it with cows, or sheep, or horses. We have our sperm banks for cattle, and there's no reason why we couldn't set them up for human beings, too. I'm convinced that within ten or fifteen years it will be possible to culture human reproductive cells of both sexes in the laboratory, and using selected strains, to produce embryos pretty well guaranteed to be of a certain type, and free of serious physiological and biochemical defect. What then?

Well, in all of these things the ethical implications are ever foremost in your mind.

Yes . . . they have become so.

In your statement of your interest in human genetics, the strain of ethical concern runs right through. It may very well be a real outgrowth of the early influence in your background.

I'm sure it is. I can't get away from that background. My whole world view is shaped by it.

Perhaps it's, in a way, searching for God in the origins of things.

True. I'm not an agnostic, although at one time I had given up any formal religious belief. I came back to a belief that you really can't explain the existence of the universe and of man without a creator. I can see that some people may be satisfied not to postulate the existence of God, but I must do so. You either have to assume that the universe has always existed, which doesn't seem reasonable in the light of the scientific facts; or you must assume that it came into existence out of nothing, by completely inexplicable material causes, which seems equally impossible to me; or you must believe in the origin of the universe as an act of spirit, of creation.

Dr. Glass, do you have a family?

Yes, I do.

Do you have children?

Yes, I have two grown children.

Has either gone into science?

My son did not. My daughter majored in biology and combined it with art in her college work, and married a scientist. She has continued to be very actively interested in science. While she's been more occupied with raising two sons in the last years, she is still, I think, pretty much inclined toward science.

DAVID KRECH

In February, 1969 we interviewed Dr. David Krech in New York City; he was on his way from California to address a regional teachers' meeting in Atlantic City the next day. Krech was on a lecture tour, and we had planned to meet him for dinner to discuss and conduct our interview. Because of his work in the behavioral sciences, he expressed a special interest in the subject of our study and had pertinent questions to raise about our interviews.

David Krech was born in Russia in 1909 and came to the United States in 1913. His bachelor's degree, as well as his master's, are from New York University. His 1933 doctorate in psychology was awarded by the University of California at Berkeley, and was followed immediately by a National Research Council fellowship in biological sciences at the University of Chicago. He has been a faculty member at Berkeley since 1947, and a professor of psychology there since 1949.

Krech's early interests expressed themselves in social psychology, and many in the field know him perhaps best for the standard text on which he collaborated. But during this period he continued to pursue his interest in the neurological foundations of behavior with special emphasis on the neural basis of learning. It is in the latter field that most of his recent important contributions have been made. Dr. Krech has been one of a handful of investigators who have done much to explore what is being considered the chemistry of learning. This is an area of research that seeks to ascertain the electro-chemical basis of learning and is concerned with the full range of conditions associated with neural changes on a molecular level brought about when humans and lower animals undergo experiences that somehow modify them.

Because of the work of Krech and others, we stand on the threshold of a whole new vista of possibilities and challenges in this exciting field.

BEHAVIORAL SCIENCES

David Krech

Because Dr. Krech is a psychologist we first suggested that he might be in a particularly difficult position in this interview since he can look at this work both as a participant and as an observer.

It would be easier for me to prepare a lecture on the creative act and discourse at length on how and why others are creative than discuss with you how *I* get an idea which, if one were generous, might be called creative. I've read some of the psychological literature on what is supposed to happen in the creative act, so I suppose I could whip that into an acceptable lecture, but when I think what happens to *me*, and what experiences I undergo prior to, or during the moments of arriving at an interesting idea, I draw a blank. My so-called psychological insight will neither be a hindrance nor a help, in discussing my own cognitive world.

Could you discuss your thoughts about the relation between fantasy and the birth of an idea?

There is no question that I do a lot of fantasizing and daydreaming about the research problems that I am working on, and in my fantasies and daydreams, I solve them all. And these solutions, in turn, lead to other and greater achievements! It's a real Walter Mitty routine. But I'm not sure that these fantasies or daydreams provide me with anything more than perhaps motivation or persistence. I doubt that I get any substantive help from them. I remember when my colleagues and I decided to investigate whether enriched psychological experience could bring about palpable, noticeable changes in brain structure and in brain chemistry. I was trying to think up a good experimental design. In my fantasies I had already demonstrated that learning leads to brain changes, and I went on to the next step. In short order, I had solved the problem I was working on and I was solving problems way beyond the starting point, problems that after ten years of constant research, we have not yet reached. Once I'm in a Walter Mitty daydream, challenges can be overcome at will. I can decide when and how I'm going to solve the problem and how long I'm going to continue worrying about it. I never really know what the solution is, but I simply decide that I have solved the problem, and then I can go on to the next one. The solution is not completely unrealistic, but it is as realistic as I can make it; it is usually related to something I can label or something that I have been thinking about. I just give it the explanatory power which I know it does not have. I suppose the reverie helps to keep salient the problems which I am trying to solve. I play with my ideas, I live with them, and fantasize about them. I build them into a big, whole *megillah,* a systematic solution to all the problems of brain chemistry. In that way I keep them salient.

The fantasies of solving monumental problems and making great discoveries fill different needs, involve different actors and represent different concerns at different times. Sometimes I solve all the problems of mental retardation. I don't see myself in that picture; the mental retardates are the focus. Sometimes I become famous, and now *I* am center stage. I don't think it's ever a matter of my making money; I'm not hungry any more. I suppose a few years ago, when I was on an assistant professor's salary, that would have played a more important role. It's not promotions either. You see, I never had any fears about promotions. I knew I could get them. I was relaxed about promotions. I suppose fame, solving problems, and understanding what happens in the brain when we remember something, that seems to be the big thing to me. When I'm stuck with a problem, I deliberately try to reverse the field. I ask myself, "Well now, suppose the assumption that I've been making is *ganz Verkehrt,* just the opposite of what everybody knows to be the truth." Sometimes this technique works, but more often it does not.

What about the place of your moods in the development of ideas and in your productivity?

At times I seek to come up with interesting new ideas about my research to take my mind off despondent thoughts. I use my thinking about research as a sort of soporific, so to speak. Indeed, I sometimes do that in an attempt to overcome insomnia, and lull myself to sleep while designing Great Experiments. I know what I'm doing, and why I'm doing it and sometimes it works. But once in a while I come through with a useful idea that way. Frequently, of course, those ideas don't pan out later on, but once in a while they do. Some thoughts arise as an escape from a mood which I don't like; often they come from just feeling bored with a research program in which I'm involved.

When a scientist is doing research, and it's paying off, he always wants to exploit it and not leave it as long as it's paying off. But no matter how profitable, a well-exploited enterprise can become boring. And so I deliberately think, "What *else* can I do." This occurs even in research in which experiment after experiment continues to yield new, cumulative ideas and valuable data for this problem. Let me give you a specific illustration: We were seeking to relate levels of enzymatic activity in the brain (acetylcholinesterase) with learning ability. It was (and is) a tough problem to attack, but almost everything we did seemed to yield something of interest; sometimes the yield was interesting because the results were contradictory. But even contradictory results set other problems before us. Sometimes we were vouchsafed a few leads on how to solve the contradiction and sometimes these leads even worked; sometimes they did not. But after about four years we just got bored with that problem. We quite deliberately reversed our thinking then. Instead of saying, "How do chemical differences in the brain affect learning," we asked the reverse problem, "How does learning affect brain chemistry." Now this was not a question which "flowed" from our research, or was suggested by our results. It was an attempt to escape boredom, although in the cover story (officially known in the trade as a "scientific paper") in which we described our later experiments, it appears that the second question does indeed flow from the first. In any event, having asked that question, a whole new world opened up. If we could demonstrate that learning affects the chemistry of the brain, we perhaps would have demonstrated for the first time what everybody assumed to be true. That is, that an experience has a physical residual in the brain. As far as I know no one denies this, but no one has demonstrated it either. So we set ourselves that task and I think we have now demonstrated it without any question. Whether the brain changes we have found are the important ones, I'm not at all sure; but we did demonstrate that there is a physical residual effect in the brain consequent upon experience.

What about the role of errors in your work?

My research for the last two decades has been done in collaboration with other people. When one of us gets an idea, each one of us plays with it himself, each after his own fashion; but before we *do* anything with it, we discuss it with everybody else. By the time that idea gets translated into an experiment, or even into a paragraph in a paper, it would be hard to say whose idea it really was because it had undergone changes in the discussion. It is in those discussions where a lot of errors are caught. I've done collaborative work all my life, and I've discovered that the glitter and originality and novelty and shininess of an idea is inversely related to the number of people who participate in it. If I work alone, the idea comes out young, alive, brave, brilliant, and, usually, wrong. If I work with two people the idea never comes out as clean and as brilliant because my colleague, the S.O.B., has discovered an obvious error, and the bravely shining new idea has to be qualified, and sobered, and brought into line with reality—ugh! If I work with *three* people it gets even worse, and if I work with seven people (as I have), then ideas come out sound and maybe even dull.

Do ideas occur to you on your own or as part of collaborative efforts?

I have often picked up a remark or an observation that someone else has made, and discarded, but which I saw as a brilliant idea meriting exploration. But, to begin with, that idea was someone else's. I then build out of the overheard remark, out of the cast-off kernel, a whole new net of ideas which I then call my own. I've even built a speech out of an overheard remark, and then I'm told that I've presented a very interesting idea! Yet the idea which I had developed was, in essence, picked up by chance from some unsung Milton.

Do you find vacations helpful or do you "hammer away" at a problem?

Well both things happen. I've had occasions where a break or a vacation helped. Let me give you an illustration: Recently, I was at Brandeis University on leave from Berkeley for ten weeks and I wasn't planning to do any research there. Of course, I wasn't in our laboratory. It was a vacation, really, for me. And for two weeks or so I didn't have a single thought about our rat work back in Berkeley. I got bored not worrying about rats. I started thinking, out of sheer boredom, and suddenly I arrived at what I thought was an insight. I had a veritable Aha! experience. I'm still working out some of the implications of that "insight." Now whether this was due to the layoff, I don't know. Let me give you a contrary illustration, one which suggests that ideas come from pressure. Shortly after I had taken my degree, I worked for a couple of years as Lashley's assistant in Chicago. After I left him, Lashley sent me a manuscript of a paper he wanted published and he asked me to read it critically because it had something to do with some of the work that I had published. I was a young squirt then and I was so flattered to have the great Lashley ask me to read his manuscript "critically," that I thought I had to find something worthwhile to say in response. So I read it with painstaking care and lo and behold, found what I thought was a horrible mistake he had made in reasoning and, as a matter of fact, in his whole approach to the experimental problem ("form-discrimination" in the rat). I wrote to him and he wrote back a very gracious letter thanking me for stopping him from "premature publication." If he had just sent me his manuscript without requesting my critical evaluation, I don't think that I would have come up with the critique that I did. It was the pressure of the necessity to come forth with an idea for Lashley that stimulated me.

What do you think about the rate of growth of knowledge in animal studies?

The rate of growth of knowledge in physiological psychology is tremendous. When I first went to work with Lashley in 1933, I learned to become a physiological psychologist in a matter of weeks. In about five easy lessons Lashley taught me how to operate on a rat brain; how to sew up the rat so that it would survive; and the minimal histology that was necessary. And there I was—a physiological psychologist. In this day and age, this would be insane. It takes about three or four years of difficult, careful technical training, because we have made so much progress. And that is why, by the way, I think the field of psychology is being fractionated. I think that a differentiated science is a sign of growth. The only sciences that are viable are those that are constantly differentiating. That's true of a developing organism too. Physiological psychology has been differentiating at a terrific rate. At Berkeley we have three separate departments of psychology with three vice-Chairmen. Each one of these three groups has practical autonomy in personnel, in promotions, in appointments and

in choice of students. Graduate students from the biological group usually
don't take any courses in personality, or social. And I consider that a sign
of growth. And this has happened really since the end of the Second World
War. Let's say in the last twenty-five years.

Because of this rapid rate of growth in science, it is very difficult for a
man to grow old gracefully in science. It probably isn't as true in the
humanities, or in the arts. But in science the individual scientist faces a
grave "aging" or "obsolescence" problem. I know very well that the newest
graduate student we have in our group knows more biochemistry, electro-
physiology, neuroanatomy, and mathematics than I do. What does one do
in a case like that? One way of escaping this kind of challenge is to move
into a brand new field where there are very few better-prepared people.
You move into a field which is new and raw, and then you can have a
holiday for a short time. Almost everything you touch turns into gold. Of
course, what happens is that within two years there is an influx of young
people who come in with all the necessary sophistication, newly developed
equipment and technical preparation. After two years you're an old,
grizzled prospector with a pan, and they are mining engineers with the
latest and most expensive hardware. And that is good for one's science, but
you can't keep up with them. I know, for instance, in the field of brain
chemistry, the only thing I can do now is to provide "wisdom." I can't
teach my students any of the skills, tricks, techniques, or even the knowledge, laboriously accumulated, because the knowledge that I have is
probably already wrong, or it's not very useful knowledge because it is
relevant to by-gone issues. So that all I can provide the students with, is
"wisdom" about experiments, and how to "think" about problems. I have
resigned myself to that role and, as a matter of fact, have lots of fun at
playing "the old man from the mountain."

*Dr. Krech, in view of your comments about the differentiation and diver-
sity in the field of psychology, do you believe that all of these areas could
really be called "psychology?"*

I don't know what that means, beyond saying that all of us are all dealing
with life. In our psychology department at Berkeley we have people who
grow gray before their time worrying about what happens when a molecule
of rhodopsin captures a quantum of light. Now what does that have to do
with the kinds of things that worry you in clinical and personality psychology? But both you and my gray-haired friends in Berkeley are called
"psychologists." Are you dealing with the same science? It all depends on

how you want to cut the cake. Psychology is a name for all kinds of professions, arts, sciences and scholarly disciplines—some of them but dimly (if at all) related to the others.

What about incidental or accidental discoveries?

Accidents do occur in science. For example, I have frequently come across a paper in a journal which I normally do not read, and found there ideas which helped solve problems for me. Perhaps I read that paper simply to occupy myself while I was waiting in someone's office, or someone perhaps sent me a reprint for reasons best known to him. Now that is pure accident. How could I say whether I would have gotten that idea without reading that material? Of course there are all kinds of instances I could cite pointing to the importance of accident.

Is there anything in your own life that might be relevant to your interest in brain chemistry, in the learning process, and in relating brain functioning with learning?

I suppose so. When I was a kid I had two objectives in life. My daydreams would alternate between them. I was either going to be a Justice of the Supreme Court of the United States, or a great scientist. I was going to be a Supreme Court Justice because Justice Louis Brandeis was one of my great heroes. I don't know why I thought I was going to be a great scientist, probably because I was so terribly impressed with the book *Arrowsmith.* When I went to college I discovered that, in the normal course of events, one does not go directly from law school to the Supreme Court bench. I saw what was involved in being a lawyer, the kinds of things one had to do, and I decided I didn't like that. Justice Brandeis lost out, and Dr. Arrowsmith won and so I went into science. My specific interest in the brain really didn't show up until my last year of graduate school. I felt that Lashley's work was going to pay off for psychology and I felt that there lay the future for psychology. I wanted to be part of that. Despite my great admiration for Tolman, my Professor at Berkeley, I thought that Tolman's approach just wasn't going to go far enough, nor was it going to get us where we wanted to go. We wanted to understand behavior in the same way that any scientist understands.

But there are extra-scientific factors that also came into play in my decision to go into brain study. If 1933 (when I received my Ph.D.) hadn't been one of the years of the Great Depression, and if I weren't Jewish, the

probability is high that I would never have gone into physiological psychology. But because 1933 was a Depression year (and thus there were
very few academic jobs open) and because I was Jewish, it was absolutely
impossible for me to get one of those very rare jobs. This is not paranoia. It
was as simple as that. Since I was interested in brain studies, and since I
couldn't get a "regular" appointment, I applied for a National Research
Council Fellowship in Biological Sciences to work with Lashley. Lashley
apparently had read my articles which I published as a graduate student
and he was willing to sponsor me. I did get the Fellowship. So you see,
there are extra-scientific factors (economics and anti-Semitism in my
case) that enter into the work you do. I think that if I had gotten a job
teaching someplace, I would probably never have mucked around the
inside of a brain.

Could you tell us about the influence of your family background?

I suspect that my father was the person who had the most influence on my
intellectual life. He was an extremely dedicated Hebraic scholar and he
prized that above everything else. That message came through clearly to all
of us. Scholarship was *it*. My mother thought scholarship was all right, but
she was more concerned about paying the grocery bill every week, not at
all an easy matter with my father's earnings. My father's interest in
scholarship fell on fertile territory with me. I don't know why, but it did. I
was the only one of eight children who went to college. I was second from
the youngest. My brother and sisters were not interested in scholarship,
though many of their children now are. I suppose my father was a little
grieved because I didn't turn out to be a rabbi. I had been his last best
hope, since my younger brother very quickly let it be known that he wasn't
interested at all in scholarship. I had been interested in Hebrew scholarship, having even studied the Talmud with the local rabbi. I suppose my
father continued to think, for a long time, that I might still be saved.
Before he died, however, it became clear to him that I would not be a
rabbi. But he did influence my attitude toward the "Word" and the
"Book," and although he wasn't terribly impressed with science, he was
pleased that I was going to be a "Professor."

He did think that the study of law was a proper study for a grown
man (and approved highly of my announced intention of becoming a
Supreme Court Justice), but not the practice of law as he saw it in the
United States. I remember that when I told him in my freshman year at
college that I had made the debating team, he said, "You mean that it's a

matter of just chance which side you're going to argue for?" He thought that was immoral, and that was what he understood the practice of law to be.

Do you think that your relation with your father might be related to your need to meet challenges and your fantasies of outstanding achievement?

I remember as a child of about eight or nine, I broke my leg playing in the schoolyard. It was a very nasty break which our local family doctor set. It soon became apparent, after about four or five days, that it just wasn't setting correctly. My mother called in a specialist who said that the leg had to be broken again and reset. I would then have to be removed to the hospital where they would have to operate on it. So in my home, while my uncle held me by my shoulders, my father and the doctor pulled on my leg and snapped it at its original point of fracture. It hurt even through the anesthetic. When I came out of the anesthetic I remember telling my father that I had dreamt of having been selected by Moses to lead Israel to the Promised Land. I can't remember whether that dream was a sheer fabrication I made up to console my father who was sitting there gazing at me, terribly upset, or whether I actually had had that dream. I identified with my father and I had to satisfy his wish that I was going to be his great hope. Dream or not it was a sheer Walter Mitty fantasy—it also made the pain worthwhile.

Because of Dr. Krech's background in psychology and the behavioral sciences, he expressed himself concerning the plan and technique of our interviews and commented on his ideas about creativity.

Prior to the interview, he raised some question as to whether our findings might be biased by the nature of the questions and by our preconceived expectations of what we wanted to find. Following our meeting, we asked Dr. Krech whether he felt that his comments were determined by our expectations. He then stated that he did not feel that this interview was determined by our attitudes and said he felt the interview was free and open-ended and that his comments were not forced. He then went on to comment further about our study of the creative process:

I wonder about the creative experiences of people who you feel are not creative, a control group, so to speak. Would they come through with some of the same characteristics that you think you are finding in creative people? Would there be any differences? I just wonder whether all people play with ideas, be they creative people or not. A control group is absolutely essential because otherwise you may be misled by the fact that whether a person is creative or not, he may try to be creative and what you are recording is not the distinguishing characteristics of the creative person, but of the effort after creativity.

It's very difficult to say who really is creative. A person may have so much regard and awe for the really creative achievement in science that he doesn't dare think of himself as being creative. Whereas one who doesn't have that understanding or awe of the creative act could be less modest, and readily confess to a creativity which he may really have. One need not be in awe of the creative achievement to be creative himself. I believe that I have had few creative ideas, but I do stand in awe of the creative act. You know, there's another thing that has interested me. It is easy to ascribe to the creator the power and the attributes which really lie in the thing which he has created. But the power of the thing created is a function not only of the creator's intellect, talents, and background, but also of such factors of time, place, and accident which do not accrue to the creator. You see, the halo effect from the thing one creates to the creator is helped because most creators are indeed bright people. So it's easy to make the transfer of the man's achievements to the man. I think that I stand in awe of the creative act and not so much the creative man. For example, I may stand in awe of a scientific or artistic or musical creation, though I may not be awe-struck by the artist or the musician or the scientist as a person. I have met many of them, and while impressed by their creations, I have also been depressed by their blundering feet of clay. I suppose that is why I don't think there's anything "mysterious" or "different" or "unique" about the mental processes of the creative person.

NOAM CHOMSKY

Noam Chomsky was born in Philadelphia in 1928, and is the Ferrai P. Ward Professor of Modern Language and Linguistics at the Massachusetts Institute of Technology in Cambridge, Massachusetts. He has been a member of the faculty at M.I.T. since obtaining his 1955 doctorate from the University of Pennsylvania, where he also completed his bachelor's and master's degrees.

Our interview with him was conducted in the study of his home in Lexington, Massachusetts, not far from where he teaches. Professor Chomsky is a dedicated scholar whose significant contributions to modern linguistic science are widely recognized. In addition, he has written eloquently on the political and social issues of our time.

Dr. Chomsky was a member of the Institute of Advanced Study in Princeton during the academic year 1958–59, and he served as a Research Fellow at the Cognitive Studies Center, at Harvard, from 1964 to 1967. These associations suggest the scope of his professional interests, which extend from linguistics proper, which he has done so much to reorient, to mathematics and to some of the central problems in the psychology of cognition.

Among his more important professional publications in linguistics are Syntactic Structures *(1957),* Current Issues in Linguistic Theory *(1964),* Aspects of the Theory of Syntax *(1965), and* Cartesian Linguistics *(1966).*

Readers of the present volume are no doubt familiar with the large body of his social and political writings that have appeared during the past decade in both scholarly and lay journals, some of which have been collected in his latest book, American Power and the New Mandarins.

Noam Chomsky

Can you tell us something about your technique? Is it a matter of plugging away at a problem?

No, I'm usually working on quite a number of different things at the same time, and I guess that during most of my adult life I've been spending quite a lot of time reading in areas where I'm not working at all. I seem to be able, without too much trouble, to work pretty intensively at my own scientific work at scattered intervals. Most of the reasonably defined problems have grown out of something accomplished or failed at in an early stage.

How does a new problem arise for you?

My work is pretty much an attempt to explain a variety of phenomena in which there is an enormous amount of data. In studying how one understands sentences, you can pile up data as high as the sky without any difficulty. But the data are pretty much uninterpreted, and the approach I've tried to take is to construct abstract theories that characterize the data in some well-defined fashion so that it is possible to see quite clearly where the theory you're constructing fails to account for the data or actually accounts for them.

In looking at my theories, I can see places where *ad hoc* elements have simply been put in to accommodate data or to make it aesthetically satisfying. While I'm reading about politics or anything else, some examples come to my mind that relate to the problems that I've been working on in linguistics, and I go and work on my problems in the latter area. Every-thing is going on at once in my mind, and I'm unaware of anything except the sudden appearance of possibly interesting ideas at some odd moment or the emergence of something that is relevant.

Would it be fair to say, then, that you have the problems you're working on in the back of your mind all the time?

All the time: yes, I dream about them. But I wouldn't call dreaming very different from really working.

Do you literally mean dreaming?

Yes, I mean it literally. Examples and problems are sort of floating through my mind very often at night. Sometimes, when I am sleeping fitfully, the problems that I've been working on are often passing through my mind.

Do they pass through your mind in a dream in the same form in which you were working on them?

Well, as far as I know, in exactly the same form. The dream life doesn't seem to have a different framework or to involve a different approach. So it's just a sort of slightly less concentrated and conscious version of the same thing as during the day.

How did you ever become interested in linguistics as a scientific field?

I think that my interest actually comes from two sources. In the first place, I sort of grew up with the study of language. As a child, I became inter-ested because my father was working on a medieval Hebrew grammar, and I used to read his proofs when I was twelve or thirteen or so. So I knew something about historical linguistics from informal background, but I wasn't professionally interested in it at all. And then, when I got to college, I was much more interested in radical politics than anything else. I became involved with Zellig Harris in connection with left-wing Zionism (more accurately, radical alternatives to Zionism). He was the professor of linguistics at the University of Pennsylvania, and I had a lot of personal contact with him. I was really a kind of college dropout, having no interest in college at all because my interest in a particular subject was generally killed as soon as I took a course in it. And that includes psychology, incidentally.

I went to college with great enthusiasm, and I was interested in everything. But as soon as I took a course in some subject, that took care of that area. By the time I was a junior, I was perfectly willing to quit college and go to a kibbutz or something of that sort. Then I ran into Harris. He was the first person I'd met in college who was in any sense intellectually challenging, and we became very good friends afterward. He was perhaps twenty years older than I, and since I liked him and liked the things he was interested in, I took his courses, just to have something to do, and I got interested in the field and sort of put it into the center of my concerns. In retrospect, although it was really an independent influence upon me, it did tie in some way with my childhood.

What sort of work did your father do?

My father was a Hebrew teacher, and he did scholarly work on medieval Hebrew grammar, as I have said. He did a book on David Kimhi, a thirteenth-century Hebrew grammarian, and this was something I grew up with. At the time, it didn't seem to have any real contact with linguistics, but I now know that it really did in the sense that some of my own work later on was modeled on it, and quite consciously, on things that I had picked up totally informally from an acquaintance with general ideas in the history of linguistics.

Some of the reasons why some of my work was successful, I know, is because it grew out of a framework different from the accepted structural linguistics at the time. It was borrowed from some of the much older sources which at the time I didn't understand very well.

Do the sources you speak of grow out of, in part, the work of your father?

In part, definitely yes. The structural linguistics that I was studying grew out of the work of Leonard Bloomfield and others. It developed in part in parallel with radical behaviorism in psychology and was very similar to it, and in some ways equally trivial and beside the point, I think. That is, I think that the assumptions were just as debilitating, and the framework just as pointless. One of its characteristics is a sort of infantile obsession to worry about explanations. This is a point of view that was expressed quite explicitly by Martin Joos, for example. The work in structural linguistics, as I knew it, was concerned with collection and careful organization of data. This can be really deadening stuff, but it was really the tone of much of the field when I got into it. I was saved from this approach to some extent by the fact that I was acquainted with a different and more informal tradition which was concerned with explaining why a form has such and such a property and offering an historical explanation for it.

From the very beginning of my work I have tried to explain the characteristics of a given stage of the language by trying to understand what a person knows about his language, not by means of historical explanation which would be irrelevant, but rather by trying to attribute to him certain mental characteristics from which one could derive the facts—just as an historical linguist would seek to explain things by looking at the historical stages of its development. I was very early conscious of this different approach.

We assume that you mean that, in studying Hebrew, one would not be interested in studying a particular work and its various forms in terms of what a rabbi might say about it but rather a particular form is used because its author has certain psychological needs to express himself in a particular way.

Let me give you a more technical example which is closer to what I have in mind. If you take the Hebrew word *Malchay,* it seems to violate regular rules in that one would expect to have *kay* rather than *chay* after a closed syllable, as in the form *Malkee.* So why do we have *Malchay* and not *Malkay,* let's say? An historical linguist might argue, and I was aware of this when I was ten or twelve years old, that the underlying form at one stage of the language was *Malachim—Malakeem* rather—and the *k* became *ch* after a vowel. At a later stage, the vowel was dropped so that you have a post-vocalic form appearing after a consonant, and that is why there is a violation of the apparent regularity that you don't have a *ch* after a consonant.

This is an historical explanation?

Yes, that's an historical explanation, but you know it's the kind of explanation that one can give for many phenomena. In the historical tradition in linguistics that I was loosely familiar with, this was typically the form of explanation offered. I have tried to ask comparable questions about how the speaker of the language organizes his knowledge so that the form is such and such or that the syntactical structure is such and such, and I think that this is the only innovation I've introduced into the field of linguistics.

Of course, most speakers of a language know nothing of what its history has been, but each, as a child, was faced with a mass of data that he has to make up some coherent theory about, and the theory has to be rich enough to enable him to carry out his normal creative use of language. It turns out, if the theories I have worked on are correct, that the theory of language the child develops has interesting formal similarities to some of the language's historical development. That is, they contain within them a kind of residue of historical evolution. What this really means, I think, is that at every stage of the language there's a very abstract theory that people who speak the language have that characterizes, through some process, the phonetic forms. What changes in historical evolution is sort of the tail end of this process, by and large. The common core of the language very rarely changes. After a long process of development, then, the language still may preserve more archaic features in its more abstract structure.

If you want a loose analogy, I ask you to think of Haeckel's theory of biological recapitulation. Suppose that it's true, for example, that in the ontogenetic development of an organism an early mutation will probably be lethal, whereas a mutation that affects a later stage of development may very well be viable. This is similar to phenomena that we encounter in the development of language. Of course you can't take the analogy literally. There are all sorts of reasons why it doesn't provide a perfect account of what occurs in language.

Has this approach led to an interest in why a particular individual, in the light of his particular history, speaks or uses a certain language?

That's an interesting question, but it's beyond the bounds of this kind of study. This is really an attempt to move into individual differences, and we don't have the tools, as yet, for this kind of inquiry. Perhaps this will some day change, but this is the present state of the field, I believe.

You mentioned earlier in our discussion that, in trying to construct a theory of something, you used abstraction and placed some reliance on intuition.

Yes, I always thought, from the beginning, that the whole scientific aura of linguistics and psychology was in part something of a fraud. And part of my belief came from the fact that under Harris' influence I became interested in school again and saw that things could be interesting. I started taking graduate courses in technical philosophy and mathematics and modern logic and began really studying some serious stuff. When you approach the behavioral sciences with this kind of background, you see right off that you've been totally missing the point. I mean it's a sort of mockery of science to use the framework of behaviorism with its narrow concept of theory and experimental design because nothing of this sort really goes on in serious science.

The work in linguistics was very similar. I mean that there was a lot of talk in the field about how scientific we were and how we were just like the physicists, and of course all that was missing was the intellectual content of what we were doing.

Is there some aspect of psychology that has been influential?

Yes. I've been very close, over the years, to people like George Miller who, I think, is moving in the right direction toward some conception of the cognitive processes that is far more abstract and deeply rooted than the behaviorist framework will tolerate, a conception that may offer some insight into some of these processes. Miller was one of the very few psychologists that I've had any acquaintance with, at least in this specific area, who was really able to see what is wrong with the behaviorist tradition and is really able to go on to the next stage.

I've found it very easy to work with him, and I've learned a lot from him and, I think he's learned a lot from me. We were able to work together very effectively. You are aware that there have been lots of changes in psycholinguistics in the past few years.

What about your book, Language and Mind?

This is based on a series of lectures that I gave at the University of California at Berkeley. They were addressed to a university-wide audience, and they were relatively non-technical. There was an attempt to draw together, in the first of three lectures, some historical developments in the study of language and mind. I really tried to show that there is a classical tradition that grows up in rationalist philosophy and psychology in the seventeenth century and continues with very interesting work to the mid-nineteenth century, when it is virtually replaced by a later "scientific" tradition. I put "scientific" in quotes because it was in another sense less scientific although it had more trappings of science than the earlier work in these fields. Of course, the newer research tehniques increased enormously the available data as well as the reliability of data, but it seems to me that they entirely missed the point of, let's say, physics. That is, one should be interested in an intellectually satisfying deep explanatory theory, and this is more important than getting data accurate down to the tenth decimal place.

I tried to suggest that, by synthesizing these two traditions, one of which aimed at a basic understanding, and the other that is concerned with making sure that your data are reasonably correct and constitute a good sample, one can make scientific progress. One can begin to ask some of the old questions when using the refined methodology that did come out of this modern tradition, and you get some interesting answers. Well, you see, I'm convinced that language is species-specific as a biological attribute and that some of its deepest properties are really genetically determined. It's quite pointless to expect animals to speak or anything of that sort: It's just like expecting humans to fly. There is a sort of dogma to the effect that the human mentality is perfectly plastic and that humans can learn anything. I don't think this is true at all. I think human mentality is very narrowly constrained, and it can develop in certain directions and not in others; and one can see this, for example, by doing a careful analysis of cognitive processes, such as linguistic processes. That's roughly what my book's about.

So this approach has had quite an impact on the field generally?

That's not the question you should ask me, but my perception is that almost all of the young bright people in linguistics are vaguely acquainted with this area. There is plenty of conflict in this area, and my students think that I'm an old fuddy-duddy who doesn't understand a thing. I suspect that anyone looking in from the outside would have to say that most of the new work going on, whether you like it or not, is within this framework. In psychology, psycholinguistics still has a very heavy residue of the old verbal behavior formulation. Take a look at a journal, say the *Journal of Verbal Learning and Verbal Behavior*. About 90 percent of it is association studies: you know, the effect on changing the list position of items, and so on.

Are the findings of psychoanalysis relevant to your field?

Well, that's an interesting question. I've been searching to find some point of contact because I'm very much concerned with unconscious cognitive processes. It seems to me that the work we've done shows as conclusively as one can show with this kind of material that in these areas most of the processing of experience, at least with respect to language, is not only unconscious but is beyond the range of conscious processes. I mean that one cannot introspect into the way in which he interprets a sentence any more than he can introspect into the way he perceives physical objects or digests his food. As far as I have been able to determine, however, I'm not able to see anything in the Freudian tradition that tries to develop a notion of unconscious processes in the area of cognitive thinking. This seems to me a real gap.

But Freud does make a great deal out of the use of language, doesn't he?

Well, you see it's a very different kind of use. He's not talking about the unconscious cognitive processes, he's not talking about the thinking process; that is, how one makes an inference or how you understand what somebody says when he fashions a sentence, or how we perceive objects in the three dimensional world. This is a whole domain of questions that involve biological processes that are to an important extent species-specific. We want to know how these things are organized.

You'd be getting closer now to the questions Gestalt psychologists ask, wouldn't you?

In many ways. Except that I think the Gestalt psychologists are too peripheralistic in their concepts. Kohler, for example, tried to relate these considerations to field properties of the brain. I think that's too superficial: I mean that there's a much more abstract processing that goes on that probably has nothing to do with closure or any of these grossly physical properties of things. I've learned a lot from Gestalt psychology in the sense that it searches for integrative processes that aren't immediately evident in behavior. And also from other psychologists, like Lashley. Or, I should have learned from them. In fact, after I had learned independently just about everything Lashley had said, I discovered that he had done some very interesting work along just the lines that concerned me. Lashley was a professor at Harvard when I got there, and he had important things to say about language. I came as a graduate student and met all kinds of people, but I never even heard Lashley's name! About ten years later, Meyer Schapiro, the art historian at Columbia who knows everything about everything, told me that he couldn't understand why I didn't refer to Lashley because he had been saying many of the same things.

I discovered that Lashley had given a very sharp critique of what was going on at the time and had very interesting suggestions about the necessity for deeper integrative mechanisms not only for language but for coordinated motion and so on. There's been something of a Lashley revolution in the last few years. His papers have been reprinted and have influenced many in the field.

What we're interested in getting through to you is the birth of ideas. Is there some way we can separate this on-going line of work you're involved in, or is it a kind of continuing process?

I just don't know. I know that the major work I've been doing for the past twenty years simply seems to be the obvious thing to do. For a long time I worked on it in near total isolation. Most of my work is published, but in fact I have a long, almost 1,000 page book, which I wrote when I was a graduate student at Harvard, that still isn't published.

In your present area?

Yes, and it has almost everything in it, in a general way, including the basic ideas. Lots of it is wrong. Nobody would read it at the time. A part of it was my doctoral dissertation which almost no one looked at at the time, that is the mid-fifties. I had been working along structural linguistic lines, following ideas of Harris, which were in some ways related to radical behaviorism. His idea was that there is no mental reality at all. The only thing you can do is develop analytic procedures which can be applied in a mechanical way, in principle programmed for a computer. You take a body of data, apply these analytic techniques, and the result is the grammar. This struck me initially as rather persuasive, and I worked for a long time trying to fill in the holes in the procedures that he had suggested, where they didn't work properly. For at least five years I worked very hard, and this was conventional linguistics. I knew more mathematics and logic than most people in the field at that time, and I was able to try more sophisticated techniques. But in spite of this it was a total fiasco, and gradually I began to work on this other approach. Because it didn't have any connection with the more conventional work, it aroused little interest. There were some exceptions. Particularly, I got a lot of encouragement and help from

Morris Halle, who has been a close friend and colleague since we were graduate students.

However, I felt I was getting some place in explaining strange things about language and in finding regularities and principles that really worked. But this was totally out of the structure of the field at that time. Public lectures and articles that I submitted for publication met with the reaction that this work was not in linguistics. When my book went to a publisher in 1955, it got the same reaction. In 1953 I took a trip to Europe. I remember on the ship thinking about what I had been doing the previous five years and recognizing very clearly that one line of approach that I thoroughly believed in was an obvious failure. Another approach, which I was following because it intuitively seemed sort of right, though I didn't really believe in it, was working out. I then decided to abandon the first and commit myself entirely to the second.

Can you tell us what made the new approach seem "natural"?

When I first got into the field, I was really doing two things: I was learning the techniques and I was asking about the kinds of questions one might deal with using these techniques. The attempt to develop and apply these techniques led in a direction that grew quite fruitless. The other approach involved asking the most naive question about what happens when you as a person who speaks a language come across a sentence you've never heard before. It doesn't take a mathematician to know that the number of sentences that you come across and try to understand is astronomical. Obviously one must have in mind, somehow, a set of principles that are sufficiently rich to assign an interpretation to an arbitrary sentence that you've never encountered before. What would this principle be? Well you go ahead to search for it. For some reason it never occurred to me that this insight refuted all the work I had been doing. It was only after three or four years that it became obvious that I was really getting somewhere.

What do you mean that you were getting somewhere?

I was able to explain things about the language. For example, if you look at English, there are some funny curiosities. Take the formation of questions. When you form a question from "John will come tomorrow," the corresponding question is, "Will John come tomorrow?" On the other hand, when you form a question from "John reads a book" it is "Does

John read a book?", not "Reads John a book." On the other hand, you say, "Is John here?" not "Does John be here?" which would look like the analogue of "Does John read the book?" Now you can look at this as some crazy fact, but I was able to show that if you formulate certain fairly general principles, generative principles of language, then it had to be that way and exactly that way. In many areas it has been possible to show that we just know intuitively, as speakers of the language, the curious forms that sentences have because of some very general principles we have internalized and use quite unconsciously. This kind of example struck me as very exciting because it is more along the lines of what we know of science in general. We are interested not only in organizing data, and we get excited when we find an intuitively satisfying explanation.

What you have just said leads naturally, we think, into the questions of the roles of mood and the emotions in your work, which has been so largely abstract. Are you aware of the roles of your emotions and moods?

I know that some things get me very excited and other things are just dull. The exciting things are what one wants to follow. I can't describe them very well.

Do your ideas emerge when you are happy or unhappy?

I think it's probably the other way around. I'm· so aware of the fact of having hit upon a train of thinking that seems to be getting somewhere that I get excited and so on, but I'm not aware of the opposite. I'm thinking of periods of my life when I've ranged very widely in mood but have not been different in productivity.

Does it ever happen that you find yourself up a blind alley?

Not too often. I've been kind of lucky in the sense that there have always been plenty of alleys that were open.

What do you do when you can't figure something out?

I turn to something else.

You don't bang your head against the wall?

Rarely, no.

You just stop for a while?

Yes, and I come back at a later time. There are still lots of things that I can't see any way to handle. Of course, you know that once I got graduate students—we have a very lively department with very bright kids—they provide all sorts of other ideas about the work. And also more blind alleys, too. There's a very real interplay here that I find very exciting.

Is Dr. Harris at M.I.T.?

No, he's at the University of Pennsylvania. In fact, we really lost intellectual contact in linguistics within a few years of our acquaintance, although we have stayed very close friends.

What about the place of visual images in your work. Are you dealing only with words, with images, or with auditory stimuli?

One part of what I was interested in for a number of years was really a kind of mathematics. It was the study of the formal properties of certain systems and rules, what kind of structures could be generated. The systems were suggested by language, but they were really considered in terms of themselves, and they were really part of the theory of abstract algebra or something of the sort. Working on these problems, I certainly used concrete models that involved visual imagery. I was interested in the formal properties of graphs and that sort of thing.

Your work appears very highly cerebral, and yet aren't you searching for meanings behind your thoughts?

As far as I am aware, it is "highly cerebral." Something that makes sense may be a very abstract principle that doesn't seem to have any direct connection with the data, and I have arrived at it through a complex series of processes. If it's surprising, it's exciting.

Something surprising is exciting?

If the principles themselves are implausible ones, in the sense that there is no a priori reason for language to be based on these principles rather than others, and if certain phenomena can be explained from the interplay of many such principles, it's exciting. There is a very intellectual relationship among the principles that one seeks.

What about the role of surprise in your work?

By searching the consequences of certain assumptions through a long process of inference, one is able to predict certain empirical results. If these results turn out to be correct, and if they do not directly reflect the assumptions upon which they are based, we have something that is surprising and exciting.

Surprising because it's not logical?

It's logical in the sense that there's a logical connection. It's very far from being self-evident. In fact, if you make slight modifications in the principles you thereby get overwhelming differences in the predictions which hopefully are false. In these cases you will discover things which yield satisfaction and really give the field life, as far as I'm concerned. If you didn't have such things, I wouldn't be interested in the field at this time.

Then your discovery of the relationships between your data and the generalizations of your principles is what's really creative for you?

Yes, that's right. That is *the* creative experience.

Are there aesthetic and affective reactions, too?

Yes, that's the whole business! It's the kind of experience I had when I was studying mathematics and logic really seriously and finally got to understand something: the same kind of excitement. Of course, I didn't discover it in that case, but in a sense you rediscover it when you finally grasp it, and it's that kind of experience that occasionally comes also from literature or music or something of the sort.

When you come upon a discovery like this, what about your techniques? Do you pursue it, do you get involved in it, is there a quality of urgency to get it down on paper, or do you just let it simmer?

This varies. For example, when I was a graduate student, I really worked out most of this stuff, although I wasn't communicating it to anyone, and I worked with a really incredible intensity. In looking back, I don't see how it was possible. In just a few months I wrote my book of close to 1,000 pages, and it had in it just about everything that I've done since, at least in a rough form.

There are some proofs over there. Do you just sit down at this typewriter, and the material all of a sudden comes out?

Yes, that's a different field, politics, and this is a 300 page book which is also the work of only a year or so really. But it's stuff that I've been thinking about for years. Ever since I was a child I've been thinking about the material in that book. For example, when I was a ten-year-old kid, I was very much interested in the Spanish Civil War, and I got to know about it through reading and friends. I remember writing an article for the school newspaper on the fall of Barcelona, for example. Since then I've been interested in the anarchist movement in Spain and other things, but I never dreamed of writing anything about it, but this book has a good bit of material on the anarchist revolution in Spain. It's a sort of distillation of things that I'd had on my mind for years and years, but had never bothered writing about.

Well, it sounds as if the pot's been boiling a long time and the soup's just getting ready to be served.

I guess so. Well, the linguistics thing was kind of like that, too, but it was over a shorter period. When I finally decided to write it down, it came very fast and freely. Most of the time I work directly at the typewriter. You know, I don't work it out and then write it up, but I sort of work it into the first draft. Even in my technical work I do that.

We have just one final question, we think. You spoke of the role of your father as a source of interest and stimulation. What about the role of your mother?

That would be more in the area of general concern about social issues, I suppose. As a matter of fact, one major part of my intellectual life has been politics. During my childhood, there was always plenty of discussion in my home about really interesting and important issues. I mean that my own linguistic work has always been a small part of my intellectual life. I have also been very much interested in philosophy and have read in it fairly extensively. For example, I have been quite interested recently in seventeenth and eighteenth century rationalist philosophy, in connection with issues that I've been thinking about in a vague way for a long time.

Have you published on this?

Yes, in 1966, a book called *Cartesian Linguistics*. It was a quite different departure.

What has your specific interest in philosophy been?

Well, it sort of converged upon a critique of empiricism.

Logical empiricism?

No, all empiricism. I got started with a critique of logical empiricism, but I really think that the whole empiricist tradition has some very fundamental flaws and these are responsible for the fact that it has had so little impact on the actual work in fields that have real intellectual content, as compared with its impact on weaker fields like psychology and linguistics or the social sciences. It seems to me that the empiricist framework has been debilitating in these fields because it tends to restrict theoretical and intellectual content, if taken very literally. That is a problem that interests me in intellectual history. That's why I'm so interested in the rationalist philosophy and its implications for biology and the human sciences.

Your interest, then, is in the conditions of thinking?

Yes, and just what it means to be human. This involves some special kind of mind, a special type of biological development, special ways of dealing with interpersonal relations and intellectual structures, and so forth. I think the study of language fits in here.

There is one final question. You got into linguistics, and you weren't happy the way the field was at that time.

That is a little misleading. I wasn't aware of this until afterward. It took me several years to come to this realization.

There's something a little deceiving about this that we ought to go into. What is the place in your life of the need to prove something, to be competitive, which appears sort of hidden in what you've said.

It's not hidden at all! Well, for example, when I had come to believe that structural linguistics was on the wrong track, I began to work very hard in an attempt to provide a definitive disproof of the claims of people working in the field. My competitiveness was perfectly obvious and, although perhaps I shouldn't admit this, there was a sort of aggressive element in it that I am perfectly aware of.

MORRIS KLINE

In a starkly modern building off Washington Square in New York City's Greenwich Village is the Courant Institute of Mathematics of New York University. Here in late May, 1968, we interviewed Dr. Morris Kline, Professor and Chairman of Undergraduate Instruction in Mathematics at New York University's Washington Square College.

Born in Brooklyn, New York, in 1908, Morris Kline received his higher education at New York University and has since had a distinguished career both in mathematics and mathematics education. Professor Kline has held a series of instructional positions at New York University, he spent two years at the Institute of Advanced Study in Princeton, New Jersey, and three as a physicist with the U.S. Army Signal Corps. In 1958–59, Morris Kline was both a Guggenheim Fellow and served as a Fulbright Fellow in Germany.

His publications include Mathematics in Western Culture (*1953*), Mathematics and the Physical World (*1959*), Mathematics: A Cultural Approach (*1962*), *and* Mathematics for Liberal Arts (*1967*).

Some of his more strictly technical works are his Electromagnetic Theory and Geometrical Optics (*1965*) *and the two-volume* Calculus (*1967*).

MATHEMATICS

Morris Kline

What are the essential factors that go into creating ideas in mathematics?

I would say that one of the major factors that has impressed me in attempting to do original work is that one must try to keep one's mind open and more or less relaxed. If one has already fixed on one line of thought and is trying to work out that particular approach to a problem, if he keeps hammering away at it, and it just doesn't happen to be the right approach, then he ends up with disappointment and no achievement. When one is mentally relaxed, ideas seem to come more freely as one works. In this state many possible approaches or at least ideas that should be looked into because they may bear fruit occur. As a matter of fact, these approaches and ideas are likely to occur with such rapidity and suddenness that one can't pursue each one seriously at the moment. A good thing to do is to jot these ideas down so as not to lose sight of them. Then one can investigate each one more thoroughly. I would say the mind has to be very much alive and very free in its ability to make associations at the time that one is trying to solve a problem. If he is tired, for example, he will find that ideas do not present themselves. I would think a happy state of mind is far better than a depressed one. A depressed state affects one's willingness to think, let alone the ability to think. One can force oneself to work only on something that's more routine or that really was worked out before and needs revision.

Committing the mind to one approach for a long period of time with no evident prospect of success is a mistake. Of course, the length of time one should devote to any one approach cannot be stated in advance. It depends on the difficulty of the problem. But if one does not seem to be making any progress the thing to do is to try to break from that pattern of thought, though it is very hard to give up once one starts to think along a certain line. There is an inertia that keeps you thinking along that line. What one should do is probably forget the whole thing and come back to it sometime later when that mental groove has disappeared. Then, try to let new plans of attack come to your mind.

Trivial examples of what I have in mind are the puzzles or brain twisters one often encounters. There is one which asks that one form four triangles with six matches. Well, the first thing a person thinks of is that these triangles must be in a plane, and he keeps thinking about how to rearrange them in the plane and form the four triangles. There are just six matches, the possibilities are not so numerous; and yet one keeps hammering away at it because his mind has gotten set on the thought that these must lie in a plane. The best thing to do is to forget the problem and try to come back to it when the mind is ready to try to start a new line of attack altogether. It turns out in the case of this particular problem, that you have to take some of the matches and build up a three-dimensional figure, a tetrahedron. Hence the new and successful approach is to get away from the plane figure and consider a space figure. Once you see that, the solution is trivial. The same suggestion of putting a problem aside for a while and then returning to it with a fresh mind applies, of course, not only to puzzles. The danger, I repeat, is that once one starts on a particular approach the tendency is to stick with it because that seems to be the only approach. One can't conceive of any other approaches at the time; but putting the problem aside for awhile and allowing the mind to relax permits new ideas to emerge.

This experience with creative work can be applied in teaching. There are a few rules that can be given to students that will help them somewhat. One is that if you try an approach and it doesn't work, don't persist in it for hours and hours, unless you know that you're working on a problem that has defied great mathematicians. In such a case, days and weeks of work may be called for. But, if it is an ordinary homework problem and you work on it for hours and hours, the approach can't be right. Textbooks don't give homework problems that require many hours of thought. The advice to the students then should be to forget the problem for a while and come back to it later. One might reread the text or do something else that will make the mind start thinking along new lines.

The greatest mathematician of his age, Henri Poincaré, has pointed out that new ideas or new approaches to problems will occur when the mind is free. He gives the example of an idea coming to him as he was about to step on a train. And he mentions also ideas coming to him in the morning just after waking up. I believe that ideas can come to people at such times because the mind is free and is open to new suggestions.

It seems as though a totally new channel starting at one cell generates a whole line of nerve impulses and produces a thought. I don't know how to connect the thought with the nerve impulses, but they seem to be connected. That is, thoughts are biologically, I believe, a series of electric currents passing through a chain of nerve cells. Now what starts such a series is hard to say, but the fact that the mind is free to accept some kind of start seems to be very important.

It isn't always true that the relaxed state reveals a solution, but it may engender another line of attack. If a suggestion does occur or even if some new relationship occurs, progress has been made because these may lead to the successful approach. Poincaré actually affirms that he saw the solution to a problem in these moments of free association. I have not experienced that. But Poincaré was one of the greatest mathematicians and his recognition of the significance of what occurred to him was surely far deeper.

The fact that new ideas may come suddenly when the mind is not concentrating on a problem but is relaxed applies to all kinds of non-mathematical situations. I was writing a review of a proposal, and I thought I had given the arguments I wanted to give about this proposal. While I was on the way home a totally new thought occurred to me which I should have put into the review. I have also found that while listening to music, ideas have come to me. In this situation my experience has been that the ideas apply to speeches or articles that I am trying to compose. It may be that one then does not really hear the music, at least for awhile, but the initial effort to listen seems to free the mind for the emergence of new thoughts.

Though I have been talking about not persisting too long with one line of attack if it does not seem promising and I have recommended putting the problem aside for awhile, it is also true that one cannot abandon the problem completely for a long time. The problem should be in mind but not necessarily the method attempted. In fact keeping the problem in mind and questioning whether as one reads related material one may use what he is reading to solve his own problem, often produces the solution. Many great mathematical papers have used ideas or methods that had already appeared in the solution of other problems. Mathematicians do not always admit this though some have. However the major point is that reading related material may be the best way to get the mind started on a new channel of thought and because the reading is related, this new thought may be the right one.

Keeping the problem in mind is vital not only in connection with reading related material. While eating or walking ideas may occur and one should keep testing them for their usefulness in the problem one is trying to solve. No matter how random these ideas are, no matter where they come from, one should keep testing them for their usefulness. The solution, or correct approach at least, has been obtained in this way by any number of mathematicians. They do not usually mention such "accidents" perhaps because they would prefer to have people believe that their minds were powerful enough to drive directly to the correct solution.

What about the place of visualization in mathematical thought?

It happens that in practically every area of mathematics one can think geometrically. Good mathematicians, in fact, do use geometrical interpretations to help them think. Visual images or visual understanding of what one is trying to do are definitely helpful. The biggest analytical results have very definite geometrical meaning, and the men who obtained the results undoubtedly arrived at them with the help of geometrical thinking. I would say understanding is achieved and results come more readily if one has a picture rather than by looking at a lot of formulas. For most mathematicians, geometry is the way of thinking. There are some men recently who came out with the slogan, "Euclid must go." What they meant was that we should stop teaching the old Euclidian geometry and that we should instead teach the modern sophisticated version, which would generally mean today linear vector spaces, which is primarily algebra. Those of us who think we know something about how mathematics is understood and how one creates feel that is the most ridiculous suggestion that mathematicians can make. To wipe out geometry is to wipe out the greatest intuitive aid we have to mathematical thinking. There is a story about a professor who got stuck while giving a logical analytical proof to a class. He went over to a corner of the blackboard, drew some pictures, thought about them for a minute, erased the pictures and then went back and continued the proof. In other words, the professor was thinking pictorially, but he didn't tell the students what his pictorial interpretation was. To the students, he gave the rather meaningless analytical relationships in a deductive chain. What he was really doing was translating his pictures into formulas.

Physical understanding is another vital aid to understanding and creating mathematics. The greatest contributors to mathematics have been either primarily physicists or leading contributors to physics. The logic of the calculus and of the most important branches of mathematics, ordinary and partial differential equations, infinite series, the calculus of variations, differential geometry and the theory of functions of a complex variable was in a horribly confused state throughout the seventeenth, eighteenth, and most of the nineteenth centuries. But the developments in these areas were enormously extensive and marvelously applicable to physical phenomena. The explanation of the correctness of all this mathematics is simply that Newton, Leibniz, the Bernoullis, Euler, Lagrange, Laplace, Legendre, Gauss, Fourier, Poisson and Cauchy thought in physical terms, in terms of velocity, acceleration, force, mass, fluid flow, vibrations and dozens of other physical concepts and happenings.

Professor Kline, what do you think about specific mathematical intelligence or talent?

I have wondered whether there is an essential difference in the intellect of people who do mathematics successfully and those who do not. This is, to my mind, the biggest issue that we have to face in determining how far anyone might be able to get in mathematical creation, and also in teaching. If there really is such a thing as a mathematical mind, or a non-mathematical mind, and one is trying to get the non-mathematical mind to understand something that is accessible only to the mathematical mind, he is wasting time. This question of whether there is a difference in kinds of intellect, I am inclined to answer negatively. I cannot make a flat assertion because we really don't have anything more to go on than the inferences that can be drawn from one's own experiences, from the experiences of colleagues, and from reading what some of the best mathematicians of the past have said about their work. For example, Gauss said that "if others would but reflect on mathematical truths as deeply and as continuously as I have, they would make my discoveries." One could say that Gauss was just being modest, but I believe that he meant it, and it is true that Gauss, from the time he was a young man worked continuously on mathematics. After he became director of the astronomical observatory at Göttingen, a post he preferred to a professorship because it left him freer to do research, he rarely left Göttingen and put enormous labor into his research. We still have thousands of calculations he made in order to arrive at a reasonable conjecture or to test a conjecture.

All the mathematicians that I've ever been able to learn anything about no doubt possessed good minds but there is no indication that there was a special mathematical talent. They devoted themselves to mathematics but could, I believe, have done great work in other fields. The converse is also undoubtedly true. Leaders in other fields, had they chosen mathematics, could have produced superb mathematics.

Could you discuss your thoughts about the teaching of mathematics?

Teachers are anxious to get results which means usually to cover the prescribed contents of the courses and to get students to pass examinations. Of course the examinations are based on what was taught and so students merely hand back subject matter. The learning is usually rote, whether in the new mathematics or the old. Mathematics is recommended because it supposedly teaches people to think but as currently taught, it does not. The professors are usually not concerned with pedagogy and since teaching how to think is far more difficult than presenting subject matter, it is the latter which receives the emphasis. The texts most widely adopted are either cookbooks of recipes or collections of theories and proofs.

We have to get away from trying to cover content. At present every course has a fixed amount of content that is extensive so that the teacher has to keep hammering away at teaching contents in order to cover the term's work. If we taught students how to think, it might be more profitable in the long run. But then the student might complete Calculus III without having learned how to handle partial differentiation, and that would seem tragic to the normal teacher because he is so accustomed to thinking in terms of content. At the very least, professors could help students by supplying motivation and psychological help. They don't do it in the usual courses. It is the unusual teacher who emphasizes the point I made earlier of warning the student that he should not freeze his line of thinking in solving a problem and that the thing to do is to get away from a problem long enough so that his mind is freer to entertain some new line of approach. Professors should encourage the student to feel that mathematics is his meat and that he can do it. When so encouraged, students do a lot better. Incidentally, many a parent discourages his children unintentionally by saying, "I could never do mathematics." The implication to the child is that mathematics calls for some unusual quality of mind and he is not likely to possess it if his parent doesn't.

Like most colleges we give a course to students who come to college convinced they're never going to use mathematics professionally, and we know that they haven't learned very much mathematics in their high schools. We don't make any strong demands on them mathematically, at least not at the outset. We make them feel at ease. We tell them, "You don't have to know much of your earlier work to handle this course. Never mind that you didn't do well in high school. We're starting afresh. We're going to review or restudy whatever we shall need to use in this course, starting even with arithmetic." We also try to awaken interest in mathematics by appealing to uses of mathematics, or associations of mathematics with areas these students know something about. And then, they begin to feel that because they know something about a related area, they should be able to learn something about the mathematics.

For example, we take up painting and the mathematical elements in painting and the questions of what makes a musical sound and how one sound differs from another. Another question raised is, "Is mathematics truth?" If it isn't, why not and what is truth? The students feel, when you talk about music, painting, or truth, that they've got something to say. They know good music as much as anybody else and so become inveigled into looking into mathematics. As a consequence though, they come to college bitter about their high school experiences in mathematics, they become converted. I wouldn't say that we're achieving 100 percent success. Some students don't care to study even though they come to college, and those students aren't going to change very much. They will not succeed, not that they lack the mathematical ability, but because they're not interested in knowledge. But to get back to the main point, I feel that if you can convince the person that he can do it, he will do it. He also has the incentive to show how great he is.

In my case, my father was an accountant, and he taught me how to do a lot of computational tricks in arithmetic. He knew how to do arithmetic marvelously well. When I went to elementary school, I was better informed in that subject than the other kids. When the teacher got around to arithmetic, instead of groaning as so many of the kids did, I thought, "That's fine. I know that stuff. I'm going to shine." I knew what the teacher was going to talk about, and that made me think that mathematics was my meat. When I decided to go to college, it wasn't because I wanted especially to study mathematics, and it wasn't because mathematics in itself meant so much to me. I remembered being good at it in high school, I ought to be good at it in college. On this account I chose to major in mathematics and, as a matter of fact, I worked harder at it in college, because I had decided to make a career in mathematics. The goal was more or less confirmed in me long before I really got into mathematics seriously.

When I tackle a problem, it doesn't matter if it's an old piece of work that I'm trying to reconstruct because I'm going to present it in class, or if I'm tackling something that is totally new, I have a feeling of confidence and I therefore persist at it. The average student when he does a home-work problem will get discouraged in a few minutes. But if he has the conviction that by spending another fifteen minutes or another half hour he could do it, he will spend the time and he will do it. Several such experi-ences reinforce his feeling that he can do mathematics and he will stay with it.

Since mathematics is a cumulative subject, students have trouble in algebra because they didn't get arithmetic straight. Algebra is no more than a generalization of what is learned in arithmetic. Then trouble in algebra makes for trouble in learning the calculus. If a student didn't learn elementary geometry properly and then takes analytic geometry in college, he is handicapped. So, if a negative attitude enters early or the student is unfortunate and has a very bad teacher, he may be defeated in mathe-matics for the rest of his life. It takes a very strong person, an emotionally strong one, to overcome the handicap of being seriously behind.

What has been the influence of your family background?

Well, my family isn't significant insofar as mathematics is concerned. My father did go to college, my mother didn't. I think making a living was far more on their minds than whether one was going to be a mathematician, a lawyer, or a good businessman. They didn't have any feelings for the academic profession, or for mathematics opposed to literature, archaeology, or any other academic discipline. My father did pretty well for a man who struggled very hard for himself as a boy, but as an accountant I don't think one learns much about the academic world. If my boy decided to become a mathematician, I think that I could contribute to his career and education, but my parents had no idea about what it means to become a mathematician.

I don't recall that I was trying to prove my ability to my parents. I was aware of the problem of finding a career of some sort and making a living. Because my parents were poor, that drive to earn a living comes naturally. Our relationship was good, but I can't recall that being a factor in choosing mathematics.

I have two girls, one of whom did work in mathematical linguistics. Now she's married and when she had her first child she gave up her professional work.

I have been a college teacher for thirty-nine years now and so I think I have some convictions about the profession. I think that what I learned from a few professors in college days, and from hundreds of mathematicians with whom I have been associated in one way or another has influenced most my feelings about mathematics.

Do you have some ideas about personal motives in mathematical creativity?

I think that in research you want to satisfy your personal ego. You want to know that you did it before the other fellow and then whether he does it or not is no longer relevant. In fact, if he does it after that, you can even believe he got the basic idea from you. You did it, and therefore even if he did it a different way, most of his difficulty was eased. That, incidentally, is a big point about mathematical research. You start to work on a problem, and one of the things that always plagues you is, can it be done? Is what you conjecture right? It could be wrong, and you could waste a lot of time trying to prove it. You have inner doubts about whether it is right, and you get to wonder whether you're barking up the wrong tree. So, if the other fellow knows that it is so because you proved it, he doesn't have to have those inner doubts about whether he's reaching in the right direction. Hence you really have helped him tremendously. In any case, there's no question that the ego is there. I think that ego is very important in all scientific research. I think that's the drive fundamentally.

Some historians have pointed out that the greatest mathematicians have lied, have stolen ideas and have dissimulated to be able to claim for themselves what was not theirs. I had to go up to see an eye doctor this afternoon and took with me all historical accounts of the work of the Bernoulli brothers, James and John. These men fought with each other all their lives as to who should get credit for what he did. When one of the brothers put something out, the other would attack it and find something wrong with it, even though it might be a trivial error. He then put out his own solution, and of course claimed that his solution was right. The history of conflicts and arguments among mathematicians, dissension about priority of creation and whose method was better, is enormous. I don't believe a lot of what scientists say about their motivations for doing research. These people say that they are working for the welfare of mankind, that they're working for a comprehension of the universe, and that they seek the harmony in nature that the mathematical patterns reveal. I think these values accompany, but are subsidiary to what they're really after, mainly doing something themselves and showing the world what they can do.

I don't know whether one should be critical of these people. The satisfaction of the ego is a natural drive; why should we expect mathematicians to be any different? The fact that they did fine work and deserve credit for what they did is well enough, but that doesn't deny the motivation. I see it all around. In most universities, the members of a department compete strongly with one another for prestige, for rank, and for salary. At our place, New York University, we have a very friendly and cooperative crowd; people help each other and yet, there is no question that when one man does something he feels pleased that he did it and not the other fellow.

Mathematicians do differ today on what kind of mathematics they should pursue. The controversy centers on pure versus applied mathematics. The pure mathematicians think that they are the cream of the mathematical world and that the applied mathematicians are merely engineers. Historically practically all the major ideas of mathematics come from the investigation of nature or from the more practical problems of engineering and technology. The pure mathematicians now insist that they can raise their own questions and seek to answer them without regard for the needs of science and engineering. To counter the argument that such mathematics is useless, the pure mathematicians assure us that their work will prove to be applicable, though in the past every major development that did prove applicable arose in response to definite real problems.

Most universities in this country are staffed only by pure mathematicians and do not seek to add applied mathematicians to their staffs. In a few places the applied mathematicians are obliged to form a separate group or department. Some universities are a little conscience stricken that they're doing nothing with applied mathematics and are trying to make efforts to build up that activity, but since the training of new Ph.D.'s has been almost entirely in pure mathematics in this country, it is very difficult to find applied mathematicians today.

The philosophy at New York University is that mathematics is a unity and that the separation into pure and applied mathematics is artificial and deleterious. Mathematical problems are worthy of investigation if they answer physical problems, shed light on the mathematics that is used directly to answer physical problems, or give promise of doing either of these. On the whole, we pursue the older tradition as to what is worthwhile in mathematics and we, unlike all other universities in this country, emphasize that mathematics must cooperate with science and engineering.

WILDER PENFIELD

*Dr. Wilder Penfield, is Emeritus Director of the Montreal Neuro-
logical Institute, in Quebec, which was opened in 1934 under his inspiration and directorship.*

*Dr. Penfield, who has devoted all of his professional life to
neurosurgery and neurology, was born in Spokane, Washington, in
January, 1891. After private school education in Wisconsin, he received his bachelor's degree in literature at Princeton University
in 1913 and, from 1914 to 1916, he was a Rhodes Scholar at Oxford.
During the First World War, Wilder Penfield, not yet a physician,
served as a Red Cross dresser. In 1918, after his return to the United
States, he was awarded his doctorate in medicine.*

*After his medical degree at the Johns Hopkins University, he
returned again to England, where he received his bachelor of science
and master of arts degrees. At this time, Wilder Penfield decided to
dedicate his professional career to neurological surgery. From 1921
to 1928 he was associate attending surgeon at New York City's Presbyterian Hospital. While at the Presbyterian Hospital, he founded the
Laboratory of Neurocytology.*

*In 1928, he accepted the chair of neurosurgery at McGill University
and an appointment in neurosurgery at the Royal Victoria Hospital.
While in Montreal, in 1931 Dr. Penfield perfected the operation for
epilepsy, for which he is well known. Many other new surgical techniques followed, along with refinements of existing procedures.*

Among Dr. Penfield's books are Cytology and Cellular Pathology
of the Nervous System *(1932),* Cerebral Cortex of Man, *with Theodore
Rasmussen (1950), and* Epileptic Seizure Patterns *with Kristian Kris-
tianson, (1951).*

*Since his 1960 retirement from the directorship of the Neurological
Institute, Penfield has written two novels* No Other Gods *and* The
Torch.

MEDICAL SCIENCES

Wilder Penfield

Dr. Penfield, what do you think about the place of emotions in discovery?

Well, of course emotions are always fleeting. They only come once in a while. Emotion never stays with you, it doesn't seem to me. Purpose stays with you and a plan, and I think every investigator certainly in the fields that I've been concerned with has a hypothesis or a set of hypotheses or possibilities in mind, and he goes on working at any time the opportunity presents itself to prove or disprove or extend the hypothesis. Then there are certain times, it may not be when he is working, it may be other times, or even when he is thinking of something else that he makes a significant step forward. Something becomes plain which was not plain before. That's when the emotion comes in and that's a thrill.

I could recall a good many such instances, but as far as brain stimulation is concerned . . . the first time I caused a patient to vocalize startled me much more than it did the patient.

It came as a complete surprise. We had never caused vocalization. Animals don't have an area in which you can produce vocalization anywhere near the motor area. There is a place in a chimpanzee, but it's hidden away in the central fissure. And I remember the man on whom I used the electrode. He began to cry in a certain tone. I took the electrode away and he stopped instantly. I put it on again and he started, without knowing what I did. Then, I put it on and kept it on, and he cried, making a sound progressively until he used up all his breath. Then, he interrupted it, took a deep breath, and then continued, and he would have continued forever if I had kept the electrode there, because he had no control of it. He and I talked then. That was rather a thrill, because that was an entirely new observation. One of my neurological friends brought in a dictaphone and held it under the sheets and recorded it. The fact that it opened up one of the mechanisms that makes it possible for a man to talk, a control of vocalization upon the cortex, that was exciting. But, that was stumbling on something. . . . The first patient to have a psychical response was a woman whose temporal lobe I was stimulating. It was in the Royal Victoria before the Montreal Neurological was built. She suddenly said she felt the way she did when she was giving birth to her baby and I've always wondered about that; whether I had produced this memory or whether it was just incidental. I put it down, kept it in the back of my mind and then it was four or five years later that I stimulated the cortex of a girl and she suddenly relived a little portion of her earlier life. That was a great thrill because then I realized there was a possibility of activating the record of consciousness.

There are different kinds of memory, you see. But, this is a continuous record of conscious experiences. It's like a recorder. The first time I did that it was thrilling, but that's not creative really. I think it happens as far as I am concerned more when I write and rewrite, and restate the evidence and the information in trying to prepare it for publication. Then, very often once I get my thoughts truly expressed, I see things I never suspected before. Although each one of them brings a thrill. That's a far more creative thing than stumbling on accidental discoveries. But, having stumbled on vocalization and been quite sure that the patient was not pulling my leg, I made sure I checked all possible errors, then after that, I just went on trying to fill out the data month after month, and year after year; any time the opportunity presented. But, I think the important thing is for a man to have in the back of his mind certain ideas and I imagine it's having that kind of plan in the back of one's mind that leads people to feel sometimes that they have made sudden discoveries. Well, I should think the prepared mind is just in the habit of having a lot of unanswered questions at the back of one's mind and then answers present themselves. Then, you get the thrill of making a step farther forward.

As far as creating hypotheses is concerned, with epilepsy, for instance, by analyzing a large number of different types of epilepsies, I realized it was absolutely necessary to hypothesize an integrative system within the brain stem and involving the cortex. By analyzing the different types of epilepsy, I found they all fitted into a general scheme. And then, after that, we adopted this theory or hypothesis; that of an integrative system which we called the centrancephalic system, never meaning, never supposing, never suggesting that it was an area of the brain, but only that it was a system of connections, and that the important part of that system was in the brain stem. We used that, all of us here at the Neurological Institute, for some years, and as each case came along, we found nothing to contradict it. So gradually, over a period of time, using a teamwork approach that is still being used at the Neurological Institute to test this hypothesis, it still stands up as a hypothesis. But the idea of it in the first place was forced on us by recording and continuing to think about the different types of patients.

I have the feeling that all you do is to get the evidence and hold it and not make up your mind, realizing the danger of making a conclusion until you have the complete truth. Then you have a framework, and you don't make the answers synthetically; it may be some little thing that fits into it that makes you realize something you should have seen long ago. I think the only really creative part is preparing the back of the mind, if I can use that expression; assembling the evidence and putting it in the form of an hypothesis and having it there along with a lot of unanswered hypotheses.

You don't remember the details, but you can remember a scheme, and then discovery is just by chance. And once it presents itself, you realize it fits. Then comes the momentary thrill, if you're looking for the thrill. That's the emotion. But the rest is hard work and good fun, of course.

Was there any single figure in your life who has played an especially significant role in the formulation of your hypotheses in this field?

Oh, yes. Sir Charles Sherrington. Actually, he played a very important role because when I had finished my surgical internship, I had the hope that I could go back to work with Sherrington so that I could learn to do in surgery with humans what he had done with animals. That was my objective in going back to him. He was the least prejudiced man I've ever known. I think he had an open mind. I divide the scientists I know into those with an open mind and those with a closed mind. Sherrington's mind was so open that he expected each of us, who was working under him, to teach him something, and he was constantly asking us questions with the hope that we would give him something. I think that must be the way he worked. He kept his unanswered things at the back of his mind and so he was constantly asking questions of the youngster who was working for him.

He lived to the age of 94, in Eastbourne. He spent the last five or ten years of his life there. I remember going to see him and he kept up on new developments. He knew about my getting this memory response from the human cortex; he said to me with his eyes shining, "It must be great fun to ask the preparation a question and have it answer!" Preparation is a word he took from animal experiments.

I had been with Harvey Cushing at the Peter Bent Brigham Hospital in Boston. He was a brain surgeon whose interest lay in brain tumors. But I thought there's a pathological physiology of the human brain, and I wanted to enter that area of investigation which was really challenging. Actually then, after finishing with Sherrington, I realized I had to cover pathology and surgery, so I was ten years doing pathology, trying to do it thoroughly. That was including the seven years at the Presbyterian in New York. Before I got back to physiology, I was doing only pathology and surgery, but always wanting to get back to physiology. Then, I eventually made the discovery which I should have made at the beginning, that no one man can cover it all—that you had to have teamwork. That's why I came up here, hoping to create an institute. And Bill Cone came with me. He became a brilliant surgeon and pathologist. I realized that it was quite impossible for one man to do it. I set out to write a pathology of the human brain, and then I realized there were dozens of people who could do, each of them, a better job on a particular aspect of the pathology of the brain. Well, that seems self-evident to begin with, and so I edited the *Cytology and Cellular Pathology of the Nervous System*. It grew into a three-volume work, eventually. It was in editing that and discovering what teamwork could do, that made me realize I had to make this move up here, or somewhere. When I was invited to come here, I thought, "Well, maybe this is the chance." So, we came here, Bill Cone and I, with that in mind. I always wanted to do physiology; the physiology of man.

I suppose my desire to work on the physiology of man came from my work with Sherrington. His was the finest mind I had been exposed to in my graduate years. When I was awarded the O.M. [Order of Merit], it seemed unbelievable that I should be the one to take the vacancy he left when he passed on.

Had you thought of bringing about vocalization by brain stimulation prior to this discovery?

I don't know whether it occurred to me, but it should have. It should have occurred to me because epileptics vocalize very often depending on where the attacks are coming from. It should have been self-evident that some-time I would find such an area, but I must admit it didn't occur to me. We never had thought of it and there was no such thing in animal research to suggest it.

The location of the motor area goes back to 1871. Sherrington outlined the motor areas in the chimpanzee, and in monkey and cat. He did a lot of work on animals. But in man, it just happened that we found we could treat epileptics and that we could do the best job by doing it under anesthesia and we found the electrode would guide us in our work; so we outlined the sensory areas and then came to what we called psychical responses.

First thing I knew, everything was set up perfectly for an experimental study; the sort of conditions I would have hoped for. I think those things just work out as far as man is concerned. You don't plan, you don't go in for creative planning; you follow the opportunities as they come along and you keep an open eye for the unanswered questions.

What are your thoughts about the place of fantasy in the creative process?

Very often, when I get into a hot bath before I get into bed at night I look back without planning to; and I've said often that good ideas seem to appear then. Very often, when I knock off, go to a movie or read aloud with Mrs. Penfield or something like that and get my mind completely away from something I've been working on; when I come back to it, it's all plain. And I think that when people say that their brain goes on working during sleep and solves problems, this is probably a false interpretation. The brain doesn't do any working on problems during sleep.

But, you come through at the end of sleep with a complete change and with a recollection of the problem and you see it suddenly simplified. Your discovery is there, but it wasn't worked on during the night.

Even if you got entirely interested in something else and have not slept, you come back to your problem and it's answered. What seemed difficult is easy.

You get rid of the fatigue, you may be going up blind alleys in your thinking and so on, and you're tired. But, if you have a complete change, whether it is sleep or something else, and then come back to it, suddenly the whole thing is answered for you. It wasn't that your brain was working on it, it was that your brain wasn't working on it. And that's what I think about the discoveries made the morning after sleep. There are people who wake up and suddenly have to write the thing down. But to my mind, it wasn't because they were working it out in their sleep at all, but they woke up, and here was a fresh brain and the problem was still there and the fresh brain made it perfectly obvious and they wrote it out. Something they should have seen if they hadn't been tired or working up a blind alley or doing something else. And I'm sure that explains a lot of the so-called discoveries in sleep.

There's so much stupidity about sleep teaching, for instance. There's no such thing and some of it was started off by the idea of using a whispering pillow. Nothing is sillier than that. I think the centrancephalic system turns off in sleep.

What led you into medicine and ultimately into neurology and neurosurgery?

I went into medicine really, after eliminating everything else. I realized I had to do something. I went to Princeton with the determination not to go into medicine.

And then, one day I sat down in the library, for instance, and wrote out all the different things a man could go into. It was my sophomore year and I had to decide. I had to choose my courses for my junior year. I remember, I stayed there all afternoon and I finally found that I had crossed out everything on the page but medicine. But I wanted to do something that served mankind, and I had discovered how pleasant and easy biology was. We had a very good professor of biology at Princeton, Professor Conklin, and I'd discovered that biology was great fun and that's how I went into medicine.

Then, after getting through Hopkins, I realized I liked to do things with my hands, and I think I had a hunch that there were a lot of brighter chaps in my class who could do well in medicine, all the bright ones go into medicine, you know, just the middle group go into surgery. So, I decided to go into surgery.

Then I had seen the field Cushing was opening as an intern, and I still had an unused Rhodes Scholarship, and I realized the only thing I could do to advantage would be to work under Sherrington, using that scholarship, and so I just went.

Could you tell us about your family background?

My father was a surgeon, trained in Chicago. But I was not stimulated toward surgery by him. I didn't want to go into medicine. But, I'm sure that the inherited tendency was probably important. My mother was the important one, as she often is in a man's career, in my opinion. She was more responsible for it than anyone else, I suppose. She was the kind of woman who expected a great deal of her children, and she had an excellent mind. It was she who started me off on my writing my first novel. In 1935, I went out to see Mother for the last time. She'd been trying to write a novel for fifteen years, and as she grew older, her plot got more and more confused and so, on this trip, I suggested, "Let me take your manuscript, and maybe I can make something out of it." She was so distressed because she couldn't get on with it. She was the kind of woman who, having set herself this problem would not give it up, you see. I thought it would relieve her if I promised to look it over. I returned here with all her manuscripts and her books, and then word came that she had died. And I couldn't use her manuscript. It was quite impossible to do anything with it. It was the story of Sarah and Abraham, which she wanted to teach. I put it away and eight years later when I was in Teheran, I picked up Sir Leonard Wooley's *Excavations of Ur.* Ur was the birthplace of Abraham, you see, and suddenly this promise to mother, to finish her manuscript was there.

That was no discovery. I'd had this thing at the back of my mind— that's the back of the mind in another way, isn't it? I hadn't thought of that. I read Wooley's book again, and suddenly I thought, "Well, I'm right here where Abraham was born," within two hundred miles of it, and I had ten days before I could get a plane on to Chungking, so I managed to get to Baghdad, to the Iraq museum, where you could see the stuff that came from the excavations, and then I got someone to take me out to the Ur excavations which were deserted. So, I sat down in Baghdad then and wrote out the plot of a novel on the story of Abraham. I couldn't do anything with Mother's stuff; it was a Sunday school kind of thing. But once I had the plot for *No Other Gods,* I worked on it for five years, off and on. Never when I was working here, never. But, off and on, when I went on holidays and I finished the book in five years; reviewed it and found it was quite hopeless. The diction was bad, the writing was stilted; it sounded like the King James version of the Bible. I scrapped the whole thing. Then I took another trip to Mesopotamia with my wife. We had two months there. Wonderful. And I took the same characters and the same plan. That was, if you like, a hypothesis. The same characters served the purpose. We went back to the places where they had lived and so on, and we went into the marshes which must have surrounded Ur in those days. Then I started all over again and the characters wrote the book for me.

The characters had had me, if you like. Well, that's what you carry at the back of your mind. During the time of the second writing while I might be operating, for example, when things were quiet and I was closing up, these characters would come to the back of my mind and we'd talk and plan. Once you get a book written like that, then you lose them, but until the publisher accepts it, they're yours.

Well, I don't think that's a discovery as it is in the few things I've done in neurology, but I don't think it's dissimilar. When I write on something difficult and elaborate it over and over again, as I do in difficult jobs, I get little thrills. I suddenly realize that this is the kind of thing I was after. This is good English; this is clear thought and I make little discoveries as I go along. I don't see very much difference between science and literature, in that sense.

Do you find that moods affect your productivity?

I'm sure that it's a matter of health and vigor. It's when you've got normal drive, particularly after exercise, I think your mind is always clearer. And I think in every day there are certain times when you can be creative and there are certain times when you are tired and you can't possibly be. I say even now, an hour or an hour and a half before breakfast is my best time. In the afternoon I never do anything worthwhile, except just patch up things. I am sure it's the drive and the feeling of exhilaration that goes with creative thinking.

Have there been times when you have missed a solution to a problem or missed seeing a problem, only to come to it later on?

The answers and the clues are staring us in the face all the time. Of course, the difficulty is recognizing what's important. I'm sure that must be true in physics or in anything else; that in retrospect a man might realize that the clues were all there: why didn't I follow them? This applies to our discovery that one could use stimulation to activate the memory record. We should have anticipated it all.

What about the place of errors in solving problems?

If you are being critical enough you are not making errors. If you're waiting until the proof is completely there, you don't make an error; you don't go on to the conclusion stage. To make a conclusion before the evidence is all there, that is the error. You may think the evidence is all there, but if you're really carefully studying a thing, you know it isn't and you know there's a chance of your being wrong. If you call it a conclusion when you recognize there's 50 percent chance this is right and 50 percent that it's wrong—that I would call an error. If you're stupid enough not to realize that you may have made a mistake when the proof is not complete, that's an error, I suppose.

PAUL SALTMAN

*In August, 1968, we interviewed Dr. Paul David Saltman at the Hold-
erness School in New Hampshire, where he was participating in a
conference on iron chemistry.*

*Born in Los Angeles, California, in 1928, Paul Saltman attended
the schools there and did his undergraduate work at the California
Institute of Technology in Pasadena. After his college training, he was
a Du Pont Fellow from 1950 to 1953, the year he obtained his doctorate
in biochemistry, also at the California Institute of Technology. Going
to the University of Southern California in Los Angeles as an instructor in biochemistry in 1953, he was, by 1961, professor of biochemistry.
He is presently Provost and Professor of Biochemistry at the University of California at La Jolla.*

*Saltman's professional interests are broad, encompassing such di-
verse fields as biological transport mechanisms, iron chemistry, photosynthesis, plant-growth hormones, and problems of communication in
science. His interest in science education and communication has
involved him in films, radio, and television.*

MOLECULAR CHEMISTRY

Paul Saltman

Have you had experiences, daydreams, fantasies, night dreams that enter into your scientific work?

I don't think night dreams really play any critical role in a conceptual sense in the work I've done and how it's come about.

I sort of let my mind wander; daydreaming I guess is closer to the concept. In a sense, fantasy has played some role in what we've been doing. I couldn't pin it down for you specifically, but usually the fantasizing comes when I've done some preliminary experiments which are getting me into a problem.

I know the problem that I want to investigate. I may have a misconception of what the answer is going to turn out to be, but I go ahead and do some experiments anyhow. As a result of what happens in those experiments which often come out completely contrary to my original hypothesis, I start to brood and wander around and don't know what the hell to do next. I begin to think idle thoughts of what the possible answers might turn out to be. Out of *that* kind of situation there have come new insights into a problem. It's ideas that are over and beyond anything that is in the data. Hopefully these new hypotheses can then be tested. That sort of situation occurs occasionally in my work.

For example, take the work we've been doing on iron chemistry. We had discovered, quite by accident and with no preconceived notion, that a complex of sugar with iron is very important for iron to get into human beings. I tried to work on this problem and got nowhere. Four years ago I ran into an inorganic chemist who was at one of these conferences. We sat down together, we started talking, then working. We worked for two months one summer. Everything we did just sort of turned to nothing, and nothing was happening. In brooding about this, I said we ought to look at the data not as if it were an inorganic chemical problem but as if it were a protein chemical problem. And we just developed a whole new approach. It was a matter of three or four weeks, and we had sort of broken a whole new field of chemistry wide open.

It was the observation of the funny color of the chemical solutions during the experiment that impressed me. The relationships of the colors began to make sense. What was true for a protein might be true of my complexes. All of a sudden I said perhaps there is some physical-chemical relationship. Why don't we look at the inorganic complexes as being a very great molecule rather than tiny ones. And it sure as hell was. This concept had really not been understood at all prior to that time.

Then it was the work that you were doing. When you came up with this idea of let's look at it like a big molecule, was this something that occurred to you while you were at work on the job or you were talking to this fellow or did it occur to you while you were daydreaming?

The idea really occurred to me while we were sort of talking and brooding about it, but I think that I had thought about it before in idle hours and in daydreaming about the work. When problems don't work well, I always go home with them and I sort of tuck them away and then I'll catch an idea when I'm shaving or something of this sort. I don't know what to do when I'm in the lab and talking with a student, but I'll go home and I'll be doing something quite different and I'll say I should have tried this, that, or the other thing.

My brooding is more of a metaphor because I'm not a very broody type, I'm not a melancholy type, but I do worry about things. I carry them around with me. I'm sort of like a ruminating cow. I'll pick data up, chew on it for a while, swallow it, pop it up again, and chew on it a little more. I don't have the capacity personally for sustaining a hard, driving attack on the problem I'm not getting anywhere with. I get frustrated and tend to walk away from it, and wait until I can have some new way of approaching it that breaks it loose.

*Can you elaborate on that more about not getting caught up in a main line
when you don't get a solution to a problem?*

Oh, for example, I guess the best way to describe it again is with our work
on iron-sugar complexes. We looked at it several ways, were getting nowhere, and instead of just sitting there and trying everything that people
were telling me to try, I just put the damn thing down and walked away
and started to work on an entirely different problem. Later Tom Spiro and
I got together. He brings in some insight, I bring in some insight, and all of
a sudden we get this brand new way of attacking this problem, and then I
go forward like hell. I have a great ability to sustain, but only if everything
is coming up roses. I'm a lousy loser.

Is most of your work called collaborative; that is, do you work in teams?

I've never been a loner in the sense that it's me alone in the lab and I shut
the door and do the work. I love to work with students. My best efforts
have been collaborative efforts. Usually with students and most recently
with some post-doctoral fellows in which we've done some very good work.
The only time I really worked alone was when I went to Denmark in which
the whole concept of collaborative effort and laboratory work is a strange
one and unknown to them. And there I just sat down by myself and went
to work and I got a nice little something. It wasn't a big something, but it
was a little piece of a problem that opened some new ideas for me. Nothing
cosmic. And yet there it was all me, and there I felt the frustration of just
sitting alone in a laboratory and trying to generate this enthusiasm within
myself, which I ultimately did, but it was a lot less satisfying to me
sensually. I get a great sensual feeling about science and finding out new
things and having fun at times. I really find it very hedonistic which I
think is a better word than sensual.

Do you see yourself as the active agent or do you see yourself as passive?

At that point I saw myself as the active agent. I went over to work on a
specific problem in Denmark. Actually I went over first to work with
people and learn what they were doing, because that's what I want to do in
a lab. Then I sat around the laboratory, and nobody wanted to work or
talk with me for the first month. Then I said I had better get my fanny in
high gear or the Public Health Service is going to be fairly disappointed. I
had had in the back of my mind for many years a little problem that I

wanted to solve about how you could measure how molecules move within a single cell, using giant algae, giant cells which are as long as four or five centimeters, and I thought maybe I could manipulate these cells to advantage. Then I just sat down and started working on these damn algae. Well, it took me just months to learn how to handle them. I finally learned the techniques and in the last couple of months that I was in Denmark I got the new techniques worked out and could do what I really wanted to do, which was to ask questions about how the cells worked. Then I felt very good. But it was hard for me, and I was a very unhappy guy in a laboratory situation for the first nine months of that year, just sort of sitting there and chipping rocks with a hammer. Maybe this is the way science is all the time.

The frustration was great. There was a lack of cooperation. There was quite a different environment from what I was used to. I think I'm a very gregarious kind of guy, and I do my science in a gregarious fashion. Unlike other people, I don't work alone so well. I know a lot of people who just don't work that way, and that's all right too; they have to do their thing. But for me it's that way.

There are two kinds of problems. One kind of problem is the direct outgrowth of the material that I was developing in my Ph.D. thesis that led me to ask questions of a different but related sort. There followed a chain of experiments that came about by my knowing that certain problems in the field needed to be solved. That was the beginning of work I did in photosynthesis which I look upon as a kind of deliberate approach. There are some nice things that have been developed that way, and I think that they're not great but we have fun and we have made some contributions. The work on iron came about in a very curious way. My first job after my degree from Cal Tech was at the University of Southern California Medical School. I felt very insecure about teaching medical students without ever knowing anything about medicine. So I went to the hospital, to talk with various physicians, asking them what sort of things they were working on from a medical point of view, and just trying to see what could be interesting. I found an interesting problem related to iron storage pathologies.

When explanations were given by the physicians about what the mechanism of the disease might be, they weren't satisfactory. The reasons didn't feel right. So I just started to do some preliminary exploration. Out of these initial experiments have grown lots of different research approaches from working with whole animals and tissue slices to working with properties of inorganic ions in solutions. Our research has encompassed just about every conceivable size range from the atom to the molecule to the whole animal. And *that* of course shows the funny way I work. I went into a specific problem and then all of a sudden found myself running around doing all kinds of different experiments distantly related to the problem. I think if I have any single major fault it's probably the fact that I like to run around and do lots of different things in a field. I guess it goes back to my bad habit that when things aren't happening in a particular area, then I want to look to see if there is something else. These scientific meetings such as the Garden Conference are good. I get exposed to new and different research areas and I talk to new people, get some new ideas, find out if somebody knows something that I need to know. I try to bring them in for summer collaboration and we go to work. I'll go to work at his lab to attack a problem. I don't feel I have to know everything in the world. I don't feel compelled to be the world's most knowledgeable guy in every field. I know that I don't have the ability or the time to do it.

The thing that I try to do is always ask what are the critical questions that have to be asked about a problem. For example, do you want to know how many different compounds will react in a solution? Or do you want to know what are the basic, dominant reasons for any kind of reaction? I try not to do the "little experiment" that makes the perfect paper. I would much rather block out the major theme. I really prefer to do the experiments which say "tilt" or "bingo." I don't like to ask questions which I have to say "well, maybe it is." If the experiment doesn't work, I just abandon the problem even though it may be very, very interesting.

When the experiment works, I get very happy and excited. I really feel terrific. I just run down to the laboratory in the morning and just jump in and start running the centrifuge, mixing up compounds or getting the kids who are in the laboratory and say, "Come on, let's do this and try to get as much done every day as we possibly can." I just want to get as much done every day as we possibly can. When the action is "on" I can't relax. I'm just terrible.

I learned once that you never tighten up. You do everything very loose, and if I get up tight, I go away and do something physical such as skiing or surfing. Literally I just walk away from it. Because I find that when I get tense, nothing happens. I start yelling at myself and my kids and my wife, and that's not good.

Many years ago we got on to some problems quite by accident. We were convinced that the old theories as to how iron got into the body were

wrong, and all of our experiments were proving that it was wrong. We
didn't know what the hell was right. Then we learned that it could be the
fact that iron molecules are held by organic molecules and then brought
into the cells. And this was known from other people's work in plants but
not in animals. So we thought, just for the hell of it, we would screen a lot
of compounds and see what would be effective. By accident we put in ten
times too much sugar in a solution we were making and as a result of this
the sugar complexed the iron. All of a sudden we had found a new reaction.
Now this reaction had never been described at all before. Out of this one
experiment we developed a whole new chemistry of sugar complexes which
is still very poorly understood but fascinating. It was strictly serendipitous.
If it had been a one-one-to-one mixture, we would never have found the
iron polymers. We would never have done a lot of things but because it just
happened, we lucked it out. One of my students made the observation
actually, and I said I don't believe it, and we did it again, and it didn't
work. He looked at his notebook, and said he had made a decimal point
mistake. We did it again, and boom it worked, and we were just delighted.
From the results of this one experiment we were able to learn much about
iron. We learned the mechanism of iron storage diseases that plague the
Bantus. We learned how to cure anemia. We learned all about iron chemistry. I could see that none of this would have come about had it not been
for the initial observation. But it was so fortuitous and so strange that it
immediately sort of captured our imagination and our attention, and we
went along with it.

Another experience, I think, was the conceptualization of how iron
might be behaving. The finding that polymerized iron exists as tiny balls
was sort of fortuitous. The initial find really was an accident in this
case, and that is the most specific case I know of. It opened many wonderful new vistas to us.

I really need someone else working with me who presents new ideas, or
I need to find a new instrument to try out in our problem, or I need to see
an article by someone else in which I find the germ of an idea. This may be
kooky as hell, but years ago I found out I could go just so far and exhaust
the method as a way of approaching a solution. When I find it is exhausted, I walk away from it and have to look for a new way for an
approach. Or just completely abandon that situation. For example, we
abandoned a problem five or six years ago. We were seeking the natural
chelating agent in the body which facilitated the uptake of iron. The more
we worked on it, the more we could not find it. Now I am ready to go back

after knowing a lot about iron chemistry. I'll look at the problem again because I think it's ready, and I understand why we lost our compound now.

All right now that's good. Would you say that you lost that compound at that time because you didn't have enough information?

Yes.

Now what we're getting at it—is there any distinction in your mind between making a good error and making a bad error in trying to solve a problem?

Some errors are good and bad. As far as I'm concerned, a bad error is that you're an incompetent guy when you stepped on a test tube or where you kicked a machine or where you asked a stupid question. I think that asking irrelevant or unimportant questions, stupid questions, that's the big error that most people make.

Experimentally, I think the error oftentimes comes about when maybe you don't understand the instrument well enough to exploit it fully. That can give you an error. But then most of the time the errors that you commit are sins of omission and not of deliberate stupidity. We didn't know. We couldn't expect why we would lose the chelating agent in the technique we were using to isolate it, because we assumed that the chemistry of iron was well worked out as the textbook said it was. It wasn't true at all. We know now that our methods would lose that molecule.

All right. But now you feel you might.

Oh, sure I know.

No I just dropped that problem and walked away from it.

Then again it's by accident that you happened to develop some new information as a result of your work afterward that brings you back to the chelating agent?

Yes, it's sort of like weaving, you know. You start out with one line, and then you put another one across. Then a pattern emerges. I think if I had systematically tried to work back and forth I'd have just still been nowhere except frustrated.

My frustration is mostly with my own children. I would probably say I'm reasonably intolerant of people. But I try not to be an intellectual snob. Sometimes I get impatient with stupidity. I find myself having a little problem. But I don't blow up. I usually walk away. I don't feel I am argumentative or aggressive; maybe I am. I would much rather play the role of the clown than the heavy. The clown I think is often a cover up for being annoyed.

My dad was an immigrant from Russia, who came over to Canada at the age of sixteen. He worked at the Hudson Bay Trading Company for several years. He taught himself English, married my mother, and came to Los Angeles. When he got here, he started selling shoes, then sold mattresses, then wound up manufacturing furniture. He came to be one of the first manufacturers of modern furniture in America. Really a pioneer in the field. A guy who had a wide range of interests, and I was very fond of him. He died, and I'll tell you about that later. He was very much of the compulsive Jewish school; you've got to learn. He taught himself all kinds of things, including poetry, literature, music. I know very little of my mother since she died when I was five. She died of pneumonia, and I was raised fundamentally by my father up to the age of fourteen when he was killed in an automobile accident. I moved in to live with my mother's brother. My father was a good human being and a compulsive guy. He really was hard driving—he drove himself hard, and he expected others to do so. When you went out to learn how to paddle a canoe, you paddled with perfection. When you went to school, a "B" was not a passing grade. Constant exposure to all kinds of intellectual stimuli. My father was very political, very much involved with the left-wing movement at that time. I try to remember the earliest exposures which were lessons at the dinner table about the Abyssinian War. We had fund raisings in my father's house. This type of situation was very much a part of our lives.

As a matter of fact it is very interesting that I was always very interested in science and in math and did well and went to Cal Tech as an undergraduate. Majored in chemistry actually, found myself bored and totally disenchanted with science by the time I was a senior, and actually was admitted to the Harvard Business School. I had decided at that point to go into my uncle's furniture business. My uncle had taken over the furniture business, and I figured, Christ, I'll go and become a multimillionaire. Make it in the world of industry. Then I got a very exciting professor in my senior year, James Bonner, and I was really captured by the man and the way he presented his subject. I went abroad to study for a year in Paris, really recaptured a whole new approach to science. Science became a creative experience. I really was bludgeoned to death by science at Cal Tech. I'm smart enough, but everyone else there was smarter. There really was no love in science there. Plenty of hard work. If it weren't for the fact that I played basketball and wrote for the paper and participated in politics, I could have gone crazy. I would have left that joint.

It wasn't the competition, it was just that they demanded so much of you. Every guy was being demanded a lot of so that if you were very very smart, fine, you grabbed the stuff, and it was easy. I had to work for all of it. I didn't really see this creative experience in science literally until I went abroad for a year and worked as a researcher. I had never really done research and understood the process of research as a creative and as a fun experience. Science was never fun. I didn't ever feel I was in the game for four years.

Have you had the feeling with science that perhaps after Paris that you have any axe to grind or something to prove? Do you feel you have something to prove in science?

I know what you're saying. I brood about this too. On the one hand, I'm an egomaniac in that I would really love to have the King of Sweden send me a ticket. That would just be perfect because I love to have peer-group recognition. I like to be recognized as something besides a clown and like to be a complete guy whose wife is a lovely gal. That's my own ego. It is occasionally satisfied a little bit, but I don't think it's fully satisfied at this time. But I'm not so driven by it that I'm willing to sell out the other aspects of my life, which is life with the family and doing other things that give me great pleasure—going to plays, reading, skiing, surfing, and being with my boys.

I may be conning myself but I don't think so. I look at a guy like Bob Sinsheimer. He is just as intense as hell. Jesus, he goes, very very hard, 100 percent of the time. Really a very hard driving guy, and I think that it's been wonderful for him, it paid off beautifully. It paid off in the sense of the discoveries he made, just terrific contributions to science, bulldozed his way. That's why I was so surprised when he agreed to take the chairmanship of biology. Anybody who takes a chairmanship today is doing it as a public service to his colleagues, and he really is doing it that way.

If you can tell me why I took the provostship at San Diego, we'll both be cured!

I like to be broadgauged. I don't think that I'm ever going to do really cosmic work so that everybody will say, gee, there goes Saltman, he's the guy who did such and such.

I'll never be a Jim Watson. I'm not built like Jim is. I do think of myself as a Class A teacher. This I discovered when I was at USC. I do like to teach, and I do it well. I guess I'm always a bit of a revolutionary too in the sense that I always wanted to change USC, I always wanted to make USC a great place, but I never could, because I could never get the opportunity to do it in the sense that I had the authority and responsibility to try to make changes. Then it happened that I could do it at La Jolla, and I felt really this is a critical time in higher education. I'm very sensitive to education and its role, and I thought this is the time to either put up or shut up. I realized it would sort of cramp my science activity, but I felt that it was a job I could do and I wanted to try. I certainly never ran for the job.

My father was really a nut about education, and he was largely self-educated. He would tolerate nothing less than the best in terms of our own efforts in school.

I got further toughened at Cal Tech. When I went back to Cal Tech as a graduate student, it was a whole new life. It was the flip side of the record. Post-doctoral fellows who were there, the other graduate students, James Bonner as the Professor, and it was as easy as hell. It was easier for me to get a Ph.D. than it was to get a bachelor's degree. But by that time I had really become emotionally involved in science where I had not been before at all.

The atmosphere in Paris was important, in the fact that I was there again in a laboratory working with other scientists. There was the opportunity to find something that made a small contribution. I published a paper of the work there. The first paper published was in French. I thought that was very neat, and I had a feeling of accomplishment which I didn't have as an undergraduate at Cal Tech. The only accomplishment was that I didn't die that day. I made it through one more year. That's no way to feel.

In all honesty, and I gave this a lot of thought before I went down there, my colleagues at San Diego are a most distinguished lot of people, three Nobel prize winners, twenty-three National Academy of Science Medals, blah, blah, blah, and they're really high-powered guys with a tradition of publishing credits. Both the system in general and that place in particular, and yet at the same time although they had played lip service to their role as teachers, they really weren't being involved, and I thought that if I wanted to get them involved in teaching, I had to do two things. I really had to be as good a scientist as they were, and I also had to teach and teach very, very well; so I tried to do both during this past year. It worked out fairly well. For the first time in my life I taught a sophomore biology course to 300 students, I had never taught that course before, never taught that many students before, and it was a pretty good course. We had a good time. And I think I feel that for two reasons. One is my own kind of ego. I still like to come to meetings like this conference despite the fact that I'm a provost and I don't want to go to meetings of the American Association on Higher Education. I just don't want to go to those meetings. I want to be here, and at the same time I feel that I am an effective leader of that gang down there in San Diego.

This is in science and also as an administrator. I've got to show my strength every day. I have to show my ability to teach, to do research, to be a fair person. Then I can say to a guy like Linus Pauling. "O. K., Linus, come on now, teach freshman chemistry this year."

Well, I love teaching and administration in the sense that I think that they make the institution great and in the sense that the institution becomes a personification of my leadership. I'm a great believer in benevolent despotism in that I am taking the authority and the responsibility for that college and how it runs, and I want everybody in the world to say, "Hey, that's a great show they have down there."

I see a great deal of similarity between my reaction there and the way my Dad used to react in such situations. He really tried to get me to learn, and I feel I did all the way up to Cal Tech. I learned there was so much God damn fun to learn, but at the same time there was a constant pressure. Boom, boom, boom, go, go, go.

We tried to put a similar kind of pressure on our professors, even on Linus Pauling. Not because he's Linus Pauling. I want to do it on the young guys. I don't like to sit alone. I don't like to see very quiet places. I like to see them in a state of creative dynamism.

I like to do what I want the others to do. When I took this administrative post, that was the first real sense that I had of having to do that. Up to that point, when I was just a professor at USC, there were two main drives. Again it was the egomaniacal pleasure of doing it, I wanted to make the big time. There are the big leagues, and the middle leagues, and the bush leagues—and there I was in the bush. I wanted to play the big league. But when it came time for me to play the big league, it turned out there was a hooker in it. I couldn't play, I could only coach here or play manager or something, and it was at that time that I decided to make a firm commitment to myself that it was imperative for me to continue as a scholar, to continue as a teacher, and to become an effective administrator. I had been

too long at USC where there were not many administrators who were
effective scholars and effective teachers.

This all had to do with my father. My old man said that he wanted to
learn how to ride horses. His knowledge of horses was that of the Cossacks
coming through the Russian village. And yet when he got enough money so
that he could afford horses, he went out and he bought a five-gaited horse
and a jumper and he used to ride the five-gaited horses in show, and I had
to learn to ride the hunter like it or not. I used to show the hunter but I
hated horseback riding. The day my old man died, I never got on a horse
again, literally. It's very interesting to me and I have thought about this
quite a bit, but he was very demanding of himself. He could go in and use
any machine in his factory as well as any of his mechanics. He was not a
furniture maker and previously had sold shoes, but that was the way he did
things. In a sense I'm sure that I was affected by those attitudes.

I think that I really have to exercise more self-discipline, especially as
to how I spend my time. I notice that what was good enough for USC is
not good enough for San Diego. The demands that are placed upon me
affect the way that I use my time. That's my biggest fault.

My sons are thirteen and fifteen years old. I see two different personalities. I'm much too close to these characters. We have a very close family
relationship. We do lots of things together by choice, I think, and not by
demand. I would much rather go skiing with them and my wife, rather
than go alone. We took the boys to Denmark. Whenever we can, we like to
spend time together. I see my older boy as being more self-disciplined than
the younger one, more like me in his approach to study. He will probably
wind up with an interest either in one of the social sciences or in law, I
think. He doesn't have that funny kind of thing that I see in the bright
science kids who by fourteen years old have ground their first telescope,
built their first oscillograph, and so forth.

That's the sort of thing I did as a youth. I used to do a lot of reading
and wrote reports about science and carried out little experiments and built
things in the house, and so forth. The younger kid is much more a personality like my wife in the sense that he's a much more artistic kind of character. For example, Josh will try anything including, for example, drugs,
and this and that and the other thing. My older son is far more conservative. Josh will just try anything whether he wins or loses. David will only
try those things he can win. If he loses, he's just really up tight. I guess
that's really my fault. I said too many times when he has made a mistake,
he's a *schmuck,* and then I say OK try again. That's my own frailty, but I

think that I'm better at that now than I was.

I've never been dry in my scientific work. I've averaged about four or five publications a year, sometimes six and sometimes two or three. I think that there were some high spots when we got some very good results, and I felt very good. Then there have been years which have looked as a sort of foundation building. Or you make the discovery and you have to spend a couple of years pinning down some loose ends, and something new will happen. Right now, I think I'm kind of in a quiescent period, but I see some problems developing in people coming to work in the lab that will make exciting things happen.

I think James Bonner was a very significant influence in my life. And I think Linus Pauling was a significant influence. He taught me freshman chemistry, and I was very much excited by this man and by the way he operates. He thinks in so many different ways. He's so smart, and he's so terrific that he makes great, great, great discoveries. I'm very impressed by him.

In college I was getting straight A's in the humanities courses. I was tempted to dump science, and I was enjoying these humanities courses and doing very well. My economics professor wanted me to go to Harvard and be an economist. When James Bonner came along, it got very exciting again. Those are two big influences in my academic career. I think my graduate students have been very important to me. They have made discoveries. I help them and they help me. That's been a learning experience. It's only been in the last couple of years that I sort of achieved any kind of a stature that would bring post-doctoral fellows to my lab, like Tom Spiro who has been with me for the last three summers, who is at this meeting. He's an Assistant Professor at Princeton, a young guy. We've been just terrific for each other.

I think when I'm happy I function a lot more effectively in the sense that my tolerance level goes up. I think I'm willing to consider a lot more points of view of the situation and make better decisions. For example, just before I left USC, my mood was very down. There had been a whole series of incidents that had occurred relative to the environment of the University which were very depressing to me, and as a result of this I didn't think I was as effective a teacher as I should have been. My scholarly production was impaired to some extent. I knew that I wasn't giving my students as much as I should, and in return getting from them the kind of relationship that had been productive in the past. I wasn't really living with my colleagues. I had lost all tolerance for them. I just couldn't walk in any more because I had lost respect for them.

My subjective experiences are interesting. I'm a pretty good surfboard rider. When I'm in a big wave and I'm riding down that wave, there's a certain kind of feeling, the adrenalin is flowing, and you feel just tingly, you feel all jazzed, euphoric. There's a sense of excitement and danger, but you're free and you feel totally removed from everything else in the world when you're in that big wave. It really is that. I get that kind of a feeling in science when the days are coming where everything is hitting and you're seeing new relationships and the experiments work and the next one works and the next one works, and oh God, this is wonderful. This is wild. All of a sudden you get so excited and you're running around and your total life is kind of wrapped up in this problem, and it feels that way. That's one aspect of the creative process which I feel very keenly. There's another aspect of science which again goes back to people. I have had many good friends in science whom I have developed human relationships with, and that's been a very important aspect in science. A meeting like this is important when I can sit down and drink beer with my friends and talk about lots of things besides science. It is catalyzed by science, but in terms of the creative process itself I see that it is important.

It has been a non-sexual quality but I think there is also a sexual analogy too in a relationship which I happen to enjoy very much with my wife. It transcends just a physical sexual relationship. It's the sense of lying in bed together when you know she's sleeping on one side of the bed, you're sleeping on the other and it feels nice. It feels a hell of a lot better than when I'm sleeping in this bed and she's 3,000 miles away. Being able to share a relationship with her is great. It's something that enriches me. This is why it was so important for us, I think, to be in Paris that first year we were married. We just shared everything, and sort of from that time on it's been that kind of relationship that we've had with one another. My wife is an artist. She majored in design at UCLA and recently turned her attention to pre-school education. She's been very active in that area, concerned with a very interesting project.

It doesn't concern the use of art, just the whole concept of pre-school education as an important aspect of child development. She worked very closely with an outfit called the Pacific Oaks School in Pasadena which has a very good reputation in pre-school education. She hasn't really been a compulsive artist. For a while she was modeling and designing, and then when the kids came, that was given up. I think she'll go back probably and teach. She's interested in people. And so am I.

ARTHUR KOESTLER

Alpbach, a small village in the heart of the Austrian Alps, was the setting of our interview with Arthur Koestler. Mr. Koestler was born in Budapest, Hungary, in 1905, but for many years he has lived in London. After education at the University of Vienna, he became a foreign correspondent in the Middle East as well as in Germany and France. He was also a member of the Graf Zeppelin Arctic Expedition during 1931. As a result of covering the Spanish Civil War for the London News Chronicle, *Mr. Koestler was imprisoned by General Franco. In 1939 and 1940 he was a member of the French Foreign Legion, and in 1941–42, the British Pioneer Corps.*

His principal works include Darkness at Noon (*1940*), Arrival and Departure (*1945*), Insight and Outlook (*1948*), The Sleepwalkers (*1959*), *and* The Act of Creation (*1964*).

The last-named work sets forth Koestler's interesting doctrine of bisociation about which he has something to say in the interview that follows.

Arthur Koestler

You know, it is not the same when one writes about the theory of creativity and when one sits down to do a day's job of writing. Fantasies, in the sense of daydreaming, or reverie, as far as I am concerned play no part in doing the job. Fantasies may be a satisfying form of autistic thinking for your private benefit, you know. But—

Autistic thinking? Or, artistic?

Autistic. I mean, just for your own benefit. I mean daydreaming is the opposite of creativity. Wish-fulfilling fantasies are just the opposite of creative work. As for dreams, I've written about Kekule, you know, how he found the structure of the benzene ring in a dream—but I never had that luck. And I think it's an extreme case. In other words, it isn't the same as when, let's say, in your bath or under the shower, suddenly you get an idea related to your work. That is neither daydreaming nor dreaming. It is a process, an idea which probably was in the preconscious, you know, and broke through. You sort of go down from the conscious level to some unconscious creative level, and then you come up again. But creating while dreaming is not in my personal experience. And daydreaming is always a shortcut.

While shaving, while on vacation, while in the bath—this comes up over and over again . . . that ideas pop up. Now, yes, it's preconscious.

It may have been close to the surface.

Yes. At the same time, there's this idea of keeping something in the back of your mind all the time. This idea of keeping ideas salient.

On the agenda.

Keeping it on the agenda. Right. And, well, we guess that's not day-dreaming.

No. Daydreaming is a whole sequence, planned; you are Napoleon and you have conquered the world. There's a sequence in it. It's storytelling on an infantile level, on an autistic level, addressed to yourself, which is the opposite of creativity. It's a shortcut to wish-fulfillment in an unrealistic way. An inartistic way. You see, you can't when you write a novel simply daydream yourself into the main character. It doesn't work that way.

As for dreams, there have been varying remarks. For example, some of our contributors have felt that dreams have played a very signal role in their work. Some have gone so far as to say that their dreams are actually part and parcel of their work, while others point out that it plays no role at all.

I would belong to the others. Dreams are not a part of the work. It would be nice, you know, but it is not the way one writes or creates. It's a burning up of calories to one's own private satisfaction.

And you don't feel that this is in any way related to the creative urge.

Oh, it must be somehow indirectly related, but very indirectly.

Could you say something about any possible indirect connection then?

I cannot think of a single case where I dreamt the solution of an artistic problem, or where remembering a dream did help me with the solution of an artistic problem; you know, when you are stuck and don't know how to go on with something, I can't remember a single instance. I know that indirectly the subconscious processes must contribute to creativity, but it isn't a shortcut.

Could you say something about the role of serendipity, of accident.

Well, whether it's real accident or apparent accident, that does enter into it quite a lot. And this may be the indirect connection between unconscious processes and actual writing. What happens is that a solution suddenly offers itself as something so obvious and self-explanatory that one wonders why one hadn't thought of it before. Not in a dream, nor in a daydream, but just in that Poincaré manner, you know.

Poincaré? Did you say Poincaré?

Poincaré. You know the classic case . . .

Foot on the bus—

Foot on the bus. You haven't thought of it before and suddenly the solution is there. That's the same thing as while shaving, while your conscious mind is occupied with something else, and this provides an opportunity for the preconscious thing to break through.

How about a slip of the pen? You write a wrong word. Or at the typewriter the wrong word comes out. Has it happened?

Well I wish the Muses would offer me a slip of the pen. Perhaps I am too pedestrian. No.
    Things which help are after-dinner drinking, when you are interested in something totally different, but somehow the blockages are broken down, you know. When you let a little alcohol into your head and you don't think of the problem in hand, then something might come through. In other words, it's really a question of breaking down blockages. And incidentally, amphetamines in small doses can have the same beneficial effect in this breaking down of barriers.

Have you had experience yourself with the amphetamines?

In very modest amounts. What matters is getting out of the rut, somehow getting out of the grooves.

Then the question becomes one of techniques, of getting out of the groove, and why it is that some people stay in the groove and why some people are relatively free and manage not to get in the groove.

Well, there must be something outside the groove. That's a precondition. That must be there. And the techniques of getting out of the groove, well you can't employ them consciously, otherwise they become self-defeating. You can't tell yourself, "Now let's abandon the beaten track and enter a new territory." It's a tricky business, you know. It's somehow achieving a balance. When you have that balance, the words become transparent to the meaning which counts, and the words themselves fall into their natural, God-willed order, instead of searching for words.

When you speak of God, what was it—God-willed you said?

Uh huh.

Now in your book on the act of creation, in the area of discussing Gestalt psychology, you referred to "demand qualities."

What qualities?

"Demand qualities." The situation demands a solution. Requires. It's a matter of requiredness. Yes. And when you speak of something as being God-willed, it makes it sound very much as if you're referring to this requiredness. That the situation itself demands that solution.

We ought to distinguish whether we talk about writing or about problem-solving in science. You see, in writing, you've got a lot of problem-solving situations, but the main job of writing is not problem-solving. Whereas if you look at science, it is problem solving. So, we ought to distinguish between those two.

You feel there is a difference in the creative act in the arts and in the sciences.

Well I have tried to point out that it's a continuum.

Yes.

Nevertheless we are in different . . .

Regions?

Yes, regions of the continuum. You see, you can say writing is problem-solving, finding the right expression and so on, but that is stretching the analogy too far. No. It's a different thing. I repeat, in writing you do come up against problems which are capable of a solution. But that isn't the essence of writing. Problem-solving is getting the idea for a story or for a book, or getting the idea for a plot. Or getting the idea for the solution of a dilemma in your plot. But, these are the milestones. In the normal routine of writing, things are different.

But how about the birth of an idea?

Well, here we are in deep waters. You see, the idea comes from somewhere, and it's very rare that you can follow the chain back to where the idea came from. But again there is a difference between this and scientific problem-solving. You see, when you write, let's say, a novel, sometimes you start with a very vague idea and let it develop by itself, and one thing leads to another.

But the vague idea has to come from something, from somewhere.

Yes. That's what I'm saying. But those are the milestone moments.

Do you have any ideas about where these ideas come from?

Well, I suppose some experience digested preconsciously or unconsciously, processed unconsciously.

An outer experience? An inner experience? Do you make a distinction between the two?

I can't make the distinction. No. The outside world has to be internalized, and the internal world has to be projected or externalized. I can't make that distinction. You see, most writers haven't got a plot beforehand. They only have a very vague Gestalt concept of what it's going to be about. It may be about an idea, or a conflict, or a problem or about some people. I start with the problems. Other writers start with the people. They start with the people and then the people come up against problems. I start with the problem and then choose the people who are going to come up against them. But in both cases, the thing develops to some extent by itself.

So you would see the stimulus as being—

A releaser, a trigger.

Of what's already there?

Yes.

When you speak of a writer having a vague Gestalt, and not really knowing how the story is going to work out, has this been your experience?

Yes.

You didn't know how a story will end.

No. Not how it would develop, nor how it would—oh, end, maybe. End. Yes. But how it would develop and reach that end, that you don't know.

You're as surprised as the reader? You feel you are as surprised as the reader is?

Sometimes. Yes. It isn't such a dramatic surprise, but a very pleasant one actually.

Would you say that all of your novels have been autobiographical in one way or the other?

Where they are not they are bad, you know. You can only write about something which you know and feel and have experienced.

When you're working, do you find a sense of urgency to get your work done? You work slowly? You work excitedly? You become . . .

Terribly slowly, terribly slowly, but occasionally, in patches excitedly, in a rush. I like to write no more than five hundred words a day, you know, and rewrite them and rewrite them. But you have to have that impatience of getting somewhere, otherwise it would be just playing around. And very often, when for external reasons you have to hurry, it helps. When you haven't got the physical time to elaborate. It helps.

You mean, like deadlines?

Yes. Self-imposed deadlines, or externally imposed. It sometimes helps. But you see creativity is such an ill-defined word. Because really there are very different mechanisms involved, in writing novels and solving scientific problems. On the other hand, in both fields you have sometimes a single idea and six months of checking or elaboration. In both cases it's the old story of inspiration and perspiration. And the perspiration is really a major part in it.

Yet when we talked, Mr. Koestler, to Dr. Wilder Penfield, the neurologist and neurosurgeon, we found upon his retirement as Director of the Montreal Neurological Institute, that he turned to writing novels. And he's already written two, he's working on another one, and they have both been published. He found a continuity in his approach, and apparently . . .

I've got the greatest admiration for Penfield. He's a great man. But I wonder . . .

He may be exceptional.

Well, Bertrand Russell tried to write short stories, you know. They were rather amateurish. That is like me taking to gardening. Do you know of any single case where a scientist took up writing as a hobby and produced something worthwhile in old age or in retirement? I don't know of any.

Well, if you think of some of the real geniuses, you know, like Leonardo. Wasn't he both a scientist and an artist of superb quality?

But he didn't write poems. Anyway, it's very difficult to talk about the people of the Renaissance. But even so, I don't know any great painter who wrote anything which is artistically worthwhile reading. I mean, Gauguin's diary is unreadable, you know. One shouldn't underestimate the craftsmanship factor in writing.

Craft or talent? What about the place of talent?

That one takes for granted. As when you say, "getting out of the groove," there must be a place to get into. But it's terribly difficult to distinguish between good craftsmanship . . . and genius. Except that genius discovers new methods of craft, new methods of expression, new techniques. But even genius, you know, often makes just one discovery in a lifetime—look at Henry Moore—that sort of holds him, and then he grows old. And that goes for most painters and most sculptors. They discover a style for themselves, and they carry on with that style to the end of their lives.

Could you say anything about the role of your mood when you're onto something? What place has your mood in your work? Perhaps your wife can tell us more about this than you can.

Well, she'll say the same as me. The mood is decisive. Isn't it? It's decisive. But, decisive only in a negative sense. It shouldn't be the wrong mood. I mean, then you can't do anything. But, the right mood doesn't guarantee that anything will come out of it. Mood merely eliminates obstacles.

Could you be more specific?

Well, to be in a writing mood means that obstacles are eliminated out of your mind. You are not obsessed whether the postman will bring a letter from a lawsuit, or whether this chap is doing his job properly, or whether the drains function, or whether the reviews of your book are good or bad. These are the obstacles.

But how about depression? Is depression an obstacle? Or does it help? Is elation an obstacle, or does it help? Is being content an obstacle?

Depression might be creative. Elation might be creative. What's important in mood is not to be deflected, obsessed with anything outside the work. So, it's an eliminatory process of your defenses against extraneous matter. I'm sorry to be so very down to earth, but you know to write about creativity is a different thing than to sit down and do a job. Alas!

You mean, writing about creativity is not so creative as writing a novel.

I didn't mean that. It's a different process. When you write a novel or when you write an essay, or when you write a treatise, or prepare a lecture, you can't tell yourself, "I am now creating." You are just doing a job. And the moment you tell yourself, "Now, here you are sitting and creating"—well, then you can give up.

But, do you find that there are any moods that go along with those periods when you find yourself being most productive. Are you irritable? Are you hard to get along with? Are you marvelous to get along with?

I am irritable and hard to get along with. Yes.

(*Mrs. Koestler*) Not when he's really sort of deeply involved in a book. No. He comes down at the end of the day. He's sort of cheerful. He's still obsessed, still thinking about it. But not irritable or bad-tempered.

No. One is too exhausted. It's a wonderful feeling of exhaustion.

A wonderful feeling of exhaustion?

A good day's work is a wonderful feeling of exhaustion. You come down. You have deserved your before-dinner drink, you know. I don't drink all day.

You've really earned it?

You earned it. And you feel an exhausted emptiness, which is really a sort of postcoital feeling. Then, of course, it might start again, and you might go on until midnight or until two o'clock. The thing turns in your head. Like a mill.

Do you work more at night or during the morning?

No. I work only during daytime.

Mornings? Afternoons?

The best time physiologically is sort of after four or five o'clock until eight.

We've got him at the right time. I think that's why he suggested five o'clock, Mrs. Koestler!

No. I had this French journalist woman here with her two children, and sometimes mixing people is a good thing, but in this case nothing would have come out of the mixture, because the interests are different, and the languages too. I find it rather exhausting, you know, up here in Alpbach to get visitors who speak different languages and have different interests, and somehow holding them together. That is a chore.

It's a chore?

Very tiring, you know.

Could you tell us anything about your own background? About your family background? And the way you feel that might in any way have contributed to your work?

Well, I think an unhappy childhood is a necessary, but not a sufficient, condition for creativity. And mine was a very unhappy one. Like most writers. Well, Hemingway says he had a very happy childhood. According to his own account, you know. But, that may have been an external happiness. One doesn't know. There was a Russian writer whose name is totally forgotten. She was called Vera Imber. She wrote one unforgettable sentence, which was, "Everybody has a given amount of calories to burn up—you either burn them up by living or by creating." You can't burn the same calorie both ways. You make poetry out of your unhappiness, and you might argue that you can also make poetry out of your happiness. But why should you make poetry when you are happy instead of living it out? So there must be something unconsummated in the unhappy moments which ask for consummation on a different level.

For expression.

For consummation in expression. Yes.

Was either of your parents involved in literature?

No. My father read only one book in all his life which was *The Three Musketeers* by Dumas.

Was he a storyteller? Did he tell you stories?

No.

How about your mother? Was she involved in anything?

She was very imaginative.

Yes?

Not a storyteller. No. I had a fairly untypical childhood. Bilingual, brought up in Hungarian and German. I repeat, I think an unhappy childhood is a necessary, but not a sufficient condition for creativity. Creativity is a secondary expression. The primary expression is living. So there must be something which demands that second outlet. You know, the not-burnt-up calories.

Do you have any brothers and sisters, or have you had any?

No. That's again typically untypical, you know. The only-child syndrome.
    How did you take to that idea of bisociation?

We think it's a very interesting idea. It's an idea which Froelich Rainey, who is director of the Museum of the University of Pennsylvania has.

Oh, Rainey. What about him?

He was the person, who, in his own way, I think, made the most of the idea.

How?

By pointing out how people from different areas, from different disciplines are necessary to bring ideas together. But that's not real bisociation.

No. It's a trivial example.

Yes. But it does touch on it. That concept, incidentally, is something we've always felt. You put your finger on it in The Act of Creation. *That somehow people who work in borderline areas, you know, really end up being the people who make the most significant contributions.*

One of the real problems in writing, whether it's fiction or nonfiction, is to have one's head in the clouds, but your feet on the earth. So in a theoretical essay, you are sometimes carried away by a purely abstract flight of thought. Now, bisociation means in this context that you suddenly say to yourself, "Well, I'm talking about real people, about real down-to-earth reality." Then you bring in an illustration of your abstract idea which pulls you down to reality. Metaphors, realistic metaphors. Or, in fiction writing, you work on a dialogue, or a description of something, and suddenly you say, "Well, this is here and now, and this person is here and now," and put your nose into it. A train of thoughts moves under its own inertia, you know, as a body set in motion goes on moving. But when you manage to catch yourself, to realize that you are up on a flight, and then manage to pull it down to earth, well that's bisociation. In the Turgenev story, when Natasha contemplates suicide, there's a fly crawling over a piece of sugar and your focus of attention is suddenly distracted to the fly; then you really have two levels of reality which are in contact, you know.

Aren't you then speaking about the relationship between autistic thinking and reality thinking?

No. No. Not autistic thinking and reality.

We don't mean autistic in the sense of a distortion of reality, but autistic in the sense of a flight of fancy.

All right. Yes.

Then bringing it down to a level of reality. And isn't there a constant exchange from one to the other?

If there is, then it's fine. But come to think of it, I wrote a lot about the tragic plane and the trivial plane of existence, you know. When you manage to get a glimpse through the trivial at the tragic essence, or you manage to get the tragic or abstract or cosmic down to the level of reality, when you get this current running between the two poles . . .

Yes. Yes.

Then you are all right, you know. Hemingway's greatness is that through his monotonously repetitive trivial dialogue, you get glimpses of eternity.

But eternity is a bore, you know, when you don't look at it through, through the window of time. So, to get those two together, I think that's really the essence of craftsmanship. That the trivial is transparent. It's transparent to the eternal. And the eternal is embodied in the trivial, in the here and now.

You've mentioned Hemingway several times, Mr. Koestler. Have you seen Carlos Baker's recent book?

I only saw the extracts of it which are a bore. A deadly bore. I mean, this is an official biography—

Because of the tremendous detail that he addresses himself to?

And it's official—

Minor.

I thought of Hotchner's book which was remarkable. It takes a long time, but in the end everybody will discover that Hemingway was the greatest writer of our century, with all his weaknesses and mannerisms and self-caricaturings, he still was. It was a breakthrough in writing.

Do you have any feeling about influences on yourself? Who do you think, if anyone, has been a major influence?

You mean writers?

Writers, yes.

Oh, yes.

Could you tell us about them.

Well, a man who you probably never heard of, Alfred Döblin, who was a German expressionist writer. And Thomas Mann. Hemingway. Although I think you don't realize it when you read my stuff. Hemingway and the early Thornton Wilder. But I do hope these influences are so digested that nobody can trace them, you know. Influence doesn't mean imitation. Influence means feeding and digesting.

What prompted you, Mr. Koestler, to do the book on creativity?—The Act of Creation.

Umpteen years ago, I had a discussion with Rapaport, the psychoanalyst.

David Rapaport?

In Budapest. I never found out whether it's the same Rapaport.

Oh, yes. He's Hungarian. Oh, yes. The same. Went to the Menninger Foundation.

Well, we had a discussion with a few writers in Budapest about humor. He told a joke, and I suddenly saw that the joke was based on the discrepancy of two scales of values applied to the same event—a bisociation. We discussed it for a long time, and he said, "I think you've got something there." I then started writing a short essay on humor showing that Bergson's theory of humor, "the mechanical encrusted on the living," is merely a special case contained in a more general rule, that the comic is the result of two incompatible codes of relevance being brought to a clash. Then I came to see that this can also be applied, *mutatis mutandis,* to scientific discovery, the synthesis of two apparently incompatible fields. So, then one thing led to another. This I think is how things really happen. When one thing leads to another. Whether the theory is valid or not is irrelevant in this context.

That was an extremely scholarly volume. You must have done a great deal of research.

Yes. That's the fun of it, you know. The research is always a kind of escapism. But a very respectable escapism. It's wonderful to dig up, to dig up things.

These two levels that you speak of in humor. You feel that this in some way led to your concept of bisociation.

Yes. That's what I'm trying to say.

That was the first chapter in the book as we recall. On humor. You told the joke, the story about the two Bronx housewives getting together.

Yes. The Oedipus Schmedipus story.

Right. And then the one about the Picasso. Yes. The Picasso story is a good one.

Picasso saying: "I often paint fake Picassos."

Right. That's right.

There is another element in what we call creativity. The ways of thinking. I see most things in diagrams, even the development of a plot in a novel. Visually. Quite a lot of people do. This is another type of bisociation, because you operate on two levels simultaneously.

You spoke of your family background as being bilingual. Would you say that it was also bicultural?

No. I would say it was uncultural.

Well, you suggested that. But I think you're being unfair to yourself.

You mean to my parents!

Yes. Or to your parents.

Here the psychoanalyst's cloven hoof comes out.

Would you say it was bicultural?

I really do mean it was uncultural.

Uncultural. What did your father do for a living?

Well, mostly he embarked on all sorts of financial enterprises which were absolutely mad.

Without success?

At times.

They were successful?

Some. For short times. But, as I said, he read one book in his life, *The Three Musketeers*. But I do not recommend that you should give your child an unhappy childhood in the hope that he'll become a successful writer, which is what is recommended by quite a lot of people.

How about omnipotence? Early childhood thoughts about becoming great, somehow. Did you ever have the thought that somehow you were going to make it?

I think that omniscience would be closer than omnipotence.

Omniscience?

Omniscience. Yes. All-knowingness. Rather than power.

Yes.

I think so. I think that can even be generalized. It's a much closer day-dream, you know. To have universal all-knowingness. Omnipotence, I think, plays a very small part with creative artists, otherwise they would go into politics; or with scientists, too, you know.

The fantasy of being a Renaissance Man?

Yes. Oh, yes. Knowing everything about everything. That is a potent fantasy.

And how!

But, power—power, I don't think so.

Well, we used it in its more general sense, what we refer to as a Walter Mitty fantasy.

But that isn't—Walter Mitty doesn't aspire to power, but to find his feet in every situation.

Uh huh.

Well (to his wife) if I were Stalin I think I would issue one decree in all my life: "Everybody has to read at least one book of mine." That's power, you see. That would be useful power.

Well, you know, you mentioned Stalin, and not without reason. It's very interesting that recently it's come to light in the Lysenko business, which you remember so well, that Stalin seems to have had a personal role in this. Having conceived of himself personally as a geneticist. You may have known that for a long time, but we think it's come out recently in a very interesting way in some publications.

Well, that's very familiar ground, you know.

There's a man by the name of Lerner at the University of California, a geneticist, who recently translated a book on the Lysenko business, in which he makes quite a point about this matter.

Whose book is it? Is it by a Russian geneticist?

I don't remember whose book it is. But he makes quite a point that Stalin personally conceived of himself as a geneticist.

Stalin thought that if one has mastered the Marx-Lenin dialectics one knows all the answers.

To everything?

To everything.

Including genetics?

Including genetics and plumbing.

And plumbing?

There were handbooks of plumbing that explained that plumbing has to be done dialectically.

Plumbing?

Plumbing. Yes. Cold and hot water pipes. It was really a revival of scholasticism, where everything could be deduced from first principles.

But, you know, the real puzzling thing is a writer's motivation. I'm surprised you didn't ask—

Well, we're very much interested in that or we wouldn't be here.

Or, were you biding your time about it?

No. We think, in our own way, the questions that we have asked have very definitely touched upon motivation.

Because, you know, that's a mystery to me . . . my own motivation. You see—you read *The Double Helix*, perhaps?

Uh huh.

Now, I have a number of friends in the sciences, including some Nobel laureates. Schrödinger spent his last summers here in Alpbach. What motivated him? What motivated X? What motivated Y and Z? This is very hard to formulate, because it's all so very indirect.

But, you see, we've touched on that by our questions—

You mean the Gestalt which cries out for closure?

Yes. Yes. Perhaps what goes into it is the unhappy childhood. What goes into it is the Walter Mitty fantasy, the omniscience fantasies.

Yes. But lots of people have unhappy childhoods and dream of being Goethe and Shakespeare. It's necessary but not sufficient.

But, we asked you about talent. And you said, "We take that for granted."

Yes. That it has to be there. But, still what motivated a writer, or scientist, is very difficult to say.

We think many of the people—

You could write a postscript and say it.

Many of them, we think, would be very defensive about that.

I see.

And they were very concerned to be sure that they were free to make any changes and so forth and so on. So we think we might have run into some difficulty there. We would be very interested in what you would have to say now about your reaction to this interview. We haven't asked this of others, but we think in view of your interest in this field, your thoughts about this approach. . . . Incidentally, of course, this is not a hard scientific study that is being done.

Well, I think your method of interviewing was sufficiently discreet, just triggering off, you know, and —but, of course, time is short and offers only limited opportunities. But, maybe you'll do a second volume. Then, the interviews should be in depth, meaning, as one shoots a film; you know, one has hundreds of feet of footage, and only a relevant selection is used. You would have to go on for two, three days . . .

Yes.

Until you really get the bloke to spill the beans.

You know, two, three days. But that's an unmanageable project. Well, actually, as you may know, this sort of thing has been done, this depth interview technique by Donald MacKinnon and his group at the University of California.

To return to the question you raise about motivation. We were saying about motivation that the ego and the matter of meeting ego needs are something that has come up over and over again, perhaps more so among the scientists. Your idea about The Double Helix *pointed the idea up beautifully; it was a good example. The competitiveness, the need to be first.*

That's very human. If you have an original idea, but another person also has the same original idea, the need to come in first. But the idea of motivation puzzles me, because I don't know my own motivation, or I don't know the prime motivation. I once said in an interview that every writer's ambition should be to swap one hundred readers now for ten readers in ten years' time and one reader in one hundred years time. I do believe in that. I'd rather be read in one hundred years than now. But that doesn't make sense. Is it a self-delusion? It sounds like it. How does that click with any known psychology? Is it some illusion that I'll be there in one hundred years to see?

We think it's a feeling and a wish for immortality.

What is the world to me when I'm no longer there to appreciate it? I don't see how it fits into any ego psychology or to any school of psychology.

We think it's an off-shoot of omnipotence, in a way.

That's a verbal explanation.

May we ask you a related question. Do you have any children?

I never wanted children.

So maybe your creative works are your children. They are your hold on immortality.

But these are verbal answers. All this doesn't enter into the practical business of writing. If you have some experience in the craft, you can write a book which will sell more. You can even program yourself to write a best-seller. So to write for posterity, so to speak, you have to avoid these temptations of immediate gratification, and I can assure you that sometimes it is a sacrifice. Nobody says thank you for that because nobody sees what one has refrained from, the cheap effects. So here the motivation becomes very abstract, becomes really a motivation of self-denial.

Now you're talking about integrity. You say it doesn't fit into ego or id psychology, but you're really talking about the superego now. If we have to oversimplify and put labels on it, it could fit into a psychoanalytic explanation.

That's verbal to a large extent.

It is verbal, but you do have a sense of integrity. If you didn't have it, you'd be grinding out best sellers left and right. You wouldn't have knocked yourself out to write The Act of Creation *which, we understand, was a sleeper for some years. It didn't sell as well as it should have. It's a magnificent book.*

But again what does integrity mean? It's a word, and superego, it's a word.

We think it explains something; honesty, a wish to maintain values, set standards. Aaron Copland put it very well. He spoke of his being an exemplar of his generation; that if he doesn't write this kind of music, nobody else is going to do it.

Now this is an essential part of motivation. That idea that if you didn't write that book, there would be a hole, a gap in the texture of the history of literature. As if on a conveyor belt, there would be a gap.

And you feel that you *have something that can fill that hole.*

Only you. If you don't do it, as Copland said, nobody else will. Now this is closer to real motivation, see.

Now, you see, Isaac Bashevis Singer said, when he writes a story, he has to have the feeling that only he could write that story.

Yes. Otherwise there would be a hole in the texture.

I got a lot of people to write their memoirs, quite a number of people; maybe twenty books have been written because I prodded the people. For that same reason, their experience shouldn't be wasted. There shouldn't be a hole, you know. And that is a genuine motivation, a vacuum which has to be filled in. It may be self-delusion, but motivationally it is real. And another thing, you know, the profession of a writer, it isn't a pleasant one.

It is really sweat and toil and you've got all the frustrations with the reviewers who either don't know what you are talking about and write lousy reviews, or if they write a rave review, then you have even more the feeling they haven't got the faintest idea of what they are talking about. But that exhaustion which you get after a good day's work, when you have a feeling that half a page which you wrote really expresses what you wanted to say and you are hollowed out, sort of emptied, that feeling is one of the most glorious feelings. Whether it's going to be successful or not, you feel that you have hit it off, and that is rarely deceptive. You sometimes have false inspirations, and you write something in a state of euphoria, and the next day you look at it and it's lousy. But whenever I had that feeling of real catharsis, looking at it next day, it was still all right. So you have built-in, you have sort of built-in critical criteria which know better than your euphoria and your mood. That's a very odd thing. Do you understand what I mean?

Can you explain it a little?

You get spurious inspirations, and you get elated and euphoric. But this inner certainty, that *this is all right,* this is different. It might be just a simple job, you know, but this is a very curious built-in control which develops as the years go by, with your experience. An unconscious censor that doesn't allow you to delude yourself. That's a very, very curious thing.

Incidentally, this has been pointed out in our interviews. Other people have pointed to this too, by the way.

It's the difference between a catharsis and that false elation.

When you have this feeling and you look back on the work the next day, or a week later, would you say you might still change it or generally do you let it stand?

Oh, you might polish here or there. But it would be only very superficial polishing.

But a concept that comes out that way with that kind of feeling—

And the formulation, not only the concept. It's a good job, writing.

Another question is, you know, money. Some people do their best work when they need the money and when they set out to do a commercial job.

Think of people like Dashiell Hammett. And sometimes when the motivation is pressing, you do a better job than if you sit down and suck your thumb and write for eternity. Sometimes an urgency helps and sometimes not. These are variables, you know. They're not constants, but variable parameters.

One of the memorable phrases which I remembered all my life is in an essay by Thomas Mann. I think it's in his essay on Cervantes, but I'm not sure. He says: "Vanity is justified, but vanity should stand behind the work and not in front of it." It's beautiful.

THE ARTISTS

JOSEPH JAMES AKSTON

There are some things that can only be spoken of indirectly; there are some answers that will always have the form of a question, a riddle, a seeming evasion. The editors of this book on the creative experience have had the courage and humility to approach their subject in the simplest, most direct way—in conversation with a variety of men in whose lives the creative experience is central. They must often have felt, while conducting the interviews recorded here, like the Zen monk's young disciple who, when he asked how he could attain true wisdom, was told to go and chop wood. For how can a lifetime of experience, or even one privileged moment in that lifetime, be reduced to a few quotable words?

Yet if the disciple had not asked his "foolish" question, there would have been no Zen riddle to puzzle and delight us. And we are grateful too to the editors for their willingness to ask questions that are, after all, not so foolish, since they serve, far better than any *a priori* theoretical discussion of creativity, to shed light on the quality of the artist's experience as he lives it day by day.

This brass tacks approach seems to us especially valuable in our second Alexandrian age of scholarship and criticism, in our era of mass information if not yet mass culture. The work of last year's novelist is dissected in this year's college curriculum; this year's well-publicized innovation in sculpture, having run the media circuit from art glossies to family weeklies, will furnish the sight gag in next year's television commercial. This rapid analysis and assimilation of the products of artistic creation may or may not be a good thing in the long run— certainly the role of the artistic and scientific creator in society is changing as rapidly as society itself—but, in the meantime, both critic and audience could profit by a closer knowledge of the process out of which art emerges. The starting point of philosophy, said Aristotle, is wonder. Wonder and humility in massive doses are what our critics and pundits lack, and what the artists who speak in these pages possess, to our good fortune.

Our approach to understanding the arts at this time is still highly verbal. We want reviews, which are written accounts of what we may have missed experiencing for ourselves. Thus, it is good to be reminded, by these interviews, that the artist is first of all someone more in tune with his senses, perhaps with his body, than the rest of us find or take the time to be. The reader will note in these dialogues a recurring tension between interviewer and subject as to the sort of question that can be answered, the interviewer wanting to know the why and wherefore (what was on your mind during that period, what did you want to express, what mood were you in?), the artist preferring over and over again simply to describe how his work came to be (I was excited by a new way of applying enamel to metal, of developing a musical theme, and so forth). Whatever the answers may be to the first type of question (and often the artist is not even aware he may have asked them himself), it has at some point in the process of creation been transposed, transformed into a question of the second type. What our vague general usage terms "inspiration" becomes, in these discussions, something increasingly concrete: a new form of receptivity to the limitations of the artist's chosen medium.

Receptivity, sensual awareness, a feeling for the limitations of one's medium; it is impossible to overstate the importance of this aspect of artistic experience for the reevaluation of social and correlated educational goals toward which our country is currently heading. Western man since the Renaissance has seen himself, in the words of Descartes, an early propagandist of millennial scientific progress, as master and possessor of nature. Nowhere has this philosophy been more deeply accepted than in the United States. Manifest Destiny in the past century, the gross national product in this—we have been the most expansionist of nations. Our folk heroes have been men who cleared forests, killed off the existing, sometimes human fauna, drained swamps (like Goethe's Faust for that matter). Now we find in the air we breathe, the water we hesitate to drink, the food we give our children, that far from possessing nature, we have been had by it; that to continue behaving as its master would be (some say, will be) fatal to our species as well as others. Sooner or later we must find a more tenable position in nature. Within present-day society we can look in the direction of the creative artist and scientist, to whom nature remains first of all a source of enjoyment and amazement, and a constant reminder of his own limitations. This we feel is a much more fruitful line of inquiry for educators and social reformers than theoretical speculation about aggressive vs. constructive, destructive vs. creative instincts in man and other primates. (We refer to the work of Lorenz, Ardrey, and their followers.)

Another cardinal point on which these discussions shed light is the artist's relationship to time and effort, to work. The emphasis those interviewed put on the how of the creative process makes it appear that they see themselves, as often as not, as artisans. Perhaps this is particularly true of the generation represented here. Whatever the case, it is clear from these discussions that the artist is one of the rare members of our society whose work does not alienate him from himself, but on the contrary, like the disciple's woodchopping in the Zen riddle, brings him into greater rapport with himself and the universe around him. Is it hopelessly utopian, in our increasingly overcrowded and undernourished world, to look to the experience here described of a privileged few, for a clue to a more desirable life style for all?

These are some of the far-reaching questions on which this book provides food for thought. The reader will be quick to discover others as he listens, along with the editors, to the words of artists, musicians, philosophers, scientists, writers. In the here and now, however, this year and next, we hope that this book will be read especially by educators and teachers of grade and high school children. We hope they will recognize in the unselfconscious playfulness, the curiosity, the con-

tinuing sense of wonder that inform the pursuits of the people interviewed here, something to respect and nurture in themselves as well,
and in their pupils. They could do much worse than to take as their
starting point the artist Josef Albers' dictum that "All learning is
through the senses." If there are any answers to our utopian questions,
perhaps the beginning lies here.

ULRICH FRANZEN

Ulrich Franzen is one of a new group of younger architects whose works are altering large sections of America's cities with striking and effective modern buildings.

Mr. Franzen, whom we interviewed in his New York City office in May, 1969, was born in Germany in 1921 and came to the United States in 1936. After taking his bachelor's degree at Williams College in 1942, and serving with the U.S. Army in Europe, he went on to Harvard for his Bachelor of Architecture. Since 1955 he has headed his own firm of architects, Ulrich Franzen Associates.

Over the ensuing years, Mr. Franzen has been a visiting lecturer at Cornell, Yale, Minnesota, and Columbia Universities. His principal works have been the Philip Morris Research Center, Richmond, Virginia (1959), the Agronomy Building at Cornell University, the New Alley Theatre, Houston, Texas, as well as current work at New York City's Cooper Union.

Ulrich Franzen has been the recipient of the Award in Excellence of Design for all but two years between 1956 and 1964. In 1961 he received the Architecture Award at the Boston Arts Festival, and in 1966 he was given the Homes For Better Living Award.

ARCHITECTURE

Ulrich Franzen

Mr. Franzen, could you discuss your choice of architecture as a profession?

I always wanted to be an architect. I can't particularly attribute it to anything. It is possible that I was led into architecture because my mother and a number of her sisters were painters. I always wanted to draw and to make things. Somewhere, someone may have indicated that architecture was a more respectable art which I don't think it is. But all through high school and college and graduate school, I never had any doubts. I went to high school in a small town in New Jersey where I endeared myself to the principal because whenever we had to make reports, I would take time and lay out beautiful title sheets, make montages and collages of the subject matter. Of course, inside the reports, it was probably the same old stuff like high school American History and things of that sort.

The lovely packaging that I did on my high school papers helped promote me at various colleges. I received a number of scholarships and wound up at Williams College. One of the fortunate things about Williams College was its closeness to Bennington. Bennington has always been a very exciting place to me, especially in the arts. So I became an Art History major. Another student and I persuaded the college to establish a pre-architecture program as part of our honors work. This was accomplished through contact with Bennington. We were able to spend half the week up there. They had a man teaching drawing and architectural design. Then I went to the Harvard architectural school which happened to be really the only school teaching modern architecture. It was at that time a school that progressive educators dream about but rarely find. The real interaction was between students. The reason it worked was that all of us had been away to war and upon our return three or four years later, we were grown up. We were serious and excited about what we wanted to do. Probably the most significant person that helped create a very exciting ambiance was Breuer. Breuer had built himself a bachelor house out in the woods and he lived like an artist. (Generally, Harvard is a place that is great for scholars, but is terrible for artists. It's just that the scholar and the visual artist are two people who work against each other.) At any rate, Breuer was the kind of person who introduced us to a life style that was appropriate and one learns from a life style. We would go to his house at night and have discussions. We had the set-up that everybody talks about having today. Every university is desperately trying to bring the professors and the students closer together. I think we were very fortunate there. The School of Architecture at Harvard was quite unusual because out of it came almost all the architects of consequence in my generation, a fairly important generation now. And everyone of us who has achieved any distinction did it in spite of Gropius. We rebelled against Gropius as an authority, as establishment, very much like what the kids are talking about now. Gropius was a very sweet and kind man, but he would puff on his cigar and he would blow smoke in the students' faces, and he would say, "Don't you think that this is going a little far? Isn't that irresponsible?" There was an effort to put us down. Despite the fact that Gropius and Breuer were both products of the Bauhaus, Breuer represented a different tradition. His tradition was a nondoctrinaire, nonideological and pragmatic approach. He wanted to be responsible to materials without recourse to theory and doctrine. The ideological approach to architecture is something that I fought all my life and I'm just getting out from under because it's taken that much out of me. I think that in the end all ideologies result in inhumanity one way or another, and when things get real rough, people even get killed, all in the name of ideology. So I react against it very strongly. But I think I reacted very strongly against Harvard. We were good students so it was very difficult for them to put us down. Architectural schools then, as they essentially still do now, work on a project basis. You get a problem, you solve it, and professors come in as critics and advise you one way or another. In order to avoid the school approach, we would run two projects simultaneously, one for the critics to see, au courant and Kosher, and the other one we would hang at the project presentations to satisfy ourselves.

The person who rescued me from the Gropius functionalism at Harvard was Mies van der Rohe. He was concerned with the poetry of building. He admitted that he could not solve all functional problems, but only certain functional ones. Mies became a great counterforce then, which affected not only myself, but also a lot of other people who were influenced by the choices the man made rather than the specific way he handled a problem. I leaned on him very heavily as I went through Harvard, as a justification for my attitude.

Could you tell us where your humanistic orientation came from?

My humanism is part of my background. My mother is a psychologist. My father was a writer. They were very liberal and very rebellious people. Like all rebellious people, sooner or later, they can pull the pieces together. But the war shaped my attitude more than anything else. I was very young when I went to college. I was still young when the war came, just barely twenty-one when I was at the Harvard graduate school. I had a fortunate job that made it possible for me to work day and night during the war. Luckily I didn't have to kill people. I knocked myself out like a fool. Everybody else was goofing off and having a good time. Then I went into Germany when the Nazis collapsed. I was assigned to a group of people who rushed around and looked for some of the remaining important documents or even important personages connected with the Nazis. This was the first time I really got out right where the troops were and it became a terrible nightmare. We were suddenly shipped off with a company of paratroopers to negotiate the retreat of some German troops in the Austrian Alps so that they would move under their own power to someplace in Munich. The German troops, including the German General Staff, not the very top guys, but everybody else, were hiding inside of a mountain and with them they had beautiful food and beautiful women. They were debauching themselves in this last big gasp. And we all got caught up in it. We were assisted by our airborne company that had been combat troops. They just couldn't stop killing even when there was no reason to kill. The whole thing was like a nightmare coming true.

I suddenly realized that anybody is capable, on an organized basis, of committing murder. I just cooled off forever on an ideological approach to life and I just concentrated on the human aspect of everything. For the first time I realized how dangerous people were, if they didn't stay close to their own humanity. And so, really right down the line I'm against all people who talk about systems. A lot of people hold the sceptre of technology as the great saviour of the housing problem. The technology obviously is a useful tool, but the basic problem I am convinced is a human one. It's perfectly apparent we don't need a new technology to put up decent housing. We just need the will to do it. If we as human beings say that a good portion of the people should be better off and should be more attractively accommodated, we can do it tomorrow morning. If we wanted to. That's my conviction. I may be wrong. Others disagree with me on it. And I think that in terms of my work, I'm just beginning to reach a level of formal solutions where one can say that this begins to represent a humanistic statement of the specific life involved, of a particular urban setting or the kind of people who might be using it. We live in a world that is to me full of ideological forms. Every form is supposed to be a formula for saving the world. That's just not the way it is any more. But it's still something that is a big pressure.

Could you tell us how ideas for your architecture are born?

Well, you know, architecture is a peculiar art. In fact, it may not be an art at all by any common definition. It begins with facts and when it succeeds, it sort of spiritualizes facts. It makes poetry out of facts. This is where a good scientist and I would see eye to eye. The lay person always assumes that if you know every aspect of the problem then the solution dictates itself. But nothing could be further from the truth. Actually I would say the relationship between the strictly immovable portions of a problem and its functional limitations is about 40 percent movable and 60 percent liberty. The trouble is that when people are not really willing to get into the problem itself they may only come up with 20 percent freedom because instead of wrapping up that 40 percent and stashing it away and knowing where their freedom lies they get it all mixed up. We go to tremendous lengths to define the immovable and free areas in order to educate the people with whom we work. Usually this is their prime fear. They know they are going to get, hopefully, something that's a little more exciting than something they would have had ordinarily. But their prime fear is that this crazy prima donna is going to come in and screw up their workings. So I pursue it right down to the last thing and that is how I gain all the freedom. I think really very extraordinary solutions are possible today. Basically speaking, the good artist does this too. The good artist limits the problem, the canvas size, the colors. And because he's been working with, say, ochre and red, he'll be rewarded with greater intensity.

Women always insist that their kitchen be functional. There isn't a single kitchen I've done that is the same as another. Obviously they are not the same because all the girls are different. What is functional to one is very different from the other. Yet these women have no complaints about their kitchens, but they all work. And so, there is a tremendous area of latitude from the imagery to the kind of life that is generated within a setting. The latitude is obviously influenced by what you set yourself as the problem to be pursued. It is never in my case, carefully spelled out. For example, the new building for the Cooper Union on Astor Place.

[At this point, Mr. Franzen brought in photographs of models of his design for the new Cooper Union in Astor Place, New York City.]

The factor that is of great importance to me is the setting. And not in any sentimental sense, but in a sense, that Astor Place with all its historic associations is visually a tremendous mess and someone has to come in there and tie it together. I was very interested in the old Victorian, very gutsy buildings that are around this area. The old loft structures and so forth. So, although this design does not look like those Victorian buildings, it plays with that thought. Further, the vista down 4th Avenue from 14th Street is very unusual because it terminates at our site. It calls for a design that recognizes this event. There are many ways of doing it. In terms of terminating this vista, for instance, I did not want to terminate it in a static way. One might possibly put the Metropolitan Museum entrance there with a flight of stairs and a classical portico. But I wanted to stop the eye and then lead it on mainly to Cooper Square, and there's a diagonal for that reason that runs through the designed volumes. The big major masses actually assert the building on Astor Place. They stop the eye just long enough to realize that this is in fact a terminal point at which one has a choice. So the concept has three different sides, each totally different and each side without shame, relates itself to the street or space it frames. Because the problems are different on each side, this is required.

Was this solution something you struggled with?

The solutions suggest themselves. It's taken me a long time to be able to put all these good words on top of it. The basic wish to address myself to these elements is there and I begin to plastically work with the problem. I work with big cardboard models and then pull them apart and then put them back together. These things begin to emerge out of it. The amount of preconception is probably limited. I play with it endlessly. And sometimes the solution suggests itself quite rapidly. For instance, I think within weeks, even while the program was being discussed, I was sketching the vertical element and the horizontal element at that scale. These elements suggested themselves immediately and they survived all the other solutions that were put into it. So there was an almost immediate response. I might add that one of the things that I've observed in myself and in a few other architects, whom I know and who are real design architects, is that we have trained ourselves for our spontaneity to be appropriate to the problem. Somehow it's unconscious or it's not on the surface. The ideas that emerge are usually in terms of the problem. There is a trained sensibility or something that is at work. I'm sure that in any other field there must be similar situations where one sizes up the nature of a problem very, very rapidly. I can foresee the major limitations of almost any kind of a problem very quickly. I mean I'm conscious of it when a client says, "Well would you be interested to do this and that." You know, the wheels spin and I see where my ball park is in terms of what I might do. On the basis of that sometimes I say, "No, I think that someone else might be more helpful to you."

Could you tell us more about what you refer to as "trained sensibility"?

I work with little sketches on 8" x 11" sketchbooks in pen and ink. The amazing thing is that designs are evolved over prolonged periods and subject to all kinds of strains and stresses, like more building money, less money, this and that. But often the first series of ideas which I make a quick clay model of, often appears to be the right choice. That is hard to wash out. Maybe it's just mature spontaneity. Sometimes this doesn't work out and I have to change my thinking dramatically. I find that my feelings were not right and I'm perfectly willing to do that if I've convinced myself of it.

What are the conditions under which your ideas occur to you?

Well, now I'm sure everybody is different. I know that for some strange reason my thoughts come the minute I have a particular pen in hand. It's got lots of juicy black ink in it, and if everything is peaceful and free of interruptions, the minute I have that pen and a white piece of paper, then the thoughts come out. There is some thinking that goes on, but it appears to be just brought about by what amounts to almost physical pleasure. In broad terms I look at programs thick and fat and I leaf through them. The minute I see the program, I begin to size it up and think about its elements architecturally. It may just be a graphic notation of the major compositional elements or the major elements that describe the possibilities of the problem. I see certain things in my mind's eye, but I don't believe it until I get it down on paper. There are times when I can and I do visualize building situations really before the paper situation comes up.

Does accident play a part in your work?

It's absolutely wonderful and I just wish I could design as if my pen had just been slipping all the time. The trouble is that I just get mad at my own rigidity. This is the great thing about the way children draw. It just doesn't have a stylized or a designed look to it. They are just bold accidents. I'm very interested in this and I find the best way to do that is to let my ideas assert themselves though they may not be fully thought out.

Ideas just introduce themselves, and I think we're the better off for it. I think accident is something really very important. In the Alley Theatre in Houston, there are a lot of what people have called "throw away spaces," and they are all the spaces that people love the most. The theatergoers come up to a landing and all of a sudden there's a little light filtering around the corner or a bit of greenery and it serves no purpose at all. But groups of people gather there and they love it. These little nooks and crannies came out of developing one part of a problem with reasonable logic. I knew when I was laying out the various levels that we had all this leftover space here and there and thought that's appropriate for a theater lobby. I didn't have any purist inclination to say, "Oh, gosh, we'd better clean up this design and streamline it and get rid of this waste square footage." To that extent I was ready to accept accident. It suggested itself without a doubt, and there's actually a lot of joy in them. They are the best spaces in the whole building.

What kind of problems arise in your work with clients?

I get hung up with people sometimes. In particular with house architecture. I don't know how psychiatrists can stand it frankly. But, I suppose they would feel that they want to get rid of a patient sometimes. And I get into those positions and I don't even have the professional knowhow to deal with irrationalities. Somewhere along the line I clam up. It's very important for me at least to feel that my work is wanted and that it gives pleasure to others. I don't have the feeling that "I'm going to make my monument in this world, and other generations are going to appreciate it," or that this is going to be built on the dead bodies of my clients. If I think that I'm not really doing a very good job and not communicating my ideas to a client, I get pretty unhappy about that. But that may be more of an emotional problem than anything else. You know, one just knocks one's self out on these things and they do take forever.

What are some of the difficulties you encountered in solving technical problems?

Generally speaking, with my experience, I know the kind of problems where I would get hung up and therefore know how to avoid them.

I would say a good 40 to 50 percent of the work that comes to my office, I, for one reason or another feel I won't be able to do justice to. I just like to select the ground of the task, so to speak, beforehand, as much as possible. One factor that determines whether I take a job or not is the realism of the client in terms of the problem. A lot of people come to me even on big projects, and they haven't thought out all the consequences. Maybe they don't have money or they think they can do something and I know that they're probably not going to succeed. At times, people have a number of preconceived ideas which they think they have seen in my work and that's probably the worst kind of problem to get into, i.e., where people don't have an open mind. They think they see something themselves and there's a big problem of having to modify something that they feel.

Do moods affect your work and your productivity?

It's not so much the mood, but I need an environment that makes me comfortable and gets me ready to work, and I know I go through a ridiculous rigmarole, hopping around and sitting on a chair, and reading a book, turning the radio off and on, asking my wife for an extra cup of tea when she has already brought me three, you know, and things like that. And sometimes that goes on for several days. But then, suddenly, I am ready and everything is clear as a bell. It just hops right along.

I have a studio attached to my place and that's really where I do all my important creative work. I would guess that probably about between 90 and 95 percent of the total amount of work that goes into architecture is administrative and technical, and it's best done in an office setting. The other 5 to 10 percent or maybe 15 percent is work that is best not done in an office setting. That building, the model of which is in back of you, has taken some fifteen people eighteen months to just draw up and specify after it was completely designed. To just draw up and specify. So I'm measuring the amount of human effort that is required in America to nail everything down. This means specifying every light fixture, every floor plug, and it goes on and on and on. During this process, there's a lot of input, and it's here that we use a kind of a critique system. The broad picture, and the essential details that make up the whole are designed and decided by myself. But there are a myriad of new conditions that emerge as the plans finally develop. With my staff, I use a process, sort of a jury room, in which everything that they have developed is displayed on walls. It may be a staircase, or the way a window sits in a wall, and we then discuss it. But this is also an essential part, because let no one tell you that architecture is not also this other effort. Without it, it's just sketchbook concepts, and one thing that an architect can't do is to put his buildings up in the attic, and hopefully have somebody discover them fifteen years later. He's got to get them built.

Could you discuss your work in city planning?

I'm interested in city planning in a variety of ways. One of the reasons is that I'm trying to continue these experiments in form. Any form is modified by something. You begin with nothing but a volume that is, in a sense, predetermined by the amount of building material that you are allowed to use. And I'm extremely interested in trying as many situations as I can to use the setting as a modifier of the form. I like to look at, for instance, adjoining rooflines and to relate them, generating lines actually that intersect, that overlap. The purpose somehow is to bind the new into a larger context. It makes sense on an aesthetic level, it makes sense on a humanistic level, it makes sense on the level of wanting to somehow be part of our larger thing, an inclusive rather than an exclusive architecture. I find it somewhat difficult because of this interest right now to relate myself, for example, to a temple setting. A temple setting is sort of like a green lawn with one or two beautiful maple trees, and on it you put some sort of a perfect object. I just don't feel very congenial to that kind of a problem right now. I would find it very hard. At one time I did build a number of temples, but I think my feelings have just changed. So, even on the most unspecific nonsite, as I call it, where there isn't a topographical situation that ties you into a larger whole, I try to invent one. I attempt to build something that will create, for instance, a topographical linkage with other adjoining settings of the land. Of course, in the city, you don't have to invent, it's all there. There's the people, the volumes, and the spaces. And they suggest all sorts of configurations. To me they do. Anyhow this is a kind of a quest that I'm on.

Which of your parents would you say has had the greatest influence on your choice of architecture as a profession?

My mother always claims that she was responsible for the artistic input, and really she makes quite lovely little watercolors, but I remember seeing on my father's walls the first really modern paintings. I remember seeing one or two modern paintings that I associated with him that excited me and so I'm really not entirely sure which one started it. I think in some ways I was very fortunate. I don't think I ever had a choice of becoming a stockbroker or an insurance man. I guess it never was considered feasible. Some kind of a professional life was always assumed to be the ball game.

My father was an essayist. I think he had a lot of potential but he never fully realized it. I think he was probably quite a frustrated man in many ways. But I think he was a very bright person.

If you sketch reasonably well, you can test a couple of things very quickly. You can see if it generates compositional tension and looks right. I think that has a lot to do with where a man winds up in life.

MERCE CUNNINGHAM

We interviewed Merce Cunningham in late May, 1969 on the top floor of a New York loft building. He had just finished a dance class.

Merce Cunningham, one of America's foremost modern dancers and choreographers, was born in Centralia, Washington. After studying at the Bennington, Vermont Summer School of Dance, he began a five year association as a dancer with the Martha Graham Company. Cunningham's first solo performance was in 1944, and in 1952 he formed his own company. In 1959 Mr. Cunningham opened his own dance school, which has been internationally significant in fashioning both new concepts and a whole new corps of modern dancers.

Among the many works choreographed by Mr. Cunningham are The Seasons (*1947*), Les Noces (*1952*), Septet (*1953*), *and* Nocturnes (*1956*).

CHOREOGRAPHY AND THE DANCE

Merce Cunningham

Mr. Cunningham, could you describe your approach to dance?

In my choreographic work, the basis for the dances is movement, that is, the human body moving in time-space. The scale for this movement ranges from being quiescent to the maximum amount of movement (physical activity) a person can produce at any given moment. The ideas of the dance come both from the movement, and are in the movement. It has no reference outside of that. A given dance does not have its origin in some thought I might have about a story, a mood, or an expression; rather, the proportions of the dance come from the activity itself. Any idea as to mood, story, or expression entertained by the spectator is a product of his mind, of his feelings; and he is free to act with it. So in starting to choreograph, I begin with movements, steps, if you like, in working by myself or with the members of my company, and from that, the dance continues.

This is a simplified statement, describing something that can take many work-hours daily for weeks and months, but it is essentially a process of watching and working with people who use movement as a force of life, not as something to be explained by reference, or used as illustration, but as something, if not necessarily grave, certainly constant in life. What is fascinating and interesting in movement, is, though we are all two-legged creatures, we all move differently, in accordance with our physical proportions as well as our temperaments. It is this that interests me. Not the sameness of one person to another, but the difference, not a corps de ballet, but a group of individuals acting together.

This non-reference of the movement is extended into a relationship with music. It is essentially a non-relationship. The dance is not performed to the music. For the dances that we present, the music is composed and performed as a separate identity in itself. It happens to take place at the same time as the dance. The two co-exist, as sight and sound do in our daily lives. And with that, the dance is not dependent upon the music. This does not mean I would prefer to dance in silence (although we have done that, on one notable occasion an entire program owing to a union dispute), because it would strike me as daily life without sound. I accept sound as one of the sensory areas along with sight, the visual sense.

How is the music chosen for the dances in view of the separation between dance and music?

At some point earlier or later in the work on a new piece, I will discuss with John Cage, David Tudor, and Gordon Mumma, the musicians connected with my company, the composers they might suggest as possibilities. Ordinarily the music I have is contemporary, more often than not a commission. The musicians ask me something about the piece, but I can tell them little, since it is about no specific thing. They may look at it naturally, but that isn't always helpful, as it isn't finished, and we, the dancers, are unable to show it clearly. There are details of course, the possible length, the number of dancers, its speeds, and so forth. The musicians make some decision from this as to who might be involved as the composer, or I myself may have someone in mind. Then we ask the composer if he would be interested in working with this. If he is, he may have a few questions. The two questions that Christian Wolff asked me about *Rune* were how long it should be and how many dancers would be involved. But the music is made to be separate from the dance. To push this a little further, the dancers on several occasions have not actually heard the music until the first performance; that is, until the audience hears it. There is no necessity for us to rehearse with it. It is okay if we do, if it is available, which with recent works hasn't been the case since it is usually not completed before curtain time, if then. As David Tudor once said, it's not music with dancing, it's music *and* dancing.

Most of the scores I now have, the works in the past six or seven years, are open-ended. The time structures of the scores are such that they can be any length, as are some of the dances. Therefore, in a work such as

Canfield or *Field Dances,* I make a decision prior to the performance as to how long a given piece will be for that playing. Then we begin as the curtain goes up and end when it comes down.

Is there a great deal of structure involved in your choreography?

Our repertoire ranges from dances which are strictly choreographed, and repeated at each performance, to dances in which, though the movements have been choreographed for the dancer, he is free in the course of the performance to do them faster or slower, in part or in toto, to exit from or return to the area freely. The length of the dance varies from performance to performance. But the movements have been given. This is not, of course, improvisation, although the dancers do have various freedoms with the materials given.

What about the relationship between the structure of the dances, and the choice of dancer?

I attempt to find in a dancer something that makes him dance in his particular way. I don't mean anything psychological about this. I mean simply that one person's body is different from another's. And each therefore takes forms and shapes differently. It doesn't mean that the shapes are deformed. He does them the way he does them. Just as you see people moving in the streets and recognize their differences. So, in training dancers in class, I attempt to see the unique way in which a given person moves. For instance, here is a photograph with two dancers in it. You can see the particular way each is in the movement-shape he shows. Now, if the two were different people, they could make the same shapes. But if the girl is shorter, it doesn't happen to look the same. But a little searching in momentum with the shorter girl might bring out the way she hits the shape. Not an imitation, but a reality.

There is a further involvement here. Being a performing company, we are often touring. This means, at times, that some dancers can't go, and other dancers have to take over parts. This makes for difficulties which all dance companies have. One has to find a way to let the new dancer do the same thing, and at the same time not make demands upon that dancer which aren't suitable to his structure and timing. So, it is a constant process of dealing with the person, not with an idea, but with the person in a given physical situation.

In my choreography I am more likely to think in terms of structure,

structure in time. I will have some awareness as to the length of a dance, and within that limit, the dance gets structured time-wise. So, if the dance is twenty minutes long, one section may be four and a half minutes, another five, the next two, and so on, although these lengths will change in the course of working the dance out. It's like going down a path: you follow it. If there's a tree in the way, you're not likely to go through it. You have to go around it. You might go over it. But that's more complicated. So you allow for these occurrences as the working procedure goes along.

What are the origins of the shapes and movements you find for your dancers?

There are many things dancers can do. For example, a girl can balance against a man who is holding her. The two people can balance with each other, and because he is stronger than she is normally, she can move much further away, and he can still allow for that. This kind of action is possible in different directions—into the air and on or across the floor. I think in movement terms. Human beings move on two legs across the floor, across the earth. We don't do very much on the ground. We don't have that kind of power in us. And we can't go as fast as most four-footed animals do. Our action is here on our two legs. That's what our life is about. When one thinks about falling, dying, or a loss of consciousness, this is a condition that is out of the normal range of human momentum. With jumping, although we all try to do it, we are again caught, because we can't stay up there very long. So it becomes virtuoso. You know, when someone jumps high and stays long enough for it to register, it becomes a virtuoso feat. This is the way I've thought of human movement, in terms of the fact that we stand and move on two legs, and every person moves differently. There is an enormous variety of movement to deal with.

My choreography is part of a working process. It is not necessarily always with the company. It may be with myself. But it is a working process. I begin, in the studio, to try something out. If it doesn't work for some reason or if it's physically not possible for me, I try out something else. And then I do it with myself, or with the company, or with all of us together. Just yesterday we had a little problem about one person's running into another, because I wanted to find out about certain momentums in space, and the only way to do it is to do it.

As you see, I am interested in experimenting with movements. Oh, I may see something out of the corner of my eye—the slight way a person climbs a curb, the special attack of a dancer to a familiar step in class, an unfamiliar stride in a sportsman, something I don't know about, and then I try it. Children do amazing kinds of motions, and one wonders how they got into that particular shape.

I have made dances that employ different compositional continuities. For instance, now I rarely make a dance in which I start at the beginning and go on through to the end. More likely I make a series of things, short sequences, long passages, involving myself alone, and maybe one or more of the other dancers, sometimes the entire company. Then by chance or other methods I make a decision about the order. So I cannot have a specific idea which starts here and goes through, that someone could pin down that way. After one performs a piece for a period though, however strange it may have seemed at the beginning, it takes its own continuity. It's as if one enters a strange house and has to follow unfamiliar paths. After a time, the paths are no longer strange.

I often use a random method to find out the order of the various sequences in a dance. This can act to jump the continuity of the dance out of my personal feelings about order or out of my memory of physical coordinations. This has been done by breaking the movement into small fragments or dividing it into big sections. I have on occasion changed the order of dances after we have performed them. This is a process of taking the given material and changing the order, which we did most recently with a piece called *Scramble*. Another work, *Canfield*, not only changes the order from performance to performance, but the various sections done at one performance can be replaced by others at the next, so though the temper of the piece is the same, the details (material, time, space) are different.

Do you attempt to express moods or feelings in your dances?

There is no specific expressive intent in the dances, although an individual spectator looking at one may decide there is something particular in it. I can give you a description of a piece we have in the repertoire called *Winterbranch*, made in 1964, which has been received by spectators in many different ways. The material of the dance is made up of a person's falling in one way or another. The structure of the piece is that one or more dancers enter an area, walking, and at a point in the area, originally figured out by random means, perform a certain kind of falling configuration. The number of dancers in any sequence ranges from one to six. Ordinarily the dancers will finish the sequence and walk out of the area. But to allow for variety in this, I saw there were several possibilities of a girl's being dragged off the stage. Then there's this terrible problem about splinters. We have to play on many different kinds of stages. So rather than make that a problem, I thought, perhaps she could fall on something, and be dragged off. I practiced with towels, tried it with the dancers, and decided some kind of material could be used.

Robert Rauschenberg did the designing for the dance, and I told him that the clothes we wore should be practical for falling. I also said we had to have something on our feet. It has something to do with the nature of the motion. I also thought of the piece as taking place at night rather than during the day, not with moonlight, but with artificial illumination which can go on and off. The lighting could change from performance to performance (as did the dance originally).

So Mr. Rauschenberg went away and came back some time later with the idea that we wear sweat clothes and dance in the dark. He put black paint under our eyes, such as skiers and football players wear. We had white sneakers. The materials on which we fall are old pieces of canvas. The light changes everytime at each performance. Sometimes the light is turned directly into the eyes of the audience. It may be strong or weak, depending upon what is available in the lighting situation. The lighting changes each time. The order of the dance could change too, except when we have to perform it often, since it is hard for us to rehearse a change quickly. I found that it's physically tiring, and there can be accidents. I try to avoid them.

As to the music part. I brought this to Mr. Cage, and he thought the composer La Monte Young might work in this particular situation. We spoke to Mr. Young. He suggested that we could use his piece which is called *Two Sounds,* which has one low decibel and one high decibel sound in it. These sounds go on continuously at the same level for about half the dance, ten to twelve minutes.

These are three separate things put together. The lighting does not relate to the movement at all. That is, it does not reveal or disguise any particular movement. There are times when the stage is in total darkness, which is difficult for us too, since we feel we might fall off the stage.

How did this treatment of lighting come about?

I thought that perhaps something about night rather than day could be tried. That's what brought that on. But then the lighting man was free to do what he liked with it, to show or not show any particular part of the piece. It's evident, of course, that it has a striking dramatic punch to it, simply because of turning on and off lights. We have equipment available now which was not available fifty years ago. We couldn't do it quite that way then. But now these things are possible in the theatre. And I hope in the future that there are going to be a few more.

Did you have any thoughts as to the origins of writing a dance about falling when you wrote Winterbranch?

First of all I don't write a dance. I choreograph a dance. Falling is one of the ways of moving. Sometimes the dances involve many kinds of movement, sometimes few. *Winterbranch* got into different kinds of falling. As to why that came up instead of jumping, I don't know. Why an apple instead of an orange?

As I have tried to indicate earlier, I am more interested in the *facts* of moving rather than my feelings about them. Naturally, movement possibilities are limited for me, since I am limited by what I can do physically or can think up for someone else to do. But I always hope to find something I don't know about. I would prefer to come upon something, whether by random means or other, that I don't know how to do, and try to find out about it. Perhaps that was the situation with falling. I didn't know much about it, and this was one way to find out.

Is your more formal kind of choreography related to the work of Ann Halprin?

One of the major differences between Ann Halprin and myself is that I work with a formally trained dance company. I accept this situation as more or less the base on which I work. From what I know of her work, she has dealt with both trained and untrained dancers in different kinds of environmental situations. But I would think that one thing we have in common is that we are not interested in the old ways or forms of making things. She is often concerned with a particular environment and the individual's reaction to it. Well, I do that in a certain way too, but it is different because we are a troupe of dancers. We are a repertory company, and we tour and do pieces over and over in changing theatre situations, so that we have to keep adjusting ourselves in a given dance anew.

How did you become interested in choreography?

When I came to New York, I was in the company of Martha Graham. I became disinterested in that work and decided to work for myself, and I began to make solos and give programs. Then I did not want to work just with myself. I wanted to work with other dancers, to have a company. I was interested in making pieces with other people involved along with myself. I began to look around and discovered that I didn't like the way they danced. It was not a kind of dancing that interested me. I went a little further in thinking of ways to train them. If one doesn't like what someone else does, then the only thing to do is to make something oneself, rather than complaining. In time, I began to teach in order to have dancers trained in the way I thought interesting. Basically it was that with just a few years in between.

In training, my concern has been to make the body as flexible, strong, and resilient as possible, and in as many directions as I could find. The human body is the instrument that dancing deals with. The human body moves in limited ways, very few actually. There are certain physical things it can't do that another animal might be able to do. But within the body's limitations, I wanted to be able to accept all the possibilities. I also felt that dancing concerned with states of mind involved one with one's own personal problems and feelings, which often had little or nothing to do with the possibilities in dancing; and I became more interested in opening that out to society and relating it to the contemporary scene, rather than hedging it in.

That was surely one of the reasons I began to use random methods in choreography, to break the patterns of personal remembered physical co-ordinations. Other ways were then seen as possible. When I talk about these ideas of chance to students, they ask if something comes up you don't like, do you discard it? No, rather than using a principle of likes and dislikes, I prefer to try whatever comes up, to be flexible about it rather than fixed. If I can't handle it, perhaps another dancer can, and further there's always the possibility of extending things by the use of movies or visual electronics. I did not want the work turned in, preferably turned out, like dancers.

Is your interest in movement and body strength related to anything in your particular personal life history?

Anyone's work is involved with his life. But I don't want to stop there. My hope is that in working the way I do, I can place the dancer (and this is involved in my student work too), in a situation where he is dependent upon himself. He has to be what he is. He has as few guides or rules as need be given. He finds his way. It's concerned with his discovery. I think a good teacher keeps out of the way. That's why, in the classwork, although there are certain exercises which are repeated every day, they are not exact repetitions. They are varied slightly or radically. Each time the dancer has to look again. The resourcefulness and resiliency of a person are brought into play. Not just of a body, but a whole person. It doesn't make a difference as to simplicity or complexity. When an exercise is presented to a group of students, each has to deal with himself, but also with everyone else in the room, to avoid, among other things, running smack into another. It's like yoga. The mind has to be there.

Who influenced your work in choreography?

John Cage has been a strong influence because of his ideas about the possibilities of sound and time. Then I had a marvelous tap-dancing teacher when I was in high school. She had an extraordinary sense of rhythm and a brilliant performing energy. I think influences are difficult to pinpoint since there are probably many of them. There are many things in one's life that serve to influence one's ideas and one's actions on them. But certainly Mr. Cage's ideas concerning the separate identities of music and dance were influential from the beginning. When we began to work together (these were during the solo program days), he would compose the music quite separately from the dance, although in those early dances, there were structure points in the music that related to the dance. Now even that has vanished. We start as though to take off from the earth and then go to the moon!

It would be erroneous to think that my work is not structured. It's clearly structured, but in a different way. The structure is in time, rather than themes or through an idea. It's not dissimilar to the way continuity in television acts. Television shows fit the time between the commercials, which are spaced so many within the allotted half or hour period. TV has trouble with movies and commercials, as the movies were made another way. Composers now write for the length of recordings. They gear the composition to be within the time of a record. The expression fits the time.

In my work a dance may be forty-nine minutes long, and the structure twenty-one, ten, and eighteen. This is the case in *Walk Around Time*. The first part is twenty-one minutes, the entre'acte ten, and the second half is eighteen. The total, forty-nine, is a seven by seven structure. In the past when Mr. Cage and I worked together, he would have written music that would be as long as the dance. At present, he would more likely make a sound situation which could be of any length, and then for the purpose of the dance, it would end when the dance ended.

Would it be correct to say that every time your company performs a dance, that at a certain time when a certain note is played in the music, that the dancers would be performing a certain movement?

In answer to your question, no. The dance movement and the musical sound would not coincide the same from performance to performance. I can illustrate this again by one of the dances. The piece is called *How To Pass, Kick, Fall, and Run*. It is twenty-four minutes long. For this I asked Mr. Cage if he would do something. He asked me how it was made. I explained the length and the structure points. After seeing the dance, Mr. Cage decided to make a sound accompaniment of stories. Each story in its telling would take a minute. He tells on an average of fifteen stories in the course of the twenty-four minutes, so there are lengths of silence as the dance continues. Using a stopwatch, he governs the speed of each telling, a story with few words being spaced out over the minute, a story with many having a faster rhythm. Since from one playing to another playing of the dance he never tells the same story at the same point in time, we cannot count on it to relate to us. Often audiences, having made a relationship for themselves, will say, it is funny when he told the story about my mother and a policeman, and I was doing a solo. But the next time, if he told the story again I might not be on stage at all.

One of the better things to do on plane trips across the country is to watch Joe Namath on the professional football reruns, and plug the sound into the music channel. It makes an absorbing dance. Probably that's something new for the spectator. He has choices to make now. Of course, he always did. He could get up and leave, and often did.

This must give dance critics a hard time in view of the departure from traditional dance.

Well, they are getting used to it now, though they do not write a great deal about the dance, and they rarely like the music. They sometimes write of the dancers, but they have trouble with the dancing so they pick out other things. For instance, one of the dances, *Variations V*, is a work involved with dance, movies, slides, electronic sound, and was given first at Lincoln

Center in 1965. Now it would be called mixed-media. The dancers had to dance over wires taped to the floor because these were attached to a dozen microphone-type poles on the stage which were antennae for sound when we came within a six-foot radius of any one of them. We triggered the sound, then the musicians and electricians on the platform behind us could change, distort, extend, and delay that sound. Behind this on screens were movies and slides. There were a few special sound-producing actions the dancers did; for example, two of us potted a plant, which was wired and, when touched, produced sound. The piece is forty-five minutes long, and for about thirty-five of that there is dancing by one or more. Probably in the middle of all the rest, the reviewers could not see the dancing, but they all saw me riding a bicycle for about a minute and a half at the end of the work. Perhaps spectators cannot see a difficult dance if it doesn't relate to the music. But we now have to relate daily to things in a variety of ways in this society, and not in just one way. Of course, the sound in our piece is difficult for audiences, too. First because it is unfamiliar, and sometimes, because it is loud. It is primarily electronic and a kind they may not be accustomed to. Yet my feeling is that the work we have done goes along with the society around us.

Could you tell us something about the influence of your family background on your career in the dance?

My family was never against my wanting to be in the theatre. My father was a lawyer, and my mother enjoyed traveling. But they had no particular awareness of the arts. They didn't stop me from tap-dancing when I was an adolescent. My father said, "If you want to do it, fine. All you have to do is work at it." There was no personal objection. It is curious perhaps, since my two brothers followed him, one being a lawyer, the other, a judge.

I think it is difficult to talk about dancing even conventionally, because it so easily becomes a kind of gossip about a particular dancer in a given work and her good and bad points. Even more so now because of the enormous changes in the way we act in space and time. We can't equate minutes with footsteps now, so much as continents. Rather than one point being the most interesting, and others relating to it, say like colonialism, any point is interesting now. Any place that something is put, is as interesting as any other place. So with time, you don't lead up to something: whatever place you are in, is fine.

I think dancing is a fascinating art, and I also feel that it lies at this moment at a great point of change. So many different areas are being explored by the dancers now, and our visual shifts have been so sharp in recent years, it gives dancing a chance to be more than just an expression of a private concern, and moves more into the everyday world of activity of people in the streets or on the stage.

SIDNEY LUMET

The production headquarters of Sidney Lumet is a bare office on West 44th Street in New York City. Mr. Lumet was working there when we interviewed him on February 26, 1969. Born in Philadelphia in June, 1924, he was educated at the Professional Children's School and for a while was a student at Columbia University. As a child, he acted in a number of different productions. After a career as a summer stock director and several years with the CBS Broadcasting television department, Sidney Lumet began work as a film director.

Movie-goers know him well for such films as Fail Safe, The Pawnbroker, A View from the Bridge, *and* Long Day's Journey into Night.

Sidney Lumet

Do you have any thoughts about the question of a birth of an idea? The role, for example, of fantasy, of daydreams, of night dreams in the creation of an idea.

It's funny because it seems it always comes after the fact, the realization of where it came from comes after the fact, in the sense that after you've done it, you look back and say "Ah ha, that was the origin point." For me at least it's never worked on the basis of the idea, of "let's do that," it's always been, "I've done that," and then looked back and saw that the idea germinated in another area. For example, when we were doing *Pawnbroker,* there was, in the form of the picture, something quite unique, what everybody refers to now as the "subliminal cutting." Now, I remember there were flashbacks indicated in the script, that was all that was indicated, and I was talking to the producer on the picture and said "No, I don't want to do it in flashbacks." First of all, that always becomes an obstacle to me, it always seems to slow a picture down. Also that's really not the way memory works, and I said I want to do it this way after—and I knew, and right away started talking about it in technical terms; "Two-frame cuts, start with six-frame cuts, reduce to four-frame cuts to two-frame cuts and then into the sequence itself." There hadn't been a moment's thought about how I was going to do it until then and then later on thinking about it, I realized I was talking largely about how my own memory works, particularly in relation to subjects I want to avoid. The nature of the resistance is that when the idea comes on an issue or an experience or an emotion that I would tend to want to block out, the idea will hit and then without my knowing it another idea will wipe it out; then depending on its persistence, depending on its importance, depending on what role its playing, it will keep intruding in little bursts, literally, and then depending on circumstances, either crash through or be wiped out. If it's of a critical nature and the circumstance is such that I'm in that emotional area, so that it's almost impossible to avoid, the memory itself will eventually actually break through and take over. In other instances where I am capable of eliminating it, other thoughts will simply cover it over, weigh it out, but essentially what was a basically creative decision came out completely spontaneously, and upon reflection I realized what its origin was for me.

Now this is a very interesting point you bring up because it's the kind of thing that requires on your part a considerable amount of introspection to be aware of the way in which your memory operates. We just wonder if this is something which you only became aware of after you had done this in the Pawnbroker, *or whether you had some other experience in your life where you had a kind of chance to observe how memory operates.*

Well, with myself, I'm particularly aware of it, having been in analysis, etc., or that I'm oriented in that direction. But basically that process as far as I remembered, was basically not any different than the pre-analytic state, I was just more aware of what went into the process. Getting back to something you brought up before—the fantasy thing plays a tremendous, tremendous role in it. Interestingly enough, daydreams and day fantasies much more than night dreams. The very nature of avoidance, which is essentially what daydreams are, for me, at least—the drift away from something and the inevitable coming back to it on this very circuitous route—is a very real sort of working energy, a very real source of things to delve into, things to fuel, literally fuel, both emotional fuel, content fuel and form fuel.

The daydream itself you refer to?

That has happened, particularly it's very interesting now in terms of the fact that color photography has become the reality. Black and white movies are over with, American companies won't finance black and white films anymore so from here on in we really have to learn to use color. Up till now because of the associations of color there was always a bit representative of Hollywood, Technicolor, and so forth. I think most directors' tendencies were to try to negate it, to try to put up on the screen what we call black and white color, an absence of color. Well, it's obviously self-defeating, color is here and we have to learn to work with it, live with it, and put it to dramatic use. It is not inconceivable, it's happened that you literally sit with the art director talking about the look of a scene and you will say "What do you see" and you'll literally on a free association level say there's something—I'd like to play it in red tones, I'd like to play it in bluish-green tones, and that's literally on a free-association level.

Where do you think that stems from, the choice of color?

Well, for instance, just as I say it now to you is precisely the way I would work with an art director and at the moment I will have no idea where it comes from, it will be totally "instinctive reaction." The scene is about— like just last Monday we were discussing—we're starting a film in three weeks—and we were discussing the color of the room of one of the important characters and I said to Gene Callahan, the art director, there are two choices and again none of this was premeditated, I'd just been thinking about the character and not about the form I wanted to put it into yet. I said, "Gene, there are two choices, three, that I'm aware of: We can: 1. Keep the walls an absolutely neutral color, slowly lose sight of the walls and finally light it so that just the face is showing and nothing else, the room just put in limbo, is one choice. 2. Second is to literally put him into hell. We could start with that thing that so often happens in Southern houses where there is a thin layer of plaster over brick and that with age, a kind of pink color seeps through (since we're starting with a naturally pink seepage in the wall) where as the plaster ages you get more of a sense of what's underneath it. As the light outside lessens, the light in the room becomes greater, the color values in the room assume more, you see them more so that as it goes on there is sort of a naturalistic justification for it. Finally, let's just drop the naturalistic justification for it and just sheerly dramatically wind up with a red room. That was the second idea. A third idea is more of an emotional response; I get a feeling of something maybe green, blue, something extremely cold, extremely sick, extremely dying, and the end result has not been resolved. I want to get it in form and Gene is giving it some thought and I want to give it some thought. But they were free-form reactions, three ways of how to do it coming out of feeling.

Well, two of them came out of feeling. Since you're talking about feeling this way there seems to be an equation between a color and a feeling. It's almost intuitive as you're describing it. Your green-blue is death somehow, the pinkish with the South, we don't know, but the green-blue as death came through very clearly so that you seem to be suggesting an emotion being tied in with color.

Oh yes, and that's what I meant before when I said we have to start using it for its emotional value rather than try to avoid it, slowly abandoning naturalistic color because very soon that will not be enough. We'll have to take further extensions of it which of course painting did long ago. I'm not talking about anything startlingly original and it's just a step that movies seem to be heading for more and more. Certainly I will look into that area and then it will be completely free-associative, personalized, because for instance that tone of blue-green can mean something entirely different to somebody else. It might be something peaceful or pastoral to them, I don't know, in those instances you're only working out of yourself and your own feelings.

Well, could we get back now to this birth of an idea—the role of day-dreams; whether you're happy or sad, the role of your moods, what conditions might be conducive particularly to coming up with something new?

I've had a peculiar mechanism all my life, since I've worked ever since I was a child. I was a child actor and started at five years old, and I've never needed a conducive condition for working to begin. Work is my norm; I have mad energy, insane energy, a kind of stamina in terms of work that's a little crazy. And in this way I'm very fortunate because I'm able to turn out a great deal of work. I turn out more films than most American directors turn out, I'm on a schedule now of three films every two years; well, some directors do only a picture every two years, I'm doing three in two years. It's something that I enjoy, the overlapping of pictures for instance, when I'm editing one picture, I can think about the next picture. I can departmentalize very simply. The only thing which ever stops any area of creative functioning is tension. I don't like it when anything starts to go wrong, any unhappiness; I stop it then and there and bring it right out into the open because I can't let it store up. As soon as I feel a lack of joy, not only on my part but with anybody working with me, we immediately stop and iron it out right then and there.

With the work itself? You're not speaking now about personal tensions in your life?

No, those have a remarkable lack of effect on my working life. Through the worst of times, the worst of personal times, the work went on as if nothing was interrupting it. The same with elation times, they don't make me work better or worse or the unhappy times don't make me work better or worse. There seems for me at least, no correlation between the two and interestingly enough the main reason I went into analysis was to—I felt as if I wanted my personal life to have the equilibrium that my working life had. It was as if I could always use the working life as a barometer of what personal life should be like because it did involve love, it did involve commitment, it did involve pain, giving of oneself; and yet all of it was essentially a joyous experience as opposed to the life experience in which things were shattering or functioning did stop. I mean there would be times when I would love to sleep sixteen hours a day, for example. Personal life seemed chaotic, the working life never did.

Did the working life become a kind of escape from the personal life?

I couldn't tell you honestly because they were interwoven only in the sense that I never did the thing of isolating myself in the work. For example, I'm the kind of man that likes to be married, the home is extremely important to me, family is extremely important to me. I have turned down work which conceivably could bust that up if it meant going to California at a time when I did not want to go. In periods when I was courting I would turn down anything just to stay with a girl, or what have you, it wasn't as if the work predominated the life and took it over. The quest was to get the personal life up to the stability of the working life, not to avoid the personal life or negate the personal life in any way so in that sense I don't feel it was ever a question of blocking out the personal life by work. The object of it always was to get home, I'm notorious about not working overtime because at 6 o'clock I want to be with the kids; so that when I talk about this energy, I don't talk about spending myself on the work so that there is nothing else in the life itself which I know is the pattern with a lot of people. It's possibly because I was trained, I was trained at work certainly before I was trained in life, that there's some kind of internal and external discipline about work which allows me to function on what I say is—that's my norm and in many ways the best of me.

So that's an area that's relatively free of conflict.

Yeah, well, let's put it this way, I've never worked with anyone who hasn't wanted to work with me again. Other directors feel tremendous affection for me because there's no competitiveness in anything. I appreciate other work, I commit myself to other people's work, there's no rancor, there's no bitterness, it's an almost ideal life in an almost religious sense. I'm free of a great many hangups that most people have in terms of work.

Now, in terms of the analytical experience that you went through, do you feel that had any impact on your productivity, your creativity? You speak of free association, you speak of feelings. I wonder if your analysis in any way made these things more accessible to you.

I would guess that without the analysis the work would have slowly run down and become a delightful "was." The cliché which says "I don't want to be analyzed because it might destroy what makes me creative" is absolute nonsense. If one functions through neurosis then you're functioning despite it, because it's like saying, "I understand when people say too much freedom can be harmful, but I know in essence freedom cannot be harmful." In essence too much peace cannot be injurious. If one has developed the habits of using tension and hostility as the fuel that doesn't mean that one cannot redevelop other habits.

The way you speak about your work, we wonder how you feel about vacations, about the break from work.

I almost never take one because the work itself has tremendous relaxation for me even when I'm under—I won't use the word tension, because I'm not —even when I'm under pressure, the sheer problem of sitting there and sweating out, for instance, a shot that we all love in what we call the magic hour, which means the light is in a particular state which only lasts about ten minutes and all different things have to coordinate. Well, there's tremendous pressure when you're going for a magic hour shot because you've got to get it just on the nose, nothing can go wrong, and so forth, but it's all essentially relaxing to me so that I don't feel a need to get away from it ever. I love being in it. I love to talk about it when I'm not doing it in the evening. Most of my close friends are other creative people. I find them the most fun, find enormous laughter in it, just great, great pleasure. I don't feel I want to get away from it.

In terms of your work, you don't create the story, you create what the camera is going to do?

Movies are essentially a communal operation and like any communal operation it literally needs direction. The function essentially is to get every single element in it working at its greatest creativity. In a way that's your creativity. Then digging the channel that gets them all pushing toward the same objective and giving them their limitations and getting the total creative burst to get the greatest expression of that limitation. It varies, various directors work in different ways. Some directors do the screenplay themselves. There are few subject matters in which I feel I could do the screenplay myself. In some instances I worked very heavily on the script; in some cases I've received scripts where I've not changed a single word nor asked for a single change. So it's varied completely. But essentially it's to extract that meaning, the script's meaning, the fullest creative expression one can muster.

And it also involves the direction of a lot of other people?

Right. And it involves very specific work, not only the directing of the actors, in some instances, very heavy guiding of the writer. In terms of camera, that's something I work very closely on. I choose the lens very often, will choose the lens, stop myself, do the setup myself. My cameraman does not do the setups, that is, the basic angle the scene is to be shot at. I do the editing myself, with the editor who does the physical labor; but each cut is done by me on a moviola, so that I ride very tight on it, very close.

Is there anything in your particular background that you think would account for the strong desire and pleasure you get out of directing others, of keeping everything in the channel, as you call it?

No, because that part of it almost cannot be learned. It can be done on two levels (and both methods can be used, it's not a question of one being superior to the other). It can be done as a total autocratic method and work brilliantly. On a human level I'm not constituted that way, I couldn't do it that way, I wouldn't want to do it that way. I do it on the other level of getting everyone's motor going on my tempo, on my enthusiasm, on my energy; people often say that they're more exhausted after working with me than ever before, because they were working at a higher tempo and a higher pitch, emotional pitch than they ever did before.

Is there something in your background, your relation with your parents, the kind of people they are or were that is somehow tied in with this?

I've never been able to find any, other than I'm tremendously organized in my work. I don't waste time. I don't waste effort. I don't waste film for example, which a lot of film directors do waste. I would think, having been a child actor, my father was an actor, and the life was—nothing in the life would create a sense of organization at all.

What kind of actor was your father?

He was an actor in the Yiddish theatre, a marvelously talented man, he still is, he's out on the road with *Fiddler on the Roof* now: There was nothing in the home that could make my kind of organization foreseeable. It's again really looking back on it now in terms of the way I've been working for the past fourteen years—it's sort of—if I had been cerebrally oriented enough to figure out a way in which I would have loved to have worked; that is, getting people functioning at their best, doing it in an atmosphere I don't hesitate to call love; if I had figured that out in advance it would have been ideal. I found it after the fact, that it has been ideal as each experience keeps getting richer and richer and better and better which is all I want to work for; and as I'm getting older I'm increasing the pace rather than decreasing it because it's just getting more fun all the time.

Was it your father that really got you into the theatre?

Yeah, because he had a radio show on a Jewish radio station, and I began acting there and acting in the Yiddish theatre. When I was eleven I began acting on Broadway and in that time there were many experiences that were essentially loving. I remember I did a play, it was Saroyan's first play called, *My Heart's in the Highlands* and I think I was thirteen or fourteen at the time. That, as a kind of creative effort, was an enormous love-fest; a loving director, a loving play, a tender cast and that one could see, one knew right away it was a rather special and perfect way to work. But those experiences weren't that many, and could not have made the discipline. It might have stayed there in my being as the ideal, but certainly not the discipline. Professional theatre then, as it is today is a fairly cut and dry thing, commercial. People get fired, you get yelled at, you yell back. It was professional commercial work and those experiences wouldn't have disciplined me to the way I'm working now. I think the analysis could have had something to do with it. I would think also very conceivably the quest for whether loving works in life could have a great deal to do with it; in the sense that one can get through a lifetime living without fear, being open, staying vulnerable, manifesting the secret tender areas, letting them come out and if they get hurt, they get hurt, but you still go on, and so forth. For me there's been an ability to do that in work since the beginning somehow, but as I say, the life experiences were not able to keep up with that and my own guess, my own conviction is that I would have closed up in the work without the analysis rather than open up in the life, which is essentially what happened during the analytical time.

About the place of your mother in this picture? Did she have a significant role in this business of getting close to other people?

I couldn't say yes or no in the sense that we were very close. She was an extremely disturbed woman, she died when I was fourteen, had not had a happy life at all. It was hard to tell what kind of relationship—I can't draw any parallel to any she could have had to the work—obviously she did to my personal life enormously, but in terms of work there is no clear parallel. It's funny because I talk about the personal life as being an essentially unhappy one and one filled with problems that have taken help to work out, and so forth, and my mother obviously belongs to that actegory and no part in what has always worked well, and that is the work which is its own clear indication.

You have some brothers or sisters?

I have a sister, an older sister, and again no particular relationship to it. Always great affection for her, slightly irritated at her that she didn't do more in terms of working with what she has, which is a lovely intelligence and a great warmth and a talent for touching people and getting close to people.

So this seems important to you, to get other people going, to light a fire under them?

Yeah, and I'm like that in my physical behavior. I'm a big kisser, a big toucher, a big clutcher. When I talk to somebody, an actor, my arm will be around his shoulder or hands will be clasped. I find that during work more and more. I find when we're working I want us to get away, live together, be together. I just finished a picture this fall, the *Seagull,* which from a working point of view is the most exciting experience I ever had and probably one of the things that made it so exciting was that we were isolated. We were in one hotel in Stockholm, families were with us in some instances, in some instances, when they had school, they had to go back, but it was a genuine communal family life, living together, eating together, and working together. It turned out for me the most rewarding work experience I've ever had.

Would it be fair to say that under such family conditions, of the group, the team, you're working with, you're the Papa?

Yeah, in the sense that . . . well, it's interesting, you're the Papa, you become it, you're the best Papa, again not out of the authoritarian thing. I have found in work, one of the things I do extremely well and one of the reasons actors want to work with me is that I do get extraordinary performances. Most actors feel that they've been at their best working with me, and it's true by the way. They usually have their most creatively satisfying times with me. There's no secret about it, nothing to hide, it's precisely that there's nothing to hide that's the secret. I'm extremely open with them, and I risk *with* them emotion from me that gives them courage with their emotion. It's not then on an authoritarian level whatsoever. I began the discussion of the play of *Seagull* with ten actors (they were not strangers, a great many of them I had worked with before) with a personal revelation of a particular incident in my life that's among the most painful ever and they immediately got the message of that. It wasn't related to the play, it had nothing to do with the play; but what I was saying in essence was that I will risk all in this film, anything you want you can ask of me, because I'm going to ask it of you. It's that, essentially, that they respond to and they respond to marvelously. It's kind of a tremendous faith in a humanistic process that if you risk it, they will respond. If you risk yourself, they will endanger themselves. Speaking of opening up to emotion as being dangerous, because it is dangerous, but essentially that's the method and they feel it from me. They feel "Papa" because I don't spare myself and then they come back in kind, and it's great and works marvelously. It's so often—my wife and I talk about it in relation to the kids, how it is not the worst thing in the world to see you arguing or the kids to see you weeping or see you unhappy, quite the reverse. They cannot open up to you unless they know you are open to them and I don't think that's "Papa" relationship, I think that's human; and it's a thing that slowly gets lost in most adult relationships, that gets lost and people see each other on the defensive level, on the plaster cast that's hardened and as soon as you can risk danger with another person they will respond well. Some people don't respond well; they turn into killers so you just don't work with them again, or you fire them if you can, or they leave.

Now to get back to the work itself. When you are confronted with a technical problem in your work, how do you go about finding a solution to your problem? Something really has you over a barrel, you can't figure it out—can you say anything about the method by which you may seek to solve the problem?

One of two. . . . For instance on our present picture I was talking to Jimmy Wong Howe, one of the best cameramen that ever lived, an extraordinary man, about this character, the same as the blue-green room character: that I felt that as he got deeper into his sickness and madness I wanted to spend more time looking through a kaleidoscope and that eventually some of the character revelations would start coming through the kaleidoscope. Now Jimmy, how do we shoot a scene through a kaleidoscope? Now the first thing we're going to try to do is shoot it through a kaleidoscope. You know, an absolutely simple thing of building a kaleidoscope to fit over the lens and try to do it that way. Now if it doesn't work, there are a million other technical things we can go to but I'm bringing it up only because sometimes the solution is so blatantly simple. Sometimes, it involves sheer reliance on your technical knowledge, of which I have a great deal, a cameraman or an audio man cannot say to me "we cannot do that" because I know how we can do it, and that training I got largely in television. Sometimes you just have to go out and try it this way and try it that way. In one instance in a film called *The Deadly Affair* I was still on this "absence of color" thing; you know, make the color look like black and white. In talking to the cameraman before the production on how do we mute the color, how do we flatten it, we went through a series of experiments and finally came up with a technical solution of pre-fogging the film, pre-exposing the film so that the color wasn't registering as brilliantly on it as it normally would, as the chemical response wasn't as high. That came through sheer trial and error. We tried four tests and finally got the idea for this and tried this and it worked.

How about the role of accident—have you found that things which have turned out by accident have turned out to be fortuitous?

Of course they have, but the funny thing is and it's going to sound—you know I don't want to start such a bloody mystique about work as it's not that mystical, and having said that I have to give you an answer with a bit of mystique about it. When you are right, when you are functioning well, all the accidents happen *for* you—you get better accidents and none of them work against you. At the times when you're at your full creative juice, when there's nothing wrong with the piece, when you attack it properly, you get all the breaks. On *Seagull* I needed six days of sunny weather and ten days of clouds: I got six days of sun and ten days of clouds. It was exact. Other times on a picture called *The Fugitive Kind* in which something had never become resolved in the script and it only became more aggravated, the hole kept opening up bigger and bigger and the accidents were against us. There is a kind of mystique about it; or maybe when you are functioning well, you can make almost anything work for you.

Like for example, a camera tilts, gets pushed, or someone puts on the wrong lens by accident?

That's never worked. No, the kind of accidents I'm talking about are either weather or performance accidents in which—well for instance one scene in the *Seagull* where suddenly she would cry with one line on a take, and it would bounce across that lake. There is an echo in it which would have taken ninety years to do in a dubbing room to put it artificially. The echo itself was so extraordinary. Or a bird cries out just in time for the right line. It's *that* kind of accident. On a technical level, very rarely those accidents—because those laws are rigid and when you know them, assuming you do know them, you've made the right selection in advance and there is no deviation from a 2.8 opening on a 35mm lens. Any 35mm lens at 2.8 will do *that* with *that* light. In the rare instances where something like that has gone wrong, I've always reshot it, that kind of accident. But the other kind of accident, the natural kind of accident, the human kind of accident, where an actor stumbles on a line, stumbles over a word, always a reason, always something going on that's good, the accident of light. I had a scene in a picture once, it hasn't come out yet, in which the actor got to the line and the actor foreshadowed the tragic ending in the tale. A cloud came over the sun and just blocked out the light. Those kind of accidents are great, just great. And those kind of accidents, if you try to calculate them, you'll ruin it; I mean if we had changed the light in time for the line it would have been obvious and meretricious and stupid. We wandered very far from what we began with actually. . . .

No, not really, we think this is all part of the material we're looking for.

I find—it's interesting the use of the word accident altogether. Often just discussing work, we talk of it in terms of all of the pre-thinking, all of the gestation, is only for a good accident to happen, is that the nature of work is to prepare for a good accident, to prepare for the one thing that takes it past reality, in such an essence that it penetrates into real meaning, not just duplication of the reality but an explanation of the reality.

Would this be comparable then to the kind of stories you choose to work on, this was the thing that was crossing our minds before.

Very possible, because I always pick stories of big emotional happening. A big joke between me and my friends is "Sidney's made a real happy picture—only two people died." They're always stories involved enormously with pain, very often with death. I find it rather hard to believe a story that ends happily in a normal sense of the word. I just don't believe it. To me life doesn't have that conclusion. *Twelve Angry Men* which some people think is perhaps one of the best things I have ever done, and I think it's a marvelous job directorially, but Reggie Rose, the author, knows how I feel about that, I don't believe that ending, I never have believed it—I don't believe one man could go in and save one boy against eleven other men.

Does that get in the way of the kind of work you do? If you don't believe the way the story is written?

In that instance it didn't only because I know Reggie's mechanism as a writer. I know that Reggie does believe that, he does believe love conquers all. I'm not putting him down in any way, he's an extraordinary, marvelous man and he does believe it, those middle-class values, and as I say, I'm not putting him down by any means, I only wish it were so. Reggie does believe that it is so. Where it manifests itself specifically in the work is that in one scene, particularly, where one of the characters launched an attack on a racial level and everybody got up and got away from the table and left him sitting there. Now that scene was actually bullshit to me. I knew I didn't believe it and just took it on a mechanical level, it was a necessary scene in the structure that Reggie had, there was no substitute, there was no way of avoiding it, and there are technical ways you can razzle-dazzle it, you can build performance on a sheer technique level in a certain way that will make it seem acceptable. Well, it was acceptable for the audience, it was never acceptable for me and interestingly enough as work goes on, that was my first film, and as work goes on I find I cannot do that anymore.

Is there a suggestion in what you're saying that most of your films have been tragedies in a way?

Yes. And interestingly enough I find my own weakness as a director in comedy. I'm a great laugher, all my comedy writer and director friends, like Doc, love to have me there opening night because boy, I go. I can start ten people around me laughing. I enjoy myself enormously. In terms of work though, I find that I cannot release the comic talent in an actor the way I can release the tragic talent of an actor.

Do you have any thoughts about that, about why that might be so?

No, because I'm at the point where I've been giving it a lot of thought, because I'd love to have it as a tool. I'd love to be able to do everything, as anyone would. I've come to the conclusion simply because I can't come to another definition of it, that it's another talent, another kind of talent. I argue with Doc about this all the time because he keeps saying, "Sidney, I'm sure you can do comedy, when Mike [Mike Nichols] and I do it we do it for real." [Explains that Doc is Neil Simon] I say, "That's because your reality is funny, you are funny, what seems real to you is funny, just like when it's tragic it's real to me. You believe it when it's funny, I believe it when it's tragic, when it's funny it becomes to me a relief from emotion rather than emotion." It seems to me that it's another kind of talent, I may be wrong, God knows that there are certainly among actors a tremendous number who can do both. Olivier is a brilliant comedian, Michael Redgrave, a brilliant comedian, Alfred Lunt, extraordinary, and yet their tragic roles have been their greatest triumphs.

And yet for you the ultimate reality is tied in with a story with an unhappiness. Let us ask this, for example: it was the last scene in the Pawnbroker, *where he puts his hand through the paper holder, was this your idea?*

Yeah, and worked out right then and there, I hadn't even thought about it.

It had a fantastic emotional impact.

You see in the script, it had a "happy ending" in the sense that it had a resolution. In the writing he had a great burst of protest against all that life had been; he tore the shop apart; smashed the windows, and so forth, and walked away from it. I thought that it was bullshit, that kind of Jimmy Cagney 1930's fake explosiveness. To me the essence of that man—this I knew instinctively, emotionally, and intellectually from the very beginning, starting with the fact that it was essentially a story of a resurrection, of a man coming back to life—that the essence of the coming alive again lay in his willingness to accept pain, to reopen himself to pain. Not only to reopen himself, but if necessary and certainly at this point necessary, to take a step *to* it, toward it voluntarily. I didn't know what I was going to do about that moment. I knew it had to come there, that was the place in the picture it had to come. I had no idea what it was going to be.

His pain was not just the reliving of the concentration camp?

No, it was his first tentative step back into life, in becoming alive again. And like all those things, it's not simple. Of course it's guilt, of course it's reliving, but primarily if he was going to be anything other than a vegetable for the rest of his life, this was the first thing he had to do and as I say, that spike had been there all during the picture, it was a prop.

And this occurred to you on the spot?

On the spot. Now what's interesting of course is the whole subconscious element of it, because I remember that I asked the prop man for a spike without having any idea that I was going to do this. I said "I want bills put on a spike on the side." That's because I've always seen that in that kind of shop, that's absolutely realistic. When the idea for the shot occurred to me, right away on a sheer storytelling technical level I checked myself, saying "Wait a minute, have I established it, have they seen it enough?" And I realized I had been establishing it all during the picture.

Have you had a similar experience?

You mean, has it happened on other pieces of work?

Yes, that something had become significant that was there all along.

Yes. And I trust that. That's why I can go into a piece without something necessarily being solved. The piece that's coming up now, the picture I've been talking about. There are still four or five major undecided things and I'm waiting for the place to tell me. I know I've picked the right things because everything fell into place, ten things more than I expected even and I know at least three solutions for the five remaining problems are going to come by just being down there.

And would you say sometimes the solutions are as much a surprise to you as anybody else?

Yes, and everyone starts screaming because you threw them a curve, there's no preparation for it, or what have you. But it's again this thing of being right, when you're functioning right it'll fall in, you'll find it. There are instances when I've failed, not many though.

That's a very interesting concept, this falling in, as if on the surface level you have nothing to do with it; yet this is a phrase that comes out over and over again—it'll fall in—it presents itself—it forces itself on you—you've noticed this over and over again.

I never noticed it until you brought it up, I guess I do use it a lot.

Could we think about it even now, can you think of other instances where a situation presents itself this way?

Yeah, for example, when you go out location looking. Lots of directors when they go out, they go out searching. I don't go searching, I go driving around and I know it'll happen, I'll turn the corner and it'll be there. And you're always prepared the other way, because you're a professional. Just this last trip, Gene took us to a house first and I found it was workable, good, we could put the slave cabins here, the levee works. Gene will have to change that and block that out, and what we were doing was preparing a place to serve perfectly for what we needed without saying we were going to use the place; and we both took off knowing, because we've worked together before, that we weren't going to use that place, and sure enough, he was showing me photographs and we turned the corner, and I said "Let's go to that one," and we went to that one and drove in and there was nothing we had to do to it. We didn't have to fix one thing, it was all there, it fell in. I really think of it, if you ask me what the association is, as literally a jigsaw puzzle of which I am a great fan.

At the same time you seem to have some kind of implicit faith that this is going to happen.

Yeah, it may be sheer egomania, I don't know.

No, it seems that in many of our meetings, this kind of thinking . . . .

No doubt, and, conversely, panic hits in the instances where it doesn't happen. Not panic in the sense—certainly in terms of movies, you can always rectify it, you can always build it, but it's a terrible feeling when it doesn't. I'll tell you something else mystic about it. It always comes early, for me it comes early. For instance, this location looking of *Long Day's Journey Into Night* which is perhaps after *Seagull* my favorite piece of work. The *Seagull* location was the first location I looked at, the one I'm going to now is the second.

But when you see it, you know it's right.

Know it, just know it, and you look around and smile and settle down to the technical problems, everybody knows it, and as I say it's always the accidents that work for you. This script originally for location had about thirty or forty pages, the rest was going to be done in the studio. The location gave me another forty pages to do on the location, not to force into, but it would be better than in the studio. There's a ridiculous example; the house has no inside staircase, all the staircases were outside. To get to the second floor you had to go outside the house. Marvelous, couldn't have been better, because one of the threats, if there's a heavy in the movie, it's the weather, it's raining, raining, raining, the Mississippi River is about to flood and the levees are about to break; and what could be better than to have to go outside and be reminded of that rain again and the wind and the fact of the elements being the enemy. Nothing better, it means that every five minutes you're going to get wet again, it's great.

But that isn't something you planned on.

No.

Well, that's what we meant by accidents happening. Well, I guess we've just about covered the areas we're interested in.

Good, very good.

The idea first and the proof came after, and essentially the exact same process, I mean it fell in first and then you went back and proved it.

Let us ask you one other question, what about the role of the times. Do you feel you have to be tuned in?

I can't conceive of working on anything in the next two years other than interracial.

What about the Seagull—*that's an old story.*

That in a strange way is also totally of time now; not just in the specifics of the boring expression "the generation gap" but the real genuine conflict between young and old now.

OPPI A. J. UNTRACHT

Oppi A. J. Untracht, an enamelist of international reputation, now living in Porvoo, Finland, was born and educated in New York City. His introduction to craftsmanship began in elementary school, and continued at Manhattan's High School of Music and Art, from which he graduated in the school's first class. Untracht continued his fine arts education at Brooklyn College, gaining a bachelor of arts degree from New York University.

Interested in teaching art, Untracht finished his master's degree at Columbia University's Teachers College, and for a number of years taught in the New York City school system. During those years, his interest in crafts increased.

He was in India from 1957 to 1959 on a Fulbright Fellowship where he studied contemporary Indian crafts. A second Fulbright Grant provided a 1963 stay in Nepal and extensive investigation of that country's crafts tradition. A third grant, this from the American Institute of Indian Studies, took him again to India from 1965–67.

He is preparing a two-volume book, The Crafts of India. *His latest book,* Metal Techniques for Craftsmen, *published in 1968, is considered the most complete manual on metalcraft ever published and covers, in text and photographs, techniques used in India, Mexico, and Japan.*

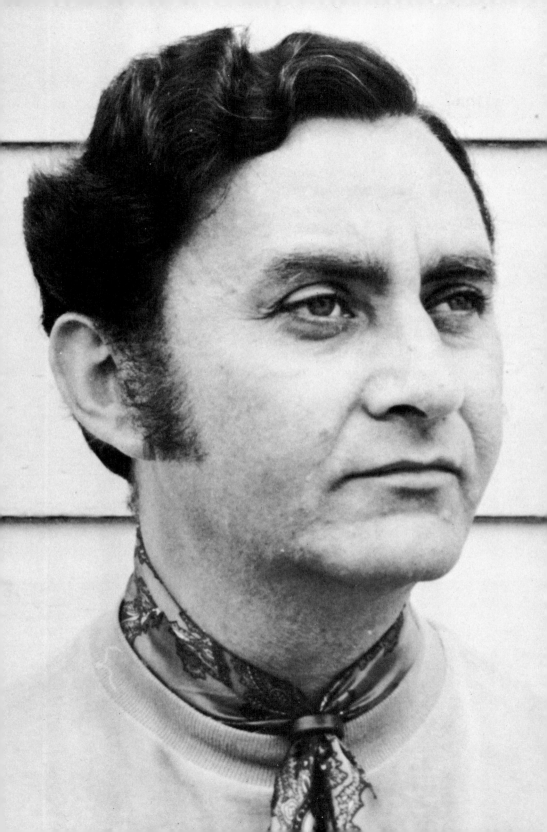

CRAFTS

Oppi A. J. Untracht

Tell us about the position of your family and the factors that may have entered into the choice of your profession?

With respect to my family background: I come from a middle-class family of three brothers and two sisters, a total of six of us, all of whom have been educated and are professionals, three teachers, a doctor, and a lawyer. I am the youngest, formerly a teacher, now an enamelist, photographer, and writer.

In connection with my interest in the arts, I would say that my first influences came through my older sister and her husband, who is an art teacher. At an early age, from elementary school onward, I apparently showed some ability in the arts, especially in drawing, which they recognized and encouraged. I remember our very early trips painting in the parks and being made aware by them of color and form in nature. With their work setting a standard, the whole world of the arts opened up to me.

In elementary school I remember several art teachers who also encouraged me by making me produce work which was of a greater challenge than that which was required of the rest of the class. It was one of these teachers who brought me to the decision to try to enter the then newly formed High School of Music and Art in Manhattan, a frightening hour and fifteen minute subway ride away from home, which later became commonplace. Also involved in this decision was my parents' agreement to provide me with fifty cents a day for travel and lunch, no paltry sum to a family with six children in mid-Depression days.

My formal education in the arts began at the High School of Music and Art in New York City. I was in the first full class that graduated from that high school, which was created during the La Guardia reign by the Board of Education for students who showed a special aptitude for music or art. Those were my happiest and richest school days, every day filled with discoveries and excitement, making college an anti-climax. At HSMA we were exposed to a variety of art subjects and crafts as well. In 1940 I went to Brooklyn College and continued in fine arts education, interrupted by the Army in 1943. After the War, I returned to New York University where I completed my bachelor of arts and also worked in the crafts, which had become more important to me than painting, in the meantime. From there I completed a master of arts degree in art teaching and in crafts, in 1947, at Columbia Teachers College, so that I am completely a product of the "education mill" of New York City. I was extremely fortunate during this schooling period to have had the opportunity of being instructed by several outstanding art teachers whose talents and qualities I fully realize in retrospect. The problems of teaching became my own when immediately afterward I started teaching art and crafts in the New York City school system, where I remained until 1965. When it was no longer possible to be given leaves of absence to study the crafts of India and Nepal on various grants, I was forced to resign.

Can you tell us something about who was the chief influence in your choice of profession?

I think I mentioned that the first influence was probably my brother-in-law who was an art-trained person and an art teacher. After entering the High School of Music and Art and being exposed to serious creative work, I found that the teachers of that school had the most influence. I am thinking in particular of a few whose imaginative teaching methods made every day an exciting adventure that was eagerly anticipated. They created an atmosphere that made art seem the only important thing in life. These teachers especially influenced a small group of students who, I suppose, they must have felt were most responsive. One in particular took a small group of us on a weekly round of the art galleries and craft exhibitions, intensifying in us an awareness of the world of arts and crafts. I am forever grateful to those dedicated, creative teachers.

Can you tell us something more about the influence of your parents on the choice of your profession? What, for example, has been the influence of your mother as you look back on this?

My mother was a person who believed very ardently in education, as did many middle-class mothers of her generation, primarily because she was never able to fully develop her own potential through education. She was really the driving force which created the situation in which each of my brothers and sisters simply had to be educated. Not that they resisted this process, but through her determination to educate her children in the best possible manner, education was an unquestioned, essential objective for us all. I remember her driving energy toward this end, and her personal sacrifice. My father was of the same feeling and made a great physical effort to provide the means.

Both of these parents, now departed, I can see now were basically quite sensitive people who appreciated any signs of talent or creative ideas in the development of their children. They encouraged music education, for instance, in my brother and sister, and were happy about my interest in the arts, encouraging me in my early years of art education by enthusiastic acceptance of my early endeavors. I think my father may have had a potentially undeveloped source of visual creativity.

The total home environment was one of acceptance of cultural pursuits. I remember, for instance, that there often was music—a brother practicing his violin, a sister playing the piano, another singing, and later at family reunions, all of us singing at the dinner table in a chorus in harmony. My early school works, paintings and sculptures, were proudly displayed throughout the house and even in the kitchen so that it eventually took on the look of an art gallery. I don't mean to imply that these were glorious works, but only to illustrate my parents' interest in the creative capacities of their children.

In retrospect, do you feel that your activities as a teacher of art in the New York City public schools had any influence, by reason of your students or by reason of your colleagues in your field, in the direction and character of your work as a craftsman?

I think a very important effect takes place in the thinking of a teacher in *any* field which might be especially valuable in the case of a teacher who also has his own creative work, while teaching a creative subject. The teaching process is basically one of communication between the teacher and the students. This makes it essential that the teacher formulate his ideas in such an organized way that they can be presented logically and understandably with the greatest impact on the student. Such a situation forces the teacher to organize his thinking, and then verbalize his ideas. His thoughts must be clarified and brought to the surface. Such a process has a very definite effect on one's creative work. Ideas mature rapidly. Also, the student's challenge of ideas broadens a teacher's thinking. In my particular development, I began as a painter, went to the crafts, and through teaching started writing about crafts. In order to illustrate the articles I presented for publication, I developed an interest in photography. My knowledge of various crafts, acquired through direct experience and teaching, plus the need to verbalize ideas in teaching which I spoke of, has prepared me for my present interest in writing about and photographing crafts. It seems to have been a logical development in my case.

To return to the reasons for my interest in the crafts. I have become increasingly aware of the fact that Western man has been assigned the function of consumer of the products produced by industrial technology. His separation from the means of production or even a simple awareness of how things are made has created a sense of inadequacy in many. Even those who are involved with industry's technology tend to be specialists. Disposability has become an important feature of what is produced, and it is constantly emphasized. Our junkpiles attest to the lack of meaning, feeling or value we give to the objects around us. My interest in crafts stems from the enjoyment of handling materials: clay, metal, fibers. I enjoy the direct experience with materials, and constructing objects whose designs grow from the basic character of the particular material which can only be learned by handling it. It became apparent to me that the field of crafts would always be most important to me in my life.

During these early experiences in craft work, I also became interested in the Far East, and especially in India, primarily because I had become aware that in India was still to be found a great craft tradition, though probably in a declining condition. I discovered that India was a country in which the crafts played an integral part in the life of the people. Industrial technology there had not yet made a permanent gap between craftsmen and consumer. I decided that I must go there to personally explore this condition. Accordingly, I applied for a grant and was fortunate enough to be given a Fulbright to study the contemporary crafts of India. I remained in India from 1957 to 1959, and started what has become a life's commitment to a study of the crafts of that country. I returned to the States, found a life-partner, a designer of crafts in Finland, and married. In 1963 after applying for another grant, this time to Nepal, we left to study the crafts of that country, India's cultural relative, on a Fulbright Research Grant.

My purpose was to make a photographic and written record of the vanishing contemporary crafts of these countries before they were swallowed irretrievably by the changes that were taking place even there. In order to accomplish this, we traveled extensively, taking thousands of photographs and gathering data and samples. I was interested not simply in the objects but in their relation to the society that produced them, and the craftsmen's position in that society. Wherever possible, photos of the objects in use were made to illustrate the use of crafts in a tradition-oriented culture. It was no surprise that forms created by the dictates of function could also be well-designed and even beautiful.

After the termination of the first grant, I realized the enormous scope of this study which would require more than one extended stay in India. In 1965 I received a third grant, this time from the American Institute of Indian Studies, in order to attempt to complete the study. My wife and I remained in India till 1967, traveling again over the entire country, visiting craftsmen in their craft village centers, and covering much territory that it was not possible to see the first time. This third grant was extremely valuable because in the interval of nearly ten years it was possible to witness the decline and even total disappearance of some crafts, as industrial advances, increased living costs, and a declining patronage took their toll. Since that time I have been living in Finland where I am actively engaged in writing the results of the study, to be called *The Crafts of India*. This will be quite a large effort, which at present seems to be taking the shape of a two-volume work. The first will probably consist of the textile and fiber crafts, and the second will cover the use of other materials. I believe the first volume will be ready for presentation to a publisher within the next year, and from there on it's a question of the mechanical process of production which may take another year. The second volume will then follow, and will possibly come out two years after the first.

Will you tell us something about the differences that you have found in the craft areas you have been working in in the Orient as compared to those here in the West?

There is a marked difference in the approach to the crafts and the creation of crafts in the East and the West. In the West, the individual artist is emphasized, and his creative experience is almost more important to him than the product. Both craftsman and artist utilize the arts as a means of self-expression, a political weapon, or a social commentary. They seek to realize the demands of their particular personalities, their creativity, and their personal outlook on the world. Though these objectives have at times also been utilized in the past in a country such as India, the craftsman there is an artisan who is following a tradition which has probably existed for hundreds and even thousands of years before him. By reason of the existence of craftsmen's castes, his training for generations has come from his family members who also are occupied in the same craft. The forms he creates are traditional, but this is not to say static—they evolve slowly in the course of many years. His expression is the essence of the ideas of the craftsman's group to which he belongs, and is meant to satisfy the needs and demands of small and specific groups in society. Essentially, he is not interested in innovation for its own sake, in individual expression, or in creativity in the sense that we think of these ideas in the West. He certainly *is* involved with aesthetics and excellence in craftsmanship.

In the West a distinction is still made between the so-called fine arts, such as painting and sculpture, and the applied arts or crafts, though this distinction is dying. These have been considered the most highly creative of the arts, and until fairly recent times, the craftsman in the West didn't have the status of that of a painter or sculptor. He was not thought to be making significant creative statements in his work. That attitude is changing in the West where craftsmen are more and more recognized as having as much creative capacity as painters or sculptors. In India, until very recent times, such a dichotomy between artists and craftsmen did not exist. Rather than being divided into mutually exclusive or contradictory groups, all were artisans, and society gave them recognition in terms of their achievements and the degree of skill in their particular fields. With the decline of the crafts and the influence of Western ideas, today both situations are occurring simultaneously there; that is, studio artists have proliferated, and in a curious repetition of a Western situation think themselves superior to traditional craftsmen, while some art school-trained individuals have turned to crafts as an area worthy of their attention. All this occurs simultaneously with the continuance of the traditional crafts which are in a state of attrition.

Can you tell us what is your principal artistic endeavor at the present time apart from your research and writing of your findings in the Orient?

My most active area in the crafts has been enameling on metal. I became particularly interested in this craft medium when I first began teaching in 1947. After a few initial experiences, I came to the conclusion that enamel was a medium that because of brilliant color, permanence, and the speed with which work could develop, appealed to me enormously. It also offered a means of expression that had been until then very little explored in terms of a contemporary aesthetic approach. At that time there was very little recent literature on the subject, and as far as I knew, no place to be introduced to such an approach to the medium in New York City. My learning experience therefore consisted mainly of trial-and-error methods and what I could extract from existing literature. I discovered that practicing craftsmen in enamel, in a manner that brought the Medieval Guilds to mind, were loathe to part with "trade secrets." Although books are certainly an aid to learning, in the crafts, the only real learning that brings one to significant conclusions in terms of the individual's development comes from direct experience. Only by spending hours working with the material, studying its physical behavior and exploring its possibilities can one's control of the medium grow and the craftsman's work mature. The material itself suggests its creative possibilities, and this is an important, basic point in all the crafts.

You mentioned that your earlier work with enameling was on a trial-and-error basis. We wonder if you can recall any errors that have had a creative outcome and have been valued by you, although they started out as errors in your work? In other words, is there a kind of serendipity about some of your errors?

Yes, it is certainly true that agreeable accidents and surprises do occur, and I might have to be a little technical to illustrate. I must start by saying that there are two important, basic types of enamel—an opaque enamel and a transparent one. I discovered, after having accidentally overheated an opaque enamel, that it reacted to the higher than normal temperature by becoming translucent or even transparent. This was an effect that I used considerably in my later work. It was an accident to start, a case of poor timing. The enamel should have been removed from the heat of the kiln in which it had been fired at an earlier time. I left it there too long, and the result to me was spectacular and unexpected. Subsequently I taught enameling at the Brooklyn Museum Art School, and this accident which I have described and utilized, became a kind of approach to the medium which I then introduced to my students. These students, in turn, made discoveries which were perhaps extensions of my original mistake.

I feel that it is a blessing for a beginner not to know too much about the behavior of a medium. He then faces it without the inhibitory effect of knowing too many "rules." It is necessary to know a few basic, physical facts about any medium, but learning directly and making "mistakes" is a desirable and even necessary experience. In the enameling medium when you use the materials freely in an untraditional manner and where coordination and judgments may be less controlled, it is common that one experiences surprise in the result. Surprise becomes an element in the work. Of course, one likes to feel that one is in control of the medium, but because of the many and varied factors to be managed simultaneously, control is never really complete. But this is part of the excitement of the medium that maintains one's interest and draws him on to other achievements.

Are you aware of your own feelings and emotions in your own creative efforts? For example, do you do your best work when you are elated or depressed or is your mood of little importance?

I think that before mood comes the simple question of physical condition. Feeling either rested or tired has a great effect on the work. It is basically a question of being physically alert or not, and one functions better when in top physical condition. Ordinarily, in work, one is not consciously aware of experiencing emotions—he is drawn along by the development of the work, and whatever emotion is experienced may be thought about only in retrospect. Emotions are nevertheless being experienced while working, at moments when the work is taking positive form. They influence decisions that become an integral part of the finished work. Emotions can also be a source of strength. I remember, for instance, that the excitement of my early experiences with enameling kept me working long hours, really beyond my normal energy capacities, but time was forgotten because of the excitement and the discoveries that were occurring. It was only when the work period ended that I became aware of being physically exhausted.

What do you do when you get bogged down with something? Do you continue with it, or put it aside and come back to it later? In other words, do you work systematically or otherwise?

Work in enameling has to be procedurally very systematic. The medium imposes the necessity for a systematic approach. An enamel can be and usually is brought to a conclusion and completed in one session, while the idea is "hot." The stylistic appearance of the work may appear spontaneous, but is the result of a more or less procedural system which must take place.

Some days in working, despite all apparent favorable conditions, the work incurs one disaster after another. Those are the days when, as my wife and I say, "The aspects are not with us." At such times, it is better to accept that state of affairs and withdraw from the workshop. What makes such a sensible decision less likely is the preparation that must precede actual work in enameling—heating the kiln, a matter of more than one hour, cleaning the metal, an arduous task, and one hates to give up the hours so spent and accept defeat. Instead, one usually continues and ends with a day of frustration compounded on frustration. What actually seems to be happening is that you are "tripping" over your own emotions.

In earlier times, at moments of frustration when a certain objective was sought and not attained, I can remember instances of physical violence when I smashed a hot enamel because it was not coming to the fruition or conclusion for which I had hoped. Today, I accept disasters more philosophically.

I must mention a situation that exists in the case of many craftsmen who earn from their work, and that is the existence of two areas of work: a commercial area and a purely exploratory and creative area. Fortunate is the craftsman who does not have to think of such a division and can dispose of everything of his work he wishes to. Realistically speaking, this is not generally the case. Frequently, there is a question of compromise dictated more often than not by economic considerations. Under these circumstances, the craftsman must adopt a systematic approach to his work which will enable him to derive the maximum benefit from it, to allow him increased time in the creative area. These two areas, of course, interact; one has its effect on the other, and the craftsman draws on his total experience for ideas. The time spent in producing "commercial" items may not be so exciting as those times spent in pure exploration. In some crafts, and this is true with enamel, certain selling standards, such as perfect finish in a product, are important considerations which may be less important in work produced to satisfy one's self. Of course, artistic integrity is the moral force that makes one produce the best he is capable of in these commercial objects.

*We're very much interested in the birth of an idea which finds creative
expression in your enameling work. Can you tell us something about how
you find ideas about your work coming into your awareness?*

I don't believe in making elaborate preparatory sketches in creating an
enamel work, though this is necessary in a traditional approach to enamel.
Following a design first done on paper to me has the effect of producing a
stilted, dead look; besides, mechanically reproducing a paper design is
pure tedium. I think of the design or subject matter before actually
beginning, but not in detail. The creation takes place during the work when
the enamel is applied to the metal.

Creative ideas for subject matter and material treatment come from
several main sources, including the intellect, the intuition, and the technology involved. All crafts involve a technology that is the main means by
which creative ideas become concretized. The greater the degree of control
and skill a craftsman has in the execution of his craft, the more varied and
developed his realizations can be. Of course, technical skill must be accompanied by creative fantasy or the result is just an exercise.

Every medium has certain technical requirements, and those requirements and their connected problems must first be studied before any
creative result can be achieved. It is necessary in the crafts to learn the
characteristics of the particular material that you are using, and this is
equally true of enamel. With enamels you are dealing with a pulverized,
granular substance in a dry form which must be physically applied to a
supporting surface, which is metal. The elemental problem is how to get
this granular stuff to adhere to the metal, and from a solution to that
problem came a means of expression. I found that by applying liquid gum
to the cleaned metal with brushes of various widths and then dusting those
gummed areas with the powdered enamel so that it would adhere *only* in
those places where there was gum, I was able to produce a result that was
very much like free caligraphy, something of an innovation in this medium.
The older and more dilapidated the brush was, the more character the
strokes had. The brush became the controlling element in the creation of a
design subject, and whatever one could do with a brush then became a
possibility with the enamel material. Even then, the enamel is not in its
permanent condition and must be subjected to a heat source, usually a kiln,
at high temperatures that may reach 1700°F. It emerges glowing red-hot
after a few minutes in the temperature necessary to convert the powdered
enamel into a smoothly fused glass-like surface which adheres to the metal.

Your work is in a visual medium. Can you tell us something about the role of visual or other images in its development or in your creative experiences?

The enamelist, unlike the painter who uses pigments, sees his medium in a condition during the creation of a work which is totally unlike what it will ultimately be. He must be able to project in his mind a visual image based on his previous experience of how the result will look, both in color and physical condition. The enamel powders give only a hint of the color they will become, and in that form do not even indicate whether they are transparent or opaque. This the enamelist must know when he selects the color he is about to use.

The work proceeds in stages, being subjected in the manner in which I work to possibly up to seven trips to the kiln, each time to make permanent what has already been accomplished. After it is cooled, the next application of enamel is done so that the enamel accumulates in strata, the number depending on the times it is fired. Each time the result is studied, and judgments and conclusions as to the next procedure occur. After the last fire, the final state is achieved, and alteration of the result is nearly impossible, outside of drastic, non-craftsmanlike means. The final surface is the hard, impenetrable glass that the heat has created. As to my approach, the number of times any enamel can be fired is limited probably to less than seven; you might say the work is created by a series of *that* number of images, each one altered by the one that follows, which is superimposed upon the last.

How about your dreams or your daydreams in your creative efforts? Are you aware of any relationship between dreams and your enameling work?

If you mean actually trying to represent one's dreams in the work, I don't think dreams have had any overt influence on me. I am not a surrealist. There are occasions when besides conscious thinking I may be thinking subconsciously about possibilities in the work as an aftermath to a work experience, but I don't think I would term these thoughts as dreams. There may suddenly come an insight into the solution of a problem or the development of an idea, but these insights occur mainly during working periods. I would not term them daydreams, which to me implies a passive state of mind. Thoughts and insights are turned into action, many times, or at least once, and if not, are stored away for future reference. But in any case, I would not call these fantasies.

The subject matter, in my case, comes directly from the medium, as I have described. This is basic to my approach. As my training and inclination are toward an abstract expression, this also influences the development of subject matter. In this case, the excitement comes from color, rhythm, variation—all the basic elements with which any creative person in the plastic arts is concerned. Decisions involving their organization occur in an intuitive manner during the progress of the work. The intuition is a sum total of all that has come before in the aesthetic awareness and background of the individual. Intuition is an important element in the creative process.

You spoke of being innovative in respect to the mechanics of working in enamels. Do you feel that you have made creative contributions with respect to your medium of expression, and how would you characterize those contributions?

Historically, enamel has been treated as a medium requiring very tight control, and was used essentially as an adjunct to jewelry and on relatively small objects. Its application and use in very small amounts gave it the feeling of being something very precious. Since those days, tremendous developments have occurred in the industrial technology of producing the raw material which is readily available for use in any quantity in a state ready for immediate use. Formerly its production was an extremely tedious and laborious process of pounding and grinding that was a part of the job of the enamelist. In addition, there is another important factor, the development of larger electric heated kilns in which enamels can be fired also occurred and became available to many at relatively reasonable prices. These two technological conditions have set the stage for the development of enameling into a new phase, formerly unheard of or inconceivable. Everything points to an increase in size, freedom in application, and ultimate use of enamels, its extension as a medium suitable for use as a mural art and even for use in architecture. Such an increase in scale demands a freer approach to the medium.

The innovations, such as they are, which occurred in my enameling, suggested at least one possibility for the expanded approach to the material. In my work, this method ultimately developed into a style of working and became a mature kind of expression. I flatter myself to think that this was an original approach to the medium. Through my teaching of enameling, this technical method I think "rubbed off" on some of my students and in turn influenced their treatment of the medium. Such a situation is common when teaching. There are not so many people working in this particular medium, and it might not be inaccurate to say, in all modesty, that a minute "school of enameling" has developed around this approach. I say this after recently seeing an exhibition in which I find myself flattered by seeing works which I believe show signs of the influence of my approach.

I have published a book on enameling which was the result of my self-taught experience with the material. Since then I have had correspondence with enamelists from all over the world. It is amazing how far the printed word can be dispersed, and with it the ideas they contain. In February 1968 another book I wrote was published by Doubleday and is called *Metal Techniques for Craftsmen*. This is a rather large work which explores the decorative processes that have been used in metal work in many cultures of the world over the centuries up to the present. In the future is a projected plan for another book on enameling in which I hope to summarize, as nearly as this can be done, the developments of the present century in the renaissance of enameling that has occurred in our time.

ISAAC BASHEVIS SINGER

Isaac Bashevis Singer was born in Poland in 1904, where he lived until he came to the United States in 1935. During the years 1926–35, Mr. Singer was a journalist for the Yiddish Press in Poland. Since 1940, Singer has been a member of the staff of the Jewish Daily Forward, *published in New York City but enjoying a national readership.*

Beginning with The Family Moskat *(1950), Isaac B. Singer has written a series of novels in the Yiddish genre, chief among which are* Satan in Goray *(1955)* Gimpel the Fool *(1957),* The Magician of Lublin *(1960),* The Spinoza of Market Street *(1961), and* My Father's Court *(1966). His latest work is* The Seance.

In addition to his novels, Mr. Singer writes frequently for magazines and journals, and in 1950 and 1956 was awarded the Lammed Prize; in 1959, Singer was the recipient of an American Arts and Letters grant.

Isaac Bashevis Singer

Do your dreams enter into your ideas for a story?

It happens that I dream about something, and, although the dream does not have a direct relation with the topic, still this dream may involve me in an idea. This did happen to me a few times. Another thing is that it might have happened more than I know. Sometimes we forget a dream, but a kind of inspiration is left. We see something in a dream which can later be remembered and become a topic. You never know how much the dream influences reality.

There are many dreams in my stories, and all these dreams are taken from dreams I really had, except that I changed them a little bit. For example, in the story *Spinoza of Market Street,* there is a dream where Dr. Fischelsohn dreams that he is sick and he thinks of an eclipse of the sun. There is a whole description of a Catholic procession. This is a dream I had. Wherever I describe a dream in my writings, it is a dream taken from my experience. There is no reason for inventing because you can get from your own experience millions of things. Millions of things in dreams and thoughts and so on and on. So, if I have in my writings one hundred dreams, they are all my dreams. And, also, some of them are what you would call daydreams. Daydreaming and writing are very, very much connected.

The only thing is that one never remembers a dream completely. There isn't such a thing as remembering a whole dream. So, we are not able to rebuild a whole dream. Even if you remember it for the first few minutes, you forget it a little later. There's some power which makes you forget dreams. I don't know why it is so. So, I would say if I have a grain of a dream, around this dream I can build things.

Your dream language is very often full of mistakes, full of distortions. In other words, let's say you have the word "telephone." In the dream you may not call it "telephone," but "feletone." I've learned from experience that in a dream we act sometimes, as far as language is concerned, like children who have just learned the language; as if your own language should be a foreign language, you distort words. You don't pronounce them in the right way, and, sometimes, when I remember, I even laugh at that. You may call a telephone a telegraph or a telegraph a telephone. It's peculiar that although sometimes in a dream you may use language very efficiently, it's very hard to find any order in it. The dream is really a riddle wrapped in a puzzle, and I'm almost afraid that it will remain so forever. I, myself, tried to create some theories about a dream, but all these theories burst immediately like soap bubbles. In some cases, a theory might last a year, a half a year, at least a day. But, not when it comes to dreams, because immediately there is another dream which reverses and bursts your theory immediately.

What has influenced your writing?

It is very difficult to say, because we are naturally influenced by everything from our childhood and by a book we read, or a newspaper. But, I don't find a single writer really, about whom I could say, I am under his influence. Maybe I fool myself, maybe somebody else could find it, but I don't. I would say that I was very much taken by Edgar Allan Poe. When I read him in Polish, I liked him very much. Naturally, I like Tolstoy, Dostoevsky, and Gogol, but I wouldn't call myself a disciple of any of these writers. My brother, I. J. Singer, influenced me a lot as far as construction is concerned. He gave me certain lessons which I still think are valid, and one of the most important rules which he gave me is that a story in itself, a story or an image, never gets obsolete, never gets stale. If you tell a story about a shoemaker who lived in the village of Frampol, this will never be stale, even a thousand years from now. Nobody will say it's obsolete, because in the village of Frampol, there did live a shoemaker, so it's eternally true. But, if you try to interpret, to explain things, no matter how clever you are, this explanation and interpretation will become stale in no time. The moment a writer tries to explain events, his explanation is immediately on the brink of becoming redundant and stale. If you tell of an encounter between a young man and a girl who fell in love, that's all right, it's an eternal truth. If you try to explain why they fell in love, you are about to fall into a pit of banality. Anyhow, school children will know it ten years from now. This is the reason why a writer like Huxley, who wrote *Point Counterpoint*, and who tried to explain his heroes by Freudian theory, looks now almost ridiculous, because children who go to public school know already about the father complex, and the Electra complex, and so on and on, and it's not necessary. Events either cannot be explained or don't have to be explained. Explanation is never good in writing.

What is the impact of your moods on your productivity?

Being depressed and being happy are so near to one another, that sometimes I really don't know the difference. It's one little step between being happy and being depressed. I would say that being very much depressed, being, let's say, in a real crisis of depression, is not conducive to one's writing, quite the opposite. I had, myself, a number of years in which I could not write. This was when I came to this country from Poland in 1935. I missed my family, I missed my friends, I missed the girl to whom I was connected. I was depressed because I didn't know the language in this country, and I often didn't have any chance of making a living. I was a freelancer; I had trouble with immigration. I came here as a visitor, and it took me a long time until I got a permanent visa. All these things worked, so I could not write at all. And not only wasn't I able to write, but when I did try to write, I suddenly discovered that I could not construct a sentence correctly. I was astonished because my language was always very fluent, but in this case of deep depression, my sentences became too abrupt, and, sometimes, not really correct from the point of view of syntax. And this lasted for years. I also played around with one topic for years, and I wrote and rewrote, and nothing came out of it. So, in this case, a real depression can make a writer impotent.

I got over it because I learned the language and I did make acquaintances. After a while I did get a job and I got a permanent visa. All these things together, which took me years, helped me.

In the beginning I was only a freelancer. To be a freelancer is not such a good thing in any case, but to be a Yiddish freelancer where there was only one newspaper I could consider, is a very bad business. My editor always used to bother me. He discussed with me a story for weeks and I couldn't pay the rent. So, all these things together depressed terribly my power of creation.

You know, when you freelance, first you send it to the editor and he will let it lay there for weeks and then he will call you up and find faults. The editor seldom thinks that the writer has to pay rent. So, when you are in such a situation, and in addition, you have to prolong your visa every three months, and then they threaten to send you back, and your room is dark, you're not in a very good shape for writing. At least, not I.

I don't need to be immensely happy to be able to write, but I must have the feeling that I have an apartment, that I have money enough to buy myself a lunch, and so on and so on. I know of some writers that say they can only write in Switzerland, they can only write in Japan, they need great luxury. This is not my case, I need a minimum. However, I know of cases of writers who wrote while they were hungry and without an apartment, and without a visa. There are no rules to this game.

How does the idea for a story arise?

In the case of writing everything can be a topic, almost everything. Not that everything becomes a topic. Sometimes you have a very important experience, but some power in you says this is not a topic for the present. Maybe it will become one later or maybe never. But, since all writing is autobiographical, in a sense, we always describe things of our own experience unless we completely invent things which we writers almost never do. So, everything is taken from one's life. You can call them emotions or thoughts. These are all names for experience, inner or outside experience which again are the same thing. Because an experience depends upon the way you interpret it, the way you see it, the way you feel it.

Every writer has his own definition of what he calls a story. What is a story to one writer may not be a story to another writer. For me, for something to be a story, it has to be a real story. I don't believe like some writers that you can just sit down and just write what they call a slice of life—just begin to write something, and something will come out. I don't believe this. You have to have a story. A story means there are surprises, where the reader does not know when he reads the second chapter what will happen in the third chapter. Sometimes even the writer does not know. But, this is not enough. The story has somehow to fit my point of view, my emotional look at things. I have three rules for writing a story. These are my private rules. The first thing is the easiest thing. It has to be a story, a real story, what I call a story. In other words, the fact that a man got up in the morning and he went to a restaurant, and ate breakfast, and he came back home and read a book is not a story for me. Although, to some other writers it may be a story. In my case, it must be a real story. There must be some surprises as I said before. This is number one. I have to have a topic. The second thing is, I have to have a passion for this topic. Sometimes I can find a very good topic, but I have no desire to write about it. I just feel I can do very well without this story. And, there are millions of such topics which I have written down, which I thought would be a very good theme. But, somehow the desire to write them was not there. But, then there comes a third condition which is most difficult. Before I sit down to write a story, I must have the conviction that only I can write this particular story, that of all the writers in the world, I am the only one that can write it. When I wrote *Gimpel the Fool,* I knew no other writer could write it. He might write a story about a Spanish fool, or an English fool, but to write a story about a Yiddish fool in a little shtetl, and such a particular fool like this one, this is my story. And this is true about every story I write. It has to be my own story. Many writers will get a topic and they will write about something which any other writer, or some other writer could write. When we see the great works in literature, we know that they were all completely unique. Tolstoy was a great writer, but he could never have written *Crime and Punishment,* never, or *The Brothers Kara-mazov,* or any of Dostoevsky's short stories. Only one man in the whole world, of all times, could have written *Crime and Punishment.* The same thing is true about many writers. When you read, let's say, a certain novel by Faulkner, only Faulkner could have done this. A writer should find what is his story, his particular story, which only one man in this life and all generations can do. I personally believe that every man has such stories to tell even if he's not a writer.

When I look over my stories, I know that no Gentile could have written them, and neither could a person who didn't live in Poland. But, even those who did live in Poland, and are writers, could not write my stories. I could not write the stories that they write, and they cannot write my stories. And I would say that the most important duty of a writer is to find what is really his story, his particular story, his unique story. If you don't find them, you can never really write and the readers will not be interested. The reader might be a very simple person, but he has a good sense to tell if you tell *your* story, or if you tell just a story.

It took me years and years for me to find my story. I wrote stories which Peretz might have written, or even Sholem Aleichem might have written in his young days. And then I tried in my young years to imitate. I read Hamsun's *Victoria,* and I tried to write that way. But, every time I saw that this is not my story. I didn't know that it had to be my story, but I just felt something was missing. Finally, when I wrote *Satan in Goray,* I said to myself, this is *my* stuff. No other writer could have written it, and until today I somehow have the feeling, at least the illusion (but even the illusion is important) that every one of my stories could have been written only by me.

Lately I write a lot about events which take place in America, in the United States. For example, in my collection of short stories, *The Seance,* I have three stories which take place in America. In my book, *Short Friday,* I have two stories which take place in America. One is called *Alone,* which takes place in Miami Beach, and then there is another one called *A Wedding in Brownsville.* In the beginning I was afraid I would never be able to connect my way of feeling with the United States. I feared I would not be able to find any stories which take place in this country, which are unique, which are my stories. But, I have convinced myself that this isn't so. After living many years here, somehow I was able to merge my personality with events which take place in this country. I had a story a few months ago in *Playboy,* which is called *The Lecture,* where I described a lecture in Montreal, and again, it's my story.

You just cannot prepare to write a story. You cannot get up in the morning and say to yourself, "I'm going to find a topic." You don't find a topic. Somehow it comes to you. It comes "out of the blue," as you say— yet it doesn't. In *The Lecture,* I did go to lecture in Montreal. I could not have described the lecture without having lectured. I couldn't have described the lecture in Montreal without having been in Montreal. I could not have described the trip there, the winter, and how the train stopped in the middle of the night, without having had this experience. But, then I described another experience of how a woman dies in the apartment where I go. This did not happen, but I knew such a woman, and I knew that she died, though she did not die there. Sometimes I sit down and write a story, and I don't know how it will be finished. In other words, I, myself, have to find a way out. It happens once in a while that I don't find a way out. I come to a dead end and there is no story. But, in many cases, somehow I do find a way out.

In some cases, you have a feeling as if some little imp or devil is standing behind you and dictating to you, but he gives it to you slowly, drop by drop. How our subconscious works we never really know. No man can ever describe how an idea comes to him. There is a book by a mathematician and he tries to explain how ideas come to mathematicians. He makes us believe that our subconscious keeps on working without our knowledge. In other words, you have a problem, some little mechanism in you, or call it what you want, keeps on pondering and calculating, and, suddenly, you get the net result. It just comes, suddenly, but, at the same time, you feel as though there's an evolution behind it. It grows and it grows. It's both, evolution and a revolution.

Could you tell us something about the influence of your mysticism?

From my childhood I had the feeling of the supernatural. Not just a fear of it, but a great fear of it. I was always afraid at night when the lamp was extinguished. I was always afraid of devils, and imps, and ghosts. My dreams haunted me from my childhood. Even in my waking hours I had fears and all kinds of fits which it would take too long to explain. Even, to date, I believe in the supernatural, though I don't know what it is. And, I think this is true not only about me, but about many people, except that most people try to deny these things. A man might say that a human corpse is not more to him than a dead chicken, and there's nothing more to it. Still, if you tell the same man to stay with a human corpse on a winter's night in a dark room, the man will shudder and refuse, and may not even do it for a million dollars. People are afraid of these things, even though they deny it. In my case, I could not deny this fear, and these feelings, because they were too strong. Whenever I write a story, the supernatural will pop up, it will come out. If I write a story, and it's not there, I'm sometimes suspicious about the story. I say, "Something is missing here." Although I have stories where the supernatural is not there, at least there is a hint of it. I seem to say in all my stories that what we know and what we experience is only a small part of the powers with which we are surrounded, and I like to dwell on this, and say it again and again. I don't feel that I repeat myself; just like a man who writes a symphony repeats the same leitmotif, because he's interested in this and the repetition enhances the symphony.

Although I was born in the twentieth century, we actually lived in the middle ages. My father was a Rabbi, and a man of great faith and great belief, not only in religion, but in everything that is connected with it. To prove that there is a God, he always spoke about Dybbuks, and about haunted houses and so on and so on. And my mother had also this kind of belief. All my life I heard from my father stories about wonder Rabbis and about the wonders which they worked and so on and so on. But, at the same time, he was enough of a skeptic to feel that one should try to prove these things. My brother always asked questions and so did my sister. It was a time of great skepticism, and my father tried to prove things as much as he could. I don't believe in everything that is written in the scriptures, and I know that all dogmas are man-made, but I feel that behind everything, there are powers. You cannot just explain life by logic or experience. My father felt that it's not enough to say you are not allowed to ask. He felt that as much as he could, he should try to explain to us, to convince us.

In my later years, I became terribly interested in what they call psychic research. I read Conan Doyle, Sir William Crooks, and so forth, and all the works which are connected with mysticism. Today I read magazines which deal with the occult, although many of them are full of lies and all kinds of nonsense. However, I always feel that there is a grain of truth in them, and I am interested in this grain. Sometimes I will take a story which I read there. Let's say a letter from a woman describes some little event, and this letter will become my story, will become my short story. I don't feel that I'm stealing anything, because hers is not a work of art, she just tells a story. These things go into my mind, and become a part of my thinking. And, in spite of it, I read a number of scientific books, and I more or less know the scientific point of view. I know about physics and chemistry, and psychology, as any other student, as any other dilettante. I still am capable of believing the most bizarre and unbelievable things. Let's say, a man would come over to me today, and he would tell me he just met his dead grandfather in the street. I would not say, "You are crazy." I would listen and be highly interested, and I would ask questions, and if I would see that he is a normal man, I would say to myself, "Yes, it's possible. Corpses do walk on Broadway." I am just quoting something out of a story of mine. It should come out, most likely, in a few months.

Though I don't practice much dogma, I am a believer. I believe in God, and I pray to God. Whenever I am in trouble, my first reaction is to say, "God in heaven, help me," without being sure of anything, because I am a skeptic at the same time. What proof do I have? There is no evidence that there is a God just as there can't be any evidence to prove that there isn't a God. I read the philosophers. I read Spinoza and Kant. I tried to translate Spinoza's ethics from German into Yiddish. I know, more or less, what the philosophers say, but, at the same time, my own feeling is that we are surrounded by millions and millions of powers of which we have no inkling, and of which we may never have an inkling. Perhaps some of them, we may have an inkling of in the future. For thousands of years men wore woolen garments, and when they took them off at night, especially in a dark night, they saw sparks. But, for thousands of years men never asked themselves what these sparks were which they were seeing. If they had asked this question, maybe electricity would have been discovered thousands of years sooner. People were afraid to ask. Maybe they were afraid they would be taken as crazy, liars, and so on and so on. And I say we, all of us, do see sparks about which we don't ask any questions. Once you begin to think about them, once you have the courage to ask questions, you are ready for a new experience.

Even though it does not fit in our sum of knowledge, it may fit into the sum of knowledge of the future generations. Five hundred years from now, children in the public schools will learn about things which would look to us now strange, unbelievable, just impossible. They will know then, they will have proof, and they will wonder how it was possible that their grandfathers, who were quite clever men, and who discovered so many things, didn't discover these truths. In other words, we are always wandering in a world full of truths which almost touch us, but to which, for some reason, we do not pay attention. The sum of all these things together I call the supernatural, maybe not the supernatural, but a part of nature. Nature and supernature, most probably, are the same thing.

I ask these questions in my stories. My novels are not answers to these questions because these questions cannot be answered. But, my heroes always ask what I call the eternal questions. They always do this, and, as a matter of fact, this is their daily bread. When I was a child of about three or four or five the questions which came to my mind actually were the questions that philosophers have asked over the years. The first is, "Could there have been a beginning to time? How is it possible that the world was created, but God existed always?" I asked, "Does it really mean always? Did he exist a billion years ago?" And my mother said, "Sure." "A hundred billion years ago?" "Surely." "How about millions of billions of years ago," I said, "as much as you can write with the whole well of ink on paper, did he exist also then?" She said, "Naturally. If he is eternal, he always existed." I said, "I cannot imagine just God remembering something which happened in a time which never had a beginning." This question was also asked by philosophers and by children. We all just cannot imagine that time could have had a beginning. The same thing is true about space. Until today the philosophers and the physicists cannot make up their minds if there is a limit to space or not. Einstein had a kind of a twist. He said it has no end, but it's limited. But it really does not make any sense to our imagination. In our imagination space cannot have any end. If you have an airplane or a rocket it should be able to go up forever and ever, it would never come to an end. At the same time, how can space be infinite in one direction and infinite in the other direction because then you have two infinites. This is a question asked by Zeno, by Aristotle, by Plato. They all tried to answer that, but I asked these questions when I was a small child of four or five years. For a time I wondered if I'm the only one, but then I saw the other children asking the same questions. They were not bothered by them as much as I was, but they do ask them. So, the eternal questions are eternal.

They find expression in everything I write. To me, a person who does not ask these questions is almost not a person. Anyhow he's not going to be the hero of a story of mine.

These questions become translated into images and into the people who ask them in my stories. They are the main topic of my work. I think, that while we eat and drink and make love, we always ask these questions, "Why do we live?" "Why do we die?" And, the main question, "Why do we suffer?" I think that almost all problems can be reduced to one problem, "Why do we suffer?" When it comes to other questions, we can say, "I don't know." "I don't know," is also an answer. But, when it comes to why we suffer, to say, "We don't know," is not an answer. When a person is really suffering, to say to him, "We don't know," is not really an answer. This problem, "Why do we suffer," naturally, is everybody's problem. Because all the answers which the philosophers and the religious thinkers and the mystics try to invent for this problem become nothing after a while. When you see a little child or an animal suffering terribly, you cannot just make peace with any of these answers. If God did it for His glory, as some say, then why does God need for His glory that a little child should have gangrene and die slowly, or a little animal. Here we really face a question which some people will ignore completely and others cannot ignore for a moment. It's always in my mind and in my dreams. The question, not only, "why I suffer," but "why does everybody suffer." Why did God need suffering for his scheme? I give answers and I will lecture and say that God cannot write a novel without describing suffering. In God's novel, He had to have suffering, for without it, His novel would have no meaning, and like an artist, He needs shadow and light and so on and so on. But, while I give all these answers I say to myself, "This is not an answer."

Nobody could write without suffering. We cannot even imagine any living creature which doesn't suffer. All living suffers. It's a question of the intensity of suffering, but suffering is almost identical with life itself. Another thing is that suffering has a function in life because if people would not suffer, they would not take care of their bodies at all. If you wouldn't be afraid that by knocking your head against the wall you will suffer, you would do it just for the fun of it. This is really the way nature makes us take care of ourselves. But, the question is, "Why couldn't nature invent something else?"

What is the manner in which you work?

Sometimes when I sit down to write a story, the telephone might ring and will interrupt. And, sometimes I have a lecture, and I have to go somewhere. Sometimes I begin to write and the so-called muse stops, the interest stops and so on and so on. But, as a rule, I see to it that I find time to continue. I get up every morning with a desire to work and to write a story, or to work on a novel, to do some creative work. This desire is made of the same stuff as the sexual desire, the desire to make money, and any other desire. The businessman's desire to go out and do business, your desire to get patients, or to write a book. This desire, even though it has millions of forms is the same desire: to do something, to create something. I don't think that only writers and painters and musicians are creative. All human beings are creative. We all have this creative desire to do something. Women have it in their own way in bringing up children, in making themselves beautiful. In men it is somewhat stronger because he has been the provider for generations. We all want to do something, to reach something, everyone in his way. When I find a person who lost this desire, such a person is almost dead.

What is the source of your wish to become a writer?

From the very beginning I wanted to become a writer. I dreamt of writing books even before I learned how to write. I remember that I told some boy in the Chedar that I am writing a book. I just fooled him, because I couldn't write even a single letter. Somehow I saw my father writing, my brother writing, and it pleased me. I believe a lot in heredity, although it's not fashionable nowadays to believe in it. Now men think that circumstances create the man. I also believe in this, but I believe that heredity, that the genes, play a bigger part than we are ready to admit.

My brother was a very good writer. I think that as far as construction

is concerned, he was a master. I learned a lot from him. He wrote in
Yiddish. He was not interested in what we call the supernatural. He was
more interested in social events. He was a very good describer of events,
and he was more interested in the sociological and the psychological than
the parapsychological.

I loved my brother very much, I looked up to him all my life. I would
never have come to the United States without him. Without his help I
would have never been connected with *The Forward*, because he was connected to *The Forward*.

Well, my father influenced me much, even more so my mother, because
my mother was not only a scholarly woman, but a wonderful story teller.
Both of them were good story tellers. My father and my mother. And both
had enthusiasm. When they told a story, they didn't just tell an event, but
it was real enthusiasm, it wasn't pointless. Because a pointless story is
always without enthusiasm. My mother used to teach me. She taught me
the Bible in Hebrew, she taught me how to write letters. She always told
me stories about her father, her family, from Bilgoray, the town where she
came from. And the same thing is true about my father. I loved them both.
When you sit with two psychoanalysts and you tell them you love your
parents, I think they must be very suspicious about it, because as a rule
one has to hate his parents, and, maybe, I wouldn't be a good patient. But,
it would be very difficult for you to convince me that I hated my parents. I
really loved them dearly, and they influenced me as much as they could.
Although they tried to make me a pious Jew they did not succeed. But,
in my older years, I see that even in this respect they did not fail completely, because what I rejected completely in my younger years, I now
accept partially, as much as it fits my spirit and my point of view. In this
respect, I agree with the psychoanalysts or with Freud or whoever, that
love for your parents is very important for a man's life. If a person really
hates his parents, he can never be a happy person. When I hear a person
say, "I hate my mother, I hate my father," I shudder. I feel there is great
unhappiness in saying this. The commandment, "Thou Shalt Honor Thy
Father and Mother," expresses not only a great duty, but a very deep truth
in life. By rejecting our parents we reject life itself. I think this is true, not
only in the case of parents, but, also, if you reject completely tradition, you
are saying that what happened until I was born does not affect me. I am
going to begin a new life completely, or I don't care for my people, for the
Jewish people, for the Irish people, they are nothing to me. Or, America is
nothing to me. The people who say this grind themselves into unhappiness.

Because you have to accept certain authority, and the group, and your parents. Naturally, not completely so, but, at least, you have to feel that you are a continuation of something. This idea that each generation should begin completely anew can make the world sick. I feel in touch with my past, and I feel also that as far as literature is concerned, if you cut off your roots, you cut off the very juices from which your talent can grow. My loyalty to Yiddish is also a part of my loyalty to the past and to my parents. It's my mother language. I feel assimilation is a terrible thing for every human being. An assimilator is always the weak one who tries to assimilate himself according to the ideas of the strong one. You never saw a strong man trying to adjust himself to a weak man. When a young man comes to this country and says he doesn't give a hoot about Poland, about the Jewish people, about his past, about his history, but is terribly interested in Milton, in Shakespeare, in the Duke of York, and so on and on, this is pure rot. Why should he not be interested in his great men, in his writers. This is nothing but a weak creature saying, "I am nothing, you are everything." Because of this, I think that the Jews were very unhappy as long as they believed in assimilation. Now that we are done with assimilation, we are going back to health.

What are your thoughts about the influx of Jewish writers into the United States right now?

There's not a single writer among them whom I could admire as much as I admire, let's say, Tolstoy or Dostoevsky or Gogol. I'm not going to admire a writer just because he happens to be a Jewish writer. I'm not so crazy about my people that I should just spit at the truth. But, we do have a few gifted writers.

As to Yiddish, I went to Chedar and I learned in Yiddish. I studied the Talmud, and it was explained in Yiddish. Many people say that Yiddish is a poor language. It is only poor in technological words. I don't know what certain parts of a car are called in Yiddish. But, when it comes to describing character, human behavior, and human emotions, Yiddish is richer than any other language I know. Actually, Yiddish is a combination of Yiddish, Hebrew, Aramaic, German, and other languages. Its idiom is very rich and colorful.

BONNIE CASHIN

In April, 1969, we talked to Bonnie Cashin in her office situated directly across from the United Nations. Born and raised in Oakland, California, she moved to New York City to design costumes at the Roxy Theatre. Three years later she was called back to the West Coast to serve as a fashion designer for Twentieth Century-Fox Studios, where she designed many of the principal costumes for important pictures produced from 1943 to 1949.

Since 1952 she has been the head of Bonnie Cashin Designs. In 1956 she was invited by the Government of India to aid in the revitalization of the handloom industry. Among the recognitions for her original designs have been the Nieman-Marcus Award, the New York City Fashion Critics Winnie, and the Sports Illustrated *Fashion Critics Award, 1961. In 1961 she had the honor of being named Woman of the Year by the Lighthouse for the Blind in New York City.*

FASHION DESIGN

Bonnie Cashin

Miss Cashin, what do you see as the relationship between your work in fashion and the arts in general?

I think that all the creative arts in whatever medium spring from the same urges . . . perhaps the urge to find new ways of shouting "I live today." Certainly all fashion is not creative by any means, but it can be so. In my own approach it is a means to personal expression first and a way to make a living second. Clothing design is only valid if it is related to environment. I feel that all the creative fields are interrelated. Each gives to the other. Perhaps I might have been an architect, perhaps a sculptor. Whatever truly captures the interest of the creative person in likely to completely involve him, and he will usually add something uniquely his own to it. We once had a painting group, and a well-known musician who had never used a brush before turned out the most marvelous things. He had rhythm, he had music in him. The paint was just another medium for expression. The mind wants to explore, and the hand wants to try. Recently math caught my attention. My uncle is a mathematician and a geologist, and all my life he's been telling me that my horror of math was unfortunate, because design is order and mathematics is order. It's too late for me to ever be even middling at mathematics, but a kindled interest of its visual aspects, forms, shapes, and relationships has been a definite influence on my work; a kind of paring down to the "elegant solution" of a design problem.

I don't know how I got on that math thing in reply to your question except that I think practically everything is a possible influence in my fashion work. All the performing arts as well as the visual arts are indeed stimuli, strong stimuli. And, certainly related. Architecture, environment, has perhaps the greatest relationship with clothing, and has been a great influence on my own work.

Where do your ideas come from?

This is hard to pinpoint. Actually my work, I guess, is always on my mind even when I'm looking at a marvelous sky or watching a play, or on holiday. I'm constantly re-designing subconsciously. I can only see in color. I look at everything in relationships. Ideas just pop into my mind out of the blue seemingly. I jot them down. Dozens of notebooks have grown. I have one called "DO-someday," filled with ideas not only for my fashion work. I'm a dreamer. I get a lot of inspiration out of reading. I read a great deal and love the feel of a book in hand. I like the rhythm of poetry and jot down some myself, mostly impressions, feelings, and wonderments. I like books about people and their philosophies. I like history and geography as human incidents, but my mind rejects dates. Ideas just come to me while reading that seem to have nothing to do with what I'm actually reading. I always read with a pencil in my hand. I love art books, just browsing through them. I buy lots of books on impulse, sometimes do not really read them through till much later. I have a theory that books wait patiently for you and I play a sort of game about this. Often when my mind doesn't want to focus on the job at hand, I'll go to the book wall, close my eyes, and pick a volume at random. It's funny, something most always of interest pops up. Then my ideas flow more easily. Some of my favorite books are by John Gardner; his *Excellence* is great. I love Thoreau, he clears my thoughts and makes me smile. I love Georges Seferis, the poet, and Buckminister Fuller with his mind-stretching theories, and Fred Hoyle's imagination and wit. And then there's that wonderful turner-oner, Bertrand Russell, the earlier Russell, that is.

What are the sources of your inspiration?

Sometimes ideas tumble upon each other. This is exhilarating. Sometimes they just don't come. I can't even draw. At those times I'll try to quit. There's no use struggling. However, when I know I have a job to finish I just get to it. I think that all professionals get the habit of meeting deadlines. I've often worked all night at something doing it over, polishing as much as possible. The simple "elegant solution" often emerges only through a lot of trial and error. I find that every so often I must empty myself, so to speak. Sometimes I pretend that I've never been here before. Then I'll try to see things with the newest eyes I can, and it's absolutely marvelous. I might just prowl around or go over to the U.N. and sit there. I can't understand the tongues that are being spoken, but I'd rather hear them than the English translation, the rhythm of voices. It's wonderful to look at the shapes of people, the way they move. This prowling, with no objectives, can greatly refresh. My ideas seem to flow more smoothly when away from my own industry and the usual fashion environment. Our industry is centered on Seventh Avenue, and to me it's an ugly environment with the congestion, dirt, and indignities that smother any creative impulse. And yet clothing itself is very fascinating, what we humans put on our bodies and why, and its relationship to contemporary life.

Years ago I felt the only way to come to terms with functioning in the fashion business was to locate my own personal working environment elsewhere. I found an old carriage-house in Briarcliff, New York, an hour up the Hudson River, which proved a wonderful "laboratory" for experimenting, thinking, and growing. Of course, I was in New York, in the market place, for certain necessary activities. The follow-through of a design concept is terribly important in my work, and I'm afraid I'm what is called a perfectionist too, which is perhaps a fault. But our standards, I think, are laid down at an early age, and my mother, who was a great craftswoman, instilled the delight of a fine seam in me as a child.

As I've matured, I've consciously tried to simplify living as much as possible. It's become almost a design project with me. Possessions begin to possess you. People and society begin to possess you. When I sold the Briarcliff studio, I made the decision to get rid of as much stuff as possible to free my wings, so to speak. There are so many things I'd love to do, so many new creative paths to explore and travel. Now I have a situation which is another experiment in living. I live "over the store." It's in a huge contemporary complex which leaves something to be desired aesthetically, but it does have certain other very necessary elements for me. It has a wide sweep of sky; it has a long reach of moving water; it has earth and trees and flowering things, and a wonderful vista of a kind of kinetic sculpture, the bustling city itself. It's easy to take care of. It's a great observation point, and the studio is below in the business part of the building, although I actually use my whole apartment to "work" in. Where does one draw the line between living and working? I love it also because there's a constant panorama of ethnic groups in this area near the United Nations. Someday

I'd like to be able to build a thing of beauty, another design problem. An "elegant solution" to meet my own emotional needs and yet be part of an intensely fascinating and changing city. As I said before, these experiments in living allow my mind to bounce around more freely and I find that the specific fashion work at hand is enriched by it. I seem to function best when I'm working on several things at once. One design area gives to the other. A principle, a theme, a concept, can take other forms in other applications.

I'm a kind of solo person, and when I'm going well, I get deeply absorbed in my work, and am very happy about it. I almost feel larky. It's a simply marvelous sensation, and I'm wondering if creativity is in some way equated with sex. I think maybe it is because it's a real joy, like being with someone you love very much. I think one should never be satisfied with one's work for long. It's good to have that wonderful elated feeling for a moment, but really never know completion. The hunger for further reaches and new insights creatively seems very necessary to me. Sometimes just playing or ambling gives ideas.

For instance, sometimes I'll take everything out of the closets, throw them on the floor, try on certain things, maybe upside down or wrong things together, and all of a sudden a certain juxtaposition looks absolutely marvelous. And thus may start a whole trend of new designs. It's an accident; yet I wonder if the accident was meant to be. Free association, free experiment, it's all part of the play thing. That's why I love to spatter paint around, cut rashly into fabric, pile up shapes in clay, throw the body around about to some loud music. It's part of creative play. People-watching is part of play too. In my wanderings and travels I've seen ragged and poor people and suddenly, quite oddly, I was inspired. Somehow the attitude of the body, the tilt of the head, the way the rags hung on the body gave me an idea. I remember an urchin boy in Spain who wore his poverty with much elegance and looked wonderful to me. Yesterday I saw a young Indonesian girl with black braid down her back, wearing her native tight shirt and a sarong skirt. She was reed slim, with slender neck, and head held high. She was more inspiring to me and more innately "chic" than all the fashion models in our publications. Actually every time I take a trip to far lands I come back thinking how inelegant we all look with our buttons and bows and our own tribal costumes.

Is there a relationship between your productivity and your mood?

Certainly there is a relationship. If I'm physically uncomfortable, working in a small, cramped, disorderly space, I feel tired and become irritable. Productive thought is slowed down. Or if I feel the perfecting of an idea to its best potential is at the mercy of elements beyond my control, then frustration sets in and discouragement from further effort. Of course, the situation reversed can spark great productivity. Sometimes intense emotional happenings have had the effect of intensifying creative action. This seems to have been the case when strong personal relationships have hit snags. I find that I attempt to kind of protect myself in a rash of work. I still have a painting I did which always reminds me of my marital split. When my mother died, which was a terrible shock to me, I applied myself with great intensity to working, and also turned to studies of a spiritual nature. The period was, in retrospect, one of strong creativity, accomplishment, and growth. Perhaps the creative person uses problems in a constructive way. Maybe this is what life is all about.

I'm a moody person I think, soaring to heights of exhilaration beyond belief and sometimes sinking low for apparently little reason. Sometimes it may be the weather. I'm a sun girl, and oppressive weather downs me. I've tried to curb these tendencies over the years. Actually an antenna-out person by nature is sensitive to all sorts of things which produce moods. For me, if my body feels good, and my environment is attractive or interesting, I'm apt to be content and able to screen out the average disruptions of a day and thus produce well.

How does your work communicate your thoughts and feelings?

I often have a difficult time communicating my feelings and thoughts in the spoken word. With certain people in certain circumstances and mood I can be very vocal; then other times I shut up like a clam or say everything that I don't mean. I think this is a hangover from my shyness as a child. I've outgrown the shyness, but I can communicate best in my work and prefer my work, whether it's design, painting, or writing, to say whatever it is that needs to be said. And this is a thing I'm most grateful for. My work seems to have communicated widely, and I have letters from women, and sometimes men, from all over. I love it when women say they feel happy in my clothes, or when men say they react to them. Maybe what I feel about naturalness and simplicity and the pleasures of texture and color comes through. Good design should have a universal appeal beyond the call of fashion, and certainly relate to contemporary living. This emphasis on relation to patterns of living and role in life, perhaps I owe in some way to my early designing for motion pictures. I considered myself sort of a right-hand to the author and tried to bring the characters in a story alive visually. I loved the book *A Tree Grows In Brooklyn*. Character designing is much more difficult than designing for glamour. You really have to dig into what the characters are, what they think, and how they relate to their environment. I remember meeting the author later on, and she said that every character looked exactly as she imagined him. I felt then that I had done a good job.

My fashion work has been successful, I think, because it does relate to a today kind of life and does communicate with a certain kind of woman. It's not just an abstract thing. It's design for a particular role in contemporary society. Our lives are so different from any other period that I don't see any reason why we should ape the twenties or thirties, Edwardians, or any other era, which sometimes is a favorite formula of the fashion industry. It's a very commercial humbug kind of formula, and certainly not creative. For the activities of our modern lives in our contemporary cities, our ways of travel, clothes have to work, and they are only successful when they really work. For instance, when I design a costume, I don't design from the neck to the knee, I visualize the whole woman, her hair, her feet, how she stands, and what kind of chair she'd sit in, and so forth. I visualize her against a certain kind of background and activity. The design comes out much more valid.

You know, when you really get right down to it, we really don't need lots of clothing to protect ourselves from the elements. But I do think that clothes are an emotional and sexual stimulus. I think we dress to attract the opposite sex. If we were in a completely female society on an island somewhere, I don't believe we'd bother. We'd not bother to put on makeup or to comb our hair much, and I think the same is true of men. The early savages and we "civilized" savages today use adornment as communication. In my work I communicate by satisfying the urge for adornment as well as relating in a practical way to today's living patterns.

What have you gotten from your travels?

Travel is a great source of ideas and inspiration for me. I prefer places out of the usual fashionable round. I've never been to a Paris collection, although this is the usual trek for people in my kind of work. For me it's much more interesting and rewarding to try to touch various scenes of living. Those scenes which are found in fashionable meccas are much the same everywhere and with the same people. I prefer, if possible, to travel on some sort of mission, because then I have the advantage of exploring slightly below the surface. One interesting experience on this level was in India—a job for that government relating to the development of the hand-woven textile export market, under the wing of the Ford Foundation. When I first got there, I didn't think I could do the job. The impact was devastating! I saw my first leper with his sick hand stretched out for a coin, and I couldn't talk for the rest of the morning. This man had a beautiful face and marvelous eyes. I saw so much around me that I knew was beyond help that I didn't think I could do a job there. It was all so much. But the job was finished, the report was written, and, we're pleased to say, is bearing good fruit. In a way I'm still involved with the India "job." It was a great source of inspiration to me and a great source of learning from the Indian friends made. The whole Eastern part of the world has always been of much inspiration to me. Aside from people-watching, the arts and the philosophies have had a strong influence. The "layered" concept of modern dressing in such vogue now has become a generic term in the fashion industry, and grew from my first studies and interest in China.

The cross-fertilization of ancient ideas with modern concepts has often stimulated whole new directions in my thought. Not a buttons-and-bows girl, I'm more interested in projecting concepts of design that might have a long life with lots of possible variations. Russia has been an inspiration to me, especially for the deep-freeze kind of clothes I seem to have been successful with. Travels to all and every kind of community cannot help stimulating and inspiring. Much of it is indirect inspiration, simply by clearing the mind and focusing the eye on new vistas.

What are your ideas about formal training and education in designing?

I'm very interested in education and do give a good deal of time to young people who communicate with me. I have a feeling that our design schools are not doing a very good or inspirational job. This is no doubt partly due to the unavailability of stimulating teachers, but I think it's much more than that. For one thing there's too much stress on specialization. A designer, to be good in any specialty, must see that specialty in relation to the whole environment. A good designer is a comprehensive designer. His eyes and ears and heart must be opened to this great new changing and challenging world. He must be exposed to all kinds of generative thought on all kinds of subjects. He must see things in relationships. I don't see much individuality or true creative play in the recent student work I've viewed. And the lack of craftsmanship is absolutely appalling. Emphasis is so strong on commercial values and so little on the creative attitude that, in my opinion, our industry is in for a bad time. I think it's partly their fault. They've been tolerating junk to death. Students feel all they need to do to succeed is to make a loud noise, get a splash in print, and isn't that what fashion's all about?

At the school administration level too, I feel there is more stress on commercial values, fund raising, publicity, and sausage-factory thinking, than on that essential oil for the industry's wheels, creativity. Although I'm not at all sure creativity can be taught, at least a young mind can be stimulated by proper exposure, and perhaps some degree of creative excitement will find its own way out. I tell young people that this industry needs them very much and what a wonderful life a creative one can be. So many kids are only interested in the money, immediately. Maybe our schools have conditioned them to this. Actually if a young person is really serious about a designing life, I think a minimum of professional schooling, if any at all, is best and then get a job. Work like the dickens, observe everything, and go to night school to take courses in the arts, logic, or anything that is mind-enlarging. He'll find his place. It's a shame our industry doesn't allow the old apprentice system, it's the best way.

How is your background related to your work?

My background was the Pacific Coast. I'm sure the sea, the mountains, the flowers, the vineyards, and all the textures of nature are indelibly a part of my being. I remember seeing my first flowering fruit trees in a vast orchard when but a small child. I felt the same kind of ecstasy then, as I held a branch in my hand and I repeated the word "blossom" over and over, as I have now on occasion when a design or drawing has turned out well. I remember eating watermelon under a grape arbor, fascinated by the play of light through the leaves. And driving out to a field of brilliant orange poppies and purple lupin . . . my brother and I losing ourselves in picking armfuls. I'm sure the undulating Sierra Madres, the rugged California coastline, the contour of that earth are all strongly related to my work in some way. In my brother's case, he turned to geology and is now a geophysicist. The rocks, which always fascinated me, became colors and forms in fashion. The rocks which fascinated my brother became clues to probing the secrets of our earth. Oddly enough, some recent paintings done by my brother as a hobby show a decidedly sensitive talent as an artist too.

My mother was a really great dressmaker. I was her apprentice. She taught me everything by doing it. Actually she could do anything with her hands and much of this rubbed off on me. I remember her building a brick wall beautifully. I remember her upholstering a wild pink-striped chair, and most vividly I remember her miracle hands in a garden. I grew up with living color. Mother encouraged me in doing all the things I was interested in. At the age of sixteen when I was working in the theater, much of it at night, she'd drive me back and forth. She was the one who cleared the way for me to grow creatively. My father considered any of the arts impractical and urged me to take up typing, a thing I've never learned to do to this day!

My father with whom I did not feel at ease was a brilliant and erratic man. I now wish I had known him better and that he had been able to communicate to us better. He had a very inventive mind, always concocting something or another, often to the family's sad fortune. I remember, when I was a small child, that he drew a lot. I remember a large charcoal drawing of Christ that held me in wide-eyed awe. I wish it hadn't been lost. He also had a photographic studio. He loved the mechanics of cars and once had a garage. I remember him mostly with mechanic's overalls on. I still think the overall is one of the most functional designs in the world, and some very high fashion things of mine spring from it.

GEORGE NELSON

The offices of industrial designer George Nelson are in an old recon-
structed building not far from Manhattan's Gramercy Park. We inter-
viewed Mr. Nelson there on May 10, 1969.

   George Nelson was born and raised in Hartford, Connecticut, and
received his undergraduate training at Yale University, where he also
took his degree in architecture. After graduation, Nelson entered into
editorial work, eventually becoming editor of The Architectural Forum.
From there he moved into the field of industrial design to which he has
made many contributions. An early book, Tomorrow's House, *became*
the first of a series in which Mr. Nelson expressed his views on the role
of industrial design and creativity in the contemporary world.

INDUSTRIAL DESIGN

George Nelson

Mr. Nelson, we understand that you came into industrial design by way of architecture. If this is correct, can you tell us something about this movement from architecture to industrial design.

Well, it was more or less forced by circumstances. I was one of the children of the Depression, and after I finished college and architecture school, I spent a couple of years abroad at the American Academy in Rome. When I came back, I think it was 1934, and it was not a very good year for aspiring young architects to get a job; in fact, I think quite a few architects were still selling apples on the street corners. I got a job in the publishing business, more or less accidentally, which turned out to be very satisfying. It went on for eight or nine years, and I ended up as editor of *The Architectural Forum*, which is a professional magazine. I worked as an architect during that period, moonlighting, and at some point during those years, this would have been the middle-forties, I was asked to write a book about houses by a publishing firm, and I worked on this with a colleague on the magazine. In the course of writing the book, we found ourselves inventing a thing that got to be known as the Storagewall. *The Architectural Forum* was part of the Time-Life group of magazines, and I described this one day at lunch with one of the *Life* editors; he became very excited, and it was published in *Life*. This led to a request from the Herman Miller Furniture Co. to become their designer.

I worked again on a moonlighting basis on this furniture for a year and a half with a technically well-equipped employee, and when the furniture came out, it was such a resounding success that I was able to quit my editorial job and set up shop as an industrial designer. Since then one thing or another has come along, and while we do function as architects here, this activity has been more or less overshadowed by what one would call industrial design. I've come to the point where I see really very little significant difference between designing a building and designing anything else.

They are both modifications of the environment, and this is your interest?

Well, I wouldn't put it quite that way, but I think more significant is the fact that they are both problem-solving activities where the result is a three-dimensional object of some sort.

In our own discussion with you, we are interested in studying and trying to understand how ideas are born—how do you come upon something new? What does it grow out of and what are the factors involved in this process?

I think the factors must be pretty common to all people who do solve problems. I think that what is loosely called "creativity" is really a description of a problem-solving activity in one form or another and where ideas come from is, I believe, rather mysterious, but I will try by hindsight at least to recapitulate some of the processes. I would say one of the main triggers is irritation. You look at a situation and suddenly see it with fresh eyes. Then the status quo, whatever it is, becomes very annoying and some kind of pressure builds up more or less unconsciously, and apparently one works away at this problem with a view to getting rid of the irritation. At some point, if one is lucky, the thing explodes. Let me give you an example. You ask how I went from architecture to industrial design. I mentioned a book which led to an invention, which led to a publication, which led to an involvement in industrial design. Well, the invention, the Storagewall, was the result of acute frustration because in this book, which was called *Tomorrow's House,* my colleague and I were trying to describe what the house could be if the dwelling as a whole and all of its parts were intelligently studied in relation to the needs and desires of the occupants. We wrote the chapters which had to do with living rooms, bathrooms, bedrooms, kitchen, and so forth, but we found that the one chapter we couldn't cope with was storage. It was rather odd because as magazine editors, we had long since learned the tricks to enable you to spin 5,000 words out of nothing, but in the area of storage, we found ourselves absolutely stymied.

For instance, we knew that many surveys indicated that one of the pet peeves of housewives was not enough storage, but you could hardly make 5,000 words out of this. We also knew that the statement of these peeves was not of not enough storage, but not enough closets—and closets are only good for certain kinds of storage. So one of the things that we did at the outset was to reexamine what one meant by storage in the house, and we concurred that if you took closets as one category, these were fine for what they were usually used for, clothes and things like that. We also observed that free-standing dwellings also need a good deal of outdoor storage, lawnmowers, garden tools, and all that, and these didn't require closets obviously, but something else, such as woodsheds or something of this type. We were then led to the residue which had to do with the dimensions of books, records, golf clubs, movie projectors or whatever.

We noticed one thing about this type of storage was that it was ten to twelve inches deep as compared to a closet which has to be about two feet deep. But at the time we didn't make anything out of it. People need bookcases but what can you say about bookcases? When we found our-selves with a virtually completed book, with a rather pedestrian analysis of storage, I remember one day I recall quite vividly, I was sitting in my office feeling quite frustrated about my inability to get this job done and was staring at the partition. For no apparent reason, I began thinking, "How thick is this partition?" and started thinking "About five or six inches, what's inside of it?" and it occurred to me that there was nothing inside of it but air. And then suddenly, as always happens, I realized that if the partition were made about twelve inches thick, inside you would suddenly have at your disposal hundreds of running feet of storage, and yet if one had a twelve-inch partition, even in a small house, one would not notice the reduction of size of the adjoining rooms because it would be, say, only three inches. Well, this was the birth of the Storagewall—the notion of a double-sided container that would hold anything that a house might need to have stored which wouldn't be more then ten or twelve inches in thickness.

It was one of those instantaneous insights which is very often the way these problems get solved. The idea and solution had a strong influence on home planning. Within six months of publication of the Storagewall con-cept, architects began to modify their plans so that houses had thick walls in them which were marked as Storagewalls. I've been fiddling with this concept in one way or another ever since. This thing we're looking at in my office is one of the many, many variations on this theme.

I've found that irritation is a very strong ingredient, but it doesn't work in the way that frustration works in a little child. In other words, you can't get rid of it constructively until you know quite a bit about the whole situation. In other words, we could say that the second ingredient in the creative act is doing your homework in one way or another, and this I think is pretty commonly overlooked. There is some notion that some people are "idea" men and that this represents a mysterious talent like being able to paint a picture without numbers, or play the violin or whatever, but what is generally overlooked is that these people identified as creative people don't just walk around and have ideas. The ideas are a result of a considerable amount of delving into the problem which then takes me to the third observation, which is the one way not to have an idea is to *try* to have one. I once had a psychoanalyst friend who was very interested in the matter of creativity, and during one of his discussions, he very abruptly said, "Did you ever hear of anyone who got an erection by an act of will?" which is a marvelous analogy because it's a perfectly ridiculous notion. You need a context, you need a situation, you need a stimulus, and I think the same is true of ideas generally.

There is also a story I'm very fond of. It's a story about Pasteur who was greatly envied by his colleagues and friends after he discovered the tuberculosis bacillus. He was very often given evidence of the acute jealousy of people in his field or in related fields. My story has to do with a big reception at which Pasteur was the guest of honor. At this reception, one of his colleagues came up and said, "Isn't it extraordinary these days how many scientific achievements of our century are arrived at by accident?" Pasteur said, "Yes, it really is quite remarkable when you think about it, and furthermore, did you ever observe to whom the accidents happen?" Again I think that this is just another way of saying the same thing I've already said.

Well, we're especially interested in your comment about this feeling of irritation because we're interested in the whole area of feeling and emotion as it may have a bearing on your own creative experience. What, for example, is the role of your mood in relation with your ability to create and be productive in your own chosen area?

The closest I can come to it, thinking of the ideas I've had in my working life—I mean ideas that have had some meaning or value and it's surprising how few of them there have been—the mood I think is always one that I can illustrate by the analogy I might use which doesn't work too well anymore because most cars have automatic gearshifts. What comes to my mind is like slipping in the clutch. In other words, you disengage the motor and get into a mood of no thought, or sort of an empty, relaxed, or detached mood. What I think I'm saying really is that you turn off your conscious mind with all its buzzing and scurrying, and just coast. Then the subconscious does the work. We've all heard so many stories: A famous mathematician is worrying about a problem; he goes to sleep and then realizes, when he wakes up, that he has the solution. Well, this is apparently quite a common experience; or you have ideas while shaving, but what you're doing while shaving is sort of disengaging because you're concentrating on this semi-automatic act.

It is my experience anyway that unless you turn off the active conscious mind, this idea quite possibly won't arrive. Again there are ideas and ideas and ideas at different levels and of different types. One can also develop ideas apparently under different conditions, where there is great immediate pressure to get a solution. I think Sherlock Holmes is a superb example of this, although Holmes would use crocheting and violin-playing to disengage the machinery. He also performed a great many feats instantaneously, and one of the marvelous things about Sherlock Holmes which has impressed me for years was the brilliance of some of his methodology. I remember one of his rules which said, "If you're dealing with a problem and none of the possible solutions work, then the only solution that works has to be the impossible solution." Once or twice I have arrived at a solution because I realized that all the "possibles" had to be disregarded and that the only one that could be made workable was the impossible.

You spoke of the pressure of having to do something, of having to finish it. Could you tell us something about how you work? If there is usually a sense of urgency to get your creative process going?

Not really.

How do you work then, functioning in this creative sense?

Very often it's a routine meeting with clients or associates, and one gets into the habit if one enjoys thinking of sifting through situations that end very rapidly, almost like flipping through a card file and I wouldn't say that either the activity or results were at the highest level but they are on a level with the work. Sometimes you come on interesting solutions very, very rapidly, and then sometimes months go by before you are able to check out these things which appear so full-blown at the beginning. I could give you examples of this too. We've been working on a long piece of Atlantic beach which belongs to the U.S. Government. It is a national park, and one of the problems that comes up in the development of this beach is that the owners, The National Park Service, have been charged with keeping such real estate in a state as close to its original natural state as is humanly possible. Now you look at a beach which is considered a very desirable place in the middle of the summer and you find yourself looking at a very impossible contradiction; one the one hand, one would like as many people to use this beach as possible, in a sense this is what it's for, being public property; on the other hand, this strip of dunes from the ecologist's point of view, is a fantastically delicate mechanism, and great crowds of people could very easily destroy a dune. Just traffic on the beach will open the possibility of wind erosion, and it could lead to the whole configuration of the beach being changed for the worse.

The other problem which comes up is that if you get thousands of people on a strip of beach, these people need various services, such as dressing rooms, restaurants, snack bars, and all the rest of it. Well this too is a contradiction. How do you keep a place in its natural state if you cover it with buildings? This is the example that I wanted to give you because this happened at a session of perhaps forty-five minutes. We had seen some well-intentioned efforts to develop very humble, anonymous buildings that would blend, so to speak, with the landscape of sand and grass. And what we were acutely aware of was not that the architects had done a bad job, but that the problem was impossible. Everytime you put a building on this half-mile-wide strip, it was no longer this wonderful natural thing. So there was quite clearly no solution if you thought as an architect. So having come to the point where there was no solution from this point of view, you disengaged your mind and let the problem simmer, and as usual all sorts of seemingly irrelevant images come to mind and this is the most curious part of the thing. It's as if you have a kind of high-speed data retriever. The retriever *knew* what to look for whereas you didn't have any idea (consciously) of what to look for. This is the really miraculous part of the whole thing. Well, my data-retriever gave me a picture of a piece of land with houses on it and boats and a harbor in front of it which had nothing to do with this strip of beach. And I thought "What am I looking at" and then I thought, "It's very funny, if you put buildings on land, something happens, in other words it's all changed, and quite often for the worse, but if you put boats in front of land, nothing happens at all, the land remains pure and untouched, and the combination of the boat and land is always very, very pleasing." So there was the answer: put everything on barges or boats or rafts, and these not being part of the dune or beach stretch, do not violate this natural thing. It's a man-made thing that moved up and touched it temporarily, and this gave us our answer. Now we have to do five or six months of research work, and I will be very surprised if any other answer comes up to supplant this image which came up in a flash. But the curious thing is that the answer comes up at all with the images that are flashed.

Well, we're very much interested in your references to images, because we want to know something about the role of fantasy, of visual and other kinds of images, and even of your night dreams in your creative work. Can you tell us something about that?

I'm afraid I can't produce anything for you out of night dreams. For years and years now I suppose I've been dreaming the way everyone does but I can hardly recall the last time I woke up and remembered what I had been dreaming. But daydreaming like any other activity can very easily and quickly be stimulated. I remember spending a couple of extraordinarily interesting years with a psychoanalyst, and like all headshrinkers, dreams were part of the baggage he liked to go through. I can still remember saying "Well, I don't dream" and he said, "That's not possible, everybody dreams, but why don't you try to start remembering these dreams; you might even, if you have a bad one that keeps you awake for a minute, keep awake and write it down because you don't seem to remember it until morning." And I got terribly good at having dreams and remembering them and could almost produce large crops of dreams on command, so to speak. Then when the professional need for my dreams ended, they sort of vanished again, but one of the things that I have deliberately used is fantasy. When you disengage the clutch and let yourself drift and what comes out of this is a fantasy you can steer, the way you steer a drifting rowboat if you're asleep, and I put tremendous reliance on this and enjoy it very much and have learned over the years that it is productive.

In other words, it's impossible that it does not have to do with something you desire, something that you would want to make happen. I'm leaving out things like "I'd like to be as rich as Onassis." This kind of thing is another fantasy that has nothing to do with reality because your talents and those of Mr. Onassis are very far apart. I'm talking about fantasy, such as images like what an ideal city might be, where any dreaming you do has to do with both your knowledge and your feelings about how people might live or should live in cities, and you can construct in these fantasies mental images, or the fantasy will do it for you. I've learned that if you deal with a fantasy as productive input instead of something which makes you blush, because here you are daydreaming and not being efficient and all the rubbish that's so assiduously fostered by the educational and business establishments, you find that fantasy becomes a component in a whole process, because a fantasy can give you certain pictures which then connected to reality, can become a plan, and a plan can be intellectually worked out and it could be made to become a reality. However, it's a stepping-down process. I might have a fantasy about redesigning the state of Alabama. I've never had such a fantasy, but I can imagine one. You would know that while you were having this fantasy you were again dealing with something like the Onassis fortune. You're not going to do this, you can't find a client—if you did find a client he either wouldn't permit you to redesign Alabama or you wouldn't be able to, so you know that the grander your fantasy, the smaller a piece of this will become a plan; and similarly with a plan where "Alabama" shrinks to six city blocks in Montgomery, it might be only a building by the time you get to the reality. Nevertheless, the dreaming that you have been doing may become an immensely valuable guide, let's say, to a breakthrough in a building. So I have come to treasure this kind of dreaming, and I think I would be far more productive than I am, which is as a half-baked and unwilling administrator—if I could become a sort of useless type, spend half my time sitting on the beach; then I think I could be far more productive than I have been to date.

What about your visual images? Do you feel that most of your images are visual because of the kind of creative work you do?

Oh, yes, but that I think is a detail. In other words, I've been brainwashed by my professional training and by my own information, and I suppose that I tend to see things as pictures. I don't know how a mathematician sees things: he may see formulas, for instance, or he may have some abstract visions that could be described in terms of images. I don't know. I think it really doesn't matter except I suspect that just as T.V. is a more complete device than radio, that probably the picture is a fuller device than words. Again, I have a sort of semi-conviction here although in a court of law I would have great difficulty backing it up, that a picture is like the words plus the music or a movie plus the sound. It's probably a more complete grasp of whatever the situation is. Again I feel very strongly about images because our entire technological culture has been starved of this faculty. We are all taught to read and write and add and subtract, but we are not taught to see except in the sense that a seeing-eye dog sees. You can see a curb so you don't fall and trip in the path of traffic; you can see the difference between a red light and a green light; and you can see a Shell or Esso sign as you're driving along the highway. I would suspect this is about the limit of most people's seeing as a result of the curiously crippled educational process.

What about the role of error in your work? Have you ever found that some of your errors accidentally had a creative or productive outcome?

Nothing comes to mind at the moment, but yet what you're suggesting must be true. In other words, if you look at something and think, "What a fool I was," and this recognition of your own stupidity might very well open the floodgates and let a better solution come through. I think this might be true. I just can't happen to think of any experience that would be relevant, and yet it must have happened. Mostly I seem to keep coming back to this role of the observer who finds himself puzzled or annoyed by something which then sets the machinery into motion. That seems to be what goes on. I can give you another example. Out in the hall you probably saw this chain of globular lamps that hangs in the stairwell. Those lamps are called bubble lamps, and I invented those or designed them, conceived them would be a better word, about fifteen years ago. The way this happened was quite amusing. We were fixing up our office and I wanted to get a hanging light with more or less a spherical shape rather than just a lampshade, and at that time the only lamps that appealed to a modern designer were being made in Scandinavia. So we went to Bonnier's which is a Scandinavian import shop because they had a sale of hanging lamps and I went with an associate of mine who by a fortunate accident happened to be a good technician. We looked at these shop-worn lamps and the cheapest one was $110 and fifteen years ago that was a lot of money for a lamp—it isn't exactly cheap today either—and I was furious that they wanted so much money for these lamps and as I looked more closely I realized that all of these were made out of a silky material which had to be cut out painstakingly and hand-sewn on wire frames. The hand labor made the $110 more believable. Well, I refused to buy, and going out of the shop with my friend I said, "You know, this is just crazy. With all the miracles of modern technology, here are these people sitting in Denmark and

Sweden sewing silk that costs $200." Well, the word "technology" apparently triggered something because I had seen somewhere, published at some point in that past year, an account of battleships being mothballed, and I was sufficiently curious to read on and found out that the Navy has some sort of plastic you could actually spray so you could literally wrap up a battleship. So I said, "Do you suppose this stuff they use for mothballing battleships would make a lamp?"

At this point I would have normally been inclined to let this question go unanswered. In this case, my companion, as I said, was an ingenious man, and that afternoon he started his research on how you mothball battleships. We found out that there was a little company in New Jersey that had fifty gallon drums full of this plastic. We made up a frame in our shop and my associate took it over there. We sprayed it up, put a light bulb inside, and found that it was a fine, translucent material. So this led to the invention of the bubble lamp. We had a client at this time who was a pleasant, permissive sort of manufacturer who made clocks, and on one of his visits to New York we told him, "You're going into the lamp business." He said, "Am I?" and we showed him this crude mockup we had made and he thought it looked very pretty and said if we showed him how to make it, he'd make it. Well, this thing came out and was immediately copied by about twenty-five other companies—we'd been unable to get a patent for some reason—and presently within the electrical lighting industry, there emerged a category called Bubble Lamps. This all happened because a lamp I wanted was too expensive, the irritation factor, but the most exciting thing about the process to me is the way your subconscious mind reaches into the memory bank, and assembles this seemingly irrelevant piece of data. What's mothballing a battleship got to do with lamps? And yet, it turned out to be the one relevant memory that made the whole thing possible.

Well, in a sense, this has to do with what you call "doing your homework," doesn't it?

Yes, had I not read about mothballing battleships, the ideas would not have occurred. This, incidentally, is one of the most difficult problems one has in a design office. The young ones cannot be convinced that an idea isn't like an apple hanging on a tree you're walking by. (They think that originality is something that happens prior to your deciding to be original. If an idea happens, then you are a lucky fellow who happened to have an idea; this is a very lazy and incomplete view of the matter, but the schools seem to foster it.)

What else can I say about this fantasy thing? Well, I've become so attached to this fantasy-to plan-to action-to reality routine that I find when I'm in a spot where I can't punch my way out of a paper bag, that just setting off the fantasy in an appropriate area (like making a paper boat and putting it on a pond) can be very helpful. I think also, and maybe fantasy isn't the word to use, if you are in a situation and say "This is not ideal, why is it not ideal?" and also, "What do you think ideal would be?". That this kind of questioning leads you to what an idealized picture would be, and this might not be fantasy but it certainly isn't reality either; such as wouldn't it be great if New York were not the dirtiest city on the planet. Then, what would an ideal New York be, where the air smelled good and wasn't full of soot and poison, and so forth. And in a way you're fantasizing because it's a little difficult to see how this is going to happen in the immediate future—but this thought could very well take you to some fragmentary answer that has some value to yourself, a client, or a survivor. But these are really techniques for solving problems rather than the root of what it is you're trying to get at. I remember some years ago running into the painter Leger, on a nice day on Fifth Avenue, and I was walking up and he was walking down, and we stopped to pass the time of day. He was a very attractive and vital man. Leger is the man who painted the women who looked like steam boilers, at one phase of his career, and I asked what he was doing and how his work was going and he said, "I'm not working. I'm doing the most exciting thing and having the best time I've had in years. I'm spending all my time at the Museum of Natural History looking at slides of micro-organisms. You can't imagine how incredibly beautiful this stuff is." Well, it wasn't too long after that that Leger's style changed from sort of a mechanical one to what we might call an organic style. He was obviously going through some internal transformation and he was seeing the world in a slightly different way, and this involved his becoming infatuated with micro-organisms which are a higher order of design than steam boilers. It was curious because I remember the incident. In my office a few days before, a couple of us had been talking about the possible or probable shift of architecture from sticks and stones to things that would look much more like oil refiners—much more organic and less rigid and symmetrical shapes. Well, what I'm trying to say is that we in my office and Leger up at the Museum had both been struck by something happening in the environment which both of us would have been hard put to identify. You know, what got you to think that we were going from mechanical to a higher order of things? But this had happened in technology, it had begun to happen in architecture, and at that point it happened to one man at least in painting. Again this is the homework department—if your sensory apparatus is working then you will apparently unconsciously apprehend changes in the surrounding situation.

We wonder, Mr. Nelson, if you could tell us something about your own family background that may be relevant to the choice of architecture as your original profession and then your move to industrial design, which you formulate as being very closely related to architecture. What was your family background like?

My father was a druggist, more or less self-educated. I doubt if he went to school after the age of fourteen or fifteen. He put himself through the courses that made him a pharmacist, working at night. I remember two things about him. One was that he was always trying to make a fortune by inventing something or other which always had to do with situations a druggist would run into. He would observe, for example, that many of his customers had back trouble and that they would come to the store and buy various kinds of back supports. Irritated by the type of back supports they were buying, he invented a new one. Or at another point he became excited about the properties of iodine and he succeeded in making an ointment with iodine which I gather is very difficult and he attempted to make a business out of that. He also tried to write. He was quite unsuccessful in all of these ventures. I don't think anyone ever published anything he wrote and I know that none of his hoped-for businesses succeeded but he was a man with a restless and inquiring mind and with a tremendous faith in progress (this was typical of his generation), and an enormous respect, almost reverence, for what one would call culture.

My mother came from a family that seemed to be mostly doctors and her great ambition was to become a singer. She was an immensely frustrated woman. Her father, quite properly for those days, said, "I would see you dead before allowing you to go on the stage." So she took these frustrations out on the children and we were all forced to play for hours at the piano and things like that. Both parents certainly set up a value system which did a thorough conditioning job on me. My father was a businessman, but a very unwilling one—he was a very good druggist. The druggist in those days was a real link between the doctor and the patient, and my father knew how to put things together, and he understood his trade very well. This activity took the form of being a small businessman but this was really imposed by the surrounding conditions. My mother had these dreams of being on the stage at the Metropolitan or something, but this never came about. But there was nobody around who said "Go out and get rich," so I followed their instructions and never did.

But you evidently did follow the creative proclivities of your father and went well beyond.

Well, they paid for the schooling which made it possible to do that.

Did you grow up in New York?

No, Hartford. I was sent to Yale because it was the nearest school and it represented something great in my father's eyes. As it turned out, Yale was a good place to go.

Did you study architecture at Yale too?

Yes, I did. I'm trying to think of what happened at Yale—I don't know if this is relevant or not. The one course I remember is a two-year course in anthropology and sociology which had an enormous effect on me then, because what I discovered to my shock and amazement was that almost everything I took for granted was either a social invention or construction. For instance, God is an invention. I mean he might also be real; but if you trace the history of God even through the Old Testament he starts off as a yowling, nasty, vengeful chieftain, and ends up as a pretty civilized guy at the end of it. We were exposed to thousands of case histories. We lived out of Sumner's casebook and I remember particularly that thing about God and curiously enough it never made me anti, or irreligious, it just made me see God as one of the nicest creations of the human animal and always an appropriate, idealized picture of what man thought he might become.

This also led to this habit of questioning things; or if I'd gotten this from my family which I don't remember because they didn't strike me as questioning people—in any event I must have been prepared for the impact of this new brainwashing. Later I hit Erich Fromm's book, *Escape from Freedom,* which introduced me to a new world of insights and made me aware of ways of thinking which were new to me. As a result of this, I determined to meet Fromm. At that point, I didn't know what a psychoanalyst is. I was so intrigued by this meeting that I became one of his customers. I had a completely naive idea of what psychoanalysis was all about, but the net result of the two years with Fromm was like another college education. What this may or may not have done to my psyche, I am not sure, but he struck me then, and still does, as a marvelous human being with tremendous integrity. It was a very productive experience.

During the thirties I'd become very intrigued with the whole Marxist thing, the way anybody who was thinking at this point did, and I did an immense amount of reading. I spent five years reading all the literature I could lay my hands on, and became very knowledgeable about Communist doctrine, Russia, and so forth, and was pretty impressed by it until the war came along, when I realized that some of their key theories about Fascism weren't working. The psychological approach of Fromm seemed to deal with Fascism in a more realistic way. I went to see Fromm because at that point I was developing a possible new magazine for Time-Life, and when I read *Escape from Freedom,* I thought, here is a new journalistic tool of unbelievable power, and I rushed to Fromm to see if he would become a consultant to us, but instead I asked him if he would take me on because I was so captivated by his thinking. So the college sociology, the Marxist involvement which was an intellectual involvement, and the Fromm experience all added up to the main things that have gotten me to move in certain directions rather than others.

There was one other thing I recall, and then I think I'm through with the background question. When I was at Yale, and this would be like my sophomore year, I was very young, almost the class baby as I was barely seventeen. I remember being terribly concerned about what my career might be. It seemed you either went into papa's business, and his business wasn't interesting to me or you became a professional, which was strongly indicated by my whole family's orientation. Teaching had occurred to me as something I might do, and subsequent experiences as a teacher indicated that this might have worked out all right, but one day I found myself in the corridor of the art school, and the corridor was lined with drawings of a problem that had been worked out by student architects and I was absolutely swept away by this stuff. They all looked to me like Michelangelos. I'd never seen anything so beautiful, and I thought is it possible that I could aspire to such skill. What intrigued me about the architecture was that you could create it. If I were like these miracle kids, I could take a piece of paper, dream a marvelous dream, and I could draw it and paint it and there it would be. The fact that you might build it didn't occur to me at the time. So I went to see the dean who at that point was hard-pressed for customers, and he told me it really wasn't that hard to be an architect, and he gave me some simple advice, and I began doing finger exercises, starting to sketch. I had never been able to draw anything, and I discovered that with no visible talent in my freshman year at architecture I was the number one student as far as making sketches. Some of these things are really hard to define because I did this the way you do pushups; between classes, finger exercises, which went back to my playing the piano. It was a pleasant shock to find that this could be learned and wasn't an innate something. It was the fantasy quality that you could implement a dream, so I think the whole dream thing has been a pretty central thing in my existence.

May we ask you if there was one predominant influence at the Yale School of Architecture as you look back? Some figure, a professor, who in retrospect seems important?

Oh yes. There was a man named Otto [Fallion] who was a partner in the firm of James, Gamble, & Rogers which did many of the Yale quadrangles. This man built dreams of a vanished medieval world with such taste and conviction that in 1969 the work still looks good. He was a very mixed up and incomplete man but with tremendous vitality and quite clearly a man of fantastic talent, and we all worshipped him. He would come in drunk, and he did all those things that we as kids associated with a great free-living, free-loving person. He was a tremendous influence. At that moment there was a system in architecture called the Beaux arts system which was based on the Beaux arts school in Paris. The Beaux arts system by the 1920's and 30's had decayed to the point where it was a ridiculous joke and later when I went to Paris and worked for a summer for one of the students who was competing for The Prix de Rome, I realized that the French training had gotten to the point of sheer insanity.

The projects that were being done under the Beaux arts system were so utterly ridiculous, nothing could have gotten further from the realities of modern life than what the young architects were doing. And this system was followed by the leading schools in the U.S. where the students would work according to common programs issued by a central office in New York and these were all shipped in for judgment to this place and medals were awarded. The value of the procedure was that you knew what the kids in the other schools were doing because they published at the end of every project or month an illustrated booklet showing what project had gotten the highest award so that all the schools in the country were in competition all the time. This I believe is very healthy. I'm saying two things; the competitive aspect, that was good because you got to know who everybody was and also what they were doing so the student didn't feel alone. He was part of a large group and on this big totem pole he could place himself so it gave him some idea of where he stood. But the projects were absurd. For instance, I remember one sketch problem—a sketch problem is a thing that lasts two to ten days. The title of this problem was "A Residence for a Western Diplomat on the Outskirts of Peking," and you were supposed to design this residence for entertainment, guest quarters, servants, and it's got to be like a huge embassy. Well, what a bunch of nineteen-year-old kids from small towns in America with mostly middle-class parents knew about an ambassador's establishment on the outskirts of Peking—this was a little difficult to figure out. However, we would do the project and get rated, and so forth. Well, years later when the Herman Miller Furniture Co. came to me saying that they had seen the designs for the Storagewall and wanted me to become their furniture designer, it really didn't occur to me that I might be incapable of coping with this problem. I realized many years later that the reason it didn't occur to me that I might not be able to do this was because as kids we were doing it—we didn't know we couldn't do it! So at that point if someone had come to me and said, "Would you like to redesign Venezuela?" I would have said "I need a bit of information, but I'll do it!" And that marvelous inability to realize that here is a project you weren't equipped to cope with was one of the things that made it possible to switch from architecture, to publishing, to industrial designing without even realizing I was making a transition.

But there's really more to it than that. There's a basic versatility that you have that comes through as you talk.

All right, I have a little baggage that was inherited and acquired. But everyone processes differently. I processed my things my way and when I say I think I've been terribly lucky, all I'm saying is that I'm happy—with reservations, one always feels inadequate—but I'm quite happy with the way I've processed what was available because it seems to suit me very well. I love this business. I love the fact that you don't know from one day to another what you'll be doing next: 10,000 gas stations, a national park, a complete terminal, an art school curriculum, or a U.S. exhibition in the U.S.S.R. There was never a shortage of problems!

AARON COPLAND

The well-known American composer Aaron Copland lives in a remote section of Peekskill, New York. We interviewed him there on March 2, 1968, in his studio, an unadorned room dominated by a grand piano.

Since 1920, after studies in Paris with Nadia Boulanger, Aaron Copland has been composing in an American idiom and concert goers are familiar with his Billy the Kid *(1938),* Lincoln Portrait *(1942), and* Appalachian Spring *(1944), among many other pieces. He is responsible too for the film score of* The Red Pony *and* The Heiress.

For twenty-five years, beginning in 1940, Copland was the music director at the Berkshire Music Center at Tanglewood, Massachusetts, and there influenced several generations of composers from America and abroad. Preceding this, he taught for many years as a Harvard Spring lecturer in music, and served in a similar capacity at New York's New School for Social Research.

Recognition and honors, both for his compositions and his teaching, have been numerous: Pulitzer Prize in Music in 1944, honorary doctorates in music from Princeton, Brandeis, and Wesleyan Universities.

Aaron Copland

Could you discuss your thoughts about the birth of ideas?

It is very difficult to describe the creative experience in such a way that it would cover all cases. One of the essentials is the variety with which one approaches any kind of artistic creation. It doesn't start in any one particular way and it is not always easy to say what gets you going.

I've sometimes made an analogy with eating. Why do you eat? You're hungry. You are sort of in the mood to eat, and if you are in the mood to eat, the food tastes better; you're more interested in what you're eating. The whole experience is more "creative." It's the hunger that stimulates you to eat. It's the same thing in art; except that, in art, the hunger is the need for self-expression.

How does it come about that you feel hungry? You don't know, you just feel hungry. The juices are working, and suddenly you are aware of the fact that you want a piece of bread and butter. It's about the same in art. If you pass your life in creating works of art in one field or another, you recognize the "hunger" signs and you are quick to take advantage of them, if they're accompanied by ideas. Sometimes, you have the hunger and you don't have any ideas; there's no bread in the house. It's as simple as that.

Mr. Copland, how does your music reflect your ideas?

It's the character of the work that reflects my ideas and it's reflected later in the minds of the people who hear the work. It isn't as if, by listening to the music I have written that you can tell what sort of a person I am. One can't be that precise. You couldn't tell that I was born in Brooklyn, but you could tell that I was interested in writing music that was suggestive of the American landscape in some of my pieces. The kind of emotion that some of my music expresses would be a reflection of the kind of person I am, because I couldn't have written that kind of music unless I was that kind of person. The fact that I don't write other kinds of music means that I am not that other kind of person. So that, in an essential way, my music does describe me. But, I wouldn't want to be put on the spot and have to say exactly what my music means, and what I mean as a person. That would be the critic's task; someone who could stand outside myself and look at the work with a dispassionate eye and then sum me up. That kind of after-the-fact judgment goes on all the time in the arts.

What conditions have you found to be conducive to productivity?

If you were to set up the ideal situation, I'd have to be in my studio, where conditions are conducive to work and where I don't have any distractions. It's difficult to write music on the subway train; it can be done, but it's not usual. If I feel in the mood to write, something starts me off. I might feel sad. I might feel lonely. I might feel elated. I might have gotten a good letter from somebody. Something starts me off.

I happen to be a night worker. There are many composers who only work very early in the morning when they get up and their minds are clear and they feel fresh and rested, but by ten A.M. they are finished. William Schuman tells me that he is that sort of composer.

I myself have always worked at night. I don't know why. Once I read a statement made by Thomas Hardy, in which he said, "Seven/eighths of the intimate letters that are written are written after 10:00 in the evening." I connected that statement with writing music and working at night, because composing is a kind of intimate letter writing. You are expressing your inward feelings in musical terms. But, as I say, it doesn't have to work that way. Certain composers only like to write early in the morning.

Whenever you write, you see, nothing will happen unless the creative fantasy is alive. On the other hand, to be alive with creative fantasy suggests, to me, improvising at the piano. But, if you merely improvise, you might never find your improvisation again. And that's where coolness comes in. You watch yourself being fiery, or sad, or lonely; otherwise you won't be able to get it down on paper. Writers probably have this same problem of writing fast enough so that they can get it all down while they are under the spell. You have a fear that you may be going to lose it at any moment. You can't be sure how long it will go on. Outside interruption is definitely out. In music, you have to get it down on score paper. Otherwise, you might forget it. Since music exists in point of time, you're "travelling" all the time. And if you want to get the music down at any one point, and you are already ahead of yourself, you have to remember what you did previously. That means that you have to observe what you're doing; and then be able to remember it so that you can write it down. The time span of remembrance is a limited one. So, if you go on being fiery all the time, by the time you stop being fiery, you will have lost the whole thing.

It's very difficult to pinpoint what creativity is, but I think it's really not very different from having ideas. I mean, what starts you thinking? It's quite the same thing. Something happens. You get a letter and suddenly your mind starts to concern itself with something. The only difference is, that the resultant idea that you get on paper in this case, is not a specific thought; it's an emotional musical thought that you can't be specific about. With thoughts, you can more directly connect what you are thinking about with the emotion that started you off in the first place.

One of the troubles about writing about music, especially music, is that there is always a tendency to make it seem more specific than it really is; and so people always latch onto those things that are most easily explicable; but the part that isn't explicable, you never read about because there's no true way of talking about it. This tendency to try to make music's meaning more specific comes about because there are people who are less instinctively musical than others and seem to need that kind of explanation.

Everyone is supposed to like music, but people who are really musically gifted don't seem to have the need for having music's significance made specific. They can think about music and enthuse about it, and that's all that's necessary.

It's difficult to convey by words what you can so much better convey by your music. You limit and lessen the significance of the musical composition by trying to pin it down too specifically to just one meaning. In a general way, anyone can tell the difference between a lullaby and a march. You'd have to be pretty dumb not to be able to do that. The minute you start trying to get closer to the exact kind of lullaby it is, the trouble begins.

In music, it's more likely to be an emotion rather than a specific idea or thought that leads to a composition. It's comparable to a person who starts to sing to himself, though he is not even aware he's begun to sing. Then, if he suddenly begins to become aware that he's been singing something with a sad sound to it, he wonders what he's feeling so sad about.

That would be a good analogy on a very elementary level of what goes on in the mind of an experienced composer.

Music is a language of the emotions. You can practice it either on a very plain and elementary basis, or you can practice it on a highly complex one. But, it generally gives off some sort of generalized emotional feeling in the concert hall.

To continue about feelings, too much depression will not result in a work of art because a work of art is an affirmative gesture. To compose, you have to feel that you are accomplishing something. If you feel you are accomplishing something, you won't feel so depressed. You may feel depressed, but it can't be so depressing that you can't move. No, I would say that people create in moments when they are elated about expressing their depression!

And, you get rid of a lot of repressed anger when you work with the arts, obviously. Every time you strike a dissonant chord fortissimo, that's an expression. It makes overt whatever it is you have inside you. When you write it down, it represents that feeling exactly.

If a composer has had many years of experience writing music, he often gets commissioned to write works for specific purposes. In that case there are ways of inducing a feeling for composing; you don't have to be absolutely passive about the whole thing. You can force yourself to think, and then, suddenly, you find that you've forgotten that you began by forcing yourself.

Of course, you have to be a composer in the first place to have that method succeed. You can't start from nowhere. You start from your experience as a composer hoping that you can induce a creative mood so that it convinces the listener. You may have to force yourself, and then you may find you can't get a decent idea no matter how hard you try. Well, when that happens, you give up.

Musical composition works best when you are in the mood. You can coldly sit down and write anything, but the results will often not be satisfactory either to yourself or to the people who hear it. Nevertheless, it can be induced to a certain extent.

I can't tell in advance when I'm going to be in the mood to write. That always gives me a sense of not being sure. One just has the need from time to time. It isn't as regular as eating, though one wishes it were. You can't prognosticate. I've always worked in terms of germinal musical ideas, which may be fairly short, not more than a few phrases. If you have a really good germinal musical idea, and you can't go on with it that day, you are pretty sure, if you are a professional composer, that the day will come when you will go on with it because it stimulates other ideas. So that the keeping of notebooks with musical ideas is an important part of the stimulus.

Few composers ever sit down and just write a piece of music straight through. That would be very unusual. Every composer will show you pages and pages of sketches and ideas he rejected before he produced the finished manuscript.

One of the reasons why cultivated music is one of the glories of mankind, one of the real achievements of mankind, is that we are dealing in amorphous, highly abstract material without any specific thought content. Incidentally it's one of the mysteries of music that there have been no great women composers. There have been great women singers, pianists, violinists, who interpret marvelously well, but for some reason or other, no outstanding composers. People have made an analogy between the fact that there have been no great women mathematicians and no great women composers. Perhaps it's the inability to handle abstract material that defeats them.

One of the curious aspects of musical composition is the fact that you don't really know what you've written until you hear it performed. And you don't really know what the effect is until you sit in an audience and listen with them. Only then can you sense how they're feeling about it. Suddenly, something that seemed all right at home, seems too long or too short in Carnegie Hall. One of the advantages of being an experienced composer and having written many things and heard them under live conditions is the ability to judge how they will sound in live performance, without actually having to hear them performed. You get better and better at being able to foretell the qualities or shortcomings of your work.

Sometimes, a good interpreter may give you new ideas about your own piece. By taking a different tempo, or by bringing out some voice in the score that you hadn't thought of bringing out quite so importantly, they may suggest new insights. I mean to say it's all subject to the actual listening experience. The notes on the paper are pretty dead things until they come alive in actual performance.

Composers, unfortunately, have a serious problem with the present-day public. It's as if you're talking a language to them which they don't fully

understand, partly because they are not professional "understanders,"
they're not professional talkers of this language. Some of them are more
gifted listeners than others, but in general you get a cross-section of the
musical public that isn't too well informed. Therefore, there is some discouragement in writing in a language that you know in advance can't be
fully understood except by people who have bothered with the language
sufficiently to feel at home with it.

But the main thing is to be satisfied with your work yourself. It's
useless to have an audience happy if you are not happy. It's nice to be
confirmed, of course. If you think your work good and the audience agrees,
that's a lovely situation. If you think it's good and they don't, you think,
"I'll show them!" That's only normal.

Of course, it's supremely important to have sufficient technical background. I mean, what's the good of having all these emotions if you don't
have the technique with which to express yourself adequately. Especially in
music. Music is a highly civilized and rather late-development art. It has
more built-in technical needs. You have to know how to handle your
harmony, counterpoint, form, orchestration. There are all kinds of things,
subtle things, that have to be learned.

Could you tell us about your family background?

My own background is a little unusual in that there was no particular
connection with music in our house. Usually composers come from musical
families. My brother and sister did play a little violin and a little piano,
but the idea of becoming a composer was entirely my own. Nobody ever
talked me into it, and no one ever had to urge me to practice the piano.

I have sketches of compositions I wrote when I was fifteen. I began
begging my mother to get me a piano teacher when I was about thirteen.
My older sister had given me a few lessons before that time. Then she said,
"I can't teach you anymore; you have to get a regular teacher." And the
family didn't want to spend any more money on a regular teacher because
they had given lessons to the older kids and without too much result. So,
they didn't want to waste any more money; but I kept nagging them until
finally they said, "If you want to get a teacher, go out and get one and we
will pay for the lessons." That's the way it happened.

There wasn't anything precocious about my piano playing. I cannot
exactly tell you why, or at what point I thought I wanted to be a composer.
Suddenly, one day, I realized I wanted to be a composer. But, I cannot any
longer remember the steps that might have gotten me that far. It was a

very unusual decision to come to. It was as if I secretly thought, "I want to make competition with Beethoven and Brahms." It amounted to that, which for a kid growing up in Brooklyn seemed like a wild idea. It had no relation to reality. After all, Beethoven and Brahms were the big shots of music!

I suppose "competition" is a rather crude way of putting it. In art, you don't compete with anybody because, after all, if you do something good, nobody but you could have done that kind of good. You can only write your own kind of music. If you don't write it, nobody else will, so you're not competing in any real sense. It's just that master musicians set standards of excellence and you feel challenged by those standards. If you can't do that well, then it's not going to be good enough to last and to sustain interest over the years.

My entry into music was instinctive. I wasn't choosing anything, I was chosen. I didn't have the choice of shall I be a mathematician, or an instrumentalist, or a teacher? That never occurred to me. It was just a natural move toward musical composition, without knowing why. Other composers had done something good in many different countries, and I wanted to do the same for America, in our terms. Especially because it could not be done by anyone else but us, here and now. You see, that's a very important factor.

We are not taking the place of anybody else when we write our music, we are adding to the combined contributions of mankind. And nobody else can do it for us but those of us now living in our time. They are the only ones who can express the spirit of what it means to be alive today.

That's what makes the creation of art seem important. You're not just expressing your own individuality. You, as a person, are an exemplar; you are one of the people living now who can put this thing down. In another twenty years, it will be different; you couldn't put it down in the same terms anymore. Because the American experience will be different in twenty years. The world experience will be different, so the need becomes very pressing. You have a sense of urgency, of being occupied with something essential and unique. To leave our mark of the present on the future—what could be more natural?

In the field of art, each country tends to produce a kind of art which somehow reflects national characteristics, and in the field of serious music, when I was a student, it was also clear that we hadn't achieved that yet in this country. From that came the desire to do something about it. It seemed a serious lack that we didn't have our own recognizably American music. Also, after all, I'm a first generation American. My father and mother were both born in Europe, in Lithuania. My mother was brought here as a child and didn't remember anything about the old country. She grew up in Texas, and I had a lot of relations who used to visit us and talked with a Texas drawl. My father was fifteen when he left the old country and spoke with an accent, but was a great American patriot nonetheless. America had made him, and he was very grateful, and the old country was nothing to him by comparison to the future in America. That permeated the atmosphere at home. I would think the two things went together; the need to create a serious American music, and this kind of atmosphere around the house that America was worth getting down into notes.

The arts in general, I think, help to give significance to life. That's one of their very basic and important functions. The arts soften man's mortality and make more acceptable the whole life experience. It isn't that you think your music will last forever, because nobody knows what's going to last forever. But, you do know, in the history of the arts, that there have been certain works which have symbolized whole periods and the deepest feelings of mankind, and it's that aspect of artistic creation which draws one on always, and makes it seem so very significant. I don't think about this when I write my music, of course, but I think about it after the fact, and believe it to be the moving force behind the need to be creative in the arts.

RAPHAEL SOYER

We interviewed Raphael Soyer in his apartment near New York City's Central Park in September, 1969. Here Mr. Soyer lives amid a splendid art collection including work by some of the world's finest and best-known artists.

Raphael Soyer was born in Russia in 1899 and has lived in the United States for many years. Together with his twin brother Moses, who is also a painter, he has achieved an important position in American painting.

His formal training was obtained at the National Academy of Design and at the Art Students League, where he studied with Guy Pene du Bois. Among other organizations, he is a member of the National Institute of Arts and Letters. For a number of years he has taught painting at New York's New School for Social Research.

Mr. Soyer is the author of A Painter's Pilgrimage, *and is at work on another. His works are exhibited in many of the leading galleries of the United States, and he is well known for a mural painted for the Kingsessing Postal Station in Philadelphia.*

Among his awards for painting are the Temple Gold Medal (1943), the Gold Medal of the National Academy of Design (1957), and the Gold Medal of the National Institute of Arts and Letters (1957).

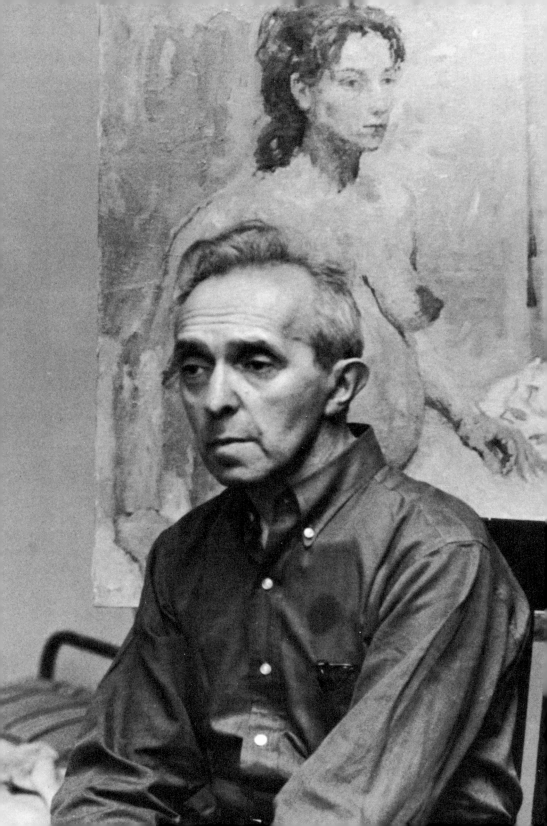

PAINTING

Raphael Soyer

Mr. Soyer, can you tell us where the ideas for your paintings come from?

From life, from what I see around me. I have also been influenced by the works of artists whom I admire, but mostly my ideas arise from what I see with my eyes. It may be men, women, or children in the street or indoors. Actually, my works are portraits of people within their habitat, within the context of their lives. I go out a lot and look. I like to look. I work on street scenes or landscapes outside, but I don't paint people outside. When I was young, I would draw out of doors, but now I bring the world into my studio. I observe. At times, I get people to actually pose for me with the gestures and movements that I have observed. But I would never stop anybody in the street and ask him or her to pose for me.

Once I picked up an unemployed man in the street. He became quite a responsible and dedicated model. He posed for me until he died, for many paintings. But that was a very long time ago. I paint landscapes too. But they are not so well-known as the pictures of people are. I painted landscapes, street scenes in New York, and landscapes in Massachusetts and Maine.

When you walk down the street, what is it that catches your eye, that becomes the basis of a painting?

Just the people. The picturesqueness of people. To me, it's a more interesting thing to go to 8th Street or Washington Square than to go to the theater. It interests me much more. I say to my wife, "Let's go to the theater." I mean Washington Square. And there, I observe. I look at people. For instance, there's one painting here, I did after we were in Central Park one Easter morning. We saw a lot of music-making young people, and some of these kids holding flowers. What I saw brought to mind paintings by a French painter, Watteau, Antoine Watteau, who painted musicians in parks. And I painted a composition which was influenced by a well-known painting of Watteau's in the Louvre, where a single figure stands on a hill, on a little hill and below are actors. They didn't happen to be musicians at that time. But this is what happened. I saw these young people in the park. I actually saw this event, and it brought to my mind the painting of Watteau. And I went to my studio and I painted this picture. And, of course, the people who posed for it were not the people whom I saw in the park. But I kind of re-created the event in my studio.

I called this painting *à Watteau* and I painted in a glass with a rose and I wrote "à Watteau."

When you look and see, you're using a particular kind of spectacle. You're using different spectacles from those that other people use. You see it through your own experience.

Through myself. My work shows that. I can't exactly explain it because it's automatic. It's self-revealing. I mean, I'm revealed in my paintings. And this is something that is very difficult to explain. I don't do it deliberately, but all my paintings have a certain character. It's possible to recognize a painting of mine because there is a revealment of myself in it. But I'm not doing it deliberately. And this part, this element is impossible to explain. It's automatic. It's like one walks, one talks, or like one's gestures.

I don't think my paintings ever come out the way I hope they would come out. I have some idea in my mind, but the result is always very different from what I really had in my mind. It never really comes out the way I imagined. For instance, now I am thinking of a large composition, and I'm making many studies, but I'm sure the painting will not be like the one I have in my mind.

Suppose you would ask, let's say, El Greco, the very same question. It would be impossible for him to answer. He just did his work. But he did it in a very, very personal manner. And it's automatic on his part, not deliberate. He was a great personality, and, therefore, his work is different from the work of other people. I just want to say that I'm not always satisfied with my self-revealment. I would want to be something else from what I am. In other words, I would like to be more objective in my work, more aloof in my work. But my work shows no aloofness and no objectivity. I admire, say, the work of Velazquez and Degas because their work was less self-revealing. They had a certain aloof quality. Of course, they did reveal themselves in their work, but their sympathies or their likes were not as evident in their work as mine are in my work. For instance, people always talk about the sympathy that I show for people. Well, I think maybe that's a weakness in my work. I prefer works which are more objective, more impersonal. I like the work, say, of Vermeer. It has a kind of an abstract quality. You don't know what the author, what the artist felt about the people whom he portrayed, whom he painted. They're very beautiful and very aloof, very abstract in a sense. You know, each one would like to be something that he is not. I would like my work to have a certain coldness, a certain abstraction, a certain aloofness, which I admire. I like those elements in a work of art. I think it connotes strength, a kind of ability to see things from all angles.

I think that Cézanne had this quality, too, this aloofness, this grandness without showing too much sentiment, too much emotion. And I like that kind of work. My work is not of that type. This conflict in me may be possibly explained by the fact that I am a product of more than one culture: Russian, Jewish, and American. As a child before I came to this country, I was already deeply acquainted with the warm emotion of Chekhov, Sholem Aleichem, and so forth. I knew the work of Russian painters. I grew up in this country and of course imbibed its culture. I am a great admirer of Thomas Eakins' integrity and objectivity.

What do you feel is the effect of different moods on your work?

I know that when I am depressed it's hard for me to work. What depresses me today are very simple matters. My wife gets a cold, or my daughter gets sick, or something like that. Those things depress me. And then, it's hard for me to concentrate and to work. But these are not serious matters. I mean, I have not really the kind of depressions that you have in mind, but I work halfheartedly, and my mind is occupied with these particular things. It's as simple as that. When I was young, I had terrible depressions. Sometimes for weeks and weeks it was hard for me to work. Then I would rather daydream. Then I would have moments of work, periods of work. But I don't remember ever having to wait for moments of inspiration nor do I remember that I ever stopped working completely because of depression. I see the world, the visible world through my eyes, through myself.

Do you find that there are times that you're, perhaps, more productive than at other times?

No. I'm very systematic and very disciplined and I go to work every day, in the morning, and I come home in the late afternoon, but every day. I paint most of the time, or if I do other things, they pertain to painting. I make drawings. I may clean the palette, I may wash the brushes. But, I mean, it's all within a day's work. It's in my studio. And I haven't any tremendous surges of inspiration or the opposite.

Well, of course, when you're young, you have more ups and downs. You're not settled. And I think that when you're young you daydream more than when you're old. You know, young people daydream a lot. They waste a lot of time, and they have surges of feelings. Sometimes they work and sometimes they do not. I remember I wasted a lot of time just by dreaming of what I was going to be and what I was going to do, rather than working, when I was young. But that is natural with young people. You also have some kind of grandiose ideas when you're young and you're more apt to become very much depressed when you're young, or very much elated when you're young. But, when you're older, as in my case now, I have a definite pattern of how to work and how to spend my hours in my studio.

I hope I still have some grandiose ideas. I mean, the desire to do important paintings. I still have that. I think I paint bigger compositions than I used to, more elaborate. You know, with time you become very deft. After painting many years you become skillful. And that's not always an advantage. And, therefore, you have to get some ideas which you have to grapple with which are more difficult to do, and not just a simple portrait.

So I do more elaborate compositions now that are difficult for me even today, in spite of the fact that I have learned how to paint. And that is because I still have so-called big ideas, but in a different sense. It may though be some kind of flamboyance that is characteristic of older painters. When I was young, I had those Walter Mitty fantasies of becoming a great artist. I mean, they're the kind of ideas that young people have in their lives. The fact was that I was very much the opposite of greatness in those days. I didn't have any confidence at all. But I would daydream. There was a basis for my dreams of becoming an artist. I come from a family that was interested in art, fine arts, literature, and poetry. My father was a Hebrew scholar and also a writer in Hebrew. He wrote short stories and stories for children. He left two volumes of Hebrew called *The Passing Generation* about the life of his time. And he wrote in the style of the Russian classicists like Chekhov or Maxim Gorky. He tried to emulate their kind of writing. He also loved art and he imbued us with love for art.

So we dreamt of being eminent personalities as children. We dreamt of being Michelangelos and Raphaels in those early days, without even having been acquainted with the work of those people. But we knew their names, because they were names that our father talked to us about, or mentioned to us. There was always this kind of striving to become artists, writers, within the whole family. Though my father was a writer, he could draw. And he actually would draw for us when we were children. He even taught us how to draw. He was our first teacher, not in a very serious way. But he would draw and we would copy his drawings. He would correct our drawings. Then he would exhibit them as our drawings. My family consisted of four brothers and two sisters. Now we are four brothers and one sister, one of my sisters having died.

My youngest brother is a teacher. He teaches homebound children, children who don't go to school because of ailments, and he goes to their homes and teaches them, but as a child he wanted to be an artist as well. My younger sister is a teacher, and my sister who died was a teacher all her life. She became very much interested in remedial reading. And she organized a clinic in Brooklyn. Unfortunately she began to do it so late in her life; even so she made a name for herself.

I think that we all in my family influenced one another. There's a family likeness about our work. And like brothers there was a great deal of sibling rivalry and competition and each one tried to be better than the other.

My brother Moses and I are twins. We are the two oldest. Then, Isaac is about four and a half years younger, and all three of us are painters. And, of course, we influenced one another. The entire family kind of influenced one another. But, you see, everybody in our family is either in art, or in education. My mother, as well, was involved in art. She would embroider whenever she had time. My father would make drawings on towels or tablecloths and she would embroider them. The color schemes were her own.

You see my father influenced all of us. His interest in art affected all of us and his interest in scholarship and education influenced my youngest brother and my two sisters, all of whom have been involved in teaching. Actually, my father was a teacher by profession and he was one of the first professors of Hebrew literature at the Yeshiva College when it was organized.

What about the effect of current trends in art on your work? Do you feel pressured by them?

No. I wouldn't let that pressure me at all. I am a representational artist by choice. I was never influenced by that kind of work. It simply wouldn't be enough of a challenge for me. I think it's too easy, too decorative. And all the profundity that's supposed to exist there really does not exist. It's a lot of speculation, a lot of talk about it rather than the intrinsic value of the painting itself. Those pictures have to be bolstered up by all this talk, by all these apologies and so on, otherwise they would flop on their faces. I am accepted and I do what I want. I do "my thing" so to speak and there is no need to compete. I compete only with myself.

Do you find that accident plays a role in your painting?

Yes. Once in a while something interesting happens, and I try to preserve it. And when in the process of painting and repainting this is lost, I regret it. You know, there are certain accidents. But, again, I wouldn't make such a to-do about it as some of the nonrepresentational painters are doing. They claim the importance of accident. Every brush stroke is, in a sense, some kind of an accident, because it's impossible to duplicate it. It has a certain tension, a certain nervousness. I painted, once, a large painting of many artists. And for that big painting I made studies from life and then I copied them onto the large canvas. And for the life of me I could not duplicate these studies. I could not get the immediate quality of the original brush stroke. They were too much of the moment, how I felt at the moment when I painted the people, from life.

What about your technical background?

I went to art school here. I went to the National Academy, Cooper Union, Art Students League, but I only attended these schools for short periods of time. I really learned by myself. I spent a lot of time in museums and I still spend a lot of time in them.

Could you tell us something about what you consider to be the major professional influences on your work?

I consider Degas a great influence, I'm passionately in love with the work of Degas and, of course, Rembrandt and Thomas Eakins. Actually, I learned a great deal from them.

SIDNEY HOOK

We interviewed Sidney Hook in his apartment not too far from New York University's Washington Square Center where he has taught philosophy since 1927. Sidney Hook was born in New York City in 1902, and received his education in the New York City public schools, the City College of New York, and at Columbia University, where he did his doctoral work under John Dewey. For years he has divided his time between homes in New York City and Vermont, interspersed with much traveling and lecturing.

Long known and valued as a teacher of consummate skill, Hook was one of the first to receive New York University's coveted designation of Great Teacher. A Guggenheim Fellow in 1928–29, and also in 1955, he spent 1961–62 as a Fellow at the Center for Advanced Study in the Behavioral Sciences.

Some years ago he was elected a Fellow of the American Academy of Arts and Sciences, and for years he has been active in professional philosophy organizations. As head of the All-University Department of Philosophy at New York University for many years, Hook has had a deep and continuing influence on several generations of scholars, both in philosophy proper and in related fields. The large scope of this influence is amply reflected in a series of symposiums of the New York University Institute of Philosophy which he has organized and directed, and which has produced an important group of publications under his editorship on continuing concerns in modern American philosophy and science.

Among his extensive list of publications are Education for Modern Man *(1946),* Heresy, Yes—Conspiracy, No *(1953),* Quest for Being *(1961), and* The Paradoxes of Freedom *(1962).*

PHILOSOPHY

Sidney Hook

I try to develop my own ideas with an accent, I suppose, on their creative aspect. I dislike to repeat or to say the obvious. Normally we think of music, literature, and the fine arts as creative, not philosophy. In philosophy vision by itself is at a discount in the sense that anybody can see visions. The important thing philosophically is the articulation of arguments and the development of a position. The result is that a good deal of philosophy consists of critical analysis rather than of a projection of original ideas. In fact, most philosophers would be suspicious if one were very original in this field. The assumption is that truths are established in other fields. The philosopher tries to clarify, evaluate, or find good grounds for what people already believe or think they believe. So subjectively I hardly think of myself as a creative person when I am engaged in philosophical analysis.

When I get an idea, I trace its ramifications; sometimes these are clear to me, sometimes they're not. I work very rapidly, I never agonize over anything I do. I think this is unfortunate for, if I took more pains, if I were more conscientious, I suspect my ideas would be more profound. But I am too impatient to test that.

I don't type when I write, I use a pen or pencil and the gravity of my thoughts seems to me to be in correlation with the pressure I put on my pen. When I type something, I always feel it's superficial because it seems to come off the top of my mind. I haven't outgrown the motor habits I acquired as a child. I don't know how it is in other fields. Some of my colleagues write very slowly and painfully. The only two people I know who composed more rapidly than I are John Dewey and Bertrand Russell. Dewey would rewrite from scratch rather that revise, often making as many as five or six copies of a draft. Russell would actually, after he thought about a position, write it out the first go. I always write out what I want to say and then prepare in better handwriting a draft for the typist, hardly making any changes. This arose because, I suppose, I always write in haste; I never seem to have leisure. Well, to be truthful, even if I did have leisure, I would write the same way. I think I'm too impatient to go over my material again. This impatience is characteristic of other things I do. I play chess, and always try to storm the opposition. I hate to dawdle and think things out. I'm no good with tools because you need to be very patient and if I don't get something fixed right away, I abandon the task. Normally, I suspect, I'm a very superficial person for this reason. If I didn't make comparisons with those who take years to excogitate, I might reach that depressing conclusion. Superficiality must be a matter of degree.

Have you discovered, because of the way you work, what you call superficial, that the results of your work are more superficial?

No, but if I didn't have other people's work to compare, I would assume that the less time one takes to write, the less profound one is, the easier the labor of creation, the more superficial. Actually I've known people who've suffered such pangs of creation and for so long that I myself would never have endured it; that is to say, the results would hardly be worth the agony involved.

Could we refer to something which was said before about when you get an idea—do you have any thoughts about the birth of an idea? Though you describe yourself as not being creative, but critical, still you refer to new ideas.

Well, that's interesting, I've never thought about that aspect of it. Ideas pop into my mind all the time. I find that when something is being discussed, all kinds of suggestions come to my mind. People are sometimes astonished and enthusiastic about what they call the fertility of my mind, but I don't regard that as much. Ideas just keep popping into my head. But many of these ideas will have no breadth or no depth. When I begin to think about, say, the student problem, I might suddenly ask, "Why has it become more acute?" Just the other day I was on a panel with Lewis Feuer who has just published his excellent, *The Conflict of Generations,* and I was presenting and praising him to the audience. As I spoke, suddenly it dawned on me that there was something radically wrong with his thesis. I don't know now whether to characterize my insight as critical or creative, but as I talked to the audience about the importance of it and illuminated something of his hypothesis, I was struck by the thought that the great difficulty the thesis faces is that it doesn't seem to explain why the present generation should be so alienated from its past. The conflict of generations was somewhat more acute in my time, fifty to sixty years ago.

My father came from a different culture. I was doing things he didn't know about, and what he did know he didn't approve of, especially my political activities. Some of his generation didn't care very much whether their children went to school or not. But, today, as I observe the experiences of my friends who have young children or grandchildren (I'm at the grandfather stage myself), I find that the conflict is not so acute. Today parents are much more aware of the lives of their children, they live the lives of their children, they are a hovering, sometimes an oppressive presence to their children by virtue of the very intensity of their concern. Perhaps they are too much aware, perhaps they empathize too much with their children. They tend to forgive them in advance for actions of which they don't approve. Consequently, I concluded that here was a difficulty for Professor Feuer that he would have to resolve. You see, I was thinking aloud, and I believe I convinced Professor Feuer, who is an enormously able thinker and scholar, that this was a phenomenon he hadn't taken adequately into account. Now what made me do that? Where did I get the idea? You know, I've had the odd experience often of not being aware of having a fresh idea or even any idea until I begin to talk. Even more often I find that I have to sit down to write in order to have my ideas flow. If I simply think without writing, I get an idea and mull over it, but I don't develop it sequentially or consecutively. When I sit down to write, the writing seems to open, what should I say, the sluices of my mind. I find it much easier to develop ideas, fresh ideas, writing than I do when speaking. When I speak, I can elaborate an idea at length or in depth, but the ideas don't give birth to each other even when they follow each other. But when I write, there is more of a ladder to my thoughts; they seem to follow *from* each other and not merely *after* each other. I also am aware of ideas crowding in when I write. I must fend them off while I develop the one I am writing down. Sometimes it is very difficult to stay on the track. I don't understand why that should be, maybe it's a matter of habit.

Well, we know we're the same way. We think you're getting feedback in your writing that you don't get in an auditory way.

I think it has something to do with the internal motor activity of the organism. It may even be rooted in the physiological activities which seem to stimulate the cortex. When I sit quietly and reflect, I get ideas and pursue them sub-vocally, but there is no explicit motor action as there is in writing and in speaking. It may be that the explicit motor actions stimulate adjacent areas of the brain so that one thing suggests another. I find, too, that when I talk before a class or audience, many things come to me and they crowd hard on each other. If I don't remember them, I lose them. I find that the only time I'm inarticulate, once I start talking, is when two ideas are fighting for expression at the same time. I have to wait a stuttering moment or so in order to determine which idea will out.

We're surprised to hear you say that because, as we recall, at the time you struck us both as being a master with the ability to take two sides of an issue and to argue on either side of the issue and make the argument sound completely logical.

That's something else, that's pedagogical technique. When I do that, and I think all teachers should do it, I play the devil's advocate. When I'm teaching a class whose students have obviously inherited their political or religious prejudices, I always challenge them. When I'm teaching a class these days which has inherited its religious disbelief or its ritualistic liberalism, I present the other point of view as plausibly as I can to challenge their dogmatism and smugness. What I was speaking of before was rather different. It was not in the pedagogic context where I know in advance pretty much what I'm going to say, presenting arguments for or against the existence of God or interpretations of mind as substantial rather than functional and so on. I was referring to occasions and fields where I hadn't developed my positions previously; for example, when I am engaged in a spontaneous debate or when I'm called on to make an extended comment. It is then that I find ideas seeming to rush at me from various directions at once. I try to order them as I speak, and I usually manage to, so I give the impression of having a well-ordered mind. But very often after I have made my points, I try to recall the ideas that had cropped up previously, but which I didn't identify. Say there are several different ideas, one, two, or three. When I am through with three, I have forgotten the fourth, even though I know there is a fourth because it struck me as I was talking about one and two. That's what I mean. That must be due to some physiological process. I tend to explain such phenomena in terms of brain physiology but I don't know enough about brain physiology. I'm kind of speculative there.

In view of what you said about the importance of motor activity in your thinking, how about the other side of the coin? Have ideas presented themselves to you while sleeping, in the form of fantasies, dreams, daydreams?

Sometimes. Sometimes striking expressions and phrases come to me in dreams. Occasionally I've used such phrases upon awakening. At a very early age I became aware of the fact that often in dreams I would speak effectively and sometimes strikingly. I recall that when I was fourteen or fifteen, I once said to my mother when I awoke, "Wake Selma (who was my sister) up, I have so many brilliant things to tell her." I wanted her to take it down in shorthand before I forgot. My dreams are very orderly: they have a beginning, a middle, and an end. When I've had dreams about others and told them, they're always surprised at how well ordered my dreams are. Maybe I don't remember the others, the disorderly and the disjointed ones. I've had fantasies and nightmares, of course, but these seem harder to recall. They have no point.

Do you ever recall using the material that has come up in a fantasy or dream?

No. Only an expression or two. Sometimes when I awake, a point will come to me, say, an obvious contradiction in a position I had been thinking about. But I didn't dream about it. I find, however, that if I don't write it down I forget it. One of the great mistakes of my life has been my reliance on my memory. How many hours I spent with Dewey and Russell as they talked about the most intimate things in their lives which I thought I'd remember forever, but when I try to recall years later, they're gone, all faded out. What I recall, I recall accurately, but many things I don't recall; that is to say, I have a sense of knowing more, having heard more than I can now recall. Sometimes something comes back. That's another interesting thing. The things that will suggest ideas to me! I can read something and get an idea while reading quite different from what has been

written, quite different from what's been expressed; sometimes it is a re-
statement or an implication, partly, I think, attributable to the stimulus
from what I read.

When I express it, it sounds quite different from what I read, and it
seems quite new. But I've always had an unconscious or uneasy sense of a
feeling of guilt, perhaps not so unconscious, that I'm plagiarizing, or that I
owe this man whose work I am reading an acknowledgment, since the idea
has come to me as a result of reading him. Sometimes I think I know what
he is trying to say even when he hasn't said it or that I can say better what
he has said or implied. I have ambiguous feelings about this which go
back to my childhood. I don't know why. I somehow got the feeling when I
was young that if you looked a word up in a dictionary, you were cheating.
I never owned a dictionary. I always thought the best and *honest* way to
get the meaning of a word was from its context. In high school, I was
astonished to find that my rival in one of these classes in which we wrote
competitive compositions admitted that he had a book of synonyms and
consulted it. "That's cheating," I exclaimed with considerable heat. Well,
you see, I was a great reader when I was young and did amass a remarkable vocabulary. Even though I couldn't define a word, almost always I
could use it properly. I read Dickens, Thackeray, Hardy, and when I went
to college, I had a pretty obsolete vocabulary. I used words like "cravat"
and "waistcoat" (which I mispronounced). One of my teachers, an Oxford
man, was very much amused. But he guessed at once what my reading had
been. Those were the days before radio and television.

Are you a fast reader today?

I read rapidly but not so rapidly as some, and I don't have a photographic
memory. Some of my friends can read like that. Though I did discover
when I gave a talk at the Naval War College when they were showing some
instruments on how to improve reading capacities, that one could acquire
the art. They flashed a series of numbers on the board for a fraction of a
second and asked me to repeat them. I couldn't. They asked me to try it
several times, and within a couple of minutes I was able to reproduce those
numbers from memory. Then, as I was reading something, a shutter came
down the page. They timed my reading speed. I was a fairly rapid reader,
but with the shutter in operation my reading speed greatly increased. I
recall that when I was a kid and went to the movies and they flashed a
legend on the screen that was funny, I was the first one in the theatre to
laugh. It was as if I could draw and shoot faster. I concluded that my

reading speed was greater than the average. But that has nothing to do with creative capacity.

What do you think the role of your mood has been in your creative work?

Now that you have mentioned it, I confess that, although half conscious about my mood, I never thought about its role. Sometimes I have a great reluctance to get down to writing something I am supposed to do. I discover myself making excuses not to write even though aware that something is pressing. Suddenly when I feel that the time is right, things pour out in sort of a gush. That's *sometimes* true. But as a rule and most of the time I can work under any circumstance when I know I have to work.

(*Mrs. Hook*) He is a true artist in a way that Koestler, for instance, is not. When Koestler talks about his writing, he tells us he gets up in the morning, never reads the mail, never talks on the phone, works steadily from nine to one, is very orderly in his working habits. When Sidney works, it is in an inspired way. Once he starts working, you could sit on his head.

And you could sense that?

(*Mrs. Hook*) Sense it? My mother sensed it, the dog sensed it, the cat sensed it. Does he have to write a manuscript? Well, get out of his way! He doesn't pay any attention to you as he paces, or sits, and you can talk your head off to him without getting a rise out of him.

Are you aware of thinking going on when you're pacing?

When I do that I'm already in the mood for working.

(*Mrs. Hook*) And ill-tempered—I want this to go on the record.

After thirty-five years or more of connubial bliss, Ann still doesn't know how I work. If she wants us to go out in the evening, she will say in the afternoon or morning: "Sit down and work now so we will have the evening free." She thinks I'm a faucet and can turn the creative flow on and off at will. She always likes for us to run off to Vermont for four-day weekends. Her excuse is, "You can do your writing in the car." And I do write in the car but, as I have often told her, my work shows it. I can read and correct term and exam papers in the car quite efficiently, but my writing is too much off the top of my mind when I have to keep one ear cocked to what she's saying and one eye out for traffic policemen and traps.

She does the driving and you do the reading?

That's the only way she can get me to Vermont! I'm not wasting time!

(*Mrs. Hook*) He's the only man I know who doesn't need a sharpened pencil or electric typewriter to write.

When you say under any circumstances, do you mean when you're sad, depressed about something, happy about something?

Yes. Independently of those moods, but some moods, rather than objective circumstances, affect me. I have moods when I don't feel like working, but I don't know why. Something may be incubating in me or I may have a distaste for what I am supposed to be doing. Right now I'm supposed to be writing a review on Marcuse for *The New York Times*. Now I should be reading that book but I have a feeling I'm postponing doing it because, on the basis of past experience, I know I won't have to tax my brain to write that review. If they want it on the twentieth, I feel I can read the book, it is quite small, and write the review on the nineteenth. I doesn't require me to stretch my imagination. Of course, if I had an important book on philosophy to review, like Ayer's new book on pragmatism, and I found myself postponing getting down to critical work, it might be because it's too big and I'm waiting for a longer space of time to do it and myself justice. Well, I suppose everybody has these idiosyncrasies.

But one trait that I wish I had, and I don't think its absence, as Ann seems to think, is a reflection of artistic temperament at all, is the capacity to acquire work and place habits. I don't have work and place habits partly because my kids were all over the house, and I never had a study. Also I grew up in a cold-water railroad flat in a Williamsburg slum, where we spent most of our waking hours in the kitchen. My brother sang in one corner, my sister played the violin in another corner, my mother was baking at the stove, and I was reading or writing either on the floor or in another corner. Brought up under those conditions, one doesn't acquire any specific time and place habits. Yet most of the people, the scholars and thinkers I admire, went to their studies or their desk at 9 A.M. and worked right through. If at the beginning they don't have anything to write, they say it comes to them in time. If I am left to myself, things don't happen that way. I never seem to be left to myself. I'm interested in too many other things—the newspaper, magazines, the telephone, my mail. My wife is convinced that I can't be a profound philosopher because she says a profound philosopher doesn't rush to answer the telephone the way I do, I can't bear to let it ring, or carry on about my mail or read it with the zest I do. I feel that if I weren't interested in my mail, I'd lose my curiosity about the unexpected. My correspondence is quite heavy, and much of it is provocative. Until recently I have felt it is a matter of simple courtesy to reply to all letters, but now it's too much of a burden. At any rate, the only experience of regular work habits I have had was when I went to places like Yaddo or The Villa Serbelloni. These are ideal refuges for scholars, for writers, and artists. I found that when I was alone—one wasn't encouraged at Yaddo to come out of his room until 4 P.M.—I did a lot of reading but I also got a lot of writing done, too. The people I know who go into their study at 9 A.M. apparently do so in order to write. I don't know whether they read, too. Now when I had that block of time, say from nine to four, I would spend a considerable part of it reading. Others seem to do most of their reading at night. Max Eastman, Arthur Koestler, and others apparently do most of their writing in the morning. When it comes to writing, I am primarily a night owl. I suppose I became one because I used to wait until the children went to bed before I sat down to write.

Somehow as I look back over some of the earlier things I've written, I'm surprised at their liveliness and freshness. They had a dash . . . my metaphors were bolder. When I was younger I was not so much concerned about logical exactitude, and I wrote with fewer qualifications and more daring. I wasn't so much concerned then about covering my flanks against criticisms. It took me time to learn that there was a will to misunderstand in controversial fields. I am not so sure that I am better understood today despite my precise and carefully qualified way of stating what I believe to be true, although I am much harder to refute. When I was younger, I used to get off some striking expressions, but as I've gotten older and acquired hosts of antagonists among different varieties of fanatics, totalitarians, and phony liberals, who seemed ready to pounce upon any seeming mistake or misinterpretation, I became more guarded, and I feel today more cramped. I can even predict who will misread me and sometimes misquote me. Of course, try as you will, you can't safeguard yourself against the will to misunderstand. But the effort to do so makes you much more cautious. It's a great pity, but I don't believe it has affected my basic positions.

I still haven't got what I believe to be the true artist's creative feeling of "What the hell, let them think what they want; *I* know what I mean, and if they misinterpret me, that's their fault!" I'm too much aware of the ways in which what I say could be misinterpreted. Perhaps partly because of my lifelong vocation as a teacher and partly because of my passionate desire for clarity, I haven't flown so high as I could or been so publicly speculative as I'm sometimes inclined to be. I'm aware, in introspecting, of a feeling of a high sense of venture burdened by a large stock of common sense. If genius consisted in being brilliantly wrongheaded, it wouldn't be in such short supply.

If we may, let us make a curious comment, because we thought initially when you began talking that you were a little bit defensive about your being creative. We wouldn't be here if we didn't think you were creative. But we wonder whether this may not be related to your own allegiance to pragmatism as a philosophical point of view. Maybe pragmatism is not given to the creative flights of certain other more speculative positions. You would know this much better than we.

I see what you mean or I *think* I see what you mean. Now pragmatism is a technical philosophy—I don't think it relevant to the creative mood. There are creative and uncreative pragmatic philosophers. The word "pragmatism" has been corrupted and vulgarized. Pragmatism is a theory which explicates the meaning of general ideas by tracing their consequences in specific contexts, but it doesn't prevent or condemn persons for having general ideas. It is all for general ideas but it wishes to clarify their meaning and test their truth or falsity by their specific and relevant consequence. You see, William James as a pragmatist was a great creative mind. Anything he touched came alive. He was one of the most creative psychologists in human history. His writings are still a storehouse, a treasure house, of all sorts of interesting things that came to him. Pedants and unimaginative critics can easily point out crude logical errors in the way he said things. But they overlook what he saw, its freshness and original vision. Lesser minds can always find the good arguments to support the valid position.

Dewey himself was very creative in a ponderous sort of way. He would always outflank arguments that seemed to meet head-on. A speculative philosopher is one who believes he can talk about the universe in general terms. But that doesn't necessarily make him original. To be truly creative, one must be original. I believe that if I had to explain my emphasis on criticism, I would have to attribute it to the influence of Morris Cohen. Morris Cohen was my first teacher in philosophy. If I hadn't been taught by him, I think I would have been more like Dewey, not in stature, of course, but in willingness to play hunches and go all out for what I wasn't sure about. Cohen was a great dialectician and had one of the most incisive and critical minds of the age. He could always find chinks in the armor of other philosophers' systems and analyses, but when it came to solving problems on his own, he couldn't do very much. He would always make you aware of what was wrong with your solution, but he never offered you a solution of his own or helped you to reach a better one of your own. He would justify this by saying, "Well, there's so much nonsense in the world, I don't have to encourage more of it." Or he would repeat his famous remark until it became a legend, "When Hercules cleaned out the Augean stables, it is not recorded that he proceeded to litter them up again." The result was the best of the students trained by Cohen were merciless in their criticism, more interested in argument than vision.

We'd go out with a sword in one hand and a dirk in another, both honed to a keen edge, and no other teacher could stand up against us. One of the reasons I couldn't get a job at City College is that when I'd go from Cohen's classes to those of other members of the Department, and when differences arose, I would stalk to the blackboard to prove them wrong; and I'd do it, too. I was written off, since Cohen never bothered with such mundane matters, as someone who had a radical chip on his shoulder. (Maybe it was a blessing that I didn't get the job at CCNY since I probably would have been thrown out subsequently.) However, when I went to study with Dewey, I found an entirely different cast of mind. Dewey was always interested in others' ideas and in how to make them right not wrong. But he carried this process of midwifery too far. No one was ever refuted. Both Cohen and Dewey represent extremes.

When Cohen was throwing his weight around awing his students by devastating repartee, he reminded me of that cartoon in *The New Yorker* in which a swordsman decapitates his fencing partner, and smilingly remarks, *Touché*. When Cohen went around the class with his dialectical sword, he'd skip me because he was afraid I'd give the right answer. But he was a critical genius and exceedingly helpful to those who were tough-minded and enjoyed intellectual encounters. For others it was a cruel and sadistic experience. But with Dewey, almost anything the student said would be greeted as a contribution of importance. The student would find himself undergirded by the strong pinions of Dewey's own thought, and he would often end up convinced he was a real philosopher. Dewey's approach was, on the whole, wiser as well as kinder. At least he found things in what students said and encouraged them. As a result some people went into philosophy who never should have done so. They felt buoyed up and overconfident. After all, if they could impress Dewey and make him think, they *must* be good. Hardly anyone was turned off or turned away by Dewey. This was true not only for students of philosophy. Anyone with an idea would be encouraged. I once asked him when we became good friends why he was so sympathetic to apparent cranks and world savers of different varieties. He told me he got more stimulation from people who were not philosophers than from those who were. But he was much too kind and uncritical. He used to write prefaces to all sorts of books that shouldn't have been published and which received attention only because of what Dewey imagined he saw in them. But I put a stop to all that with a burst of indignation after he wrote an introduction to a book called *The Lazy Colon.* For a long time after that he wrote no introductions. But at least pedagogically Dewey's approach had more virtues than defects because there are a lot of late bloomers among students and others, and there are people who are not glib or articulate. Cohen's approach, which I am ashamed to say I enjoyed when I was young and a student, I found cruel after I got to know Dewey. It's so easy for a mature mind, especially a teacher, to ride herd on students. Temperamentally perhaps I am more like Cohen than Dewey in my delight in argument, but when I began to teach, I was careful to avoid his methods.

(*Mrs. Hook*) No, you're really more like Dewey.

My students sometimes say that I'm too sarcastic or too sharp, even when I take pains not to be.

Too much of a logician!

As I said before, Cohen had the ability to take two sides of any argument, depending on what the student said. This would often be annoying to students. But it really is excellent training when it is done impersonally and objectively.

(*Mrs. Hook*) I know Sidney used to infuriate me, too, when I was his student. He's made a lot of people philosophers who shouldn't be philosophers. He used to make everybody imagine he had great ideas.

I'm afraid a good many students didn't feel that way. It's a pity because it meant that sometimes they felt hurt. Students often don't distinguish between analysis or repudiation of what they're saying and disparagement of them for saying it. It's partly a result of their imagined relation to the other students in the class. If a student makes a statement and the teacher shows it's wrong, other students often are glad they didn't speak up. They don't appreciate the importance of making a contribution, whether it's sound or unsound; they fail to realize that the progress of discussion, like the discovery of the truth, consists in eliminating false starts, hypotheses, and alternatives.

Could we pick up on what seems to be an apparent contradiction to something you said? On the one hand, earlier you were discussing your way of working and thinking; you described yourself as not mulling things over, you get an idea, you write it down, and you think your work could have been more profound if you hadn't done this. On the other hand, you're talking about the fact that you wish you could take flight more freely. You feel that you're too tied down with a concern about criticism or about how other people are going to misinterpret what you're going to say.

Well, those are two different points. They don't really contradict each other. The first point refers to the rapidity of composition. The second point refers to the style of composition. If I were more speculative, I would write everything without any kind of self-criticism as I write. I'm critical of what I write but, nonetheless, even though I'm critical, *when* I write, I write fast. As I write, I'm performing critical operations on the ideas that are coming to me, rejecting this one or that, this formulation or that. If I were more speculative, the rate of writing would be the same. I would let myself go, but my mind-set would not reject so much. I think fast whether speculatively or critically. My trouble or difficulty is that whatever I do doesn't seem to take much time. After I get through writing, I should try to re-write and re-think what I have written, whether it is in a critical or speculative vein, but I don't. My first draft, whatever it is, is practically my last draft.

But that's tying you down more—

No, you see—suppose I wrote something speculative or wrote something critical or logical. It would be written in the same space of time. After putting my draft in a clear hand for the typist—perhaps one can consider that a second draft—I'm too impatient to do anything more. I can't bear to read it again. When Ann types my manuscripts, she will often find expressions or sentences that are too long, and I'll make some changes at that point. But, if she doesn't say anything like my secretary who used to type most of my manuscripts, I let it go. Most people I know, except those who are professional journalists, after they write something, whether speculative or logical, will muse over it or make several drafts. John Dewey, who was very speculative, would make six or seven drafts sometimes of essays and chapters, starting afresh. I always marveled at his patience, especially when he would discard a version of what he was writing and make a fresh start. Here's another interesting thing. Once I make a first draft, I can't depart from it too much once I try to make a second draft, unless someone were to steal it and tear it up. I seem to be too much a creature of the first strike, more acute perhaps than profound, whereas Dewey would make three or four drafts with *different* approaches to the same problem. That seems to me to be evidence of a real creative mind. Sometimes I'd think his earlier draft was much better than the one he ended up with. They were so different in emphasis and organization. There are other people I know who work with a pen as if it were a chisel. They labor over their copy, weighing each word and sentence. They are wonderful craftsmen, polishing the same idea, trying to find the *mot juste,* almost rejecting different ideas, if they have any, as distracting.

Don't you think that approach sort of ties one down, puts the blinders on?

No, not necessarily, it may make the thought more profound. You rethink it, and in philosophy in particular, one should do that. Many of the arguments in philosophy are subtle and require thinking. Nonetheless, Bertrand Russell never did that. His technical ideas would come out in a steady even flow, he once told me. Sometimes the ideas didn't come. But once he was ready or felt ready to write, he never agonized over any scripts. He wrote them as if they were letters. This may all be a matter of habit. Why is it that people who work on newspapers, journalists, are able to compose so quickly? Perhaps it's sheer practice. There used to be a columnist years ago by the name of Harry Hansen. When he began to write, I wouldn't have passed him in a composition class in high school. But after several years, he developed a passable style. I used to try this notion out in giving advice to students who complained they couldn't write. I used to say, "Write three hundred words a day, every day in the year, and at the end of the year you'll get over every writing block you ever had." I still think that's true. If a person keeps on writing, he will develop excellent writing ability but, whether he has ideas or not, good or bad ideas, that's something else again. That depends on grace, from nature, from God, or what not. Fluency in writing is a matter of habit, but the flash of insight into truth is a gift from somewhere.

Will you tell us a little bit about your early background, your family relations? You mentioned your sister, brother, your father and mother.

I don't think they had a bearing on my creativeness or lack of it.

(*Mrs. Hook*) Sidney's mother once told me that, as a young boy, he concentrated very much on whatever he was doing. This was in their small apartment with guests coming and going, walking in and out. When he was reading, and very often when he ate he read, too, and there would always be a lot of commotion in the kitchen. Once he was sitting there reading and eating, and someone got very annoyed at his apparent indifference to what was being said. He took a jar of mustard and emptied it over his head.

I was a great reader, and my mother would chase me downstairs to play, to get fresh air. The ghetto life, it was no different for me than for any other boy. These days are gone. The ghetto life was a real community life, ugly and cruel, but vital and interesting. I played with boys who became notorious gangsters. Others became lawyers and judges. No one had anything much except large hopes for the future, especially the parents for their children. I grew up in the Williamsburg ghetto. It was a tough ghetto; it didn't have any social service. There was so much unnecessary suffering. I still remember when toilet facilities were in the yard, when electricity was not used, and when we chased the first automobiles shouting, "Hire a horse!"

My father was a factory operator. He was a man of great potential intellectual capacity, but he lacked the courage to leave the ghetto. He was an autodidact. He taught himself to read and write English without a day's schooling, but he never lost his foreign accent. My mother had a very good ear, and her diction was excellent. She spoke English at home. She was all heart. My father was very reflective, although sometimes very choleric. My mother was very emotional, and she was usually the cause of his impatience. They had the typical culture syndrome: "Go to school! Education is important. Make something of yourself!" Of course, they wanted me to be a physician or lawyer. My mother would threaten to beat me if she ever caught me with a thread and needle. She feared I might become a tailor. And although I loved cats, dogs were not kept in our ghetto, she would not let me fondle them for fear of my becoming a "Katzenkopf."

Who ever heard of a philosopher in those days? I remember that when I got my Ph.D., my father asked me what I was a doctor of. He'd tell his fellow workers I was a doctor, and they wanted to know whether I was a children's doctor, a woman's doctor, a general doctor, or a specialist. He would reply, "a doctor of philosophy." "What's that?" they persisted. He couldn't tell them, and they were puzzled. They could understand the ministry. You could translate it to them in religious terms. I never thought too much about those early days when I lived them except in consequence of my school experiences. Some things happened that seemed to result from emotional drives. Perhaps the greatest single influence in my life was an event that occurred when I went to high school in the spring of 1916. By spring of the next year, we were at war with Imperial Germany, and I had become an enthusiastic young socialist. And, as a young socialist at that time, I was firmly opposed to the First World War. Opposing the First World War at that time and subsequently meant risk to life and limb quite literally. When people talk about the terror of McCarthyism and present backlash reaction, they don't know what they're talking about. I used to get beaten up at school for criticizing, mildly, American war policies, for refusing to sell Liberty Bonds. I'd get up in class during the discussion period and advocate a capital-gains tax and get a zero, despite my logic and eloquence. I very often would do things that were risky and invited punishment, because I felt some force moving me almost against my will. I spoke up when I shouldn't, if I valued safety, and sometimes refused to stand and applaud when I disapproved of a speaker, knowing I would be yanked to my feet and punched and kicked.

Was this force in the direction of getting yourself hurt or in the direction of expressing a rebellious idea?

Expressing an idea. It was a force that brought me from the back of the room to the front of the room. I couldn't sit still to argue. But it always was in terms of argument, in terms of positions. We received blows, not counter arguments. Of course, at that time, the radical movement prided itself on the fact that its arguments were unanswerable. You didn't go to the meetings to break them up, only hooligans did that, but to ask questions. That remained the tradition among radical students right up to and through the Second World War.

I never got much stimulus from my teachers in high school. Until I met Morris Cohen, I never met a teacher whom I respected intellectually. And I don't think it was a matter of arrogance on my part. The teachers were a poor and timid lot.

But were you a rebel in your thinking? It sounds very much as if you were.

Well, in my thinking I was a rebel. I was following a socialist point of view, but only because it seemed more reasonable to me. I wasn't very original, but I was not a conformist. I thought the war was an imperialist war between two different sets of capitalist powers. I was anti-capitalist, I soap-boxed for Morris Hillquist for mayor of New York in 1917. I became quite knowledgeable politically by voracious reading. I knew that the world was hostile. If you lived in a ghetto, you couldn't help knowing the world was hostile, but it didn't have any bad effect upon you. You felt sorry for those outside the ghetto who were persecuting you. Not that I have any religious beliefs about being a member of the chosen people, but one naturally expected to be persecuted. It was part of the rain and snow like death and taxes. You didn't suffer from it, and your ego didn't suffer from it. There was no self-hatred as a consequence of that.

When I went to high school (and college, too), I organized a group and ran for president of the general organization on a platform. It was the first time of student self-government, all classes were to elect representatives to meet together, for the benefit of the school. *The Brooklyn Daily Eagle,* the borough newspaper, came out with an editorial entitled: "Soviets on Marcy Avenue Red and Black Guards at Boys High." We called ourselves the Red and Black Party because these were the colors of the school. *The Eagle,* our opponents, and the administration said the colors were red for bolshevism and black for anarchy. The Superintendent of Schools, Dr. Campbell, came down and asked me where I got my money from. This was at the height of the nationalistic fervor which followed the Armistice in 1918.

They weren't teaching in those days. We were planting potatoes or saving peach pits. The young teachers were in the army, and we were taught by some scholarly types who were quite old and who taught by rote and drill. Ideas were at a discount. I still remember a Latin teacher I had, by the name of Hopkins. We were reading Cicero, and I was called on to translate and wasn't prepared. I was too busy fighting against the war. When I was called on, I stalled, waiting for the bell. I said I didn't agree with Cicero. The teacher looked startled. He said suspiciously, "What do you disagree with?" I replied, "Cicero is unfair to Cataline." "Unfair to Cataline?" he echoed. "Yes, it's quite obvious to me that Cataline was organizing the downtrodden slaves and freemen. He was organizing the opposition to the ruling class in Rome. Cicero's denunciation of Cataline is a class judgment because of the incompatible class interests." I was all of fifteen at the time. An intelligent teacher would have said, "Now that's a very interesting notion. Why not go to the library and see what you could find out about Cataline and make a report to the class. Perhaps you will learn something and be better prepared next time." I, of course, was applying the class-struggle notion a priori, and was only half serious. Instead, he flew into a fury. I can still see him, he was appalled, his face went red to the top of his bald head. He shouted, "I've been teaching Cicero's orations for forty years, and this is the first time I ever heard anybody defend Cataline—you Bolshevik! Out." And he drove me from the class.

What part of Europe did your father come from?

Well, I think the name as he spelled it, Huk, is a Czech name. I think it's on the Czech-Austrian border.

The reason we ask is that many of the generation from Russia had a strong socialistic bent.

No, my father was a Republican. In 1912, he voted for Taft. I remember we had a straw vote in primary school—Roosevelt, Wilson, Taft. I still remember his reasons. He was for a high tariff. In the school straw vote in 1916, I voted for Benson, the socialist candidate.

So how do you explain such a discrepancy between your orientation?

I got my socialism from reading. My family was very hostile to my socialist activities. My mother used to say, "Let someone else fight. You were cut out for better things. You talk about workers, what do you know about workers? Nothing. They are just as mean and selfish as other human beings. You're glorifying workers out of your ignorance. They're no better than anyone else." "Of course," I replied, "they're not better than others but we want them to become better by improving their conditions." My parents, however, were never reconciled to my radical ideas, and thought I was naive and foolish for all my book learning. They would fall back on their experiences. "People's ideas change depending upon their conditions of life. Workers and socialists in power act like other people in power." And there was one illustration they were fond of quoting. My bosom boyhood friend was a socialist, as was his father. Over the years there was a change in fortune. His father became comparatively well-to-do. Before long they became extreme reactionaries and brutal cynics.

That was my first great disillusion. Of course different people react differently to the same circumstances, but this case was so abrupt in its

cynicism that everyone attributed it to the change of status. My parents
felt I was a foolish idealist in not realizing that most people were the same,
and that if they reversed conditions with their oppressors, they would act
in the same way. Well, in those days, your boss of today was very often a
worker yesterday. Interests naturally clashed, but when he couldn't make
out he gave up ownership of the shop and rejoined the union. Or the
landlord, there were no corporate landlords in the ghetto. People would
borrow money, buy a house, and hope to make money or live cheaply.
Since there was natural opposition between landlord and tenant, no matter
who the landlord was, yesterday's tenant was today's penny-pinching landlord. These phenomena explained my parents' attitudes, but they didn't
influence me because I was concerned with the conditions which oppressed
everybody, and my parents hardly understood what I meant.

*Except it sounds as though there was quite a bit of rebellion on your
part.*

I rebelled against their whole culture. Even earlier I broke with them on
the religious beliefs because I had discovered, like most intelligent children,
"the problem of evil," and they could give me no sensible answers.

You mean the religious problem of evil?

Yes. While my people were conformists in religion, they were not fanatical.
My father, interestingly enough, rediscovered Pascal's famous argument.
When I said to him, "I can't think of a good God that permits such things
to happen that do happen," he replied, "Look, suppose there isn't a God
and you believe in him, what have you lost? But if there is a God, and you
don't believe, what do you think the consequences will be?" But I said,
even as a child, that I don't think that would appeal to God if there is a
God; He wouldn't like the reason for the belief. The argument indicated
first, his ingenuity and, second, that he was not really religious but more
concerned with the reaction of the neighbors. And I did find him late one
Friday afternoon, smoking a cigarette, when a religious man shouldn't
smoke a cigarette. Nevertheless he never worked on Saturdays, went to the
synagogue faithfully, kept the High Holy Days, and my mother, too. But
if something got into a dish that shouldn't, she would use it. She wouldn't
break it. We were too poor. She used a kind of woman's common sense.
But what she couldn't do was eat bacon and ham.

And you can?

Oh, yes. The only thing I acquired as a result of my mother's culinary
devotions is a partiality for scorched meat. If I were a literary man, I
would try to do justice to her. She wasn't the Jewish-mother type one reads
about; she was much more likeable. She would forget the whole world,
engrossed in her novels, while the meat and everything else would get
overdone. But, you know, scorched meat has a good taste! When I go into
a restaurant, I tell them, "I can't eat rare meat, it has to be well done."

Well, someday I'm going to write my political autobiography if I find
the time.

EDWARD STEICHEN

Edward Steichen met us at his office at the Museum of Modern Art in New York City where he was preparing for a retrospective of his work.

Mr. Steichen, who is also an artist and plant breeder, was born in Luxembourg in 1879, and came to the United States the following year. He is considered one of the first to have realized the full possibilities of the art of photography, and for many years he served as chief photographer for Condé Nast publications.

Steichen served in two world wars. During the First, with the rank of Lieutenant Colonel, he directed the photographic air service of the American Expeditionary Forces; during the Second, in the rank of Captain, he functioned in the capacity of director of the U.S. Navy Photographic Institute.

Among his more formal recognitions as a leader in his chosen art are his honorary master of arts from Wesleyan University and a doctor of fine arts from the University of Wisconsin. Not the least of his awards has been the Fine Arts Medal from the American Institute of Architects, awarded to him in 1950; his honorary fellowship in the Royal Photographic Society is another sign of international recognition.

Mr. Steichen has written A Life in Photography *(1963), and he has edited* Photographers View Carl Sandberg *(1966). Those interested in photography know him best, however, through the many exhibits of his work, and especially for his most famous effort, the 1955* Family of Man *exhibit.*

PHOTOGRAPHY

Edward Steichen

How did you become involved in photography?

My family was not interested in the arts. My father was a farmer in Luxembourg and my mother went to school at Arlon, France, and she was the one who had great sensitivity. My mother was a real source of inspiration and encouragement.

For instance, when I first had a camera, that was before the "automatic," and daylight loading, there was a roll of film that had fifty exposures and you had to shoot the fifty before you saw what you had. When that fifty went to Rochester, it came back with only one photograph printed.

My father said that was a pretty poor investment, to get one picture out of fifty. My mother comforted me by saying, "Such a wonderful picture, it's worth fifty misses." So that's a very good idea of how my family background worked.

I was sixteen years old when I got my first camera. Of course, you have to have something to start you off, to spark you, a challenge, or a duty to perform.

The first real experience I had in photography was a job I got as an apprentice in a lithographic poster-design department. I worked one year for nothing; the next year for $2; then $3 a week; then $4. My apprenticeship completed, from there I jumped to $25. I was considered graduated. That's a typical old German apprenticeship as it took place in Milwaukee then.

As assistant in the poster-design department, we had a lot of old magazines and books, chiefly old German publications with woodcuts and we used their woodcuts as copy material. On my trips and on my vacations in the country, I observed things looked entirely different. I saw that they didn't look anything like the scenes in the woodcuts, so I suggested to the boss that I observed the differences and we ought to photograph them. My employer said, "Well, if you get yourself a camera, you'll be given time off to photograph them." Well, I started taking pictures of wheat and rye in sheaves. When I saw a bunch that looked nice, I photographed that. And then I really became interested in photography. The streetcar in Milwaukee used to go from our house to the end of the line that was right in open country. I often would go to the country right from work. It got me interested when I would see things in the twilight and then I would come back and see them by sunlight, being of romantic disposition. Then once while I was photographing, it was raining a little and when I looked on the ground glass I saw everything was an interesting blur. I looked to see what it was, and I saw water on the lens. I went back and wiped off the water and then I experimented; spitting on the lens or getting more water. I used spit when water wasn't handy, and this became a useful tool. At another time, I accidentally kicked the tripod during exposure and I got a nice blur from that, so I kicked the tripod whenever I wanted a blur.

You see, when I took up photography and got bitten real hard by it, I believed that there wasn't anything that couldn't be done, and I attempted to show things in photography that painters did. It took me a long time to go through that mill. I remember once when I went to Chicago with a friend of mine, he took me to see Frank Lloyd Wright, and I took my portfolio along. He looked at all the things and then he said, "This is all interesting, but it's not photography." He dismissed me with that. Well, I thought Frank Lloyd Wright was a great architect, but he was old hat as far as photography was concerned. Many years later, I met Frank at a dinner at the Plaza Hotel in New York where we were sitting next to each other, and he leaned over real warmly and said, "Ed, I understand that you think that I 'saved' you ten years of your life by your talk with me." "No," I said, "you've got it wrong, it's just the opposite." And then I told him the story. Later on, after the dinner, he leaned over and said, "So you really think I could have 'saved' you that?" I said, "Yes, sir." He said, "Perhaps you're right, but I was so immersed in my own problems and work, it never occurred to me."

Photography was a challenge. It wasn't until many years later that I realized I was imitating what other mediums could do, to show that photography could do it too, and easier. I just felt that there were unlimited potentialities in the photographic medium.

And then when I first came to know about color photography, my interest was sparked further. You see, at that time, there was no single process for color photography. You had to make three separation negatives. My first color photographs were taken in 1901, or 1905. The first color photographs I made were with a German camera with a repeating back; when you made one exposure, the back dropped until finally the three exposures were made, and I made quite a number of those. They were difficult to make prints of: you had to make three prints and superimpose them and that took a lot of "invention" because there was no process available then. It was in 1907, I think, that I exhibited my first color photographs. I much prefer color to black and white. There's practically no way of rendering the early part of an autumn landscape, when the leaves start changing color, except, of course, with color. And the same thing goes for photography of people. Color adds so much to a picture, gives much more of the facts.

Photography was never a hobby for me. It was always a means to an end, to show what could be done by photography. It was a stupid reason, but it was really important to me at the time. This was the overriding purpose and goal in all of this, to show that "I could do with my camera what the artist could do with his paintbrush."

That was the beginning, in the early stages. When I got a better understanding, I realized that photography was doing something that the painter had no business doing, and no training to do. They didn't realize it, but the modern boys do. There's Op and Pop, and all those schools, and they are photographing absurd things, but the photographers are now trying to copy the painters again, they're even trying to do abstractions.

How did this philosophy affect your productivity?

My productivity is affected more by my age than by anything else. I don't have the control I had with the large camera. I don't take it as seriously as I did then.

Everybody has a creative kind of an urge. Some use the creative effort. I don't think in photography that plays as big a role. "Hunch" is a better word. You get a hunch about something; or you fall in love with something. You can fall in love with inorganic things just as well as you can with human beings. Certainly that little tree I'm photographing so much—

there's a distinct love affair between us. It's a tree I planted outside my bedroom window. Anytime it looks good or interesting, I photograph it. I actually get up in the morning, and I think, "Well, you're putting on a fine performance today, little girl." And when that little tree bursts into bloom in spring, God! People in the old times that though they saw angels have nothing on me . . . it's my little tree.

I don't think very much creativity enters into photography. You don't have enough control of it. If you are a good photographer, you automatically rely on what mechanically happens; what the light does and what the developers do and so on. But, I say, if you start with the definition of creation of a life, you know, the original problem of creativity is a tough nut to crack. It's an awful big word—"created." I don't know whether anything that I have done can be called creative. Some people might call it that, but the little woman who goes along for nine months—that's creation! Photography turns into method in the process, but I don't think I ever created anything. You know, when you get going on something and doing it one way, it's awfully hard, it takes a powerful push to smash it. Habits are bad. All habits are bad. *There are no good habits.*

I didn't know I was, but I think I was a rebel. That's the thing that sparks you to do something. It's the fact that they are done so stupidly. Oh, I'm in favor of all revolutions. *All* of them. There is no such thing as a bad revolution. And 1776 was not the only revolution that took place in this country. There's one that is taking place right now, and that's good.

I think creativity is never accidental, though it may be unconscious. *Genesis* took a long time, several chapters before they got to human creation.

I am not a man of religion, but I believe I am a *very* religious man. True reverence, but not for the dogma of the church. I can't follow that. I did when I was a boy, and my family were Catholics. And when I was eleven or twelve and I made my First Communion, I remember feeling and believing that with that first wafer put on my tongue, I took in Christ. But, I can't follow any of that anymore. But my religious feeling grows and grows. It gets richer, and enlarges my experience. It's a reverence for life and for change and growth. It's sometimes hard for me in my garden to pull out a weed. If it's a very fine weed and only grown a little, and then I think if I leave it there, next season I'll have more, so out it comes! But I can understand the beauty even of a weed and I have a certain reverence for it even if it is growing in the wrong place in my garden.

You see, I am active in plant breeding. Now, that's a form of creativity. For instance, I have produced a new type of delphinium which is now being distributed all over the world. I call them Connecticut Yankees. It's a new plant, unlike any other delphinium, or anything before it. *That* is a creation!

I think the exhibition and the book *The Family of Man* was a creation. That's the best thing I've ever done. And, I was very much moved when I found the State Department had presented the original large-size edition of *The Family of Man* in shows in sixty-nine countries and refurbished several times. They gave the original to Luxembourg, the country of my birth. It's supposed to be permanently installed in a beautiful chateau there. And while I was there, while I was looking the chateau over, the mayor of the city came over the air and announced that he was making me an honorary citizen; but of more creative importance came a telegram from the minister of finance saying that money was allocated for restoring the chateau.

SELDEN RODMAN

At his home in Oakland, New Jersey, which houses a most impressive collection of art and sculpture from the Caribbean and Middle America, we met with Selden Rodman in May, 1969. Born in New York City in 1909, he has a bachelor's degree from Yale University.

He spoke of his experiences not only in poetry but also music, psychobiography, painting, and sculpture, as well.

Rodman's early works include Lawrence: The Lost Crusade (*1937*) *and his* The Airmen (*1941*), *which refer to his interests and experiences in the early years of the Second World War. In 1945 he served as the editor of* A New Anthology of Modern Poetry (*Revised Edition*), *and in 1947 he edited* One Hundred American Poems. *His* A Diary in Verse *appeared during the same year, followed in 1951 by* Portrait of the Artist as an American. *His 1957* Conversations with Artists *revealed an intimate understanding of the contemporary art scene. An important achievement to come from Rodman's many years as a music lover was his* Heart of Beethoven (*1961*).

Selden Rodman

So, we're interested as much as possible in hearing your ideas about the birth of an idea—how ideas come to you.

Only in relation to poetry, or in relation to all kinds of writing?

Well, we think it should apply to all kinds of writing, certainly.

I've been very deeply involved with other kinds of writing, as you know, histories, art criticism, travelogues, and so on. But now I am coming back to poetry in a sense in the one I'm working on now, to be called *South America of the Poets*. I discuss each of the countries of South America, not only in terms of its poets but of the poetry of its culture, its people, its buildings, its landscape and so on, in a much broader sense than just the poets. However, the first two, the first and last chapters of this book, are concerned with Jorge Luis Borges of Argentina and Pablo Neruda of Chile.

Six books on Borges are coming out in this country this year, with six different publishers, so he's probably at the moment the most discussed South American writer. In fact, his conversations are being brought out in a month. I've just reviewed them for *The Saturday Review*. My chapter involves my conversations with Borges, a discussion of his work and his country, Argentina.

Do you feel that there would be a significant difference if you were to speak about the birth of an idea between writing, generally, and poetry, in particular?

Not really. They may be different kinds of ideas, but you reach them by more or less the same process, I suppose.

Do you have any other ideas about how ideas occur, how they come to you?

Well, my own writing, both in poetry and nonfiction, if you want to call it that, came to me in a series, usually based on my particular preoccupation at the time. For instance, during World War II, I wrote a good deal of war poetry, and that was published in my book, *The Amazing Year.* And it was all written, more or less, during the years 1944 and 1945 when I was involved in the war in one way or another. And with my new book, *South America of the Poets,* the ideas come to me in the course of traveling through each of the South American countries; in looking up the people whose ideas interested me, and in drawing them out on their poetry and the poetry of their country, and the culture in which they operate. To go back a little, in *Conversations with Artists,* I was very much concerned with the divorce between content and style in modern art. I had already written *The Eye of Man,* a reevaluation of Western art, in terms of the confrontation of form and content, and occasionally the divorce between them. I spoke to a great many artists on the subject. And just naturally in the course of doing this I made entries in my journal, which I've been keeping most of my life, and those conversations, almost verbatim, became the book, *Conversations with Artists.*

You're placing a heavy emphasis then on the stimulation of the times or where you happen to be. At the same time, in order for the things that you're exposed to, to take root, there must be a process within yourself to do something with them. Thousands of people travel to South America, but they don't come back with ideas the way you do.

That's part of a lifelong habit that I have. Wherever I go, I put these things through the filter of my own mind and consciousness and so on and comment on them in one way or another. Either through poems, through prose, through conversations, or through photography. These are all ways in which I express myself. On this particular trip, for example, I took hundreds and hundreds of photographs. You'll be seeing some of them in *The New York Times* shortly.

Are you writing some of the material for the Travel Section?

Well, I did a piece on Easter Island, which was the last spot that I touched belonging to South America. And I also did a piece on Belo Horizonte, Brazil and the colonial villages around it.

You spoke of the filter of your mind, this is what we're interested in. Can you tell us more about this? About what you do with these things and how they occur to you.

I'm not given to analyzing my own mind. In fact, I have a block against psychoanalysis, or anything else that tends to break down one's interior or internal processes, so that they just don't perform naturally. I prefer to let mine be uninhibited, and I prefer to live with my complexes. I recognize that I have many. And I prefer to let them produce whatever I am and whatever I have to say, without analyzing and analyzing and so on, which I think destroys any kind of meaningful creativity. Though I admit it creates a great deal of what passes for art today in all the arts. To my mind this is a kind of sick phenomenon. This preoccupation with one's own ego, and with one's own capacity to shock one's contemporaries, either through invention or pornography or whatever doesn't interest me.

Well, we are not attempting to do any kind of analyzing in that sense. We think what we're interested in is trying to discover what some of the dimensions are that do lead to creating ideas, and the thing you've emphasized up to now is the stimulus from without. Again, what we say is that for that stimulus from without to go through the filter of your mind is a very interesting phenomenon. Anything you can tell us about that would be extremely helpful.

That's exactly the point that I was making. In order to have it go through the filter of my mind and come out in a fresh way involves *not* analyzing it. Not that I don't think when I'm writing. Naturally, everybody does. But I tend to approach a book the same way I approach a poem: by not having any fixed idea of what I want to write, or what I expect to come out of it. I have no rigid idea about this book on South America. I do know that I took a lot of notes because in doing something as extensive as that you have to take notes, and you also have to take down conversations, and I don't believe in tape recorders, so I put them down the night I have them, in order to be sure they're accurate and fresh. But what it's all going to add up to, and what it's going to turn out to be, in terms of a book, is just as much of a mystery to me as the poem, which may be suggested by just a phrase that has gone through my mind, or something I saw on a billboard, or something that was lying on the ground that I stumbled over, and I make a note of that particular phenomenon or idea or sensation, or impression, and one day when the spirit moves me, I use it and make something out of it or perhaps I don't use it at all.

When you make something out of that phrase, is it—could you tell us, does it take a pencil and paper for you to get going—or a typewriter—so you take that phrase and you sit down with a typewriter, you have no idea what's going to come out of it. But you—

Not usually. Maybe with a long poem. That's somewhat different. But, with a book . . . I mean, if I'm doing a book about *South America of the Poets,* for example, at the present time, I at least know that it's going to be a book which is going to involve all the countries of South America. I know the individuals who will appear in it, because they're the people I saw and spoke to. I know that there will be a lot about Pablo Neruda and Jorge Luis Borges. I know that there will be a lot about the architecture of Bolivia, and the politics of Peru, and the jungles of Guyana and so on. But other than that, I don't have any specific idea of what shape it's going to take until I actually start writing. Because I feel that if I did plan all that then the book would tend to have a very artificial feel to it. And it wouldn't have what Alastair Reid, the poet in England, wrote me about in terms of my last book, *The Caribbean.* He said, in effect, "The great thing about this book is that it has the feel of having been drawn and written by hand." And I think he added something about the fact that, "You're one of the few open minds still left who allows himself to be played upon and impressed by what he actually sees, instead of trying to prove some ideology, or some theory of art."

So, this is it. You go in with a free and open mind as much as possible.

As much as I can.

And you let happen what happens.

Right.

Do you feel that the ideas that you finally come up with, even these nuclear ideas that will become the basis once you sit down at the type-

writer, that will become the basis of a larger work—are these prompted by daydreams of yours? By fantasies or nightmares?

No. No. Never.

It's always by what you see.

And hear and feel. Because once you start analyzing your fantasies, and your daydreams, and your nightmares, then essentially you're turning in on yourself, and you're doing exactly what I said I think the artist should not do. And that is to analyze his internal motivation. I think that is one of the reasons that so much of modern art and modern writing is ephemeral and incapable of communicating with any audience except that of other artists and intellectuals. I think the great artists of the past may have been just as neurotic, and just as upset, and just as sexually complicated and abnormal, but they were never concerned with investigating that or making that part of their art. Leonardo da Vinci may have been homosexual, but his art is not a homosexual art. Michelangelo the same thing. Walt Whitman. The latter's least effective poems perhaps are the ones in which he actually tries to put himself on record as a homosexual. The effective poems are the ones in which he just let the world and what he saw of it, and his relation to it as an outgoing human being, operate, producing a work of such great magical intensity as "Song of Myself." He never got back to that. I was talking to Neruda and Borges about that this winter and about how Whitman seemed never able to recapture what he found in that early poem. And I think part of it was that critics and people in the outside world made him conscious of what he was doing, and then he became a great theorist of poetry, and felt obsessed with the ideology of making America in his image and so on, and he became an entirely different kind of person. He became the kind of person that, as Borges put it, "seems obsessed with proving that America needs to be happy." For example, for one thing, in "Song of Myself" he was happy, and he expressed it, without any of this probing into his own subconscious mind. It just welled out of his subconscious mind, if you like because it was there. It's there for a great work of art, in the same sense that the Sistine Ceiling is.

Well, Mr. Rodman, do you think that there's anything in your life that you could characterize as a creative experience that you've had. An awareness in yourself of something bubbling up, whether it's a poem or an idea for a

*book, or something of that sort. Do you become aware of this, in any
subjective way, while you're having the experience? At your typewriter, or
somewhere on a trip. In Haiti, or anywhere in the Caribbean or South
America. Does this seem to be something that's coming from within you,
as well as all the material from without.*

The creative experience takes place with the typewriter or with the pen,
when I've decided that I want to write something, whether poetry or
prose.

The rest is registration.

A process of registration.

Uh huh.

When I'm in Haiti, traveling in Haiti, or working with the primitive
artists, or something like that, I'm devoting my whole thought and consciousness to what I'm seeing and what I'm doing. It's only later when I
feel moved to write about it, that I begin to have what is, if you want to
call it that, a creative experience, a sense of inspiration and so on.

*Now, is that before you get to the typewriter or while you're at the
typewriter.*

While I'm at the typewriter.

*You get to the typewriter first and then you start working on it, and then
you start getting carried away, so to speak.*

Yes. I've never understood people like, well, Jim Agee, for example, who
was a very close friend of mine. He was sitting in my office once, when I
edited a political magazine, back in the thirties, and I said, "C'mon,
haven't you written any poems lately." And he said, "I just haven't had
time to get them down. I've got them in my head, but I haven't written
them." And I said, "If you haven't written them, why don't you start
working." And I shoved a typewriter in front of him, and he wrote down
word for word, without a single change in punctuation or spelling or so on,
a complete poem, which he had in his head. And I took this poem out of
the typewriter, read it once, put it in an envelope, and sent it to Random
House, and said, "Put this in the new anthology of modern poetry. This is
obviously it." And it was. But I never could understand how these poems

just formed themselves as complete finished wholes in his mind. To me, it doesn't work that way at all. I write something down, and then maybe go over it and work on it and polish it a great deal. But it never forms itself as a whole in my mind.

Do you feel there's something in the—

I know that this is true of many other artists in other fields, because I've talked to many great painters, as well as poets, who say that their greatest works are as a result of working, not as a result of anything of which they had a complete vision to begin with, or even more than just the germ of an idea. I know that's true of Rico Le Breen with whom I spent a great deal of time when he was actually working. And his greatest drawings always took place in the course of being in his studio and making sketches of this and that and so on. That doesn't mean that he didn't have a lot of very complete ideas, or that I don't either. And complete thoughts about every aspect of modern life. But those come into play, and I use them in my work in the course of producing what I hope is going to be a work of art. In other words, I have very specific political ideas and so on, but they don't begin to have a bearing on any book that I do until I'm working the book, and then the political part of that book is affected by the general feeling that I've built up as a result of all kinds of experiences, reading things, seeing things, reading the daily newspaper and what not.

Once you're working with the typewriter on something, do you feel a sense of urgency to complete it? Is it the sort of thing you can get up from, have interruptions and so forth, or is it the kind of thing that you really keep working at?

I have a great sense of urgency to finish whatever I'm working on, whether it's a poem or a chapter of a book, or a particular episode in a chapter of a book. But I'm perfectly capable of dropping it if something important comes up. If one of my children comes into the room and wants to talk to me, or if I want to go out and play tennis, which maybe comes ahead of anything else in my life, I'll go and do it, and I'll come back. But the sense of urgency is still there, and I go right back and resume the sentence or the following sentence, without any feeling that anything has been interrupted in my mind at all. And I'll stay with that particular chapter, or that particular poem, or whatever, until it's finished. And I hardly ever revise. I mean, I do my revising in my head as I go along. That doesn't mean that

I don't do any, but on the whole, when I write a chapter, or even when I write a book, I write it straight through from start to finish and make very minor changes thereafter. And I do it in such a way because I have a command over the unit with which I'm involved—a command I hardly understand. Last year, for example, I did a book on the history of Mexico and I did a very long chapter on the Mexican Revolution. Let me think a minute. I've lost my own train of thought. I thought of something else. Yes, I was starting to say, I have so much of a command over that material that when I decide arbitrarily that this chapter must not be too unwieldy, must not get out of hand, that it should be sixty-seven typewritten pages, then to my amazement when I've finished the chapter I look at the page number, and it's page sixty-seven! In other words, somewhere in the back of my mind, as I'm going through and writing this chapter, and I'm very excited about it and the material, and the way that it's all being put together and so on; something in the back of my mind is arranging it in such a way that it falls exactly into that number of words, and it's a mystery to me how it happens.

Did the chapter on the Mexican Revolution involve a great deal of research or did you have it at your fingertips?

I had it pretty much at my fingertips. I'd done the research before. I had references to certain books when I needed a specific fact, but most of it has been pretty well assimilated, so that my main creative effort was in giving it style and giving it the kind of excitement that it has to me as a subject, in the writing.

So the creative process or experience does have a quality of excitement for you.

Tremendous excitement. When I'm working I'm constantly stimulated and excited by the whole thing. And I want to finish it, and then read it over. And I get a great deal of enjoyment out of reading it over, or reading it to somebody else. To one of my friends, or to my wife.

Do you read it for feedback from the other person?

No. I think more just to satisfy myself that it's hanging together, and that it has the same tremendous impact on them that it had on me.

That it really conveys a sense of excitement to them.

Yes. I'm usually sure that it's going to, but I'm happy to find out that I was right.

Let us ask you, Mr. Rodman, what in your background, in your life experiences, predisposed you, as you see the situation, to your interest in poetry, to your interest in Haiti and the Caribbean, and all of the things that you've done so much interesting work with?

That's a long story, but I can go into it very briefly. I suppose the fact that I was brought up by my mother, without a father, and had many problems in connection with that, and felt very isolated from other boys and so on when I was young. I felt very rejected. I grew up here in the East. Mainly in New York City. I must have gone to a dozen schools, and I deliberately refused to be taught. Either they failed me or they told me I was hopeless, and I would never be able to pass. And all during this period the thing that I really wanted to become was an athlete. I didn't want to become a writer or have anything to do with it. And it was only when I was fifteen or sixteen years old, when I was in prep school, that I discovered that many of the things that I had been reading and looking at and had registered in some degree suddenly had a great meaning to me. I had the feeling that I could do this myself, and I wanted to do it. And I began to put that together in my mind. But I was still very unhappy. In fact until I got to college, to Yale, I was still a very frustrated and unhappy person for all these reasons. And suddenly in the exciting atmosphere of that university, I discovered that by both the students and by the teachers I was appreciated for qualities that in prep school had no value at all. And I had a sudden surge of confidence, and a feeling that I was being appreciated for what I really was. And I broke loose from the whole thing. I was able to get extremely high marks in every subject without doing too much work, and still play tennis, bridge, and poker far into the night if I wanted to.

I put out a publication at Yale which attacked practically every institution in the college at that time. And it was tremendously successful. I think that that was one phase of my becoming a writer. My awakening, as it were, but another phase had been the fact that when I was told my last year in prep school that I had no chance of getting into college and passing my entrance examinations, I made a decision to leave, which was opposed by my mother and most of her family and so on. But I left anyway, and I went and lived with an aunt, who was very close to me, and who was very much concerned with the arts, particularly painting and Renaissance Italy. She had spent a great deal of time in Italy. And I went and lived in her house for six months and just studied by myself, and talked with her about painting, listened to music, Beethoven especially, and wrote things about painting, and even had things published, even in local newspapers and magazines. When I came to take the examinations I passed them all with very high grades. And I had no problem at all. And I went into Yale the next year. So it was that experience with this aunt, to whom I dedicated one of my books incidentally, *The Eye of Men*. And this produced a feeling of great liberation that took place when I got to college.

Was there anyone at college who was particularly influential?

I don't think any one person. I found many stimulating professors in the English Department. I'd finally specialized and taken honors in English, which made it possible to drop most of the other subjects. There was one in sophomore year though, a young English teacher who had just come out of Yale, and was very brash and full of exciting, nonconformist ideas, Lewis P. Curtis. He may since have become a member of the Establishment as far as I know, but at that time anyway, he was a great liberating force. Then there was another teacher who taught Greek and Latin in my sophomore year, named Hank Rowell. He was also just out of Yale. He became a well-known archaeologist and a professor since. But at that time he was a gay blade around New York Society, knew all the glamorous actresses, and nightclubs, and so forth, and led a very exciting life. He made Greek and Latin poetry very exciting. He would lecture to us on the importance of nudity and the importance of complete sexual liberation, and so on, in the course of making Catullus and Horace alive. But I don't think I would have been prepared for that if it had happened in prep school probably, because I was still much too insecure myself, and too much in rebellion against the whole idea of even receiving such stimulus. Then there was another great professor at Yale, F. S. C. Northrup, who wrote *The Meaning of East and West*. His course on the philosophy of science was very stimulating and exciting.

But, on the whole, while I was at Yale, I was already moving, in my own mind anyway, far beyond anything that was being taught me at Yale, which I don't attribute to my own brilliance or farsightedness, but to the stimulation of the environment itself and to these teachers. For example, in junior and senior years I was reading poets like Hart Crane, Allen Tate, and Williams, who were not even considered in the curriculum, or even known to the people who were teaching me. These were the people who were important, and I was translating Rimbaud and so on, and doing all kinds of things that were related to the creative world outside of the university. And with my friends at Yale I was discussing these people, and we were formulating all kinds of ideas for our own creative life once we got out of college and what we were going to do then. We were writing poems all the time and publishing them, and we would never have shown them to a professor. We showed them to each other because we assumed that we were the only people who could understand them.

Were you disinterested in the anatomy of poetry in your courses? The classical, academic approach to poetry. From what you said earlier it would seem to us that you had no patience with that kind of thing. You know, the technical aspects.

Well, I think by that time I was sufficiently interested in becoming a poet to be interested in everything having to do with poetry. And there was no aspect of it, even the critical and analytical one that really bored me. Although in one course that I had we were supposed to write an analysis of the poetry of Blake, the poetry of Donne, the poetry of Herrick, the poetry of Browning, and so on. And in each case I asked this professor, Bill De Vane, whether I could skip that assignment and instead write a poem in the style of that poet. He always said "Yes," and I always did so. He always gave me a high mark on it, because I wrote one that was pretty much like the original, at least on the surface.

We wonder if we could get back to something you said earlier. Do you have any idea what it is that might prompt you to sit down at the typewriter and get that going?

The deadline. The fact that the book has to be done by a certain time, and I want to have the chapter finished. Yes. I commit myself. And I find that very valuable as a way of not wasting any time. I would like to have a deadline for everything that I write.·

So while you're traveling throughout South America you have it in your mind that you're there and you're going to write a book about this?

Yes. And that I'm going to absorb more information and more impressions in the eighteen days that I'm in Brazil than anybody else absorbed in maybe a year or two years. That I'm going to have to, because I'm limited by the financial aspect of it to that amount of time. I can't afford any more time. I just haven't got the money.

So, even before you make this trip to Brazil, you do a considerable amount of reading before you go.

Everything that I can get my hands on about the country and about its art, and about its writers and so on. Of course, there's a difficulty in the case of Brazil where I don't even speak the moderate amount of Portuguese that I do Spanish in the case of the other countries. In the case of Brazil, I'm almost totally at the mercy of what has been translated. But as soon as I got to Brazil, I became acquainted with the young poets and with the artists in certain of the cities, and talked with them about the literature, so that at least I had a feeling of what it was that they were after, and what they were concerned with themselves.

Did you commit yourself to a publisher before you took the trip to Brazil?

Yes.

Did you tell him what your book was going to be about?

I told him it was going to be a travel book about South America. That was all.

Do you have any idea of how you came about to have the desire to write a book, a travel book about South America?

Well, yes. Because I'd already written one about Central America, *The Road to Panama,* and one about the Caribbean. I'm talking about books that enveloped the whole area. So I wanted to do the same thing in South America. But since somebody like John Gunther had already written a book called, *Inside South America,* which dealt with the political aspects of that experience, minutely, and with a degree of reportorial savoir-faire that I wouldn't even begin to approach, I thought right from the beginning that I would concentrate on what I know better, what I could understand better perhaps, although politics fascinates me too—namely, the arts, and the culture of each country, which are practically unmentioned in his book.

Well, if we could go back to your first book on this subject. What we're trying to find out is where did the idea come from for you to write on this particular kind of subject.

Well I'd have to go back through every book that I've written on Latin America until I got to the first one, which was the one on Haiti. And that came from an experience of going to Haiti on a two week vacation from work on the political magazine that I edited in the thirties. I became very interested in the revolution of the blacks against the whites in Haiti in 1793. As a result of that two weeks' experience, I came back and wrote a play in verse, *The Revolutionists,* which was later produced on the stage by the Haitian government. They invited me to come back to Haiti and see the production of it. I was given a two weeks' lease on life from my draft call. This was during World War II. I went back and saw it produced. Then I went into the Army, and after I got out of O.S.S., the first thing I did was go back to Haiti. And when I got back to Haiti I discovered that the art center, the Centre D'Art had been set up in Port-au-Prince by Dewitt Peters. And I became his collaborator, and we became co-directors of the art center. And it immediately fitted into my whole preoccupation with art which had gone on underneath the surface. It was almost as strong as my interest in poetry. In fact, during the war when I was in the Army, I started collecting works by Horace Pippin. The first art book that I wrote was called *A Negro Painter in America.* A book about Pippin. So then in the course of working and directing the mural painting of the cathedral in Port-au-Prince in '49, '50, and '51, I directed the work of all the mural painters in the Cathedral St. Trinité

That was an idea that had come right out of the experience that I had with my aunt in Newburgh, New York, when I was sixteen years old, because I was obsessed even then with the idea of painting murals. And not that I wanted to paint them, but I wanted to be close to that kind of experience. That kind of collaborative work of art. A work of art that had impact over and above a purely personal one, I guess, is the thing that I am talking about. Anyway, to come back to what I was saying about Haiti, just as a by-product of that experience, it began to occur to me, "I now know more about Haiti, I've traveled in this country more than any Haitian, I know the country better than anybody, and I might as well put it all together and write a book about Haiti, since there is nothing good available in print." So, in '54, I came back and wrote, *Haiti, the Black Republic.* It was very successful. I went on from that to other books. I'd always wanted to do a book on the Dominican Republic, but after Trujillo's secret police picked me up and threw me out of the country, because I'd written a poem satirizing Trujillo, I decided that as soon as that man is assassinated, which is bound to happen, sooner or later, I will go back and write a history of the Dominican Republic. Because there isn't one, either in English or in Spanish. It has never been done. The same with Peru.

There was no history of Peru in English. Imagine that! One of the most fabulous of all histories. I went down there and wrote the only one.

Do you have any thoughts about what it is that draws you to South America and to the primitive?

Well, I suppose one thing is that when I was a boy I spent a lot of time in Europe. I guess I had the feeling that Europe had been pretty thoroughly combed and that it was no longer an adventure, no longer exciting to go to those countries and write about them. South America was a great unknown continent.

Do you have any thoughts about this desire to open up the unknown— open up unknown territory—expose what nobody else has gotten to?

Well, of course, that's one of the things that I am interested in doing and which excites me very much. Possibly, it's a somewhat egotistical thing. I have the feeling that I'm there first. I want to say whatever I can to make that country vibrate, to make other people as stimulated by it as I have been.

So, there's a real quality of challenge . . .

Right.

What was your father's profession?

He was an architect and a painter. But I never knew him. You see, he died when I was one year old. But I loved his paintings, and I knew that he was an architect. Other than that, I had no contact with him.

What about your own painting, Mr. Rodman?

I don't paint.

You don't paint at all?

No.

Never tried it?

I've tried it. But I decided right in the beginning that you can't spread yourself too thin. It's not really the thing that I wanted to do most. The thing I wanted to do most and which I was best equipped to do, by my whole background, was writing.

But I've had a great rapport with painters. And I think I've done a good deal to stimulate them and to focus them on what they're doing. And not just with the primitive painters of Haiti, but with highly sophisticated painters like Seymour Leichman for instance, who painted the murals in this house. He wanted to paint something large, and I said, "Well, here are the walls of this house. Paint them. I'll pay for the paints." And he did. And this became a great challenge to him, and made him a much bigger painter. He's now painting things far beyond these murals in scope. I helped him get a commission to do one for the government of Jamaica. And he's done a magnificent mural for the Jamaican government, which is going to be discussed in an article by the poet, Sandra Hochman in *Look* Magazine in a few weeks. And same thing in Mexico, where a whole generation was in revolt against the social realism of Rivera, on the one hand, and against the noncommittal abstraction of the fashionable international style on the other. Those young painters read my book, *The Insiders,* which discussed this whole problem of alienation from commitment, and called themselves "Los interioristes." My book had become a kind of bible for them. So they asked me to come down to Mexico. They forced the Mexican government to invite my whole collection to be shown in the San Carlos Academy in Mexico City. And this undoubtedly, for better or worse, had a good deal of impact on their styles and what they were trying to do. On their direction maybe, not so much on their styles as on their direction.

Murals seem to be very important.

Well, they interest me more, because perhaps they're necessarily more related to large ideas and to societies than an easel painting which can be produced in a closet by an artist or as a private joke for his friends. For a mural you have to do a good deal of planning in advance and establish some rapport with your audience. It's like anything else on a large scale. Like an epic poem or a book on *South America of the Poets.* You have to do your homework. You have to do a great deal of research before you can even understand what you're seeing. The same with a mural. It's not enough to just either go into a frenzy, or decide that you're going to go one step beyond the latest gimmick in the gallery world. Or, perhaps, have a psychedelic experience and make something of that, and so on. That's the tendency in all the arts today. But with a mural you're brought back down to earth, if you want to put it that way, and you've got to say something meaningful, on a large scale, and to many people. Particularly, if it's exposed in a public place. It's just not enough to shock the bourgeois, explore your psyche or explain your rejection of the world you live in, and why you're a dropout. In great art there's no room for self-pity.

We've seen the murals you directed in Port-au-Prince, and they are magnificent.

Well, the murals by Leichman in Jamaica are on a much more sophisticated plane and perhaps say more about the world we live in. The Haitian murals, after all, are religious murals on traditional themes.

Where are the Leichman murals?

In Kingston's Memorial Park. When Leichman was painting these introductory murals here on my walls, we used to have constant ideological battles about what was going to go in it, and what ought to go in it, and how it ought to be presented and so on. And we remained the best of friends throughout the whole thing. We didn't ever get to fighting about it, you know. But, he would defend his position to the death. And I would try to undermine it if I thought it needed to be undermined. And he admitted years later that sometimes he felt like killing me, but that in the end he had profited tremendously by having this constant necessity to justify what he was doing, even if he stuck to his own guns. This was always the relation between *patron* and *maestro* in the past. In some cases, of course, maybe I did influence him and he made some rearrangements in his material that were effective.

Was this in terms of content, or color, style, or what—these arguments that you had with him or these discussions?

Perhaps largely content. But you can't divorce content from style and color and all the rest of it completely, because painting at its best, as my book *The Eye of Man* indicates, is always a perfect equilibrium between content and form. But with an artist who has as much genius for painting as Leichman, and had it right from the beginning, there's never much you can say about form. I mean, he finds the inevitable form to say whatever it is he wants to say. So it's more a question of relating ideas and saying things pictorially, in terms of what we feel about the world we live in. And these three murals are highly ideological. One of them is called "Liberation"— liberation from all that is worst in the society that we live in. The second one, based on Walt Whitman, is a kind of a God-figure—the serenity achieved by a poet. And the third, "The Earthly Paradise," is a kind of synthesis of all the things in the world that we consider valuable, lasting, eternal, worth fighting for and all the rest of it.

To change the subject for a moment. Let's go back to your work at the typewriter—

But one more thing about that mural and about my whole feeling about content in art. I feel, and I'm sure that Leichman feels the same thing, and perhaps a few other artists, too, like Artemio Sepulveda in Mexico, that one of the most important elements in the greatest art, not necessarily in art in general, but in the greatest art, has always been a quality that perhaps can best be described by the word "nobility." And that this is the most rejected element in art today, and one of the things that causes this tremendous abyss between the general public and art. It's a quality that is never rejected by the greatest artists. In the case of painting, Michelangelo and Breughel and Goya and Orozco had it. In the case of music, Beethoven supremely about whom I wrote the book you may know, *The Heart of Beethoven*. Beethoven is the supreme key example of a man who projects this quality completely out of the torments and the unsatisfactory nature of his own life.

I wrote the book about Beethoven at the time when I was doing these studies of art because it was the most extreme example of an artist who was completely unable to solve any of the problems of ordinary life and living. He led the life of a beatnik, a dropout, a drug addict, a neurotic, whatever you want to call it. I mean, he had all the worst qualities that you associate with the artist today who is rejecting society and rejecting the Establishment. And yet, the thing about Beethoven is, that though none of these problems were solved in his personal life, all of them are solved in his music, which allows none of this irritability, meanness, and violence, and various other qualities which are so repulsive in Beethoven's life, and were found to be repulsive by his contemporaries. None of these emerge in his music. His music is the resolution of all these conflicts, and the projection of this encompassing, majestic acceptance and nobility. With the result, that Beethoven's music, uniquely, appeals not only to the other musicians and the intellectuals who are able to appreciate the subtleties of the last quartets, let's say, but to the common man, who responds to the symphonies as no other composer has ever been able to reach them and touch them.

Could you speak of that in your own work in any way?

Well, obviously I'm not putting myself in a category with a man I consider to be the greatest artist who ever lived.

No, but this quality of nobility that you referred to . . .

It's something that I want to project in my own work, of course. Just as an artist who interests me like Seymour Leichman is obsessed with projecting the same quality. Although he has almost as many problems as Beethoven. And I'm sure I do too.

Could you tell us about how you go about resolving conflicts?

Well, for example, in this book, *South America of the Poets* that I'm working on—I'm concerned to show why a poet like Pablo Neruda is able to project this kind of nobility through his work. He does, and it makes him perhaps the only universal poet in the world today. This is completely at variance with his politics which are on a very partisan and even, perhaps, mean level of factional in-fighting, but somehow, this doesn't affect his art. He's able to either divide these two worlds completely, or rise above the partisan nature of his life as a propagandist or what have you. And I'm not talking about the specific fact that he's a Communist, because it's completely unimportant whether he be a Communist or an extreme fanatic of the Right. It would have the same bad affect on his poetry if he allowed it to become the meat, the projection of what it is that he has to say. But he never does, for some reason. He has this miraculous ability to be able to separate the two. Borges, on the other hand, is a much more single-minded person than Neruda. You don't have this division. You don't have any compromise with a self-service political clique. Borges is extremely humble, and has even a doubt whether his work, and his life, and life itself is too important. And this kind of humility and a great kindliness in his nature are the things that project themselves so beautifully in his writing, which has this absolute clarity and honesty, in spite of the great subtlety of his thought.

Do you have any thoughts about how a person comes to resolve some of these problems that you speak of so that they don't foul up his artwork?

Well, I think it's partly because, in the case of these artists, they have a very high and demanding notion about the responsibility of the artist, and of the vocation of being a poet, or a musician, or a writer. Your responsibility is not just to yourself, but to the past, to the world in which you live, to the future, and to everything that you consider to be valuable and important in the world. Or, in the case of a religious artist, to God.

Though in his own personal life he may not really act what one would ordinarily call responsibly.

I think in the case of Beethoven, it may have been partly a religious thing. The fact that Beethoven recognized his sinfulness, and his meanness, in his more lucid moments when he was not being completely, you know, hysterical about what life was doing to him, that he knelt to God, and he asked forgiveness for being such a terrible, mean, ugly human being.

Through his music?

No, he never apologized in his music.

No.

He recognized at best, well, in his music . . .

Yes—

He put into it the same kind of humility and faith that he felt in his rare moments when he was able to actually speak to God and identify with Him. I wouldn't call him a particularly religious man either. I mean, he was not like Bach, for example, who is a man whose problems were resolved almost from the beginning by his complete religious identification with his religion and his particular time, and so on. In the case of Beethoven, it was much more as it is with the artists today. A constant struggle.

To go back to your sitting down at the typewriter and working, does it happen as you write? You said before that you don't yourself know what's going to come out. Do you ever end up being surprised at what you write?

Oh, yes. I'm surprised at the moment of writing a phrase or a sentence that it worked out that way; and that it perhaps produced something that I hadn't anticipated at all. And I'm rather amazed by it and happy about it. And then when I read over the chapter, perhaps I'm surprised by the way the whole chapter hangs together and expresses—in the case of that example I gave of the Mexican Revolution, how completely it expresses that phenomenon. Better than I had anticipated was possible. And in writing about something like the Mexican Revolution, for example, one of the things that certainly guided me more than anything else, since it was an event in which I hadn't participated myself, was the way it affected poets and writers. The greatest insights into the Mexican Revolution are provided by novelists like Martin Luis Guzmán, for example, and Manuel Azuela and painters like Orozco, and poets like my friend Octavio Paz. Those are the real insights. Those are the ways of understanding the Mexican Revolution on a level that the politicians and the professors can never even approach. So that when I wrote about it I had these artists before my mind. I don't think of Pancho Villa, not in the stereotypes of the Hollywood movie, but in the acute moments of insight available in such a novel as Guzmán's *The Eagle and the Serpent*.

Do you have any other thoughts at this point. We would be interested in pursuing, if we could, this question of the artist whose personal life is a mess, or is troubled, but who is able to use his art to resolve it. It might be a terrible imposition, but again, if there were any way that we could kind of tie this down to you?

Well, I don't see how you can tie it down more unless you read one of my books, for example, *The Heart of Beethoven*, which goes into it, perhaps more than any other, and this book that I'm working on now in which I try to do the same thing in relation to Borges and Neruda. I can't do it in regard to myself because my own life is relatively well organized and relatively happy. I would say that I had so much unhappiness in the first sixteen years of my life that I developed a way of making life what I wanted it to be after that, and that I've been able to do. I wasn't prepared to have children, perhaps, until I got into my fifties—late forties, early fifties. When I was ready for them, I had them. And they're exactly what I wanted them to be. So far. And I'm very happy with them. And, I'm happily married for the first time, I might also say.

How old are your children?

They're three, five, and seventeen. And this place in Oakland that you've seen is also, I think, a work of art. Not only indoors, not only the collections, especially the extensive collections of Latin American and Haitian painting and sculpture, but the way the whole outdoors has been shaped. I've been able to do it with these five acres of ponds and woods and make out of it exactly what I wanted.

Have you done it yourself?

Yes. But I get people to help me whenever I can, naturally.

ROBERT ENGMAN

Robert Engman was born in Bellmont, Pennsylvania, in 1927. He studied art at the Rhode Island School of Design, where he obtained his bachelor of fine arts degree. In 1952 he enrolled in the Yale University School of Art and Architecture, where he came under the influence of Josef Albers. After he received his master of fine arts degree at Yale he was appointed an instructor and subsequently Director of Graduate Studies in Sculpture. Since 1964, when he left Yale, Mr. Engman has been Professor of Sculpture and Director of Graduate Studies in Sculpture at the University of Pennsylvania in Philadelphia.

Engman's work, which is chiefly in the structuralist idiom, has been included in virtually every major survey of contemporary sculpture, such as Aspects of American Sculpture (Paris, 1960), the Bienal of Sao Paulo (1961), and a number of exhibitions at New York City's Whitney Museum. Engman has been a lecturer and visiting critic at Princeton University's School of Architecture, the Carnegie Institute in Pittsburgh, the Rhode Island School of Design, the Cleveland Institute of Art, and elsewhere.

Robert Engman

In 1951 I joined Josef Albers at Yale, as a student. I knew of him because I had been interested in the work of the Bauhaus. When Albers went to Black Mountain I intended to go there, but he left Black Mountain and became associated with Yale, so I went to Yale.

Some men have a peculiar ability to attract a vital student body. Walter Gropius did at Harvard, Mies van der Rohe at Chicago, and Albers at Black Mountain and Yale. Hans Hofmann was the same way. Theirs was a strange pedagogy. Albers' students didn't do the kind of work he did. They went through a series of disciplines which were impossible to put to any use other than to point up the principles of art and the reasons for creating. I think that our fascination with studying people who have done things with their lives, whether in mathematics, in physics, in painting, sculpture, or poetry lies in the fact that these men have found the proper discipline which allows them to penetrate themselves, to become unshackled, to see who they are, by writing, or by organizing themselves in terms of color, or in terms of sound or in terms of substance.

A piece of sculpture or a painting is never a finished work. Simultaneously it answers a question which has been asked, and asks a new question. It answers the question of refinement or self-refinement and asks the question of possible future refinements. This kind of rapport with oneself which the created work reveals is essentially what artists are involved in. I think the whole purpose of creation is to unshackle oneself, to be free, to find out what you are and how you relate to other things which are. Without this self-questioning and self-refinement, there is no process of elevation possible for man. Making one's mark, or forming a substance, or a symbol is as old a process as eating or building a shelter. Unfortunately most people today don't "make marks" in the old way. They have discovered they can make a living at it. I think current works of art are pleasant to look at but I do not think they serve the prime function that making or substance-forming originally meant—a life force as basic and as real as procreation, and eating, and self-protection.

Expressing oneself and understanding oneself are synonymous with asking and answering a question. Expressing oneself through art is answering one's own questions. And if man has made it, man can understand it, so it is not really "oneself" who questions, it is mankind.

Of course, when I work on a piece, I'm concerned with the piece itself. It is the reason for the substance taking form. Recently I've become involved with a sequence of works, which has extended to over a hundred now, and these are like time-lapse photography. In time-lapse photography a frame is clicked off every minute or so for several days. When the film is shown at normal speed one is able to see a flower open and bloom and wilt within a very short space of time. The works I have become involved with have been expressed in terms of distended surfaces. These surfaces expand and contract necessarily in reference to the works which have preceded and which will follow them. This becomes an evolutionary sequence of experiences in form, not unlike what takes place within us from moment to moment. We are constantly undergoing change. At no time can a single photograph of a man be a true indication of what he is. Man is in motion and coincident with change. Sculpture and painting appear as single works but in reality they are not. They are more or less interrelated phases which do not necessarily follow a clear pattern. They move ahead of one another in sequence or become retarded, depending upon all of the emotions operating in the artist and on his general feelings during the day or week. When he stretches them out they seem to make more sense and that is the reason for doing it.

Feelings and moods have a direct relationship to productivity. When I moved to Philadelphia in 1966, I got up at a normal time in the morning. I live ten to twelve miles outside of Philadelphia and by the time I arrived at school I had spent nearly an hour driving through congested traffic. At this time also I was having increasing difficulty thinking of or producing anything. I had always been extremely productive and suddenly this had come to a stop. I was concerned. After eighteen months, out of sheer desperation, I got up at four in the morning and drove the twelve miles to town almost uninterrupted. An experience that had been very ugly became quite pleasant. I found that under the previous circumstances the drive to Philadelphia had so influenced the way I felt that I couldn't come to grips with things which required a certain kind of conditioning. That rush hour commute twice a day was just enough to keep me from entering the kind of psychological condition I require to do serious work. I fooled a lot, made little objects, but nothing was in keeping with the kind of work I had done. For the last three months I have been getting up at four, starting work at five, and working right through until about 2:30 in the afternoon and the production has come back. I know now that for as long as I live in this area I am going to have to sustain that relationship to the city. Up until this time I had always lived in the country. Getting in and out of New Haven was never a problem, country roads all the way. I found myself able to solve certain problems while driving and observing changes in the landscape which were compatible to that. But Philadelphia was so radically different that it literally disturbed everything I was about. I was so desperate I was willing to leave my job. Now I'm going to stay, on the basis of the past three months. The whole reason for "making" has come back.

I don't think we pay enough attention to feelings. I think we should be led by our feelings. Society in large measure tells us to suppress them and I think that they are much too important, much too significant to be controlled and subdued. The business of feeling is terribly serious and difficult and I think that it makes sense when a person is fortunate enough to discover the system that best serves his psychological make-up.

I painted for a long time and was told I could draw well. All the time I went to school people encouraged me to be a painter. When I was at Yale and met Albers, and another painter, Diller, who is dead now, I was given a job in the woodshop. I started to make toys for my little girl and Diller said that if I could make things like that I ought to consider sculpture, because my painting wasn't quite as impressive as I may have thought. My contact with sculpture was pasting little clay balls on an armature and I really didn't want to do that. But then Diller brought in de Rivera. There was no reason for him to have a particular concern about me. I was one of about thirty students he had to see each week, but he sensed that he could really help me. And he prevailed upon his friend, de Rivera, to bring a piece of his sculpture in, and when I saw it, then my whole life changed.

My stepfather had taught me to be a blacksmith, and up until the war broke out I was going to be a blacksmith. Then, under the G.I. Bill I went back to school. I could make things as well at fourteen as I can now, but then I had no reason for "making" and consequently it was difficult. When I moved from painting to sculpture I had an intense desire to work. All of a sudden someone gave me something to do which related to my old craftsman's world. That world and art crashed together. It was a fine feeling and after I finished my second work under de Rivera's tutelage there was no question about what I was going to be for the rest of my life.

That's what I mean when I say that systems are sometimes very specifically related to people. It isn't a question of training anyone. A person has to move around until finally he finds what best suits him. It is absolutely essential that a person have purpose. And purpose has more to do with the idea than with its articulation. I think, for example, that a man inclined to express himself musically is in need of a vehicle and so he picks up a single instrument. He may try one and then another and another, and then finally he discovers that it was not the violin or the piano, but the flute which allows him to have an experience musically. This instrumentation and technique, as far as the sculptor is concerned, is the instrumentation which allows him an adventure in form, an adventure in form compatible to him. The sculptor gives *substance* to thought, not symbol, not color, not sound.

I suppose a person's instrumentation is formed at a very early time. I would imagine that in our process of stabilizing ourselves, our potential is established, at least in terms of a direction. I don't suppose it is established at a conscious level, except in the case of a prodigy. Possibly prodigies, at the time of their formation, know the instrumentation best for them. Most people have to shuffle around after that knowledge. I don't know why, for example, I am inclined to give substance to thought rather than sound or color, and my recognition of myself as a sculptor was long in coming.

When I was young I caused considerable trouble in school because I didn't want to learn. I couldn't see the sense in learning facts and figures and I think I was what one would call delinquent today. I left high school and enlisted in the Navy. When I got out of the Navy I went to work in a factory. I worked twelve hours a night for a year and I was terribly unhappy. I used to complain to my older brother about how miserable I was in the factory and he finally said: "Why don't you quit? You have the G.I. Bill. You can quit and go back to school." I went to the authorities and they said that I needed a high school diploma and would first have to complete high school. I was twenty years old, and I thought, "God, I've got to get out of the factory. I've got to get out even if it means going back to high school."

After a summer of secondary school, although I still didn't meet the standards, I asked the Rhode Island School of Design to admit me for a semester. I chose that school because of my brother. He had always drawn a great deal and received much recognition as a child. He won all kinds of contests, decorated everything and drew incessantly. I went into painting simply because he got me out of the factory. The Rhode Island School admitted me on the condition that if I did well I could stay. I did do well and I did stay but all the time I was there I kept shuffling around. I tried architecture for a semester, and this meant learning elaborate systems, tensions, stresses, and materials. And I had not had any calculus so it was difficult for me.

In 1950 I married, and my wife, Margaret, who was also a painter said that if we were going to spend the rest of our lives in art we ought to go to graduate school and get jobs teaching. So I went to graduate school as a painter and moving from painting to sculpture was just good fortune. I could have been unsuccessful, easily. I mean unsuccessful in terms of understanding myself. I could have been lost for the rest of my life, easily. The one thing which I am consistently pleased with is that I am absolutely a sculptor. I know that.

I don't think you can prevent an artist from being and I don't think you can cause one to be. Artists have come from every conceivable situation and from the best and the worst living conditions. No one knows what makes an artist. They seem to be the consequence of teaching and the consequence of no teaching at all. I know at one time I became furious with the Rhode Island School of Design for not having realized sooner that I was a sculptor. I went back and delivered a couple of blistering lectures on how I thought they had failed. But then I began to think about Albers and some of the people whom he had taught and on whom he had had no effect as a teacher. It had to be more. It had to be a set of circumstances already existing when I came to study with Albers which allowed the miracle to take place. You can't teach artists and you can't not teach them. I think artists happen and sometimes they will benefit from a school and emerge sooner, sometimes the school will retard them a bit. Princeton has run a series of tests on architects for a long time now, fifteen or twenty years, and they can accurately predict who is going to perform well in client relationships, who is going to run the most efficient office, who will best invest his money. But the Princeton tests cannot predict who is going to be the best designer, which is the creative aspect of architecture. Every aspect of growth is predictable but that.

I feel I could be an architect now. I would approach it as Kiesler does. I can dream of building. I can suspect structural relationships in a thing. When Nervi, the Italian engineer-architect, makes a building, it comes out the way it would grow if it were a plant. The tree's trunk is bigger than its twigs and you know the tree is not going to stand on its twigs. Structure is based on just simple good sense and it only becomes difficult when we are technically unable to structure something which is sensible and have to force it. Nervi found a way of working out problems in terms of absolute good sense structurally and I can do this in my head. I can look at a thing in terms of structure and know certain things must be so. This is a question of intuition and is completely divorced from the question of style.

My concern for certain relationships in form is related to parallels in nature. My attitude toward form is simple. I have a feeling about scale. I make things as large as they need to be in order for me to understand the formal relationships that exist within. When the scale is unnatural it fails. The idea of a human being fifteen or twenty feet high and serving no other function and accomplishing nothing more is an unnatural affair. When the scale of the dinosaur became unnatural the dinosaur ceased to exist. The efficiency and naturalness of scale and being are what prevails.

There is a relationship of a substance to an idea as well as of a scale to an idea. When an idea becomes profound, when one is at the core of something, when there is the generation of something new, then everything becomes important. Then the material is important, because when ideas become precise and the notion is of a high order then the substance has to be very particular and the scale has to be particular. It is like the man who plays or composes for the violin. There is a precise relationship of the tone to the instrument. If it's another tone that's wanted, then it's another instrument and that is why different instruments exist. The range in tone cannot be described by a single instrument or a number of instruments which are the same and so it is with sculpture. It isn't a question of blowing it up or reducing it or working in a certain substance for the hell of it. It is all important in a real sense, not in an arbitrary one.

I've learned to rely on intuition. I've learned that it is fundamental for me. At first I didn't pay much attention to it, at least not as much as I do now, because it poses some practical problems. For example inspirations and solutions are apt to come to me at night. Perhaps because everything else has been dispensed with and certain inhibitions are no longer there. I'll wake up and be wide awake and know what that thing I've struggled with has to be. If I don't write it down, or work on it, then it may not be there, so I have pads of paper and sometimes clay around all over the place.

I have to keep working. Vacations are not good for me. I take my family on vacations, but I have to work just the same. The place has changed, that's all. Whenever I don't work with consistency I'm impossible to live with. I'm not kind to my family. I get wrapped up in all sorts of complications. As long as I work as a sculptor I'm straight and honest and unafraid. I can coast for about a month fooling myself with puttering, but if I'm not soon active then I start to get irritable and into real difficulties. When I work I'm straight. When I get distracted I start to question everything. I don't know how my inspiration is triggered. All I know is that I have to hammer away at it all the time for a good portion of each day.

My productivity is heightened when I solve things. The easing that I sense in myself is intensified when I solve something. It can't be just digging a hole, or something like that, because I've done that too. It has to be peculiarly related to a measurement of myself to myself. I think it is one of the reasons why I as a sculptor have confined most of my activity to relatively small things—small in the sense that they are only large enough so that I can complete all of the transitions that go on in them. My works are not illusions, they are actual things.

Albers came along and put red and green together. That had nothing to do with what he had observed in nature. It had to do with what took place when he put those colors down. So this became like actual art as opposed to illusory art and it meant that everything prior to it was abstract. The artist has primal things, active things, and my works are part of that. They are an act of twisting and turning of surfaces which are consequential.

In a funny way my works are almost like solutions. They are like seeing how many sensible sea shells you can make; not just with added points and swirls, but with formal transitions. A conch shell is not the same as a snail, a land snail is not the same as a sea snail, because their environment and the relationship of each to the environment is different, and there is a commensurate difference in the form itself. The principle in art and the principle in nature is the same. What an artist creates is real in the same way that nature's creation is real. Not an imitation of it but comparable to it. I think that in this sense man dignifies himself and this is what my form is about.

We teach our children to write according to the Palmer method, or some other method, and no matter how hard we press them to make the A and the O in a precise way, the letters come out each with its own individual twist. And of the millions of people there are are millions of different twists to an O. So predictable is this that we can contract business over a signature. I think this is the real essence of the individual and that it cannot be suppressed. It is there and the artist is simply a person who has found out what caused that variant and has given it precedence in his thinking. He has found a way of allowing that to temper his thoughts. This is for me the justification for being. It is why we are cut free. To some degree it comes out in every man's life. He furnishes his house the way he likes, eats the food he likes best. Each man has his own self, but in some men the need to be distinctive is greater. These are the men who make an addition. I think they distinguish themselves. They say, "This is the way I relate numbers, and this is the way I put colors together, and this is the way I organize substance."

My own need to be in control of my work is very strong. My work is brought to a very high finish, which is already expressive of this need. Why would anyone want to bring anything to a particularly high finish where not even a tool mark is allowed to appear? Along with that, why do I teach? I believe it is a need to dominate something, to control. My concern for meticulousness, in terms of craftsmanship, is I think attributable to this. I can make that substance do anything. I've learned to do this and the only time I haven't done so is when a substance is new, when I have never encountered it before and had to find out how it was made and how it responded to my notions. Invariably, in the end, I could make that substance take my forms. I've avoided working on materials where, as in violently strained marble, there was a vein of some sort going through which would dominate my carving. If I want that interruption, I want to put it there. I wouldn't think of allowing my carving to be predicted by a knot that might occur. The only times that I've taken advantage of a grain is when I can laminate up a number of even thicknesses so that when I carved a certain way the grain would respond to my carving rather than my carving responding to that grain. I've carved thickly laminated pieces so that when I cut shallow through these laminations the changes are accentuated and when I cut sharply they are less accentuated. I have a need to completely control the situation.

When I was a child I was often alone and I found myself constructing things at a very early age. I made all my own toys when I was a child and when the neighborhood in which I lived was developed and there were other children to play with, I made toys for them too. As long as they didn't tell me how to do it. And they played with my toys.

In a sense I have always been a rebel, even in the art world. I've associated only with a handful of artists in my life, yet I have taught at two schools which were flooded with critics from New York and I have had every opportunity to meet the most prominent painters and sculptors alive. But I've had no interest in that. There has to be a place for everyone and I've found the place for myself. I don't think of art as being more or less important than anything else, except as a way for an individual to make his mark. I consider it one of the great privileges of my life to have met Albers, to have worked with him and to have been taught by him. I have no feeling about the art world as a whole, except that every artist I have known has had an intense ego. And some use this more as a force than others. It's exhausting. I'm sure that mine is the same.

My rebellion to people is just to leave them alone. When I first met Albers I did all sorts of things for him, just so that I could be with him, just so I could learn from him and we developed a friendship which I think will last all our lives. When he retired and left teaching I continued to see him whenever I was in the area. Then I went to Europe for two years on a grant from Yale and at that time I felt as though somehow I didn't want to go back there. It might have been the last few times I had talked with Albers. He started to talk about the formal aspects of sculpture and I found myself in disagreement with him. There seemed no longer to be a need for me to associate directly with him. I have kept tapes of the talks that he gave at Yale and there is a core of what he talks about which is the highest I've run across, ethically.

The artist is an ethical being. This is part of the question he asks of himself. What is of concern is to give some notion of yourself to yourself, to know when you are in or out of phase with things, and how to handle being in or out of phase. To make a demonstration of being an artist I don't think is important. I don't know any good artists who do that. Most of the artists I know are absolutely sane. They are not strange people. Oh I know a world of people in the art world who are peculiar, but the artists I've known are clear.

Artists have a peculiar concern for other artists, which comes from what they have learned about themselves. When a young person says, "Is there anything you can show me which will help me to find out where the hell I am," I'll listen. It's never a question of creating a group of followers. I've had students who couldn't tolerate me for a minute, and at that point you can do one of two things. You can either get very angry or you can say, "All right, now I want you to go and talk to this other fellow, because he is of another sort and maybe he has the key, or whatever it is." We have three teachers at Penn whom I work with and we are all different one from another. That difference embodies most of what sculpture seems to be about these days. We have had quite a good fortune in reaching the students. The sculpture department is composed of fifteen people, and not one works in the same way. You go in and you can't believe anyone is teaching there because it is so diverse. And yet, that diversity is being taught. The privilege of each person to be himself, is being taught. And that is what being an artist is.

If you are not going to live for those reasons, what are you going to live for? Not to ever find out? No, I think the whole point is to find out, and in a strange way I envy the people who aren't concerned, who can go to work and put the same fender on the same car every day, and always paint it blue.

There isn't a single thing that I don't have a feeling about. There isn't a single thing I'm not interested in, regardless of whether my feelings are right or wrong. I have them. I have contact with every damn thing I put my eyes on. That constant contact sharpens and intensifies the business of being alive. It is the one thing that's consistent with being alive. You touch it, you see it, you taste it, you hear it, or you smell it. To sharpen those senses is to make life full and rich. Not to sharpen them is to deny yourself life. Such a sharpening takes place within any single discipline and is nearly impossible to sustain well in more than one discipline. You will find, sometimes, that a second-rate pianist is a first-rate mathematician. Unless he's of an unbelievably high order he's almost never a first rate musician and mathematician simultaneously. You need only one road, really.

NEIL SIMON

Neil Simon was born in New York City in 1927. His career began in the mail room at Warner Brothers after his discharge in 1946 from the Army Air Force, where he served in various capacities including sports writer for the base newspaper. The route to Broadway led via radio and television. He worked as a publicity writer and part-time member of the stable of comedy writers who supplied material for Goodman Ace, Phil Silvers, Jackie Gleason, and many others.

During the summers of 1952 and 1953, he and his older brother Danny, wrote sketches for shows given at Camp Tamiment in Pennsylvania's Pocono Mountains. These later were worked into Simon's first Broadway offering, Catch a Star, *in 1956.*

In the years that followed, Mr. Simon wrote a musical fantasy, Little Me (*1962*), Barefoot in the Park (*1963*), The Odd Couple (*1965*), Sweet Charity (*1966*), Star Spangled Girl *in the same year, and* Plaza Suite (*1968*). *His latest theatrical effort is* Last of the Red Hot Lovers. *Still playing on Broadway is his musical,* Promises, Promises.

THEATRE

Neil Simon

Perhaps we could take off on the issue of the role of fantasies or dreams that may trip off in you an idea for a play. Whether you feel that dreams, fantasies, daydreams may have any role in giving you ideas.

That's such a complicated question, because I have found out, over the years, that I'm beginning to lose track now of what is fantasy and what is reality. In the beginning, I was experiencing and living things, and then writing about them. I've found out in the last few years I've been writing about things and then experiencing them. Now, maybe it's not true that they're not actually happening that way, but, somehow, mentally, they're all getting mixed up, and I'm beginning to really lose track of the difference between fantasy and reality.

Well, when you say you write about something and then you experience it, is there any way of getting more specific about this? Like The Odd Couple.

Well, in one instance, it's too personal, at this point, I think, to get into a specific—well, *The Odd Couple* was based on a situation in real life that I did not participate in. It was actually about my brother and a roommate of his that he lived with in California. But, there were other people involved in that. He had at different times, two or three people that he lived with, and always had the same experience with each of them. I sort of placed myself in his position, as I did in all writing, in all the plays. I usually place myself in the position of the character that I'm writing about, and that's where I get mixed up, because sometimes I get so involved in that character that I begin to think like that character. And somehow it gets imbedded in my own thoughts, and I begin to think that I have many of the characteristics of that person. In a way, I consider myself a little bit of almost every person that I've every written about. And they are so divergent, all the personalities and characters, that it really becomes confusing sometimes.

Then you're saying there are many facets to your own personality.

I think so. Well, I think so of all personalities. The early plays were completely autobiographical. *Come Blow Your Horn,* my first play, was literally about the experiences of my brother and myself leaving home. The second play was *Barefoot in the Park,* which was about my wife and myself in the early days of our marriage. In those plays I was able to be much more objective. I knew clearly then who was me. I was the boy, my wife was my wife, the mother was her mother, or, not really her mother, but a composite of many of the women that I knew. But, as I grew older, the plays got more complicated, and I began to see myself in many of the other characters. In *The Odd Couple,* I've said to myself, people have said this to me, that I'm both those characters. I'm that compulsive, neat man, cleaning up. I am very neat. Also, I'm occasionally sloppy. And I find myself being both of those characters. Take *Plaza Suite.* It's the story of a marriage between a fifty-one-year-old man, and his wife, who's about forty-eight, and after twenty-three years of marriage, it's going on the rocks. He is now straying, becoming vainer and more self-centered. In a way, I felt myself being that man, although I am ten years younger. I find myself looking in the mirror and saying, "Gosh, I'm putting on weight. I better be careful." On the other hand, I could put myself into the position of the woman, and understand what she is going through. And there again, the reality becomes fantasy and vice versa.

But, now you're talking about empathy, about your ability to put yourself in somebody else's shoes. Do you find this characteristic, for example, in your social relationships with people? Have you been described as being an empathic person. In the way that "Gee, you can, you can somehow feel what I'm feeling, or you're saying, you just said what I was thinking."

Well, I have never quite put myself in the right category in the outside social world. I always picture myself as that person at a cocktail party standing in the corner and watching. And I've always felt, and I think this is very true of most writers that I know, we are observers rather than participants. Even though I do participate in life, I don't consider myself participating. I'm always sort of on the outside, watching it all, noting it, not necessarily with an eye to putting it down as an experience in writing, but just as a human being, because I find it harder to relate to life personally—much easier to go upstairs, put a piece of paper in, and live my life there. Although, that too, is a fantasy in a way, because I do participate in life. I have friends. I have problems. I have a marriage. I have children. And I'm involved in all of these things. Still, I consider myself on the outside of it. When I am sitting and having a conversation with a friend, I hear the conversation. I become the third person at the table listening to the two of us. And I think that is what gives me my ability as a writer, really. To observe this objectively.

It's a way of transcending yourself and observing yourself in interaction and with the other person.

Yes. Exactly.

And how about the idea then of all of these multitudes of experiences that you go through. What determines, while you're sitting there, and you know, you're in it and you're out of it at the same time—that prompts you then to say, "This is an idea, and I'm going to go upstairs now and work on this?"

Well, somehow, you know, this is the part that's mysterious to me. Somehow I have the ability to take the everyday, ordinary occurrence and realize that dramatically it will work. For example, I've just written a film that we'll be shooting in New York soon, called *The Out-of-Towners*. And it's the experiences of a couple who come from the Midwest, and this man has this big job offered to him, in a big company, and it's what he's wanted all his life, and he comes to New York, telling his wife about how marvelous New York is going to be, and how wonderful. They get to New York and their plane is diverted from Kennedy and goes to Boston. They lose their luggage. They come to New York. They lose their hotel room. They get mugged. Well, all of these experiences have happened to me one way or another. When they happened, they were all tragic and terrible. When I relive them, they're all funny. For example, in *Barefoot in the Park*, there's a scene at the end of the second act where the husband and wife, who are married now for a week, have this violent argument, where she says, "I made the worst mistake of my life. We have nothing in common." They have this disastrous terrible fight where they scream at each other, and decide to get a divorce. When you see this onstage, we know that this young couple are in love with each other and that this is just a fight, and we're able to laugh at it, even though we sympathize with them. When it happened to me, in real life, it was tragic. In *The Odd Couple*, this is related through someone else's experience, the man's wife says, "I can't live with you any more. Get out of the house." He leaves, and he goes to his friend's apartment, and says, "What am I going to do?" It's tragic for him, but really tragic. He's contemplating suicide. On the stage it's funny. How I am able to do that, I don't quite know.

But then, what you're saying is that when the argument and talk of divorce after a week of marriage actually came about, were you still able to split yourself this way?

Oh, no. No.

Were you still an observer, or were you really in it?

I was in it. Completely.

So then, only in retrospect do you become a third party observer in a situation like that . . .

Yes. Yes.

Where you're really emotionally involved . . .

Well, when I am that involved with it, in the situation, and when it is seemingly so tragic, then I become very much involved. In the business of this out-of-town couple's coming to New York. Well, I recently went to Jamaica, and I arrived there in my winter suit, my winter overcoat, ready for three weeks of fun, and there's no luggage. Well, it was not very funny then, but still it wasn't that tragic. And I said to myself, "I could use this in the film." So there I can be objective about it.

Do you have any thoughts about this observer—being an observer and a participant at the same time. When you noticed this part of yourself, or how do you think it might have come about?

Well, it goes back as far as when I was a child. I remember always sort of being on the outside of things. Mostly, as I got into my teens, in most social situations. I had a very close friend of mine. We would go to dances, a boy and myself. We'd go to dances and never dance. We would just sit there on the side and comment and get hysterical laughing at this whole ridiculous scene. And yet, when we went home at night, the both of us were very miserable that we didn't dance and meet this very pretty girl over there. And it was a bane of my life, my whole existence that I was always sort of on the outside of things. And somehow I have, I think, this may not be true at all, but I have lived a fuller life writing than experiencing things. It isn't quite true. But it just seems true.

How about the role of comedy then? The idea of laughing at these things that you're really not happy about.

I think it's a mystery to most writers of comedy. I think it may go back to being a defensive trait. I mean, it has to do with a whole Jewish background too. Things get so terrible going back 2,000 years, if you don't laugh at them they become so impossible you can't bear up to it. Like the new humor today is Negro humor. It's just suddenly coming out. We're hearing it now because they have the opportunity to voice it finally, through television and the stage, and so forth. But, it's all those years of persecution, and they have found the ability to laugh at this, rather than to buckle under it. Maybe that's much too intellectual a thought of why I, myself, am able to laugh at these things. But, it may have to do with the whole sociological background. I don't necessarily laugh at these things when they're happening, nor do I see the humor when they're happening, but retrospectively, when I sit down I see it all. I am at my funniest, even personally I would say, in the face of danger or in the face of tragedy. Not real tragedy. But, one of my great fears, being a claustrophobiac, or, at least a retired claustrophobiac, I'm pretty much over it now, is the great fear of being trapped in elevators. Well, it's happened to me twice, and I was funny on both occasions with other people in the elevator, only as a safety valve to keep myself from going completely to pieces. We had a trip recently, my wife and myself. About two years ago we were flying to Tokyo and the plane crashed in Honolulu. It didn't crash, but it aborted the takeoff, and we skidded along and had to go out the emergency chute. It was one of the most horrible experiences I've ever had and one of the funniest, because the minute the real danger was over, I was able to look at it objectively and make myself laugh, make my wife laugh, and all the other people around us. And in telling the story to other people now, it's one of the funniest stories they've ever heard. And yet, what is the story. It's about a plane crashing in Honolulu. It's not very funny. So, somehow I'm able to translate these things into terms of humor.

It's a kind of tragic comedy.

Yes. It's what I look for more and more now in my plays. To find more tragic things to write about. In a way that first act in *Plaza Suite* is that.

Do you find that you've written about things that you have never experienced?

I've done it once, with not very good results. *The Star-Spangled Girl* was a completely contrived play, and a play born out of my fantasies in a way. Fantasies going back to my adolescence about the all-American girl, the girl with blond hair who is the olympic swimmer. I never met that girl, but I fantasized about it. And in looking for an idea for a play which I didn't have that particular season, much to my mistake, I wrote this play. It was manufactured. It was contrived. And not nearly as successful as the other plays. It had no basis of truth really. So, I find I do not, any more, try to write about things that either I have not experienced, you know, observed close-hand.

This new play that you're working on for next season that was written about in the Times *last Sunday.*

The *Last of the Red-Hot Lovers.*

Now this is something that, also, is not born strictly out of fantasy.

That's right. The specifics I have not experienced, but it's based out of my own thoughts, out of people that I've met, women that I've met. I found another thing, too. That in almost all of the plays I'm writing about myself somehow. I am always the central character in all of the plays. In *Promises, Promises,* an adaptation of *The Aparment,* I had to find something that was new. And so I put myself into the play. And myself being the facet of the man's character that talks to the audience. And the things that he says to the audience are exactly what I would say, if I were onstage in that position. It's being very frank and honest and personal. And so there I am again in a play.

The choice. After all, you experience a great many things in the course of a day, a week, a year. The choice of what you are going to write. Is it fair to say sometimes you experience something and it just kind of grabs you, and you say, "This is it." Is it that kind . . . ?

Well, sometimes I just sit there for months and months. The idea. . . . There is always one thing that I always look for in the beginning of a play, and that is an event, an important event in someone's life. For example: the first time he's had relations with a girl. The first time he leaves home. Their twenty-third anniversary. Moving into their new apartment. It can't be just an everyday occurrence. At least, not for me. And so, somehow they go hand in hand. When I experience it, it becomes an event, and I say, "This would make good material for a play."

But, not any event.

No, not any event. It has to be something quite important in their lives. Very important. A turning point. That's why I get nervous about my future. I say, "How many turning points are there in your life?" But, there are enough to go on writing about.

How about the mechanics of your writing? Do you find that you work in a methodical way?

Well, in the beginning, I didn't know how to write a play, and so I asked people. And they said, "Well, you make outlines." And, so I would make— in the very first play, in *Come Blow Your Horn*, I made an outline of the entire play, of the first act, the second act, and the third act. Then I started to write it, and I found that the characters were heading off in one direction, completely in opposition to where I was heading to in the end. And I said, "What will I do? How will I get them there?" And so, I found myself twisting and pushing for them to get back on the path that I was heading for, and there came the contrivances. And the play was not working that way. So, I would do it again and again, and I would change the ending a little, so that I wouldn't have to divert them too much to get to that ending. Well, I did this twenty times over, from beginning to end. And I found that was not the way to write a play, because that's not the way life is. You don't know what the end is going to be, so you don't twist and push it. It just carries you along, somehow, predetermined by your character. And so, now in plays, I don't make an outline at all. I have a very brief outline in my head about what the play is about. But, I would like to be as surprised and entertained as the audience is. And so I begin—I just put the paper in and start to go, and discover it. And I can sit there in that first writing, laughing at the play as much as an audience eventually will, because I'm amused by what is going to happen. And I find it very difficult to talk about new plays. People ask me, "What's this new play about?" Well, I've only written one act, so I can't tell them what it's about, because I don't know where it's going. *Plaza Suite, The Odd Couple,* I had brief ideas about where they were going, but I just let the characters take off. So, there are no more outlines.

All right. So, you've written the first act. You don't know what is going to happen in the third act.

Well, basically. I mean, I know who the characters will be, and what the situation will be. But, what the result of it is, I don't know yet.

You're just going to let it . . .

Let it happen . . .

Can you tell us about letting something happen?

Well, I don't even know the next line that the characters are going to say. People always figure because I have so many funny lines in the play that I must put the lines down first and then try to find a way to get to them. Well, I don't. I just write the line, the next line comes. And the next line after that comes. What determines that process I just don't know. Maybe I do. I just can't explain it right now. I guess I would have to be doing it, come to that line, and then tell you. Sometimes I go over it. It's not all quite that instinctive. I mean, they just don't flow that easily. I'll write a line, and I know that the next thing that she says must have a certain point to it, must push the story along, and yet I have to say it amusingly. But, it can't come out as a joke that you could just take out of context and tell anybody, because then it's just a joke, and it's not coming out of character or a situation.

The best way to do it, for me, to find the amusing people, is to take somebody who has an amusing characteristic, an amusing twist of thought, or the way he phrases things. I guess, maybe, in a way, a lot of my things relate to the Greek plays, in that there's always someone relating something to the audience. It's the Greek chorus. There's always a character in my play who's the Greek chorus, but is the central character. For example; Oscar, the Walter Matthau character in *The Odd Couple,* was the Greek chorus. He told the audience everything that's going on. He says, "Look what this idiot is doing now. He is cleaning up my poker table. I don't want him to clean up my poker table." But, instead of saying it to the audience, he says it directly to that character in the situation.

In all of the plays, *Barefoot in the Park,* the husband says to the audience, "Look what my idiot wife did. She took this apartment that's five flights up, and it snows through the ceiling." "Look what she did," again, talking to the audience. For the first time, I literally did it in *Promises, Promises.* I had him talking to the audience, explaining his thoughts. Now this may be a key thing, because I know it works. That character always tells the truth. He never lies. In *Promises, Promises,* he says one thing to a girl, and then tells the truth to the audience. For example, the girl says to him, "All I do is think about you, and dream about you. You're the only man in the world for me." And then he says to the audience, "It's not true. That's a daydream. I made it up." What she actually said is . . . "Hello, how are you. I'm sorry I can't stop to talk to you now." So, he's being truthful again. The Oscar character is completely truthful. The wife in *Plaza Suite* is completely truthful. The husband comes home. He is quite obsessed with himself, about his physical being. He's just come back from having his teeth capped. And he bares his teeth to his wife, and he says, "How do they look? Do they look too white?" And she says, "No. It looks perfect with the blue shirt." She's putting him on. She's saying, "'You fatuous idiot. You know, having your teeth capped. You're fifty-one years old. Why don't you grow old gracefully." But, she says it to the audience. And the audience laughs at that. So, that's usually the key process for me.

Yes. So there's a bifurcation here, between reality and laughing, and between—well, is it reality and laughing at reality?

I guess so.

The splitting. The splitting here of the thing happening and laughing at it again as you described it there.

It doesn't pertain, I guess, to all kinds of comedy. It pertains to my kind of comedy. Being truthful and real. The things that really make me laugh are people who are so frank and truthful, even in social situations. And then it becomes shocking and very funny. Someone once told me that Elaine May was at a dinner party. Elaine May of Nichols and May. And she was sitting there at this party, and someone was talking to her, and just droning on and on, as happens at all these terrible dinners. And finally she said, "Would you please excuse me. I'm very bored." Well, I mean, that's kind of shocking, but it's so truthful, it's funny. There's a designer, a set designer I know, who's also the same kind of person. Walking along the street and someone met him and he said, "My gosh, how are you? Haven't seen you in so long." And he wanted to get going, and the person said, "Can we have lunch sometime?" He said, "No," and walked away. That's funny to me. I mean it's so shockingly truthful and frank. Nobody ever says these things.

Then you're cutting through certain social niceties.

Yes. Exactly.

Well, does this trip off any thoughts in your mind about like where it comes from—this laughter in cutting through things.

No. Why it's funny—

Breaking open what's hypocritical and what's phony.

I don't know why it's funny because in the real situation without putting it so succinctly, saying, "No, I won't have lunch with you," people who are that truthful are not necessarily funny. But, I think that just sort of pointing out the ridiculousness of ourselves as human beings and trying to point it out to the public, to the audience. . . .

Do you have any idea where this comes from in you? For example, is there something in your background that may tie in with this in some way?

Well, it's just something that's always been with me, my whole life. I've always been in opposition to pomposity and to society.

Were you a rebel?

Not really. No. I was a rebel in my mind, again. I didn't actively participate in it. If I were a young kid today, I don't think I'd have long hair and be one of those kids. Because I don't think those kids are on the outside of it looking in. They're all participants. Most of them. Because I have never been able to conform, I haven't belonged to a club in my whole life, any kind of group. I can't do things on a regular basis. Thursday night poker. Nothing. It just has to be always on the outside. And as far as where it all came from I'm not quite sure.

Could you tell us a little bit about your background? Your mother . . .

Well, I come from a middle-class Jewish background. I was brought up in Washington Heights, with my brother, who is eight years older than myself. It's funny. I've just been reading about myself. Philip Roth's *Portnoy's Complaint*. And I think it's a brilliant, brilliant book. You ought to read that, and then you can put it down for me, because that's what it's all about.

Is it biographical of you?

What? *Portnoy's Complaint?* Well, it seems to be about every Jewish middle-class young boy that I know. But that's interesting, too—about in my plays. I always think that I'm writing to a very specific group. Only those who have experienced what I have experienced. But then I found out, in my world travels of seeing some of my plays in all places in the world, that people have identified with these same situations. So, there seems to be something universal about human relations. When you get into specific incidents, it doesn't necessarily work, and that's why I only like to write about people confronting each other with some kind of problem, rather than writing about sociological problems. I will never be that kind of writer. Writing about the contemporary problems. With the exception of this one film that I'm doing, about the troubles of New York, or a big city.

Is it a documentary?

It's a documentary comedy in a way. Yes. That's what's funny. Because that's the name that I've applied to it. A documentary. In trying to relate it to the director and to the cameraman and the producer by saying, "I would like to shoot this as a documentary rather than as a performance of a film, a play."

You were telling us about your background. Well, what did your father do?

My father is now dead. He was a salesman in the dress business. There is no theatrical background in the family. My brother was seventeen years old, and he wanted to become a radio writer. That was his great ambition,

to go to Hollywood, and become a radio writer, for Jack Benny, or, you
know, one of the comedians. I, being eight years younger than he, I was
nine years old at the time, wasn't much help to him. So, he would look for
other people to write with. And then, as we grew older, when I was about
fifteen years old, we started writing together. Then I went into the Army. I
got out when I was twenty. And I went to work in Warner Bros., in the
mailroom. And then the two of us got a job at CBS, working on a radio
show. And we worked together for about ten years.

What kind of work in radio?

Writing comedy. Radio shows.

*That's remarkable, that you could break in that way. Isn't that difficult to
break into?*

Yes, it was. But my brother had given up a much more lucrative job to do
this. He was making about $250 a week working at Warner Bros. And
he quit that to take this job writing a radio show where we got $50 a
week each. For me, it was a $25 increase, so I didn't mind. That was
pretty good. But, we did that for a while. Then we started writing special
material for nightclub comedians. And then started to get some reputation,
and worked in television shows. And eventually, I worked on the *Sid
Caesar Show of Shows* and the *Sergeant Bilko Show*. And then, nine years
ago, I wrote my first play. But that's when everything changed for me.
Because, as a writer, when I progressed and grew as a writer, I stopped
writing about other people's experiences. For example, *Bilko,* or whatever
particular show I was writing about, and writing through their eyes. I
started to write through my own personal experiences. And, again, writing
with truthfulness. You know, being frank about things.

What about your brother now?

My brother is still a writer. He's working in television now. He directs
occasionally, too. He's done a number of my productions in national companies, touring companies.

Is he here or on the Coast?

He lives on the Coast. Right now he's here. But, he mostly lives on the
Coast. He prefers it there. I hate it there.

But, apparently, you feel that he's had a significant impact on you, on your career in writing.

Oh, yes, the most. He was responsible, I think, for my becoming a writer. He encouraged me as a very young boy, ten, eleven, twelve years of age. I guess I had some indication at the time that I was funny. I was never a clown. I could never be funny with my friends, but in a very small, select group, my observations on things, I guess, were funny. My brother was the first to spot this. And I remember, at the age, when I was about thirteen or fourteen years old, he told me then. He said, "Someday you're going to be the best comedy writer in America." He used to say that to me then. And it was, you know, pretty young to spot any talent then.

What about your mother? What's been the role of your mother in your life?

Oh, is this going to get into analysis now?

Well, no, not quite. Particularly your creative life, you know. What you've been doing in the last nine years that you've been writing plays.

No specific role, really. I mean, I've used her as a model of the woman in *Come Blow Your Horn.* But, I think I'm naturally a product of my environment, of my life with my mother and father, which was pretty hectic, and quite terrible at times. And I think that has been instrumental in building my character and personality in a negative way.

So, in other words, their relationship with each other was not too good.

Oh, terrible. Stormy.

Did you find yourself laughing at it?

Oh, of course not. Oh, it was the worst. Suffered terribly. Terribly.

But, now again, now, in retrospect you can take a situation in a marriage, where it's stormy and you can write about it.

Yes. When I did write about marriage, which was my mother and father in *Come Blow Your Horn,* not completely, but to a greater extent, I wrote about their better times together. When they were close together, and their main problem in life was their sons, and were they going to grow up to be successful, good young men. But I would never write about the terrible times between them, because that really was just too horrible. And what I have done, and it seems to be a trait of mine, is that I have blocked out almost all the experiences of my past. It only comes out under prodding. My mother remembers every instant, every moment of her life, and she relates things to me that I've completely forgotten. And so, most, I always consider that my life has started around the age of twenty-three, twenty-four. Before that, it's a sort of blur to me.

Is that about when you got married?

I got married at twenty-six.

If we can get back for a moment to the more specific things about the way in which you work. Such things as do you feel that your mood is important in your productivity?

That's pretty interesting. Well, usually I can just turn it on almost at will. And it's almost like plugging in an electric typewriter. Sometimes I can't think of anything until I sit down at the typewriter. And the minute I do, it's on. It's like I'm paying for this now, so I better get busy.

You plugged yourself in.

Plugged myself in. Yes. And the current is running, and you're paying the bill. But I can work almost anywhere, if I have to. During the past few years I seem to work less than I did in the beginning when I was really so obsessed with becoming a playwright. During the time I wrote *Come Blow Your Horn,* I was writing a television show six days a week. I wrote *Come Blow Your Horn* at night, on the weekends, every spare moment. I don't have to do that any more. But I still write about seven months out of the year. The rest of the time is involved either in production, or in traveling, hobbies, whatever it is. But, I'm able to go upstairs and sit down at the typewriter, after having breadfast, and I'll read the paper, without the least bit of thought of what I'm going to do, then go over what I had written yesterday, read it, put the paper in, and BANG, go right off on it.

Regardless of any other mood that you might be in. If you come down at breakfast and you have a fight with your wife, then you can still go up and plug yourself in.

Yes. I've been able to do that. Only recently I've been in a sort of de-pressed state. A few months ago. And I found it difficult to work. But, mostly, even having a fight with my wife, I'm able to do that. In a way, it's an escape. That's always the best part of it. The writing. Production is not so much fun. Rewriting is kind of fun, because you're getting a second chance at your life again. Seeing it onstage is not very much fun, after the first time. After the first experience of audience acceptance. I rarely go back to see them any more. It's sort of, you know, reliving something. I want to go on to something new, keep it going. But, doing the actual writing is the best part. That's why people always ask me, "Would I like to direct?" I wouldn't because directing is *re*creating. The creating part is the only real fun for me. It's, in a way, giving birth to something.

Right. Well, that's what we're working on. This whole idea of the birth of an idea. And again, we want to get back, if you will, to the fact that you experience a great many things in the course of a week, or in the course of a year. And yet, out of all of these things, you manage to choose a single one that's going to become the kernel of a play. And what we're particularly interested in is, you see, what the progression is from having that experience to the awareness on your part that this is going to be the topic of the play. Is it something that you dream about? Is it something that you work over in your mind? Is it something you wake up in the morning, and you say, "Damn it, that's it. That experience can be worked over."

It's all of those things. It doesn't happen in an instant flash . . . suddenly say, "Hey, that's an idea for a play." Although it has happened to a degree. *The Odd Couple* came about that way. It was something that my brother had been experiencing many years. Usually, I am working on one thing and thinking about the next thing, which is also part of that life process of keeping it going, always afraid it's all going to burn out, and so I have something to go on to. I get the idea and if it's a really solid, firm idea, it will stay with me. The development of the ideas and saying, "This is what's going to make a play," comes to me at the strangest times. I could be shaving, you know, and say, "My gosh, that's it!" Never—no, I won't say never, but once I went upstairs at the typewriter without an idea for a play, and said, "What could I write about." And, I wrote *Star-Spangled Girl*. And that's why it came out the way it did. All of the others have presented themselves to me. And while working on something, just sitting around thinking about something, and I say, "That's a good idea for a play."

"Has presented itself to me." Could we work that over a little bit. Take that phrase. "It has presented itself to me." Like, how do you experience "that it presented itself to you?"

The thought just occurs in my head.

As if from nowhere?

Well, I'm trying to recreate it now. I'm trying to think in each of the plays when it happened, and I can't go back to any specific moment. *Plaza Suite* was about—the first act about that couple, middle-aged couple, was about a specific couple that I knew. And just talking about them to other friends, discussing it with my wife, I guess, just one day I said, "I'd really love to write about that, because she's a fantastic woman. I'd really love to put that down on paper." And that's about all I would do because I would be working on something else. Then, I would keep thinking about that. Then, I'd say to my wife, "You know, I think it would be a great idea if I showed them on their honeymoon night, or something." And somehow, somehow it just grows and develops.

So, you take something that happened, but your fantasy then elaborates on it.

Yes. But, almost always it generates out of a character I know, rarely out of a situation. I'm talking about a full-blown play. There's an incident in *Plaza Suite* which is a sort of manufactured farce, which is really based on an incident about a husband—did you see the play?

Is that the one with the hole in the ceiling?

No, that's *Barefoot in the Park*. In *Plaza Suite*, the third act, there are three one-act plays. In the third act, they all take place in the suite in the Hotel Plaza. And in the third act, it's the wedding day of a young girl, and she locks herself in the bathroom, refuses to come out, and it's the horrors that the father is going through in order to get his daughter out of the bathroom, and the whole play is about that. That's an incident that has nothing to do with my own experiences or life. It's a farce. And the rules of farce are quite different from the rules of writing something that is real. A manufactured situation like that will only hold up for an act. But, even there, once I got that idea, again, I drew from my own experiences what I would be like if I were that father, what my father's own reactions were to panic and tragedy. What my mother's reactions were. Her reaction to all sorts of panic was, "If I could just keep peace in the family. If I keep my father happy, and him happy, then I'll be happy." She didn't care about the situation itself. And that's what this woman does. But, the moment that that came to me, I don't know either. It just—bang, it happened.

We'd like to ask you about the role of accident.

Accident?

Accident.

In writing?

In writing. Whether you find you're in the middle of something today, you go outside, and, quite by chance, something happens, and like whether this might become part of the play.

Rarely. Rarely will I be writing something, and then I go out, then something happens, and I say, "I will use that in the play." Mostly, maybe contrary to what I said before, they have all happened, and they're all imbedded here, in my mind. And the accidents happen all at the typewriter. It's all ad lib sitting up there.

You really let it flow?

Yes. It just comes out. There is one specific incident that was a pure accident, and it's a line in *Odd Couple*, and it happens to be the biggest laugh in the play. What happened was, I think, in the third act, when they have already had the blowup, the two of them, and Oscar, the sloppy one, is saying to Felix, "I can't stand living with you any more. You are driving me crazy. I want you out of this place." And now he starts to recapitulate all of the terrible things that have been going on since they have been living together. And he starts to itemize all the things that he does that drive him crazy. And one of the things that he mentions is that—he says, "You always leave me little notes on my pillow." He says, "I told you a million times I can't stand little notes on my pillow." Then, I thought: I'm sitting and writing this now, and saying, "What kind of a note would he leave him?" So, I say, "Well, he would leave him some innocuous, silly note, like, 'we are all out of corn flakes.' " So that Oscar should go buy corn flakes, which would irritate him no end. I said, "Now Felix, being such a peculiar person, he would sign the note." I mean, there were only the two of them living there, but he is so orderly that in order to write a note, it's an orderly thing to do to sign it. So, he would sign it. So I said, "How would he sign it? His name is Felix Unger." So, I said, "Well he would sign it 'Felix.' " "Well," I said, "that's not funny. Too ordinary. He would have some more of a flourish than that." I said, "He wouldn't sign it 'Felix Unger.' " So, I said, "He'll just put his initials down." And I put his initials down. They were F.U. And, then Oscar's line is, "It took me three hours to figure out that 'F.U.' was Felix Unger." Well, there was an accident. I said, "My gosh, look what I fell into. F.U." People think that I wrote the F.U. and then made up the name Felix Unger to fit. Well, accidents like that occur all the time in writing. You know, you write something and then relate back to it, and say, "Oh, he did this. Now I can have him do this."

That's a good example of serendipity.

The first act is always the hardest to write, in that you have nothing prepared for you. The audience knows nothing about the characters. But, once it's established in the first act, the second and third act feed on the first act, on all of the things that we built, on the characters. And so, you're always going back and feeding on it.

Are you considered a funny person, socially? Are you as funny?

Well, I think, basically, I'm a shy person. So I am not funny in social situations, except with my close friends. And, then again, my humor is on a certain level that it would only pertain to people that know me. I think the only times that I am funny, perhaps, as I said before, in those horrible situations, like trapped in elevators and airplanes. I used to try to be funnier, when I was younger. Now that I'm more secure as a writer, I leave it for the typewriter. And, I try not to be funny.

He's hit the things we're interested in.

You know, it frightens me, too. The whole aspect of, "Where does the creative urge and the instinct all come from?" Because, when you don't know where it comes from, it's a mystery, and it frightens you. Say, it could turn off at any moment. You think. It's not true. I know inherently, it's not true.

Isn't that largely a fear of people whose livelihood depends upon it?

Yes.

And, the reason you feel this way is because there's no way of predicting.

Uh huh.

That's right. But, that's what keeps you from being a hack.

Yes.

If you're a hack, you're sure the bread is going to keep coming in.

Well, I don't think I'm ever going to run out of ideas, really. Because, when you take from life, there's enough going on there. It's that business that I said before of taking events, specific events. Now, I've used so many, there are things that I can't go back on. The beginnings of marriage. The ends of marriage. So many things like that, and I always have to look for specific things. Also, I keep forgetting how to write a play. Every time I start, I type the title of the play, or the tentative title, just to get my typing going. Just to, you know, get going. Then, I write, "ACT I." Then, I sit and rub my hands for a while. And, then I say—I really get into a state of panic. I say, "Maybe I should go to some college and learn how to write a play." Or, call up another playwright, and say, "How do you do it? Quick! Tell me." 'Cause I forget. And, then I just plunge in, and I start to describe the character, and try to think of that initial sequence, which is very important. I've always found that in the writing of a play, in the first five or six pages, if you can get the audience to feel secure that they're in good hands, that they will then relax. And I think that opening sequence is terribly important in a play. And in almost all of my plays, the opening sequence is, has been, some of the best things in it. Like the poker game in *The Odd Couple.*

Well, your plays have been remarkably successful. Maybe, with the exception of Star-Spangled Girl.

And that, too, had some degree of success, but nothing like the others. But, yeah, they've all been . . .

Yes.

That's something else. I don't even think about that though, about, "Will this be successful? Will it be good?" I have to first use myself as the barometer of what's good. Like, when I worked in television, I did not say,

"I think this is funny, so I'll write it." I had to write it because the comedian thought it would be funny, and I was going, specifically, for the laughs in the audience. But, I don't do that in working for myself, as a playwright.

Did you find that stifling?

Oh, terribly. Yes.

Yes.

And, I had to get out of it. I write now for myself. And, also, I pick an imaginary group of my most discerning best friends. Mike Nichols, or a few other people. And I say, "Would this amuse them?" And if it amuses them, and if they'll think it's funny, in my mind, then I'll think I'm on the right base.

Conclusion and a Review
of the Literature on Creativity

The preceding interviews were conducted with creative artists and scientists. Yet it must be admitted that these contributions represent derivatives or epiphenomena of the creative process itself. The content of the interviews, as well as the ambiance during the interviews, reflected the nonintellective and nonselfconscious urge to create. Perhaps a creative person is so close to this urge that the causes not only elude him, but are of little real concern to him. For this reason, we have attempted to study the phenomenology of the creative experience itself rather than issues of specific substance or content in any particular work.

We undertook the study assuming that the creative process is not a mystical one, but an experience that would lend itself to investigation. Our chosen method for such an investigation was that of an open-ended, free-expression interview with specific scientists and artists. Also, we assumed that the creative urge is present in everyone (an assumption that was spontaneously verbalized by a number of the contributors), but that biological, historical, psychological, and sociological determinants serve either to enhance or to constrain the realization of these urges. In our study, we could not investigate the biological aspects, except insofar as an interviewee's life history might reflect possible inherited capabilities.

In our attempt to integrate the contents of the preceding chapters, it was necessary to consider whether we would be justified in discussing creativity in the arts and sciences as if it were one and the same process or whether it would be necessary to separate the arts and sciences and to treat them individually. Further, since our study is not quantitative in nature, nor the sample large enough to warrant firm conclusions, a question could be raised as to whether we could arrive at a theoretical framework that might encompass the material presented in the interviews. Finally, in view of the open-ended, relatively unstructured interviews, we were not at all certain what areas would emerge by means of which the content could be evaluated. Following are some conclusions we reached.

The comments of artists and scientists concerning the creative experience (i.e., the birth of ideas, factors facilitating and deterring productivity, etc.) suggest that the process is very similar in both disciplines. Dr. Penfield, who is both a scientist and a writer, suggests that the process is similar, and the interviews with contributors in areas of philosophy (Professor Hook) and linguistics (Professor Chomsky), suggest that their experiences in creating and working are not very different from those in the arts or sciences.

Consequently, we believe with Brewster Ghiselin in *The Creative Process,* that general conclusions about the process of creating in the arts and sciences can be viewed in a unitary manner despite certain obvious differences in content, adherence to specific steps dictated by specific disciplines, and the process in science of subjecting findings to acceptable proof. R. L. Wilder, a mathematician, states in *Science,*[1]

> The role of intuition in research is to provide the "educated guess," which may prove to be true or false; but in either case, progress cannot be made without it and even a false guess may lead to progress. Thus intuition also plays a major role in the evolution of mathematical concepts. The advance of mathematical knowledge periodically reveals flaws in cultural intuition; these result in "crises," the solution of which results in a more mature intuition.

Indeed, in the process of categorizing some of the remarks of our contributors into specific channels, we found it difficult to distinguish artists from scientists simply by their statements.

To provide for such variations in personalities among our subjects, we feel that a field theoretical approach is most practical. In this framework, the person and the environment are placed within the same universe of discourse, and the "inner-directed" man and the "outer-directed" man may be viewed along a person-environment continuum.

The interaction of the individual with his environment is a recurring theme in the interviews. There is repeated emphasis on the effect of outside influences. Cashin speaks of the new perspectives she gains in walking around New York and in traveling; Engman refers to his drive to work in the morning as affecting his frame of mind and his productivity; Soyer paints from the life around him. It is, however, recognized by most interviewees that while the surroundings provide stimuli, such stimuli must fall

[1] Vol. 156, 5 May 1967, pp. 605–10.

on fertile territory. They must be processed "through the filter of the mind," structured through imagination and scholarship into a concrete achievement. In short, the sense organs which perceive the external stimuli must be supported by a creative mind.

Despite our efforts to keep the interviews as free and open-ended as possible, no doubt as interviewers our biases determined the questions we asked, the leads we followed, and the areas we wished to emphasize. The dimensions to be discussed below, however, were not preconceived, but emerged as common denominators out of the interviews. Indeed, the areas that were spontaneously covered in many of the interviews and that emerged as significant to the creative process came as a surprise to us. In addition, the remarkable extent of agreement by the contributors on certain themes was also unexpected.

We have made no attempt to quantify the data of the interviews. Our approach has been more qualitative and impressionistic.

The interviews generally seemed to cover topics such as: the affective aspects of the creative experience, factors that favored or hindered the creative experience, sources of stimulation, the relationship of mood to creativity, the place of self-expression in creativity, the ego and the creative experience, the contributors' philosophy of working and manner of working; and, finally, the place of their life history in their creativity.

To begin with the emotional aspects of the creative experience, it was found that feelings of excitement and pleasure accompany creative work. In many instances, this excitement is associated with arriving at insights, seeing new principles, and discovering relationships which were not fully expected. Such excitement is also experienced when one finds a satisfying explanation.

This sense of excitement, which some refer to as sensual or even sexual, is experienced by both artists and scientists. A sense of urgency is also present, stimulated by a fear that unless the idea is worked on immediately it will be lost. Under the fire of inspiration, one must not lose control so that the theme or idea can be grasped. Saltman sums it up well: "Those days when everything is hitting and you're seeing new relationships and each experiment works—this is a wonderful, wild whole life."

Implicit in what has been said is a sense of mystery which stems from not knowing where one's work is leading. This feeling is so strong that the creator may consider himself passive, as if the solution were not really to come from him. Resolutions are often referred to as coming from the "unconscious." I. B. Singer speaks of an imp that inspires him drop by drop. Others refer to "something in the back of my mind" that is arranging the material in a particular way.

The element of surprise and mystery in the creative process is not uncommon. Both Simon and Singer admit that often they themselves do not know how a piece of writing will end. Surprise is an experience that plays a part at the birth of an idea and during the work itself.

Yet along with a sense of surprise, is the feeling that nothing is really "created." Ideas may emerge unexpectedly but it is implied that they have been available all the time. One feels the process is one of discovery, of evolution.

A necessary adjunct to this process is the willingness of our contributors to trust their hunches, to remain open to surprise and accident. They speak of random events: Steichen utilizing the accident of a drop of water on his camera lens to obtain certain effects; Franzen saying, "I wish I could design as if my pen had been slipping all the time." Saltman refers to an accident during an experiment in which he put in too much sugar and arrived at a whole new chemistry of the sugar complex. Untracht speaks of poor timing in enameling "with spectacular results." Rainey speaks of accidents concerning the location of digs in archaeology.

Our contributors recognized that certain individuals have a knack for having all the good accidents happen to them. There is, therefore, a suggestion that accidents are not really accidents. As Lumet put it, "When you're in top form, you get all the breaks and all the accidents go your way."

Open-mindedness, flexibility, willingness to trust hunches, and curiosity are factors that emerge repeatedly as facilitating and favoring creativity. However, our contributors recognize the importance of structure. Sidney Hook speaks of "a sense of adventure burdened by a stock of common sense."

Of these qualities perhaps the most consistent factor that emerges is that of keeping an open mind. Penfield refers to a "fresh brain" as enabling one to see things that fatigue or rigid thinking would otherwise obscure. Other contributors speak of attacking problems with a mind free of preconceptions, premature conclusions, and patterned responses. They call for a free and relaxed state of mind. When faced with a seemingly insoluble problem, most of our contributors leave the task temporarily and go on to something else. This grows out of a recognition that nothing is to be gained by pursuing a problem doggedly. "The worst thing I can do is to force something and to bang my head against the wall," and again, "When things don't happen in the area I'm working on, I go someplace else."

Confidence and boldness are stressed. Several interviewees refer to the fact that had they carefully weighed the extent of their lack of knowledge before beginning a project, or had they realized the boldness of their expectations, they would not have done what they did. Instead many of the contributors refer to the "blessed state of ignorance" in which they pursued their careers with confidence not considering their limitations. In order to maintain their open-mindedness, a number of people, when faced with difficulty in their work, turn the problem around and reverse the field. Krech speaks of viewing the question in a manner "ganz Verkehrt" or Nelson states, "If none of the possible solutions work, then the only solution has to be the impossible one."

The creative mind is an active mind, constantly questioning. Contributors spoke of the presence of many thoughts converging upon the mind at once. However, this does not prevent focusing and selective perception. The mind filters certain observations, not necessarily in an orderly fashion, during the period preparatory to creative work.

Obviously, a necessary condition for the creative experience is intellectual independence. A number of our contributors refer to having to depend upon one's self with no prescribed guides or rules; of "finding one's own way." On the other hand, we come across references to what may appear to be passivity on the part of the creator, as if he or she had nothing to do with the ideas and work. One cannot help but notice phrases such as "the idea came to me," "the solution presented itself," and "it was in the back of my mind." Given a certain modesty factor, it still appears that some individuals do not consider themselves to be the prime movers, but simply the instruments through which certain operations take place. Of course, there is no question that the individual is responsible (though the phenomenological descriptions are enough to start one thinking along mind-body dualistic lines). The organizational processes within the brain function autochthonously once the material itself is present as a stimulus. The insights that emerge from the influence of these central processes on the stimuli are experienced as if they were outside the individual, as if the stimuli "demanded" or "required" a given solution.

Conditions that stimulate the creative act are varied and may be viewed from the vantage points of stimuli arising from within the individual, stimuli arising from the work and instruments of work, and stimuli arising from without. Ideas arise and solutions to problems emerge from within, often in a spontaneous, enigmatic and mysterious fashion. Statements such as, "ideas just introduce themselves" or "ideas just rush in from various directions," or "I just feel that something wants to assert itself" all point up the enigmatic quality of the inner stimuli. From what has already been said, it appears likely that the ideas that rush in or occur when working, relaxing or listening to music are the end result of a prepared mind. The stimulation in some instances can be pinpointed more precisely. Some interviewees attribute a relationship of their ideas to their dreams and fantasies. Others do not feel these influence them to the slightest extent.

The contributors have repeatedly emphasized that they are stimulated by the processes of their craft—writing, talking, using their hands, experimenting. The tools of the craft must be present to offer the immediate opportunity for translating ideas into concrete form. Music is usually composed at the piano; architecture takes form with a pen and sketchbook; a novel takes form on paper.

Collaboration with others appears to some as a significant source of stimulation. The opportunity to exchange views with members of other disciplines is also considered productive.

The environment provides important stimuli, and plays a significant role in enhancing or impeding productivity. Of crucial consideration here is the interrelatedness of the self and the outside world. Stimuli are absorbed, integrated, and organized by the creative mind. A walk around the U.N. may offer Cashin new ideas for design, a train trip to Montreal may become the basis of a story by Singer, or a walk through Washington Square may inspire the painter, Soyer, while for thousands of others such experiences would go unnoticed. To repeat, what is outside must be reseen through the imagination in order to become part of one's work and experience.

In addition, meeting deadlines, the need to get a job done, to earn money, etc., are seen by many as spurring productivity, though to others these are seen as encumbrances. Perhaps we are referring more to motives for work than stimuli for creativity. Inducing work in order to meet a commission or purely for monetary gain may place the individual under pressures that are alien to the relaxed, free, and open-minded spirit necessary, though history can supply examples of major work accomplished under these circumstances.

There is widespread agreement as we have cited, that rigidity and becoming set in a particular thought pattern stand in the way of the creative process. Such factors as being too concerned about the future, concerned about failure, or preoccupied with problems of everyday reality can also hinder one's productivity. These all seem to work against the kind of open-mindedness required.

In this regard, of course, mood plays a significant role. Some contributors refer to desperation as spurring them on to work, and suggest that extreme depression may be necessary. Others speak of a sense of irritation and dissatisfaction as inducements, and still others speak of creating in a state of motor agitation in which they walk nervously around the room. This spectrum of activities appears to be preparatory to actually settling down to work. Of course, many produce quite methodically without going through this stage of irritability.

There is general agreement that during the work phase, depression is deleterious. We may make reference to tension-release when working and to depression as impeding the work itself. To paraphrase Copland, art is an affirmative gesture. You create when you're elated, even if you're elated about expressing depression. Actual depression can make a writer impotent. Some are able therefore to remove their personal life from their work. That life may be chaotic, but it does not affect the working time.

Some contributors feel that self-analysis and concern with one's motives hinders creativity and leads to self-consciousness. Others, such as Sidney Lumet, feel that awareness of psychological factors aids them in their work. It seems as if the analysis of motives in the second group, however, occurs after the creative period and not during it.

Self-expression is one of the significant motives behind creating. The German poet Heine wrote, "By creating I could recover: by creating I became healthy." Repeatedly, during our interviews the theme emerges of finding release in creative work. Cashin states that, "Perhaps the creative person uses problems in a constructive way." Engman refers to his desire to put in concrete form the answer to the question, "Who am I?" Others speak of their work as being the best of themselves. Work is also viewed as an escape from boredom and despondency and as a soporific. All these statements point clearly to the fact that to these individuals, their work is essential to their psychic economy. They feel that they lead a fuller life through their work, and that work keeps life in balance. Some say that it is easier to express themselves through their art or science than to relate to the world outside. The writers (Singer, Simon, Rodman) admitted readily that fiction is generally autobiographical in one way or another. In that sense, the expression of the self is seen most directly.

The desire to prove that one is making a significant contribution to the world, that one's work is meaningful, is important to creative people. Our contributors spoke in one way or another of longstanding feelings and fantasies of greatness, Walter Mitty fantasies, so to speak. They were able to speak of these with tongue in cheek, at the same time believing in them. The desire to leave a significant mark on the art or science worlds is revealed in such statements as, "If I don't write it, no one else will," and that "Only I can write that particular story." Engman speaks of the need to dominate the materials of his craft, to make a substance take the form he desires. Steichen emphasizes that photography is not a poor relative of painting, but a form of great artistic potential. Saltman wants to make the institution of which he is provost a personification of the best in himself.

Several of our contributors referred to their feeling that everyone is creative to some degree and that the creative experience is not reserved for a few. There was little mystique about creativity evident when the contributors spoke, and nearly all of those we interviewed had a philosophy toward their work. For example, Engman views art traditionally, as an imitation of nature in principle, everything being related organically. The scale from which he works is dictated by nature. Cunningham is an avant gardist. He points out that in life our experience of movements, sounds, lights, and colors is not necessarily synchronous, and he questions why in dance one should be concerned with an artificial coordination of these elements. Among scientists, Glass is one of a rapidly growing number who do not view their achievements as independent of their effect upon humanity. He is concerned with the ethics of genetics and how it benefits mankind. Rodman speaks of great artists as being "noble people." Apart from their personal lives he feels great artists usually have a sense of responsibility not only to themselves but to the world and the future. They see themselves in the role of exemplar of their age.

In relation to family background, many of our contributors viewed their fathers especially as individuals with unrealized potential, and as men who placed a heavy emphasis upon education. We may conjecture that, though our contributors did not enter their father's chosen field, their own ambition expresses the frustrated ambition of their fathers.

Often the mother is recalled as a great source of encouragement, and some feel their mothers were more significant in their careers. The impact of an older or younger brother as a source of inspiration or as a colleague is seen in a number of instances.

For the most part, the family background cannot be specifically related to the field that was chosen. A history of shyness and feelings of isolation as children appeared not infrequently. The loss of parents early in life is encountered in at least three instances, and an unhappy home life is observed in several other examples.

Although the emphasis placed on education by the family was frequently strong, our contributors generally viewed formal schooling as stifling, and in a number of instances were ready to quit school, but stuck with it because of a single inspiring professor.

The material contained in these accounts agrees essentially with the findings of other investigators in the field. For example, Bruner speaks of "effective surprise" in creativity and of the presence of antinomies of "detachment and commitment, passion and decorum, freedom to be dominated by the object, deferral and immediacy." Mary Henle, in her paper, "The Birth and Death of Ideas," refers to correctness, novelty, freedom, harmony, receptivity, immersion, seeing questions, the utilization of errors, and detached devotion as significant characteristics of creative thinking. Newell, Shaw, and Simon point to the significance of novelty and value, motivation and persistence, and the unconventional in creativity.

McClelland, in his study of physical scientists, points to their obsession with work, their discomfort with complex human emotions, their needs for mastery, their childlike perception of humans, and their perception of nature as an extension of themselves. "In other words, we need only assume that the young scientist has enjoyed his fantasy life as a means of expressing blocked impulses, to discover a reason why he continues to pursue such 'immature' fantasies when he is confronted by anxiety in adult interpersonal relations. So his interest in nature not only represents a flight from people and a turning of aggression into new channels; it also permits him to continue indulging childlike fantasies originally developed out of a frustrated impulse life. His goal may be power-dominion over nature—but the means to the goal—the continued pursuit of childhood fantasies in which nature is a kind of extension of the self—is in itself pleasurable."[2]

Ghiselin designated the following issues as significant to the creative process: transcending the old order, a vague confused excitement, a sense

[2] D. C. McClelland, *The Achieving Society* (Princeton: Van Nostrand, 1962), p. 171.

of adventure, self-surrender and automatism; oppositionism, a wish for novelty, dedication, and discipline, and a sense of promise and patience. Taylor and Barron found that a high degree of autonomy, self-sufficiency, and self-direction, as well as a preference for mental manipulations involving things rather than people, were traits present in study after study of productive scientists. They found a somewhat distant or detached attitude in interpersonal relations in these people, who also showed a preference for intellectually challenging rather than socially challenging situations. In addition, these investigators found their scientists demonstrated a high degree of ego strength and emotional stability, a liking for method, precision, and exactness, and a preference for such defense mechanisms as repression and isolation in dealing with affect and instinctual energies. Other areas that they designated as significant in their study were the presence of a high degree of personal dominance, but a dislike of personally toned controversy, a high degree of control of impulse, amounting almost to overcontrol, and relatively little talkativeness, gregariousness, or impulsiveness. They further found a liking for abstract thinking, with considerable tolerance of cognitive ambiguity, marked independence of judgment, rejection of group pressures toward conformity in thinking, superior general intelligence, an early broad interest in intellectual activities, a drive toward comprehensiveness and elegance in explanation, and a special interest in the kind of "wagering" which involves pitting oneself against uncertain circumstances in which one's own efforts can be the deciding factor.

Since about the middle fifties, an important body of research findings has made its way into the developing literature on creativity from the Institute of Personality Assessment and Research of the University of California at Berkeley under the direction of Donald MacKinnon. There are five criteria, some or all of which had to be satisfied by the Berkeley investigators, if assessment of creative persons was to be undertaken by the group. These included the testing and observation of individuals in a group setting, with a multiplicity of tests and procedures, by a number of staff members and observers. Through a pooling of test scores and subjective impressions they sought to formulate psychodiagnostic descriptions of the assessed subjects, which would permit predictions of the assessees' behavior in certain types of roles and situations. Among others studied at Berkeley were architects and engineers. The Berkeley study of architects found certain traits significantly correlated with the subjects' creativeness in architecture. These included: intellectual competence, curiosity as a habit of mind, cognitive flexibility, and aesthetic sensibility. Further, there was a sense of destiny, an ability to evaluate ideas, independence, originality, personality stability and adjustment, and responsibility. The Berkeley team has also studied poets, novelists, and essayists, as well as research scientists and inventors.

With respect to the relationship between creativity and intelligence, MacKinnon and his co-workers at Berkeley found a positive link between the two variables, but it is simply not true, according to their findings, that the more intelligent person is the more creative. For example, architects had a median I. Q. of 130, research scientists, 133, male mathematicians, 135, and female mathematicians, 132, on the Full Scale of the Wechsler Adult Intelligence Scale.

The study at Berkeley provided some of the following as characteristics of creative persons—we take the liberty of paraphrasing: Creative persons are intelligent, but creative giftedness is not to be equated with high verbal intelligence. Creative persons are original, but only in the sense that originality is only one aspect of true creativeness. Creative persons are independent in thought and action. A fundamental characteristic is that such persons are strongly motivated to achieve in situations where independence in thought and action is called for; they have much less interest in or motivation to achieve in situations that demand conforming behavior. Creative individuals are sensitive both to their inner states and to the outer world. Such individuals are open to and receptive of experience and seek to know as much as possible about life. Creative persons are intuitive. Such individuals are capable of going well beyond sense-perception and are alert and responsive to deeper meanings, implications, and the possibilities for using that which they perceive through their senses. In short, they are not stimulus- and object-bound. Creative individuals have strong theoretical and aesthetic interests. Their theoretical interests are expressed largely in abstract and symbolic terms. An aesthetic viewpoint permeates the work of the creative persons studied. Creative individuals have a strong sense of destiny that includes a degree of resoluteness and almost inevitably a measure of egotism.

Any review of the literature on creative thinking must include the early and significant attention paid to problem solving and productive thinking by the Gestalt psychologists. Members of this school attended to the characteristics and qualities of problems such as their "demand quality," "the requiredness" of a problem, and the forces emanating from the task itself. In addition, the Gestaltists focused on cognitive processes, such as insight, understanding, good and bad errors, resonance, and so forth, as well as on deterrents to insight, such as *Einstellung* (mental set), rigidity, functional fixedness, and mechanization, all representing efforts at understanding higher level solutions. This approach served as an important antidote to the atomistic, stimulus-response, conditioning, and associationistic approaches of the time. Further, the Gestaltists attempted to relate the findings of perception and learning to a unified theory of brain functioning instead of dividing man up into a series of discrete functions.

Neither can the contributions of psychoanalysis to the study of the creative process be overlooked in any work on this topic. Almost from its inception, psychoanalysis has concerned itself with the place of unconscious processes in thinking. The central place given to dreams, fantasies, and free associations naturally led to an interest in and involvement with innovative thinking and perception. Among the early practitioners, men such as Freud, Rank, and Jung made major contributions to the study of creativity; and the more recent studies of the ego psychologists such as Kubie, Eissler, Kris, Hartmann, Lowenstein, and Erikson serve to fill a void which purely academic and cognitive psychology has left open.

Kris, for example, has made a significant contribution in his discussion of creative activity as being characterized by shifts in psychic levels and in the degree of control exerted by the ego. In so-called psychotic art, the art appears to communicate only between the artist's inner psychic levels, while in "communicative" art, the artist is able to relate between his own psychic layers while also communicating to others. This, Kris refers to as "regression in the service of the ego." He suggests that the artist's ability to regress to more primitive modes of thought and feeling, while maintaining sufficient control, enables him to keep his own defenses intact while helping him communicate. In the so-called psychotic artist, the regressive processes supersede ego controls, and art becomes primarily a personal fitting-in with the artist's autistic thinking or delusional systems.

In science, mathematics, and the arts, there is widespread recognition of the significant place occupied by intuition, unconscious promptings, inexplicable insights, and the sudden awareness of relationships. Scientific discovery and artistic creations are hardly the result solely of rational considerations. The repeated references in our own interviews to "I don't know where the idea came from," and "It just came to mind," attest to functions in operation beyond the level of consciousness.

Koestler, who was keenly aware of a distinction between routine thinking and more creative ways of thought, coined the term "bisociation" to describe the latter. Routine thinking, he points out, is on a single plane, while creative thinking always operates on more than one plane, and involves a more fluid state of unstable equilibrium. The bisociative thought or act relates previously unconnected aspects of thinking and experience by recognizing and placing those events on several planes at once. As Koestler states in *The Act of Creation*, ". . . ordered, disciplined thought is a skill governed by set rules of the game, some of which are explicitly stated, others implied and hidden in the code. The creative act, insofar as it depends upon unconscious resources, presupposes a relaxing of the controls and a regression to modes of ideation which are indifferent to the rules of verbal logic, unperturbed by contradiction, untouched by the dogmas and taboos of so-called common sense. At the decisive stage of discovery the codes of disciplined reasoning are suspended—as they are in the dream, the reverie, the manic flight of thought, when the stream of ideation is free to drift, by its own emotional gravity, as it were, in an apparently 'lawless' fashion."[3]

In our interviews, with the exception of a few (Singer, Chomsky) there was a general underemphasis, and with some, a refutation of the significance of the dream life to creativity. There are a number of possible explanations for the denial of the significance of dreams. One is that dreams do not play a function in creativity, despite the findings of others. However, this is unlikely both theoretically and in accordance with the autobiographical reports of many creative individuals. It is possible our interviews were not sufficiently deep to actually probe the role of dreams. It is also possible that the nature of our questioning was not sufficiently broad to elicit this information. Another reason is the contributors may have failed to recall their dreams and just think they do not play a role. We believe this to be highly probable. In psychoanalysis, for example, an analysand will often announce at the beginning of a session that he has had no dreams. However, later in the session, forgotten dreams and their significance occur to him. In terms of our interviews, the contributors were under the impression that we were asking about a direct connection between dreams and their work. Although the manifest content of a dream may not be significant to the creative person's work, the latent content, which may be repressed, could be. On the other hand, the manifest content, in some instances, may be of utmost significance. As Singer indicates, he is

[3] Koestler, A. *The Act of Creation*. New York: Macmillan, 1964, p. 178.

certain that his dreams are important to his stories, perhaps to a degree of which even he is not aware.

Thus, while the authors of this study are aware that not all aspects of the creative experience yet lend themselves to systems of questions and categories, nonetheless those areas that are subjectable to verbal understanding may be summarized in the following diagram.

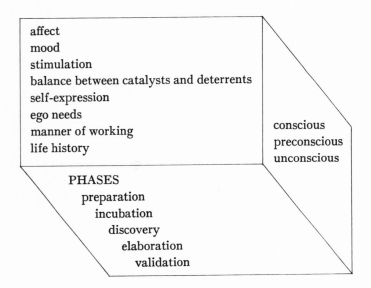

Bibliography

Adorno, T. W., E. Frenkel-Brunswik, D. Levinson, and R. N. Sanford. *The Authoritarian Personality.* New York: Harper, 1950.

Adrian, Lord. "Creativity in Science," *Perspectives in Biology and Medicine,* 1962, 5, pp. 269–74.

Allport, Gordon W. *Pattern and Growth in Personality.* New York: Holt, Rinehart, and Winston, 1961, pp. 564–65.

Anderson, Harold H. (ed.). *Creativity and its Cultivation.* New York: Harper, 1959.

Baker, J. R. *The Scientific Life.* New York: Macmillan, 1943.

Barnett, H. G. *Innovation: The Basis of Cultural Change.* New York: McGraw-Hill, 1953.

Barron, Frank. *Creativity and Psychological Health.* Princeton: D. Van Nostrand, 1963.

Bartlett, F. *Thinking: An Experimental and Social Study.* London: Allen and Unwin, 1958.

Becker, Ernest. *Beyond Alienation.* New York: Braziller, 1967.

Bergson, H. *The Creative Mind.* New York: Philosophical Library, 1946.

Bernard, C. *An Introduction to the Study of Experimental Medicine.* New York: Macmillan, 1927.

Beveridge, W. B. *The Art of Scientific Investigation.* New York: Norton, 1937.

Boring, E. G. "The Psychology of Controversy," *Psychological Review,* 1929, 36, pp. 97–121.

Brandwein, P. F. *The Gifted Student as Future Scientist.* New York: Harcourt, Brace, and Co., 1955.

Bridenbaugh, Carl. "The Great Mutation," *American Historical Review,* 1963, pp. 315–31.

Brown, R., and D. McNeill. "The 'tip of the tongue' phenomenon," *Journal of Verbal Learning and Verbal Behavior,* 1966, 5, pp. 325–37.

Bruner, J. S., Goodnow, J. J., and C. A. Austin. *A Study of Thinking*. New York: Wiley, 1956.

Cornford, F. M. *Plato's Theaetetus*. New York: Liberal Arts Press, 1949.

Crawford, R. P. *The Techniques of Creative Thinking*. New York: Hawthorn, 1954.

Drews, Elizabeth M. *The Creative Intellectual Style in Gifted Adolescents*. East Lansing: Michigan State University, 1965.

Duncker, K. "On problem-solving," *Psychological Monographs*, 1945, 58, No. 5 (Whole No. 270).

Ehrenzweig, A. *The Psychoanalysis of Artistic Vision and Hearing*. London: Routledge and Kegan Paul, 1953.

Eiseley, Loren. Film No. 7, "The Being and Becoming Film Series," produced by Elizabeth M. Drews. Portland, Oregon, Portland State University, 1967.

Frankl, Victor. "Self-Transcendence as a Human Phenomenon," *Journal of Humanistic Psychology*, 1966, Fall, p. 104.

Freud, S. *Leonardo da Vinci*. London: Routledge and Kegan Paul, 1948.

Fromm, Erich. *Escape from Freedom*. New York: Farrar and Rinehart, 1941.

Gabor, Dennis. *Inventing the Future*. New York: Alfred A. Knopf, 1964, p. 186.

Getzels, J. W. and P. W. Jackson. *Creativity and Intelligence: Explorations with Gifted Students*. New York: Wiley, 1962.

Ghiselin, B. (ed.). *The Creative Process*. New York: Mentor, 1955.

Goertzels, Victor and Mildred. *Cradles of Eminence*. Boston: Little, Brown, and Co., 1962.

Gruber, Howard E., G. Terrell, and M. Wertheimer (eds.). *Contemporary Approaches to Creative Thinking*. New York: Atherton Press, 1964.

Hadamard, J. *The Psychology of Invention in the Mathematical Field*. New York: Dover, 1954.

Harrington, Michael. *The Accidental Century*. New York: Macmillan, 1965.

Heist, P. "Personality and Scholarship," *Science*, 1961, pp. 133, 362–67.

Henle, M. "Some Effects of Motivational Processes on Cognition," *Psychological Review*, 1955, 62, pp. 423–32.

Henle, M. "On the Relation Between Logic and Thinking," *Psychological Review*, 1962, 69, pp. 366–78.

Henle, M. (ed.). *Documents of Gestalt Psychology*. Berkeley and Los Angeles: University of California Press, 1961.

Henle, M. "Some Problems of Eclecticism, *Psychological Review*, 1957, 64, pp. 296–305.

Henle, M., and M. Michael. "The Influence of Attitudes on Syllogistic Reasoning," *Journal of Social Psychology*, 1956, 44, pp. 115–27.

Heywood, R. B. (ed.). *The Works of the Mind*. Chicago: University of Chicago Press, 1947.

Hoffer, Eric. *Ordeal of Change*. New York: Harper and Row, 1963.

Humphrey, G. *Directed Thinking*. New York: Dodd, Mead and Co., 1948.

Hutchinson, E. D. *How to Think Creatively*. New York: Abingdon-Cokesbury, 1949.

Isaacs, N. "Children's why questions," in S. Isaacs, *Intellectual Growth in Young Children.* London: Routledge and Kegan Paul, 1930.

James, William. *The Principles of Psychology.* New York: Henry Holt, 1890, 2 vols.

Johnson, D. M. *The Psychology of Thought and Judgment.* New York: Harper, 1955.

Jourard, Sidney M. "The 'Awareness of Potentialities' Syndrome," *Journal of Humanistic Psychology,* 1966, Fall, pp. 139–40.

Koestler, Arthur. *The Act of Creation.* New York: Macmillan, 1964.

Kohler, W. *Dynamics in Psychology.* New York: Liveright, 1940.

Kohler, W. "A Perspective on American Psychology," *Psychological Review,* 1943, 50, pp. 77–79.

Kohler, W. *Die physischen Gestalten in Ruhe und in stationaeren Zustand.* Braunschweig: F. Vieweg and Sohn, 1920.

Kohler, W. "Psychologie und Naturwissenschaft," *Proceedings of the 15th International Congress of Psychology, Brussels, 1957,* Amsterdam: North-Holland Publishing Co. 1959, pp. 37–50.

Kris, E. *Psychoanalytic Explorations in Art.* New York: International Universities Press, 1952.

Kubie, L. S. *Neurotic Distortion of the Creative Process.* New York: The Noonday Press, 1961.

Kohn, T. S. *The Structure of Scientific Revolutions.* Chicago: University of Chicago Press, 1964.

Leithaeuser, J. G. *Worlds Beyond the Horizon.* New York: Alfred A. Knopf, 1955.

Lewin, K. *A Dynamic Theory of Personality.* New York: McGraw-Hill, 1935.

Lowenfeld, V. *The Nature of Creative Activity.* London: Routledge and Kegan Paul, 1952.

Lowenfeld, V. *Creative and Mental Growth* (3rd ed.). New York: Macmillan, 1957.

Luchins, A. S. "Mechanization in Problem Solving: The Effect of Einstellung," *Psychological Monographs,* 1952, 54, No. 6 (Whole No. 248).

MacKinnon, D. W. "The Nature and Nurture of Creative Talent," *The American Psychologist,* 1962, pp. 484–95.

Manuel, Frank. "Toward a Psychological History of Utopias," *Daedalus,* 94, Spring, 1965, pp. 293–322.

Maslow, A. H. *Toward a Psychology of Being.* New York: D. Van Nostrand, 1962, p. 177.

Maslow, A. H. *The Psychology of Science.* New York: Harper and Row, 1966, pp. 124–25.

Maslow, A. H. *Motivation and Personality.* New York: Harper, 1954.

May, Rollo. "The Nature of Creativity," in H. H. Anderson (ed.). *Creativity and its Cultivation.* New York: Harper, 1959.

McKellar, P. *Imagination and Thinking.* New York: Basic Books, 1957.

McKeon, R. (ed.). *The Basic Works of Aristotle.* New York: Random House, 1941.

Michael, Donald. *The Unprepared Society*. New York: Basic Books, 1968.

Morgan, J. J. B. and J. T. Morton. "The Distortion of Syllogistic Reasoning Produced by Personal Convictions," *Journal of Social Psychology*, 1944, 20, pp. 39–59.

Mumford, Lewis. "Utopia, the City, and the Machine," *Daedalus*, 1965, 94, Spring, p. 271.

Murray, H. A. "Vicissitudes of Creativity," in H. H. Anderson (ed.). *Creativity and its Cultivation*. New York: Harper, 1959.

Parnes, S. J., and H. F. Harding (eds.). *Source Book for Creative Thinking*. New York: Scribner's, 1962.

Planck, M. *Scientific Autobiography and Other Papers*. New York: Philosophical Library, 1949.

Polanyi, M. *Personal Knowledge*. Chicago: University of Chicago Press, 1958.

Polya, G. *Mathematics and Plausible Reasoning*. Princeton: Princeton University Press, 1954. 2 vols.

Raser, John. "The Failure of Fail-Safe, *Transaction*, Jan., 1969, pp. 11–19.

Reed College. *Life or Death: a symposium on The Sanctity of Life*. Seattle: University of Washington Press, 1968.

Roberts, C. *The Scientific Conscience*. New York: Braziller, 1967.

Roe, Anne. *The Making of a Scientist*. New York: Dodd, Mead and Co., 1953.

Rogers, Carl. "Toward a Theory of Creativity." In H. H. Anderson (ed.). *Creativity and its Cultivation*. New York: Harper, 1959.

Rosenthal, R., and L. Jacobson. *Pygmalion in the Classroom*. New York: Holt, Rinehart, and Winston, 1968.

Rossman, J. *The Psychology of the Inventor*. (rev. ed.). Washington, D.C.: Inventors Publishing Co., 1931.

Rush, J. H. "The Next 10,000 Years," *Saturday Review*, Jan., 1958, pp. 11–13.

Schwartz, G., and P. W. Bishop (eds.). *Moments of Discovery*. New York: Basic Books, 1958. 2 vols.

Schweitzer, Albert. *Out of My Life and Thought*. New York: Holt, 1933.

Smith, P. (ed.). *Creativity*. New York: Hastings House, 1959.

Stein, M. I., and Shirley Heinze (eds.). *Creativity and the Individual*. Chicago: Free Press, 1960.

Stephens, J. *Irish Fairy Tales*. New York: Macmillan, 1920.

Summerfield, J. D., and L. Thatcher (eds.). *The Creative Mind and Method*. New York: Russell and Russell, 1964.

Szent-Gyoergyi, A. "On Scientific Creativity," *Perspectives in Biology and Medicine*, 1962, 5, pp. 173–78.

Taton, R. *Reason and Chance in Scientific Discovery*. London: Hutchinson, 1957.

Taylor, C. R. "The Eland and the Oryx," *Scientific American*, 1969, 220(1), pp. 88–95.

Taylor, C. W., and Frank Barron. *Scientific Creativity: Its Recognition and Development*. New York: John Wiley and Son, 1963.

Temko, Allan. "Man at War With Nature, Which Guide to the Promised Land: Fuller or Mumford?" *Horizon*, Summer, 1968, pp. 24–31.

Time Essay. "Metaphysician of Madness." Feb. 7, 1969, pp. 64, 66.

Tuska, C. D. *Inventors and Inventions*. New York: McGraw-Hill, 1957.

Vinacke, J. E. *The Psychology of Thinking*. New York: McGraw-Hill, 1952.

Von Frange, E. K. *Professional Creativity*. New Jersey: Prentice-Hall, 1959.

Wallach, M. A., and N. Kogan. *Modes of Thinking in Young Children*. New York: Holt, Rinehart, and Winston, 1965.

Wertheimer, M. "Untersuchungen zur Lehre von der Gestalt: II." *Psychologische Forschung*, 1923, 4, pp. 301–50.

Wertheimer, M. *Productive Thinking*. (enlarged ed.). New York: Harper, 1959.

White, R. *Lives in Progress*. New York: Holt, Rinehart, and Winston, 1952.

White, R. (ed.). *The Study of Lives*. New York: Atherton Press, 1963.

Whiting, C. S. *Creative Thinking*. New York: Reinhold, 1958.

Wilder, R. L. "The Role of Intuition," *Science,* May 1967, 156, No. 3775.

This book was set on the linotype in Old Style No. 7.
The display type is Latin Bold.
Composition and binding by H. Wolff Book Manufacturing Company.
Printed by Halliday Lithograph Corporation.
Designed by Jacqueline Schuman.

DISCARD